YEAR OF THE WOLF

STEVE VENTON

"Human greed knows no bounds, except
the restraint of God's sovereign power."

Steve Venton

"For the love of money is the root of all
evil:…"

The Apostle Paul
1 Timothy 6:10

INTRODUCTION

It began on May 31, 2025. The wolf population in the Adirondack Mountains of upstate New York had outgrown the number of prey in that same area. What happened next was an ecological disaster. As the predators eliminated the remaining remnants of their natural prey, they began to turn toward other prey by encroaching onto human territory. The residents of this Park were about to find out what such a disaster would be like, from May 31, 2025 to May 30, 2026. This time period would become known around the world as the "Year of the Wolf".

All of the characters in this novel are fictional. Some, but not all, of the roads, places, and descriptions of places are also fictional. This novel is a work of fiction. The intention of the author is to entertain the reader, and at the same time, send a message that there is a spiritual dimension in human existence that is one hundred percent real.

The reader may notice that within the main thrust of the story are isolated incidents involving people who are living or vacationing in the Adirondacks. The purpose of these descriptive accounts is not meant to throw the reader off of the main direction of the story, but rather to give the reader an idea of what it would be like to face danger in a huge wilderness area inhabited by roaming packs of ravenous wolves. To make matters worse, most of these wolves have been chemically altered, making them far more aggressive than normal.

This story, as mentioned earlier, has a spiritual dimension; and the desire of the author is not just to entertain, but to show the reader something beyond the natural: Someone Who is sovereign over all,

Someone Who cares, Someone Who is willing to meet the reader at his or her point of need. May this book do more than entertain. May it effect a profound change for the better in the lives of all who read these pages.

CHAPTER ONE

PHARAOH LAKE—June 30, 2025

The party boat was steady in the water, anchored near the shore. It had been there for twelve hours. There was no sound but the sloshing of water against the hull. The engine was turned off, and there was no movement on board.

The paramedics raced to the site. They had had to approach by helicopter, for there was only a hiker's path leading to this side of the lake. What they saw would make the evening news.

"Look, Daddy! I see something moving in the bushes over there!"

Harry Oswald picked Natalie up quickly, and got back into his 2020 Hybrid Toyota Matrix. He'd decided that taking a little hike off of this rural Route 8 was not such a good idea after all. Those "things" moving in the bushes had been stalking them for the last twenty minutes, and he was afraid of them—whatever they were. They had not attacked; but he didn't want to stick around any longer. Seven-year-old Natalie was enjoying it all, unaware of the danger lurking back near the hikers' path.

Either these "things" were curious; or they had eaten already; for surely they would have attacked by now. But Harry wasn't staying around to find out.

He turned the key, looked around again, locked the doors, and shifted into DRIVE. He slowly took off, curious about what those creatures were. The brush in which they lurked was thick and tall, and concealed whatever it was that they were. But no sooner had Harry left, than the predators came out of the brush.

The beasts were indeed very dangerous, but had already eaten their full. They were not hungry now; but it was their natural instinct to track potential prey. So they had silently tracked Harry and Natalie for twenty minutes, playing a game of "cat and mouse".

Harry began to experience an anxiety attack; and he had to deliberately breathe deeply to calm himself down. He began to accelerate the car rapidly in his panic. Then, once his apoplexy passed, he began to ease off the accelerator, for he was driving way over the speed limit.

The pilot had landed in a field nearby the lake, next to the police chopper. From there, the paramedics ran to the tragic site. They ran down a short pathway through a patch of wooded area, and into a small clearing. From there, they walked down towards a small beach at the edge of the lake.

On the beach, they could see several police detectives examining the remains of seven people and one small dog. It was the most sickening thing that Julia Wilde had ever witnessed. She had been a paramedic for over twenty years, and had never seen such a horrifying sight.

"What a mess. Unbelievable!" Fred Arness exclaimed.

"This is surreal," Julia remarked.

"A real nightmare," said Jerry.

Jerry Springer was a new recruit, but very outgoing and popular among the paramedics. And, of course, his fellow medics "roasted" him about his name over and over again. He enjoyed the humor, and told everybody that he was "still the Mayor of Cincinatti."

Sergeant Carl Weaver met them. "We found a survivor on board the party boat. I don't think she'll make it."

"How long have you been here?" asked Julia.

"Got here just a few minutes before you arrived."

Julia had been scanning the scene while talking to the Sergeant. She was wondering what could possibly have done this. There were no tracks, because a heavy rain had washed them away. Whatever the attackers were, they were not human. They were animals—vicious and powerful. And they must have moved really fast.

Jerry, Fred, and Julia took one of the rowboats, and paddled to the party boat. There was an eerie silence as they approached. They lashed the rowboat to the side of the party boat, and climbed up the side ladder.

What they saw made Julia gasp. A young woman lay still on the deck. She had not been attacked, but she had hit her head. Blood had coagulated on the right side of her face. She had evidently fainted and fallen, hitting her head, and had gone into a coma.

They started to communicate with her; and she blinked her eyes twice to tell them that she could hear them. She couldn't move her arms and legs; but she could move her lips and eyes. She contracted her lips as if she was trying to kiss someone; but she was trying to tell them something. But she couldn't make any sound. The paramedics didn't understand what she was trying to say.

They checked her vitals, and then carefully lifted her onto a gurney. They then transported her, lowering her into the rowboat. They moved her to the shore, and checked her vital signs again. They noticed that her heart rate was much faster. And her eyes grew really wide. Julia could see that there was fear all over her face.

Sergeant Carl Weaver turned to Julia.

"Just one survivor. This is so sad."

"Yes, and just barely. She must have watched the whole thing, called 911 on her cell, and then fainted."

"I remember we received a call last night; and it was impossible to make out the words. Then the phone went dead. It was strange. We thought it was one of those prank calls we have been getting lately. But then we received a second call less than an hour ago. Somebody fishing in a rowboat saw the party boat and the remains. That's when we dispatched you, in case there were any survivors."

Sergeant Weaver looked at the young survivor. He was all choked-up.

"We'll stay here, investigate, and clean up this mess. You go on ahead, and get her to the hospital."

"Thank you, Sarge."

The paramedics carried her to their chopper, quickly loaded her inside, and took off.

John Talin was a world-class biker. He happened to be vacationing in the Adirondack Mountains for the past three weeks. He was riding his bike up and down Route 28 between Old Forge and Blue Mountain Lake, enjoying the hilly countryside. He was coasting down a big hill, when suddenly he saw a deer jump out of the woods and across the road in front of him. He slowed down, swerved, and stayed upright in a situation where most bikers would have fallen.

He looked in the rearview mirror, and saw a large animal crossing the road behind him. He could hardly believe his eyes. Was it a mountain lion? He would report his sighting to the DEC, the Department of Environmental Conservation. Would they believe him? He didn't know. He contemplated that for a few moments.

Suddenly, a number of shadowy figures moved to his right, in the woods. They were large and threatening. John didn't dare look directly at them; but he used his peripheral vision to keep track of them. He could hear the throaty growls as they stalked him from the right, running beside him in the woods. They were fast. He was traveling at about thirty-five miles per hour; and they kept up with him.

He could see another hill up ahead. Would this hill slow him down enough to make him vulnerable? Instinctively, he pedaled hard as he approached the base of the hill, and brought his speed up to forty-five miles per hour. As he pedaled, he steadied the bike. He knew that he couldn't afford to fall. At his present speed, the shadowy forms were falling behind; but as he started up the hill, he knew the animals would gain ground.

John pedaled for dear life; but as he ascended the hill, he slowed to thirty-five, thirty, twenty-five, then down to twenty-two miles an hour as he approached the crest of the hill. Then it happened.

The animals began coming out of the forest to get him. He could see them gaining behind him. If only the hill was a little shorter! He pedaled with all his power; his heart pounded; and he felt that he was going to die. He reached the top of the hill, and kept accelerating as fast as he could. By the time he reached fifty miles an hour going downhill, the animals gave up and went back into the woods.

Glens Falls Hospital had a helicopter pad on the roof of its main building. The paramedics landed the chopper, and rushed the comatose patient inside. They then gave all the pertinent information: Susan Downing, age twenty-two, New York State license number *********, no health insurance. She would be placed into the sliding scale for the uninsured. As Julia gave the patient's information, the other paramedics rushed her down the hallway and into a room where a team of doctors would soon be ready to examine her.

A nurse quickly plugged an IV drip into her, and checked her vital signs. Her blood pressure had gone back down, and her other vitals had improved. But she still couldn't move anything except her eyelids and mouth.

Nurse Darlene Brown noticed that she was making a motion with her mouth.

She said, "Look! She's trying to tell us something!"

"Aw, come on. People in a coma make facial twitches sometimes," one of the nurses said.

"No, really."

"Do you think so?"

"Yes, look!"

Suddenly, the comatose woman began to shake. And then her pulse got louder and stronger and faster; and she sat up straight and spoke real loudly:

"Wooooooooo!"

Then she spoke again.

"Wooooooooo!"

Nurse Brown, age forty-two, had never experienced anything like this in all of her sixteen years here; and her face was turning pale.

"What are you trying to say, Susan?" she asked.

"Wooooooooo!"

Susan flailed her arms, pulling out of the IV. One of the nurses moved to get her to lie back so she could reattach the IV.

"Wait a minute, Leslie," Nurse Brown said. She turned to Susan.

"Help me understand, Susan. What did you see?"

"Woooooooo!! Woooooooo!!"

Susan took a deep breath.

"WOOOOOOOOO!!!"

Her vitals were getting dangerously out of control; and she was obviously agitated. Suddenly, she locked eyes with Nurse Brown, and with all of her strength said:

"WOOOOOO!! WOOOOOOOOOOOO!!"

Then she blurted it out:

"Bi—Ba— WOOOOOOOO!!!"

A chill went up and down Nurse Brown's spine. She felt a fear she used to have as a child whenever she walked in the woods. She knew what Susan saw that night. No one else understood her attempts at words. Nurse Brown looked into Susan's eyes and nodded in recognition.

"I understand you, Susan. I know."

Susan didn't reciprocate, because she was going into cardiac arrest.

The team of doctors was just entering the room; and two of them started CPR. Nurse Brown looked at the screen, and tensed up as she saw Susan's vitals getting weaker and weaker. Then, for a short moment, she stabilized. Then her body shook violently; and once again, her heartbeat line went flat.

CHAPTER TWO

May 31, 2025

The Barclays had lived on a farm just outside of the township of Blue Mountain Lake all of their lives. Their huge farmhouse was built in the late 1800's. They had over a hundred acres for farming, and produced corn, cucumbers, potatoes, squash, tomatoes, and a number of other crops. They also had a sizeable herb garden. And they had several pigs, a lot of chickens, four milking cows, and two riding horses.

Ben and Shirley Barclay had three sons and one daughter. Their oldest son, Ben Jr., was in the Air Force. The daughter, Jennifer, was a Sophomore at Princeton University, studying law. The younger children, Joshua and Jesse, were ages ten and eight, respectively. Joshua was very athletic, and big for his age. Jesse was just the opposite. He was a small, sickly child. Yet, despite their physical differences, the two brothers got along extremely well. Joshua, the strong one, was very protective of his younger brother; and they did everything together.

They were more than just brothers. They were best friends. Joshua was the leader. Jesse was the follower. When Joshua was telling Jesse what to do next, he said it in a kind and respectful manner. Jesse would happily comply, because he liked being a follower. He knew instinctively that Joshua was directing him for his own good, and not to take advantage of him.

The two boys had finished their chores on this warm and sunny last day of May. And they were playing with one of the tractors.

Actually, they were studying the parts of the engine, and how to drive the tractor, if only they had a key to start the ignition.

In two months, on July 30, 2025, Joshua would get a key to the tractor for his eleventh birthday. He could hardly wait. His Dad promised him the key, as long as he didn't allow Jesse to drive it. That was fine with Joshua, because he liked being the leader.

The brothers were about one hundred yards away from the big barn, and a quarter of a mile from the edge of the woods. Between them and the woods was fallow ground. The boys enjoyed being out in the sun, and loved playing with the tractor, and dreaming about when they would be able to drive it around. Normally, the tractor was left inside the barn; but it had broken down for some reason; and Dad had just left it there, minus the key.

Clouds were beginning to come in from the west. They looked a little ominous; but there was no rain coming down from them. The clouds made the forest to the west look a little darker.

The boys were staring down at the woods, and even thinking about walking down there, when they saw something move at the edge of the trees. Instantly, they knew what it was. It was large, and looked scary, even at that distance.

Joshua saw it first. He motioned with his hands for Jesse to be real quiet. The two boys hid behind the tractor and scanned the trees. Jesse had a pair of binoculars; and he began to tense up when he looked through them.

More of the animals came out of the woods. They were gathering right at the edge of the treeline. The boys watched for several minutes as twelve predators gathered together. Then the animals began to look toward the two brothers; and that made Joshua really nervous. He whispered to Jesse:

"Jesse, start crawling toward the barn, and when I say 'Run', give it all you've got."

Jesse nodded, didn't say a word, and started to crawl toward the barn. Joshua knew that Jesse could not make it to the barn in time without a head start; and he also knew that once they started to run, the predators would attack. Joshua had to stay near the tractor for now, to make sure the predators didn't start to attack early. He needed Jesse to move at least sixty feet closer to the barn before he would be able to run to safety. This race for survival was going to be close; and Joshua knew it. He kept watching; and what he saw made his heart pound faster and faster.

The wolves began to lope slowly toward the tractor. Joshua had hoped that they would wait a little longer. But they were coming! Jesse had not crawled far enough yet. Joshua didn't know what to do. He waited a few more seconds; and then his fear got the best of him.

"Run! Jesse, RUN!!"

The wolves' ears stood up straight. Joshua knew what was coming next; and he backpedaled away from the tractor in fright. He could see the wolves picking up speed. He knew they were incredibly fast. He screamed to Jesse:

"Run, Jesse! RUNNNNN!!!"

Jesse was plodding along at his six-mile-an-hour pace. He was painfully slow. Joshua ran past Jesse and turned around, his body trembling with terror. He could see the wolves closing in. He saw the powerful legs moving effortlessly, the heads bobbing up and down, the tongues hanging out, and the mouths gaped open, revealing their razor-sharp fangs.

Jesse had gone only thirty yards, running at full speed. The wolves, moving at thirty-five miles an hour, would catch Jesse about the time he got to the barn's door. This was going to be a race to the finish; and it was frighteningly close.

Joshua ran to the barn, opened the door, and called out to Jesse.

"Hurry, Jesse! PLEASE! Hurry!—HURRRRRRYYYY!!!"

Jesse was still almost twenty yards away from safety when the wolves passed the tractor.

Joshua was about ready to cry. He didn't want to see his little brother killed like this. He knew he couldn't save him if he slipped and fell. And he didn't even know if he would make it in time. The angle of the door was such that he could close it quickly and block the wolves' entrance. He just needed Jesse to get there in time.

Jesse could hear the footfalls behind him. He was terrified. He couldn't see how close the wolves were; but he could hear them coming. And he could hear his older brother screaming at him.

"Please, HURRRRYYY!!! They're right behind you!!!"

Suddenly, he felt a surge of adrenaline, with goosebumps all over his body. He picked up the pace to almost twice his normal speed, and surged forward.

The wolves were rapidly closing the gap. They were just a few seconds away, when their prey picked up speed.

Jesse dived through the doorway; and Joshua closed the door. There was a loud thud as the lead wolf hit the big door. The door started to open again. He pulled it shut, and bolted it. They were safe!

Mr. Barclay heard a commotion, and looked out the living room window, thirty yards to the east side of the barn. He could hear yelling, and then the noise of growling, and of frightened livestock. Then he saw wolves pacing around the barn, looking for a way to get in. Then his cell phone rang.

"Dad! Dad! Can you hear me?"

"Yes, son. Where are you?"

"In the barn."

"Is Jesse with you?"

"Yes."

"Is the door locked?"

"Yes."

"Stay there. And keep Jesse safe."

The fifty-year-old farmer grabbed his rifle and a pistol. Distance and close-range.

"How many are there, son?" he asked.

"We counted twelve."

"You sure that's it?"

"I'm sure."

"Okay. Call me if you need to talk more. I'm coming to get you. Don't open the door until I give you the okay."

"Yes, Dad."

"See you soon."

Ben thought to himself: "Illegal to shoot? If I call the authorities, I won't be able to shoot them. I'll play this real carefully."

He opened a window, put on his ear plugs, aimed the rifle, and fired. He aimed again, and killed a second wolf. Three. Then four. The wolves began to gather around the four dead. They began to feed. Ben counted seven more. Where was number twelve?

The twelfth wolf had found a way he could almost squeeze into the barn. A part of the wall on the south side was rotted out; and there was a gaping hole which had not been repaired. The wolf began to dig.

Mr. Barclay kept firing. He was surprised that the animals didn't run. They were fearless. That wasn't normal. But it meant he could kill them all. Twelve shots; eleven kills. He was still a near-perfect marksman.

Carefully, he opened the door. He left the rifle in the house, and exited with his pistol drawn, ready to fire. He wasn't going to take any chances. Plenty of firepower for the last wolf.

The boys were trying to quiet down the two horses and the milking cows inside the barn. Then Joshua looked toward the south wall, and saw the wolf slowly squeezing through a hole. He froze. Then he remembered the hatchet that was hanging on the west wall. He ran to the wall, grabbed the hatchet, and ran toward the south wall. The wolf was almost through the hole! Joshua took careful aim, and hit the beast on the top of its head.

The wolf pulled through the hole with the hatchet stuck in its head, and began to move spasmodically like a bronco trying to throw its rider. The hatchet made it look like a unicorn jerking its head back and forth in a spasmodic dance. Then, after a few more seconds, the animal collapsed.

Joshua heard a knock on the door.

"Josh! Jesse! Are you okay?"

Joshua ran to let his father in.

"Yes, we're all right, Dad."

He unbolted the door and let him in. The wolf was about five feet to their left, lying dead on the floor, the hatchet still embedded in its head. Ben looked at the wolf, then looked at Joshua, and smiled.

"You did that?"
"Yeah."
"I'm proud of you, son."
They hugged.
"Dad!" Jesse yelled, as he came out from one of the empty stalls.
"Jesse!"
Ben reached down and picked up his youngest son, hugging him as if he didn't ever want to let him go.

June 30, 2025—Plattsburg

Bob and Steve Dutcher were twin brothers who loved to hunt. They were in the woods south of North Oak Street. All of a sudden, they heard a commotion a distance away. They quietly moved in the direction of the noises. What they witnessed was both fascinating and chilling.

A huge black bear was defending her cub, in a terrible fight. There were six wolves surrounding her. She was flanked. One wolf would attack her; and she would go after him. Then another wolf would move in. Then another. They would continue to take chunks out of her until she weakened from loss of blood; and then they would finish her off. It was a noisy battle with the bear roaring, the wolves growling fiercely, and branches snapping all around them. The bear cub was up a tree, wailing loudly at the interlopers. At one point, the mother bear broke free from the inside of the circle of wolves and charged toward the two teenage boys. Then, she turned, grabbed one of the wolves, and shook it violently.

"Let's get out of here," Steve said quietly.

"Nothing more to see here," Bob whispered back.

Both brothers were thinking the same thing: "The woods are becoming more and more dangerous! We have to be more careful!"

They quietly moved away, and made sure they were home before dark.

CHAPTER THREE

July 10, 2025—Athol, off of Bowen Hill Road

Mark Duggan walked up the pathway to the picnic area. He had parked his father's 2019 Hybrid Ford Explorer at the base of the mountain path, and walked up to the flat area on the western side of Sugar Loaf Mountain. His girlfriend, Tammy Wade, was sick and couldn't make it.

Sally Ellenbridge and Kathy Reinfield were there with their iPods, listening to the most recent musical hit songs. Siblings Ron and Diane Reitner were there, quietly talking over a couple of grilled burgers. Several other teens were there—Tom, Jack, Toby, Cory, Toni, Tammie Jo, Marianne, and Liz. And the fourteenth picnicker was Ron and Diane's brother, Robbie, who was mentally challenged but very well-liked.

There was plenty to eat; and they just wanted to all get together. "It'll be fun. It's nice to see whom I'm talking with, rather than just texting them all the time," one of the teenagers had remarked the day before. The teens talked for hours, in four different groups. Sally, Kathy, and Mark talked about what they wanted to do in their Senior year, starting in September. They would help with the Yearbook and do whatever they could to make their class activities exciting. They had already organized a special fundraiser to help them get to Sydney, Australia for their Senior Trip.

"Will we meet Paul Hogan?" Sally asked.

"Sure, Mate!" Mark replied.

Toby, Cory, Toni, and Tammie Jo talked about what they wanted to do with their lives. Toby wanted to be a professional athlete. He was Warrensburg's top basketball scorer. At six-foot-eight inches, he could stuff the basket, rebound, and pick off practically any pass that was nearby. He could also hit his three-point shots once every other attempt, on the average. And whenever he was close to the net, he would score four out of five times. With Toby as their top forward, the Warrensburg team was undefeated, winning by an average of over twenty points per game.

Cory was a star football player. At six-foot-three inches and two hundred and sixty pounds, he doubled as running back and wide receiver. He was so fast that none of the opposing players could guard him consistently. He averaged over three touchdowns per game. The 2025-2026 school year was looking very good from a sports perspective.

Tori and Tammie Jo were both cheerleaders, and were part of the "cool" crowd. They were Toby's and Cory's dates; so as popularity goes, they were at the top of the social ladder. The two girls were enjoying the conversation, and looking forward to the football and basketball seasons. Of course, Toby and Cory also played baseball; and their phenomenal statistics, especially home-runs, were on record for all to see.

Tom, Jack, Marianne, and Liz were the third group of talkers. They were discussing some really deep subjects. Then the questions came up:

"Tom, how do you know evolution is true?"

"Oh, come on, Marianne. Everybody knows it. Don't you read your Science textbooks?"

"What about the other side of the argument?"

"They're all a bunch of stupid religious bigots!"

Ron and Diane and Robbie heard that remark, even though they were not in on the whole conversation. It hurt them to think that some of their fellow-students thought they were stupid and bigoted, simply because they believed in Jesus Christ.

Tom kept talking about how people who go to church were all hypocrites, and how the pastors of their churches enjoyed taking their money. He then described a real-life account of a so-called "Christian" who had mistreated him when he was a lot younger. This experience left him very bitter towards all church-goers. It ratcheted up his hatred for "Christians" to the level of irrationality. He could not—or would not—be objective and rational whenever he discussed the topic of Christianity.

Marianne spoke, "Tom, how can you blame everyone for something one person did to you? ONE person!"

Tom was closed-minded. "I don't want to talk about it anymore!"

Marianne retorted, "Well, excuse me for being rational!"

Tom was hot-tempered. "Enough!" he shouted.

Jack and Liz had been quietly listening to this conversation. Both of them had serious questions about what they had been taught in school. Liz remembered what Diane had told her—that evolution's main premise is "Spontaneous Generation": that "something can come out of nothing". That premise didn't seem logical to her, since Louis Pasteur disproved the idea of "Spontaneous Generation" over two hundred years ago. Jack also knew that evolution was based on a false and unscientific premise. In fact, the "Theory of Evolution" was NOT science at all, but a metaphysical philosophy: a religion that made man into God, and made God into "Blind Chance" which "produced" a Big Bang out of nothing ("ex nihilo"). To Jack, it made more sense that a Supreme Being made the universe "out of nothing" rather than blind chance. He couldn't escape the idea that "something can't come out of nothing". There has to be a CAUSE for every effect, according to scientific law.

"Life can't come from non-life," he said to no one in particular.

"Whatever," Tom said.

A howl in the distance stopped all the conversations. Then another howl. And another.

"I thought there were no wolves in the Adirondacks," Mark said.

"I guess they're wrong about that," said Toby.

"Yeah," Toni agreed.

They heard another howl; but it was closer this time.

"This is getting creepy," Tammie Jo said.

"I think we should leave," said Cory. "Now!"

Mark, Sally, and Kathy were already practically running down the path to get out of there. Toby, Cory, Toni, and Tammie Jo were right behind them.

"I'm scared!" Toni said.

"Shhh!" Cory said. "Let's not make too much noise."

They could hear the crashing of branches nearby as they got to their cars. They wasted no time in getting into their vehicles. Everyone had a cell phone; and most of them dialed "911".

"Tammie Jo. Do you have Diane's phone number?"

"Yes, Toby."

"Call her. I'll drive us out of here."

Fortunately, there were a lot of receiving towers around; and cell phones picked up well, even at the base of Sugar Loaf Mountain. Tammie Jo called Diane's cell number.

"Hello, Diane?"

"Hi, is this Tammie Jo?"

"Yes." She paused. "Diane, get out of there! Climb a tree. Anything!"

The seven who were left on the mountain could hear the crackling of branches, and realized that they were too late in getting ready to leave. The wolves were coming up the path. There was no escape.

"Trees!" Tom yelled.

Tom, Jack, Marianne, and Liz got up and headed for some trees; but they were not in time. Ron and Diane were also trapped.

"O God, I'm not ready to die!" screamed Marianne.

Diane shot back, "You've heard the gospel, Marianne. Accept it."

"Dear Jesus, save me from Hell. Please! Forgive me. I'm sorry," she sobbed. "I know You died for me and rose again."

As she pleaded for her salvation, the wolves jumped her. She fell, hit her head, and immediately entered into the presence of her Savior.

Jack and Liz trembled in fear. They were back-to-back, surrounded by wolves. They both had heard the gospel from Ron and

Diane; and both of them prayed and received the gift of eternal life by faith, and died, entering eternal peace and rest.

Tom ran for his life, refusing to listen to his need for God. He didn't get far; and he cursed God to His face as he died.

Ron and Diane looked at each other.

"I'm ready to die, Ron."

"So am I. See you in Heaven."

They faced death valiantly, and awoke in the presence of their Lord and Savior.

Robbie had walked up to the top of the mountain. He had sensed the danger before anyone else, and had left the area early. His keen ears had caught sounds, even before the wolves started howling. He was mentally challenged; and he didn't know why he headed up instead of down. But he kept going, and hoped that Ron and Diane and all the others got away safely. Robbie couldn't speak; and so he used sign language. He believed in Jesus Christ; and he knew where he would go when he died. He was afraid he would slow the others down; so he had taken off. He decided on the way up that he would climb a tree at the top and use his cell phone to text for help.

The eastern side of the mountain was a cliff with a two-thousand-foot drop. Robbie saw some trees ahead at the top of the mountain. The wolves had not noticed him yet; so he had time enough to get to the top. He reached the highest tree, which literally hung over the cliff. He began to climb the tree. Now, he could see straight down. As he climbed nearer to the top of the tree, his ears picked up the sound of wolves approaching.

"This is it," he thought. "God is going to take me to be with Him."

It was a premonition. He was not afraid to die; but he did wish that he knew how his brother and sister were. The thought came to him that they were already with the Lord. A feeling of comfort came over him.

Robbie could see down to the base of the tree. He had not realized how flimsy and weak the roots of this tree were; but now he could see the wolves digging at the roots; and he could feel the tree beginning to sway eastward over the two-thousand-foot drop. As the roots gave way, he gave God the sign language for "I love You!" As the tree swayed further downward, he lost his grip and fell out of the tree. He sign-languaged "Jesus, I love You!" several times as he picked up speed. His eyes were looking upward toward the sky as he fell. He had no fear: just a sense of great expectation. He would not be disappointed. His body smacked the ground at nearly two hundred miles an hour; and he instantly left this world of sorrow, and entered into eternal peace and rest in the presence of God.

CHAPTER FOUR

February 15, 2023—Albany

Glen Hastings was the assistant head of the New York State Regulatory Commission. He was just finishing up his work in the east wing of the municipal building in Albany. It was about 3:30 PM and twenty degrees Fahrenheit outside. He was a "creature of habit", and always left his office at 3:30 sharp.

He filed his last document, logged off, and said "Goodbye" to his staff. Then he put on his winter coat, and walked out into the cold. He proceeded down the sidewalk of Municipal Street, turned the corner, and moved down the stairwell to the underground garage.

He noticed that there was a different Security guard today; but he thought nothing of it. "Maybe old Joe got sick today," he thought. He walked confidently toward his black 2023 Hybrid Lexus. He didn't have the perks of his boss, but still made a great salary—one hundred and fifty thousand dollars per year. His boss was chauffeured to and from his office, and worked an hour less per day than Glen.

Glen noticed some movement to his right; but he thought it was an employee of the Municipal Center. Even so, he had this "eerie feeling" come over him.

"Mr. Hastings?"

Glen practically jumped out of his skin. He turned around to see who was speaking to him. It was the new Security guard.

"Yes?" Glen asked nervously. He hoped the guard could not hear the noise of his heartbeat.

"Is that your car over there?"

"Yes, it is. Why?"

"Somebody was prowling around near your car. I'm here to assist you if you need it."

"Well, just walk me to the car."

"Okay, Mr. Hastings."

They walked to the car; and a tall man carrying a clipboard approached them and said:

"Hi, Mr. Hastings. I'm from the FBI. We have reason to believe that you're in trouble."

"What do you mean?" Glen asked, visibly surprised.

Suddenly, he felt metal pressed against his side.

"Don't be alarmed, Glen," the Security guard said. "If you cooperate, no harm will be done to you or your family."

"Wha…w-w-what are you talking about?" he mumbled. He began to feel panicked. "What do you want? I'll do what you say," he said quickly.

"My friend has a clipboard. He just wants you to sign a couple of documents."

"Documents?"

"Yes."

"About what?"

"You don't need to know."

"But—I can be incriminated," he said softly.

"You won't be."

Glen was sweating; his heart was racing; and he was shaking like a leaf. He could feel his blood pressure going up.

"Promise you won't hurt any of us?" he asked in a high, weak voice.

"No harm at all. We promise."

"You won't kill me after I sign?"

"There's no profit in it. I have no desire to harm you if you sign these papers."

"Hurry up! People will be coming soon," the man with the clipboard said.

"Okay. Just—please keep your promise. Please," Glen pleaded.

Glen had to really concentrate on signing the two documents, because he was shaking so badly. Then the man took back the clipboard and notarized it with a stamp. Glen was not allowed to see the Notary Public's name. And the documents themselves were covered with blank paper so that Glen could not see what they contained. He had no idea what this whole affair was about.

"This incident didn't happen," the man with the clipboard said.

"Tell no one," the Security guard warned. He added, "We know where you and your family live."

"You understand?" the man with the clipboard said.

"Yes. I won't tell anyone. I promise."

"We'll know if you do; and we'll come after you," the guard said.

"Okay, okay, I've got it."

"Thank you, Mr. Hastings," the clipboard man said.

"Be safe," the guard said.

And they walked away. The two thugs had knocked "old Joe", the regular Security guard, unconscious near a back room. When he woke up, the documents had been signed; and Glen was gone. Old Joe Farrell would never know what had just happened, or why. He would never know it was part of a setup for a very devious plan.

October 15, 2025—Albany

New York State Governor Bruce Devane was sitting in a computerized back room, in a house owned by Todd James. The Governor and his co-conspirators were watching a result of a multi-generational plan: a photographic demonstration of its success. Mr. James wanted to show the Governor that the wolf population in the Adirondack Park was at a dangerous level; and that this master plan really could culminate in the next year, at and beyond the target date of August 14, 2026.

Todd James had set up a series of cameras to show the Governor how workable the plan really was. All five conspirators were there.

Todd said, "Harry, Sam, Scott, watch this."

He knew the drama was about to unfold. It was a scene only a few hours past. The cycle was about to begin.

"Here you are, Governor. About twenty seconds to start."

Sure enough, the drama began right on time.

Harry Reynolds was the New York State Police Commissioner. He was an ambitious politician, who had a shrewd attitude toward life. He was unscrupulous, and did not care about the welfare of others. He was willing to circumvent morality, truth, and the laws on the books to attain his self-centered goals.

He was the man behind a massive cover-up, designed to keep people from learning about the wolf attacks in the Adirondack Mountains. When seven teens were killed in Athol, he initiated a massive cover-up, labeling their deaths as "unsolved murders". He pulled some very valuable and powerful strings, with the help of Sam Lowell and Scott Franklin, and kept the media virtually silent, and compliant with the idea of "unsolved murders". This case was eerily similar to the party boat incident at Pharoah Lake.

It was on the evening news, but the three conspirators had just caught the incident in time; and so the media reported it as a "grisly multiple murder", which investigators were looking to solve. They had downplayed the report of wolves in the area, and had cordoned off the whole area to avoid having "outsiders tampering with the evidence": namely, discovering that there were wolf tooth prints all over the dead bodies. They also had Susan Downing's cell phone, which Julia Wilde had willingly and unwittingly handed over to the authorities. A nurse, Darlene Brown, had filed a report of a "wolf attack" witnessed by said Susan Downing; but that testimony was discredited and buried.

Police Commissioner Reynolds hoped that he wouldn't have too many more of these "close calls". It took a lot of hard work and mental concentration to keep these incidents from getting reported truthfully. All loose ends had to be dealt with. If it was necessary, he had a last resort to use to silence people: four men on his personal, secret payroll whom he used to clean up "messy" problems. All four had nicknames which described them well. And all four of them were dangerous, ruthless criminal-minded men.

Sam Lowell was a very powerful lawyer who provided crucial legal counsel for Governor Devane. He had served on the Second Circuit Court of Appeals for nearly twenty years. He knew a lot of powerful people in the federal and state judiciary. He was a master at deflecting lawsuits against the Governor, the Police Commissioner, and even the Governor's campaign manager, despite numerous questionable and even downright corrupt associations and activities. And he had master-minded the plan to get the necessary contracts signed in 2023 on February the fifteenth by the Assistant Head of the New York State Regulatory Commission. He told the Governor that these contracts would give him the authorization and the cover he needed to put in motion his so-called "mining rights" to an area that contained some artifacts worth hundreds of millions of dollars at the very least, and possibly worth billions. He had also helped create the company, based in Nicaragua, which would "officially" have the mining rights. The Governor had given the Nicaraguan government stolen identity off of a deceased individual to form a bonafide owner; and because he possessed the stolen information, he possessed this company officially.

Once the artifacts were "mined", he would dissolve the company and close out the accounts. And then he would have the stolen identity deleted completely. Sam Lowell had guided Governor Devane through the whole process up to the present time, and would continue his "legal" counsel until the whole process of this conspiracy was completed. The Governor knew that Sam Lowell was indispensable.

Todd James, nicknamed "Roamer", was the genius behind all of the computer technology needed to successfully complete this plan and make it work. He guarded the DIAC (Department of Indigenous Animal Control) websites from potentially inflammatory language. He scanned the chatrooms for any hint of communication concerning any of the "incidents" that had occurred in the Adirondack Park area. A warning light would flash in his head if someone in a chatroom mentioned "wolves" or "predators" or "unsolved murders". That "warning light" indicated to him that someone was getting "too close" to the truth and would have to be identified, monitored, and possibly "eliminated" if the rhetoric went too far. Roamer had already silenced a number of people. He believed in the old adage: "Dead men tell no tales."

Besides guarding the DIAC websites, Todd James also set up all of the software needed for the Governor to carry out his plan, using only the information that the Governor wanted revealed. And Roamer set up a mechanism that would transact the sales of the artifacts through a shadow website made accessible only through a series of temporary disposable URLs built exclusively for the intended bidders. These URLs were hidden within special icons which would self-delete once the bidder clicked on it twice, and the URL would not appear even for that short moment between the double click and the appearance of the next icon. The bidder would double click on six consecutive icons before arriving at the desired bidding website. In addition, Roamer set up an elaborate scheme to hide the completed transactions. The money would go through several banks to make the initial transaction difficult to trace. A second shadow company then received the money and the transaction was hidden by a firewall so complex that Roamer calculated that no hacker on earth could decode it. Roamer had personally created this firewall; and he knew it was virtually impenetrable, because he had tried to crack the code himself without using the decoding information which he possessed. He was unable to do it; and he was one of the best computer hackers on the planet.

The Governor had several shady goods dealers at his disposal, who would come up with buyers: mostly people overseas who were heads of state—dictators who loved to buy expensive and rare articles, using money which was given to them by the United States' government to help provide food, clothing, and shelter for their countries' poor people. Of course, the dictators would take most or all of this "foreign aid" money for themselves while their citizens starved to death.

Once a transaction was negotiated, the Governor would use a private delivery service owned by a shady character who asked no questions and was paid huge sums of money for his services.

Once the buyer expressed an interest, he was given a secret access code to the shadow company's bidding website. The bidding would begin, and it would continue for 48 hours. The highest bidder would then make the electronic transaction on this super-secure site, which was automatically coded contingent to a time-sensitive delivery code. If delivery was not completed within 72 hours, the transaction would be reversed and the deal cancelled. If delivery was successful, then the delivery code would confirm and validate the transaction, sealing and completing the deal.

Sam Lowell had also provided another layer of protection for the Governor. Once the Governor's Nicaraguan-based company acquired the mining rights to the specified area of the Adirondacks mentioned in the "contract documents", that would be sufficient to claim ownership of anything mined in the area, thanks to the brilliant work of the lawyer. There was a law in the New York State books which still allowed the state to claim historical artifacts as its own. Sam Lowell, with the help of some friends in the New York State Legislature, snuck through a provision which struck that statute down. They hid it inside a huge bill that the Legislature was intent on passing. It was a huge success for Sam Lowell. The bill passed almost unanimously in December of 2023, just before Christmas recess.

Scott Franklin was Governor Devane's campaign manager. He was brilliant, a Summa Cum Laude 2014 graduate of Siena College, majoring in Political Science; and a 2018 Doctor of Political Science, earning a degree that was newly incorporated into Siena's doctoral program. Mr. Franklin then proceeded to successfully manage the Governor's campaign in 2022. He was a political genius who had in his college years written down some recently unused but "found-to-be-successful" ideas and programs (both positive-defensive and neg-ative-offensive) to win an election. He was boundlessly ambitious, and actively sought out Mr. Devane. He told him that these political programs would get him elected.

Devane decided to try the new procedures, because he was ten points behind in the polls. Sure enough, through the use of Scott's resurrected old-school-successful ideas, Bruce Devane became Governor Devane, winning narrowly by two percentage points. Of course, a little cheating didn't hurt, but that was done behind the scenes; and his opponent couldn't seem to find a way to stop him.

Mr. Franklin continued to guide Governor Devane during his tenure as Governor, and built his image up to the level of a "rock star". He now had a seventy percent approval rating in the political polls, and was expected to win by a landslide in the 2026 election. Scott Franklin had continued to boost his image, all the way to the present. He was a tremendous asset to the Governor. For such good work, the Governor had promised him a ten-percent share in the profits generated by the sale of the artifacts. That was tens of millions! Or more!

Sam Lowell, Todd James, and Harry Reynolds had also been promised ten percent each. With potentially billions of dollars being generated, there was plenty to share. This was a potential windfall where everybody was a winner—as long as you were one of the favored five who were in on the conspiracy.

The computerized counter was at "ten, nine, eight…"

"Just wait till you see this," Roamer said. "Three, two, one…"

A white-tailed deer ran through the forest; and the cameras turned to follow the path of the animal. Once the deer was out of range, other cameras would pick up the image. It was running with reckless abandon, heading for a large field. As the deer entered the meadow, other cameras picked up the action. It was a young buck about two years old. A beautiful sight to behold!

What the cameras picked up next was not so beautiful. It was the reason the buck was running so fast. About two hundred yards behind the deer, a pack of wolves was racing to catch up to its prey. The chase would last for several minutes, and cover over three miles of land. As the deer ran, the pack closed the gap. Whenever the deer turned slightly from its straight path, the pack would fan out and move more to the side to get closer. It worked, because soon there were wolves running almost alongside the deer, but at a distance. But they didn't close in yet.

The pack formed a semi-circle with their prey in the center of the circle. And then the predators gained even more ground as the buck began to tire. Some were now ahead of the deer; and they were almost ready for the kill. They would swarm the deer from both sides; and there would be no escape. As the pack drew closer, they were cutting off the angles, forcing the buck to run straight ahead. Half a mile ahead was a stream. Four of the pursuers crossed the stream first, and waited for their prey. They swarmed the buck on the other side of the stream, and dragged him down. The rest of the pack joined in, and finished the kill.

"Beautiful!" Governor Devane said. "It's working. The area is becoming more and more dangerous to live in."

"That's what we're looking for," Todd replied. "A reason to evacuate the residents. Then we can move in and do OUR job."

"We'll recover the artifacts and we'll all be unbelievably rich!" the Governor said.

"And it will be our secret, because the area will be evacuated," Sam added.

Scott Franklin and Harry Reynolds were also very pleased at this demonstration of the unfolding of this plan. The Adirondack Park would be ripe for evacuation by August of next year.

CHAPTER FIVE

August 16, 1951—Northern Adirondacks

It was a beautiful sunny day. George Devane, a self-made millionaire, was looking to explore the Adirondack Mountains for oil. A number of his friends had rumored that there were huge oil deposits under the Adirondacks. If he could tap into it, he could make tens, maybe hundreds, of millions of dollars. He was excited about this surveyor's expedition. He owned a mining company which had already made him millions of dollars.

The group traveled up to the northern section of the Adirondacks and parked their trucks near a cluster of mountains. They walked from there, moving deeper into the wilderness area. They could hear the hooting of a black bear in the distance. Varieties of birds populated the area in great numbers. The explorers walked through a half-mile mountain pass which opened up into a huge meadow. This was unpopulated territory.

"Perfect," Mr. Devane thought.

In the next few weeks, the group began to test-drill the area, and found nothing. Mr. Devane was really disappointed. He was so upset, he decided to take a walk—alone. There was a small forest at the base of the northernmost mountain at the edge of the meadow. He decided "on a lark" to walk through that forest and go to the edge of the mountain. He crossed the tree line, and motioned to the others to "stay put".

"Wait for me here," he said.

He walked briskly through the forest, and noticed some tall brush growing right at the base of the mountain up ahead. He was curious, and walked up to the brush. He noticed a small entrance behind the bushes: a hole that a man could crawl through. He had a flashlight with him; and he turned it on, and crawled through the entrance. He found himself standing in a large open space. Then he stepped forward, and felt something break under his foot with a crunching sound. He pointed his flashlight downward; and his heart skipped a beat when he saw the broken human skull under his boot.

After the initial feeling of fear left him, he began to wonder what this cave-space was. He carefully walked forward, shining his flashlight right toward the ground in front of him. He came to a wall; and there were shelves on it, filled with some dusty artifacts. They were wooden, and carved into the shapes of animals and humans. He stared at them for a while, and then moved to the left.

He saw what looked like a doorway. It appeared to open up into another room. He walked through the door, being very careful to check where he stepped. He stopped, and shined the flashlight around the space that surrounded him. What he saw left him in a state of outright shock and delight.

To the right, he saw a huge mass of gold artifacts. He couldn't believe his eyes! Yet there they were, amassed like a tree full of plums ready for him to pick. He grabbed several of the artifacts, but didn't want to tip off the others about what he had found. He placed them in his backpack, and decided to keep them a secret.

"George! Are you okay?"

That was Harry. What was he doing here? Did he see the entrance?—What to do? George's mind was racing, moving, calculating.

"George! Where are you?" The voice was closer now.

Harry Reimer was close to the entrance. He couldn't see it yet. Then he saw a squirrel race behind the bushes. That made him curious; and he drew closer. He saw the entrance.

"George? Are you in there? Are you okay?"

George stood perfectly still, hoping that Harry would go away.

Harry turned on his flashlight, and crawled in. He gasped when he saw the skeletons to his right.

"George, are you hurt?"

George decided that he had better reveal himself and get Harry out of there. He walked back through the doorway and spoke to Harry in a feigned weak voice:

"I'm okay. Thanks."

"Wow, George! This is quite a place. An Indian burial ground?"

"Yeah, maybe. This place is creepy. Let's get out of here."

He grabbed Harry's arm, and started to pull him towards the entrance to the cave.

Harry pulled back. "Wait a minute! I want to look around."

"No, Harry! Let's get out of here. This cave gives me the creeps."

"No way! I'm looking around."

He waved his flashlight. And noticed the wooden artifacts.

"Uh-oh," thought George.

"What's this? Carved wooden deities?" He picked one up.

"George! These could be worth a fortune!"

"If only you knew what was in the other room," thought George.

Harry turned to the left, pointed his flashlight, and saw the doorway.

"Anything interesting back there, George?"

"Nothing. Just a bunch of skeletons."

"Maybe you missed something. Let's have a look."

"No, let's not!" George was getting very agitated. "I'm the leader of this expedition; and I say we're leaving!"

Harry ignored him, and walked toward the doorway. He looked in, swept the area with his flashlight, and stood in awe of what he saw. He didn't see the right jab that George threw at him. Harry reeled to the left, staggering.

"What—?"

George hit him again; and Harry hit the wall.

Large chunks of dirt fell from the ceiling; and the cave reverberated. They heard echoes of the noise farther and farther into the distance.

"This cave must be massive!" thought George.

Harry hit him with a right hook, and knocked him down. More dirt fell. The two men struggled, bumping and crashing into the western and southern walls. It looked and sounded like the place was going to cave in.

"I need to finish him off, and get out of here," George thought to himself.

He hit Harry across the face, grabbed one of the golden artifacts, and brought it down on the top of Harry's head, knocking him unconscious.

He dropped the gold piece, and stumbled toward the doorway. He could hear booming sounds all through the cave, while massive amounts of dirt were falling down. He had lost his flashlight, but had grown accustomed to the darkness. There was a little light coming through the entrance to the cave. He moved toward that light, hastily, in a desperate attempt to escape with his life. He tripped over a skull, hurt his knee, and limped toward the entrance. Dirt was pouring down on him. He knew he had to get out of there quickly. He finally made it to the entrance, and scrambled out into the light. He heard a huge rumbling sound as the walls caved in, and tons of dirt and rock buried the place.

Harry was either dead, or would be. George knew where the treasure was; and he had five golden artifacts. He would be back. If he had to dig by hand, he would get to the gold.

George walked back to the rest of the group. He told them that there was a cave-in, and that Harry didn't get out in time, and ended up buried under tons of rubble. George was a credible person when he talked; and they all believed his story. Actually, he was telling the truth, but not the whole truth. The whole truth was buried in that ancient Huron cave, filled with golden sculptures and wooden artifacts, all of which together were worth—at the very least—hundreds of millions of dollars.

George planned to return to the cave before the winter to look it over and see how he could best dig down to the golden sculptures. But he ended up getting seriously injured in a car crash. He was paralyzed from the waist down; and he gave up the idea of himself personally going to that wilderness treasure site.

In September of 1965, George revealed his secret to his twenty-year-old son, John. He showed him the directions to get there, a diagram of the area, and where the cave entrance was. He described the interior of the cave, giving him approximate estimates of measurements, so that he could know about where the golden artifacts were buried. George reasoned that if he wasn't going to get to the golden treasures, at least his son John could.

George knew how valuable his five artifacts were, because he had them appraised secretly before his accident. They were worth about five-hundred thousand dollars each. Why so valuable? Because they were historical and unique. And because there were diamonds folded into the gold. He did a mathematical calculation. The massive pile of golden sculptures—there must have been thousands of them—could be worth a billion dollars or more.

"Wow!" he thought. "What a nice addition to my only son's inheritance!"

John Devane visited the area in 1966, excited about the prospect of digging up the gold. But there was a new problem: the area was populated now. A whole town, aptly named "Mountain Meadow", had grown up where previously there was only the wilderness. How could he get to the gold secretly with a whole town right there to watch?

It was true that the people there had not disturbed the cave, but that was because it was caved in, and also because the townspeople were not aware of the great treasure buried inside. But the proximity of the town was disturbing. There was no way that he could unearth this treasure without someone seeing it.

Consequently, John asked himself, "How can I get rid of this town so that I can operate in secret?"

He could not find an answer to that question for four years. Then in 1970, he saw a headline in the local newspaper that caught his attention. It read, "WOLVES RELEASED INTO THE ADIRONDACKS".

"Huh! Interesting," he thought.

He let his imagination run wild.

"What if I could influence the DIAC to go too far, and release an excessive number of these dangerous predators into the wild? Since they are an 'endangered species', the people of Mountain Meadow would not be allowed to shoot them; and so the burgeoning wolf population would pose a serious threat to the people there. The townspeople would end up leaving the area; and then I can move in and get to the gold in secret."

The idea sounded crazy. He would need a number of influential people in his corner to make it work. And what if the townspeople refused to leave? Maybe the state of New York could declare the Adirondack Park a disaster area and force them to leave. Could the state authorities use the principle of "eminent domain" in a relocation case like this, and take possession of at least part of the Adirondack Park? Or would the federal government step in? And how would he get permission to get to the gold site?

John had a lot of thinking to do. And planning. This was a complex problem; and he had to figure out a way to solve it. Somehow.

It would take a long time to put a plan like this into action. He figured that a future son of his might be the one to eventually succeed in this endeavor.

"After all," John thought. "I'm already rich. So are my future heirs. We're not desperate. We've got plenty of time."

And so, a plan was hatched in 1970 which would reap a "reward" much later. In 1980, John's son Bruce was born. By 2025, Bruce would be forty-five years old, and the Governor of New York State. Together, Bruce and his dad would figure out all the details of this sinister plan.

CHAPTER SIX

December 10, 2025

Jonathan Wilkes was a thirty-seven-year-old computer analyst, who had worked in Washington DC for ten years at the Pentagon. He was more than a technician. He was an inventor. He had invented numerous programs, and placed them into the Pentagon's computer centers. He remained anonymous to the outside world, because he would be immensely valuable to hostile countries. He was afforded top security clearance by the U.S. government.

But now, he had decided to go back home for a time. He had some unfinished business he needed to accomplish back home: back to his roots. He had left twenty years ago, after a bitter fight with his parents over money issues. Now, ironically, he was successful, with a six-figure salary of over three-hundred thousand dollars a year. He wanted to reconcile with his parents—to make up for all of those lost years. He was excited about going home; and he decided to surprise them.

He was a single man who led a quiet life; and he was immersed in his work. He didn't go out to parties, didn't drink or smoke, but spent most of his time at the Pentagon and in his DC suite. He was a deep thinker, immersed in Biblical and philosophical studies, in addition to the innovative process.

Jonathan had one invention that he had worked on in DC; and he kept this prized invention with him. It was a unique global positioning system (GPS): the only one of its kind. He had shown the plans for this invention to his superiors, but they rejected the invention as being impossible to build, and too risky, because of all the complex unsolved variables involved in constructing and using such an invention.

But Jonathan constructed this unique machine anyway. Unbeknown to his superiors, he worked out the glitches, and had a very useful and workable product. But he decided not to go back to his superiors with the workable, finished product. Instead, he made up his mind to start his own company, patent his GPS, and then sell it to the Pentagon.

There were codes that activated the GPS; and Jonathan was the only person in the world who knew them, by memory. He could command this system with his voice or by pushing virtual buttons suspended as a hologram in the air.

The GPS could take control of any vehicle, and drive it to its maximum capacity. It could make maneuvers that no human being could possibly accomplish by himself. It could calculate percentage of survivability in a tight situation. And it was in constant contact with satellites in a unique pattern of numerical sequences. Nobody could crack this complex matrix, because it was spread abroad unevenly between numerous satellites traveling around the globe. If one satellite was destroyed, the piece of the matrix which the satellite controlled would transfer to a random satellite. There was a code which allowed all these satellites to communicate with each other concerning ONLY this matrix; and only one man on the globe had this code: Jonathan Randolph Wilkes.

The GPS had multi-functions: much more than controlling a vehicle. And it was open to new functions not yet added to it. There were seemingly endless possibilities for the use of his invention; and some of those possible functions were undoubtedly futuristic.

Jonathan chose to name the vehicle control function of his GPS. He called it the world's first "Land Traffic Controller", or LTC. It was his favorite function: his favorite part or piece of the most advanced GPS in the entire world. No other GPS came close to this one. And there was no other LTC anywhere else in the world. And he kept it a closely-guarded secret.

Jonathan didn't like to use the LTC, because he was so secretive and protective of it. But in a few tight situations, he had used it to test it out. It worked beautifully. When not in use, he would put it in sleep mode, but untraceable. To awaken and activate it, all he had to do was to speak or punch in the twenty-three-letter activation code and a seventeen-digit shadow code. What made the twenty-three-letter code unique was its composition of English, Greek, Russian, and Hebrew letters all combined, and accessed primarily through a second keyboard, which was hidden inside the hologram and accessed by pressing several icons in precise order.

Jonathan calculated that it would take an army of computer hackers over a hundred years to break this twenty-three-letter code. One of the reasons that the odds against cracking this code were so great was that the shadow code was repellent toward the twenty-three-letter activation code. It had a built-in function that reversed the search for the twenty-three-letter code and presented a dummy code to mimic the real code. Consequently, if the hackers were searching the alphabetical matrix for the code, the mimic letters would appear. And they would appear only in English letters, thereby keeping the hackers in the dark concerning the multi-lingual nature of the activation code. It obfuscated the fact that there were not only English letters in the code, but Greek, Russian, and Hebrew letters as well.

Additionally, the shadow code was virtually untraceable, hidden randomly among mimic numerical codes, which in turn reversed the search for the shadow code. There were seven levels of mimic codes, immersed in a complex matrix of their own. Only Jonathan knew these codes. He had a photographic mathematical memory. The only place where all of the LTC codes could be found was in Jonathan Wilkes' mind. The LTC function was, in fact, more secure than the gold in Fort Knox or the computer files of the Pentagon.

The GPS was located inside a small box attached to the car below the dashboard. And the LTC was one of the multi-functions placed into it. Jonathan had also developed a cell phone that would bring up any of these functions. He had only to punch in one number to produce the keyboards to activate the functions. All the functions could be activated by using the same two keyboards and speaking or punching in the twenty-three-letter code and the seventeen-digit shadow code. And all of the functions could be accessed through the cell phone or the hologram.

Jonathan realized that the more he used the LTC or any other function of his GPS, the more likely someone might try to trace its location; so he had a twelve-letter code that hid its location—an invisibility code. He didn't have a shadow code to hide this other code, because he was sure that even though the GPS was detectable when activated, nobody would know that it was anything other than a regular GPS; and therefore, very few people—if any—would be interested in finding it.

Jonathan had a preference for antique cars. He loved the old 1984 IROC-Z Camaro, in the red version. He had the engine souped-up to almost the equivalent of a ZR1 engine of a Corvette. It had unbelievable pick-up power, and could go from zero to sixty miles per hour in less than three seconds. Once in a while, the big engine would stall for a second or two; yet it would always start. Once it did, the Camaro rode like a race car. It was super-fast and close to the ground. Its hug-the-road maneuverability made it a joy to drive.

When he was in high school, he loved to race; and his favorite stretch of road was "dead man's run", a stretch of six miles of nearly straight road. It was well-kept and easy to use as a race-track. Back in 2005, in his Senior year, he raced one of his hot red cars, an older Ford Mustang, at one hundred and forty miles an hour. Nobody else dared to keep up with him; and he became known as the "Roadway Ace", or "RA".

One day, when he was in Purdue University, a fellow-student invited him to a meeting featuring one of his favorite race-car drivers. This driver had won a number of recent races, and was ranked second-best in the world. So Jonathan went, got his autograph, and then sat down with the crowd to listen to his life's story.

This man had a fascinating childhood, which began with his being born into a poor family in Detroit, Michigan. His father was a machine operator; and his mother was a traditional housewife who raised five boys and three girls. He was the oldest son; and everybody called him "Junior". "Junior" was best friends with Jerry Anusewicz, the son of a race-car mechanic. At eight years old, both "Junior" and Jerry were excited about cars, and learned all that they could about engines, transmissions, and all the other parts of a car.

A couple of years later, Jerry's dad, Tom, took Junior aside, and told him that God loved him and wanted to give him eternal life in Heaven as a free gift.

He quoted Romans 3:23: "For all have sinned and come short of the glory of God." Tom told Junior that the punishment for sin is a place of suffering called Hell, or "the lake of fire".

But God loved people in the world so much that He sent His Son, Jesus, to become a mortal man so that He could suffer and die for the sins of the whole world.

Tom said, "Our sins were placed on Him; and He was punished for all of our sins, in our place, so that we would not have to be punished forever for our sins in that place of punishment called Hell or the lake of fire.

"Jesus then rose from the dead; and He is able to save anyone who receives the salvation that He offers.

"All that anyone has to do is admit that he or she is a sinner deserving of Hell, and believe Jesus died to pay the penalty for all of our sins—past, present, and future. He rose from the dead; and we can receive Him as our Savior by asking Him to forgive all of our sins, and asking Him to save us from going to Hell."

And Junior did just that. He asked Jesus to forgive and save him. And God gave him the free gift of eternal life; and Junior knew he was forgiven from that moment on. He now loved God, and wanted to serve Him for the rest of his life.

Junior, the race-car driver, then completed his story, saying God led him to be a race-car driver, and has blessed him every day of his life. Then, he invited the people in the audience to receive this gift of eternal life.

Twenty-year-old Jonathan gladly received this gift, asking Jesus to forgive and save him. From that moment on, he wanted to serve God. And he continued his studies in computer technology.

Jonathan's one sore spot was that he didn't get along with his strong-willed parents. He had left them to go to college, and then he went on to earn his Masters and Doctorate degrees in Computer Science by age twenty-five. He became so knowledgeable, that many perennial and accomplished professionals came to him for answers. He easily landed a job as a "Computer Analyst" at the Pentagon.

But now, after ten years of success in the nation's capitol, he realized that he needed to have a good relationship with his parents. God used His word to convict him one night. He was reading Luke chapter 15, which contains the story of the "prodigal son". Even though this story was different from his story, there was enough similarity to bring him to tears, realizing that his parents really did love him and miss him.

The truth was that he had been so deeply hurt by the perceived mean-spiritedness of his parents that he had stayed away from them, and broken contact with them, for twenty years. For twenty years, he felt that he couldn't bring himself to communicate with his parents. Now, he was coming back to visit; and he couldn't wait to see them.

Susan Morehouse was a supervisor for the Department of Indigenous Animal Control (DIAC). She was a 2006 graduate of Bolton Central School. Energetic and cheerful as a student, she had been a cheerleader, a Ski Club member, a field hockey player, and a Yearbook organizer.

After graduation, she went to Adirondack Community College (ACC) and then to Yale University, earning a BA in Biology and a Masters degree in Chemical and Environmental Engineering. During her college years, she worked part-time as a waitress. She graduated with high honors at both educational institutions.

Then, she started to work for the DIAC, first as an assistant secretary, and then in higher-level positions until she was promoted to Second Supervisor of the Glens Falls branch of the DIAC in upstate New York. She was more efficient than the Head Supervisor, but chose to support him rather than criticize. The two supervisors got along very well. The Head Supervisor was planning to retire in two years, and then Susan would become the new Head Supervisor of the Glens Falls branch of the DIAC.

Susan was ambitious, but patient. She was strong, yet kind. She was the type of person one would want to have as a best friend and ally.

And she had a great relationship with her parents. She kept in constant communication with them. They had brought her up in a firm but loving manner. She learned from her parents how to work hard, to study effectively, to express herself, and to care about others. Her parent's moral values were effectively transferred to her; and she was given a sense of self-esteem, not to the point of arrogance, but to the point of healthy self-confidence.

Soon enough, Susan would cross paths with Jonathan Wilkes; and they would make a near-perfect match. The super-genius would meet the super-efficient hard worker. The one hurt by his parents would find the one encouraged by her parents. The deep thinker would become friends with the energetic person who lived life to the fullest in the sense of productivity. Separately, they were two opposites. Together, they would make a "dynamic duo".

CHAPTER SEVEN

December 20, 2025

Jonathan Wilkes was driving up Highway 787, the New York State Thruway. At age thirty-seven, he still loved racing. But he kept himself in check, choosing to drive at sixty-five miles per hour, despite his constant urges to go really fast. A few other Camaro drivers had come up alongside of him and revved up their engines, tempting him to race. He would race for a few seconds, wave at the driver, and then slow down. When a Ford Mustang driver wanted to race, Jonathan simply looked toward the driver, smiled, and slowed down. The guy got the message: "Thanks, but no thanks."

He was busy thinking about his parents, and how he would reconcile with them. He knew they missed him, because he kept in touch with his two sisters, who told him so. They understood why he stayed away, but had urged him, especially in recent years, to come back home and see them. Finally, he "saw the light" and made a decision. He would take a "leave of absence" from his career at the Pentagon. He knew he would not be fired, because he was so valuable to them with his super-genius mind. Firing him would have been like the head of the Manhattan Project firing Albert Einstein.

And now, here he was, headed to see his parents for the first time in twenty years. He was both excited and apprehensive. He knew they missed him; but were they angry? It was weird to be afraid like this at age thirty-seven; but he still had the "issue" of having been intimidated by them so many years ago and still retaining that fear all the way up to the present time. Yet he was glad that he was coming home. He believed that God would work everything out. He thought about that, and realized that he had been away from fellowship with God for so long. He suddenly realized why.

The verses came to him—"Forgive us our debts as we forgive our debtors…" "…forgiving one another, even as God…has forgiven you."

Jonathan thought, "I need to FORGIVE Mom and Dad! If I don't, I'll never be really close to God!"

He started to pray: "O God, I've been so wrong. I'm so very sorry. Forgive me for not forgiving them, and being so bitter and angry for so long."

He continued praying; and yes—he forgave his parents. When he did, he felt as if a one-hundred-pound burden was lifted off of his shoulders! He felt free—much like he did in the first year of his Christian life. Joy flooded over him, and washed over his whole being! It made him so happy, he felt like he would break out into uncontrollable laughter.

"Thank you, God," he said. "I left my first love, didn't I?"

He paused. "Well, I'm coming back to You now."

Susan Morehouse, the DIAC Second Supervisor, was driving home from work at about 5:00 in the afternoon. She would be glad to get home to Warrensburg, where life was very peaceful and serene. Many people considered a small town to be boring; but Susan enjoyed the peace and quiet of this small, beautiful town known as the "Queen Village of the Adirondacks".

A nagging thought stuck in her mind: one that had bugged her all day. She had a casual friend named Marie Trombley. They hadn't talked for months. Then, yesterday, she saw her in Walmart, and they struck up a conversation.

"Nice weather we're having, huh?"

"Yeah, if you're an Eskimo."

"How have you been?"

"Not very well," Marie said.

"You're crying."

"I know. I'm sorry. I lost my daughter five months ago."

"What?"

"Yeah."

"That's awful. I'm so sorry. I don't know what to say."

"I'm still trying to cope with this."

"How did it happen?"

"The authorities say she was murdered."

"You sound like you don't believe it."

"I don't."

"What then?"

"She and six others were killed by a pack of vicious animals. Wolves!"

"What?"

"They were killed by wolves.

"That's horrible! I am so sorry."

Then Susan added, "Marie, how do you know it was wolves?"

"I believe the kids who survived. They said they heard wolves."

"Did they see them, too?"

"No. But they were so close! They had to get out of there, or they would have died, too."

"I see."

"I think the police are covering it up."

"But why?"

"I have no idea."

Then, she added: "Susan, it hurts so bad. I hurt right now as much as I did when I first found out she was dead. Even more."

"I'm so sorry, Marie. Is there anything I can do for you?"

"I'm not sure." Marie paused, obviously distressed. "Let me think."

"Okay, Marie. Take your time."

Marie was processing in her thoughts, searching for an answer to Susan's offer to help her. Suddenly, an answer surfaced.

"Wait a minute! You work for the DIAC. Right?"

"Yes, I do."

"Could you check into this?"

"Into what?"

"You know, wolves."

"Do you think I could help you?"

"Yes."

"Well, I can try. I'll check on the internet, and see what is posted on the websites connected to my numerous search engines."

"Would you?"

"Sure. I can do that tonight. Or at the latest, tomorrow night."

"Thank you."

Susan had gone on the internet that night, and checked on "wolves in the Adirondacks". What she found startled her. There was a project which she had not been aware of, because it had ended before she started working for the DIAC in 2015. She was fascinated by this project, which lasted for forty years: from 1970 to 2010. Over that time-period, there were over eight-hundred wolves released into the Adirondack Park.

"Wolves are very dangerous," she thought to herself.

Then she thought, "How many wolves are there now?"

And, "Can the Adirondack Mountains support all the wolves?"

She figured that there had to be at least two or three THOUSAND wolves. And a scary thought crossed her mind: "When predators run out of space, they cross over into human territory."

"I hope not," Susan muttered softly to herself.

Jonathan Wilkes was now finally on the next-to-last stretch of road towards home: I-87, the Adirondack Northway, part of which was voted in as being the most beautiful, scenic stretch of highway in the United States back in the 1960's. He was feeling that anxious feeling in his chest that many people feel when they are taking a long trip. He was thinking about what to say to his parents, and the words, "I love you" and "I'm sorry" came to mind.

Susan had decided to print out a lot of pertinent information. Who was involved? Any reports of attacks by wolves? Or are they all suppressed? Who would suppress this information? And why?"

She found only two wolf attack reports. One was an unidentified hiker who was killed. The second was a biker who came up from Connecticut for a couple of weeks to tackle the mountain roads to prepare for racing competitions. That was it. There were no relatives listed, because the biker was from Belgium. His body had been flown back to Europe. An undisclosed amount of money was paid to the surviving relatives. So both cases—the hiker and the biker—were considered dead-end streets.

Susan segued to another thought: "If people have died, did the reports attribute their cause of death to something else? Would they call it murder, unsolved murder, or in some cases where there was no body present, maybe even a kidnapping?"

Then she remembered Marie's words: "The authorities said she was murdered."

She decided to look under "unsolved murders". She found forty unsolved murders for 2025, in the Adirondack Park.

She clicked to 2024. There were only three "unsolved murders" that year in the Adirondacks.

That was suspicious.

"Thirteen times, plus one!" she thought.

She began to read the reports, and printed them out to keep for her files. All but one of these reports had grisly results, with only parts of bodies recovered. The latest report was a total disappearance, except for a pair of the victim's shoes.

One of the reports caught her attention. The title read: "Seven Teenagers Believed Murdered". The report went on to describe the grisly scene. The names of the victims were given. One name stood out: "Elizabeth Trombley, age seventeen".

Jonathan Wilkes turned onto Exit 18, drove down the ramp, and turned left. He pulled into McDonald's and ordered a Fish Filet value meal at the Drive-thru. Once he received the meal, he drove onto the Northway, heading for Exit 23. The last five exits. About fifteen minutes to go, to get there.

She was much larger than a wolf, and very hungry. She had not eaten in a couple of days; and she was ready to hunt again. She wandered out of her den, and began to look for prey.

Susan was planning to continue her research tonight; and she decided to finish her last-minute duties. She was way ahead of her work, and would be home by about 5:20.

Jonathan Wilkes turned on the radio and heard some rap music. He switched it to another channel, and got some country music. He kept it there. And he passed Exit 21 at 5:10 PM.

"Three down, two to go," he said to himself.

She picked up a scent and moved forward. She was sleek and powerful, a formidable predator. The rabbit was nibbling on vegetation available just under the snow, unaware that it was being tracked.

Susan had pulled into a gas station, filled up her tank, and then drove onto the Northway at Exit 20, in a hurry to get home. She passed a lot of drivers. After passing Exit 21, she passed a beautiful red Camaro, an IROC-Z. She looked at the driver. He looked like he was singing along with the radio. And she noticed that he was a handsome man. He looked familiar, but she couldn't place him.

She thought to herself, "He should be passing MY car, not the other way around."

And with that, she sped away.

Twelve rapacious predators moved like rampaging monsters, bent on destroying everything in their path. They were tracking a large animal and moving methodically. They were fearsome, and moving forward at a steady lope, with tongues hanging out and fangs showing.

Jonathan pulled off at Exit 23, and turned into the nearest gas station. He failed to notice that his back right tire was quickly leaking out air, and would be flat a few miles down the road.

Susan pulled into her driveway. She remembered that she was supposed to make an important call at 5:20; and she grabbed her cell phone. It was dead. She looked at her watch, and saw that it was

5:19. She took her cell phone and plugged it into the charger. Then, she walked over to her land-line phone, and called Marie.

Jonathan got back into his car, and headed toward Athol. His car felt bumpy; but he didn't really pay any attention to it, because the road was rough.

"Hello?"
"Hi, Marie?"
"Yes. Is this Susan?"
"It is. Here is what I found out…"
After listening to Susan, Marie decided to go to the same websites which Susan had visited. She would do some legwork herself. She suspected a huge cover-up, and was hoping she could find some collaborative information to validate her suspicion.

The predator continued to track the rabbit. The rabbit was a half-mile away; and the scent was getting stronger. So she picked up speed.

Jonathan crossed over the bridge that separated Warrensburg from Athol. He noticed that the ride was becoming more and more bumpy.
"Aw, no," he thought. "Not now."
He hoped that the tire would last for another three miles to his parents' house. So he kept driving. He crossed the railroad tracks, and turned left around the corner. He drove straight, and then turned right onto Athol Road. He could hear and feel the flat tire wearing down to the bare rim. He knew he had to stop, or do more damage to the car. He drove past the initial turns, and came to the straight part of the road, and parked to the right.

The rabbit heard a noise, sensed that he was in danger, and scampered off. The huge predator kept on tracking him.

Jonathan stepped out of the car.

He thought, "Serves me right for driving this car in the winter."

He picked up his flashlight, and opened the trunk. He was planning to change his tire quickly, because it was really cold outside.

The twelve predators were picking up speed, as the scent of the large animal grew stronger. They were natural killers; and no animal in the woods could stop all of them.

John removed the lugs and tire, and reached for the spare. He saw a rabbit in the field next to him. It was moving rapidly, and hopped across the road in front of his car's headlights before disappearing into the dark of night. He continued working. He could feel the cold, even though he had on a thick coat, scarf, and pullover hat. He thought he heard a crackling sound in the distance, but paid no attention to it, because he was fully focused on attaching the spare tire. He started placing the first lug nut back on. Then, he heard a noise from inside the woods: "Crack. Crackle! Crack!"

He couldn't ignore the sound. He felt his hair stand on end. His whole body felt warmer as his heart began to pound heavily. He hoped it was just a stray dog, but wasn't so sure about that. Even if it was, he still had an eerie feeling that something else was out there. Something dangerous. He had no weapon with him for defense. His imagination began to run wild. He was so nervous, he dropped the lug nuts.

The massive predator came to the edge of the woods, and saw something new. She left the rabbit scent, and approached the human prey. Something had stepped on some branches and scared off the rabbit; but this new victim was a much larger meal. Her approach was completely silent.

Jonathan was searching frantically for the lost lug nuts. His back was turned toward the woods, toward the direction of the sounds. Whatever it was that was out there: he didn't want to see it. He began to pray: "Please God, help me!"

The marauding predators were closing in on the scent. They were now less than a half-mile away. They picked up their pace.

She was out of the woods, and halfway across the field. She crept closer, silently. The prey was in her sights, kneeling in the snow, face-down: an easy kill.

Jonathan felt a feeling of panic creep over him. He sensed imminent danger.

"I must do something. Maybe I should get back into the car," he thought.

He fumbled for the key. He sent up a prayer of desperation: "God, help me!"

She crept closer, getting ready to spring. She was less than forty feet away.

Jonathan stood up and tried the passenger door. Locked! "Oh no!" he thought.

He fumbled for the key. He sent up a prayer of desperation: "God, help me!"

The predators were so close to the edge of the wood line, they could almost taste their prey. They were ready to strike. It would not be long before they would be satisfying their appetites.

Jonathan slipped slightly in his panic.

She sprang, her powerful legs propelling her twenty feet through the air.

Jonathan felt a mass of hard muscle hit him and knock him flat. Fortunately, he didn't feel the full blow, because he had slipped. But he knew it was a large animal; and his natural instinct was to fight for his life.

The big cat was momentarily stunned from the impact. She had expected her prey to remain upright. She bounced off the car, and landed toward the hood. She shook off the pain, and roared.

Jonathan was on his back against the snow. His left shoulder was throbbing in pain from the impact. His flashlight was still on, facing away from him, the light shining into the darkness.

The lion pounced on Jonathan, and bit into his coat, pinching his chest. Jon screamed, and slapped the cat's head with his right hand. She tore off a piece of the coat, and spit it out.

Eamon and Julie Billings had spent several hours visiting with their son Mark and his wife Linda, and having an early dinner.

"Goodnight, son."

"Goodnight, Linda."

"Goodnight, Dad. Goodnight, Mom."

The parental couple had walked through the door, and out into the cold. Now, they were on their way from Mark and Linda's house on Bear Pond Road in Athol, and heading for their home on Library Avenue in Warrensburg. At this moment, they were on High Street, and had just passed the EMS station on the left.

Jonathan tried to defend himself by raising his arms in front of his face. The big cat opened her huge maw, and chomped down on his right arm. Her jaws were so powerful that they crushed his forearm. Then the cat tore into his coat with her deadly claws, ripping the fabric all the way down to his flesh.

"Awwwwwwhhh!!!" he yelled.

Then she raked his face.

Jonathan knew he was going to die; and he felt sad, because he didn't get to reconcile with his parents. His visit was to be a surprise; but now he was the one who was being surprised—with premature death.

The wolves watched the attack, waiting. One of them let out a howl.

The lion turned instantly. And let go of Jon's arm. The prey was her prey; and she would fight to defend it. She turned to face the invaders.

The Buick Regal passed the Post Office on the left. Eamon turned on the radio to the "easy listening" (really old music) station. But Julie turned it off.

"Sorry, Dear. I have a headache," she said.

Jonathan saw his chance to escape. He struggled to get up. Slowly, painfully, he rose to his feet. His body was trembling; and he could hear the terrifying growls of the wolves, and the piercing scream of the big cat.

Suddenly, he saw the high-beam lights cresting over the hill. A car headed this way!

"I've got to get them to help me!" he thought.

And he staggered out into the road.

The lion lurched forward, and tore into the nearest wolf, biting down hard into its neck, and ripping its belly with her razor-sharp claws. Then, she turned to a second wolf; and a ferocious battle ensued, as several wolves attacked her as a unit.

The light was getting closer. Jonathan could see the Buick now, and felt almost blinded by the headlights. He moved out of the direct path of the oncoming car, unsure whether or not the driver would stop. He was desperate, and waved his left arm frantically.

One of the wolves broke away from the pack and ran towards Jonathan.

Eamon was driving at thirty miles an hour. Suddenly, Julie yelled "Stop!"

They saw a man who looked half-dead, limping up the road and waving his arm.

"What do you want to do, Dear?" Eamon asked, as he slowed to a stop.

"Help me, PLEASE!!!" Jon pleaded.

"Well, let him in," Julie said.

"Get in the car, son," Eamon said.

Jon opened the back door and jumped in as quickly as he could, looking absolutely terrified. He quickly closed the door behind him.

Suddenly, there was a loud thump; and Jon saw a mouthful of teeth and the menacing eyes of the lone wolf that had pursued him.

"Let's get out of here. Please!" Jon said.

"Is it safe to travel down the road?" Eamon inquired.

"Probably in the car, yes," Jonathan answered.

They looked to the left as they passed the red Camaro; and the flashlight on the ground helped illuminate the scene. Several wolves and a huge mountain lion were locked in deadly combat. Two wolves were dead, and a third was badly wounded.

All of a sudden, the big cat shook violently, and broke free. She had been wounded, but not mortally. She bounded across the field, jumped on top of the Camaro, and let out a piercing scream. Then, she leapt across the road, and disappeared into the blackness of the night.

"You're lucky to be alive, Johnny," Julie said.

"You know my name?"

"Yes," she said, and turned around so he could see who she was. "I was your tenth grade math teacher."

"Mrs. Billings!" Jon exclaimed. "Geometry!"

"That's right," she said.

She paused for a moment and smiled. "And you look the same as you did when you were in my class."

The mortally-wounded wolf staggered on the snowy field, whimpering, and instinctively knowing that he would not be alive much longer. Several wolves surrounded him, attacked him, and finished him off.

CHAPTER EIGHT

December 20, 2025

Jonathan and the Billingses talked non-stop on the way to the Glens Falls Hospital Emergency Room. When they got there, he walked in on his own power, and then collapsed. Julie Billings had called in earlier, so that the hospital medical staff would be ready for Jonathan; and fortunately, they were. A doctor was waiting for him; and Jon was brought immediately into Intensive Care.

At 6:30, the Wilkeses got a call from Julie Billings' cell phone.
"Hello?"
"Mrs. Wilkes?"
"This is she."
"I'm calling about your son. He's fine, but he's in Intensive Care at Glens Falls Hospital."
"What? Who's this?"
"Mrs. Billings, the Math teacher."
"Oh, I remember you. Julie, right?"
"Yes."
"What happened?"
"Johnny was attacked by a mountain lion. No arteries were severed, so he's stable."
There was stunned silence as Mrs. Wilkes tried to process what she had just heard. Julie waited patiently for her, knowing how much of a shock this news must be to her. Finally, she heard a response.
A weak, trembling voice spoke. "What room is he in?"

"Room 417."

"Thank you. We're on our way."

Marie Trombley was on the DIAC website, and typed in "unsolved murders". She read all the reports, and then checked around for a link that might be helpful. There were a couple of links; but she didn't think the advertisement link would help her, so she clicked the other link: the chatroom.

She entered the room as "Antoinette". And she began to watch. There was a lot of environmentalist talk going on, along with political talk. But she didn't care about that. She wanted to know what happened to her Elizabeth.

Nothing. She stayed on for an hour, and found nothing of interest to her. She was disappointed. After another ten minutes, she logged out.

Susan Morehouse saved her files on the computer, and also kept printed copies in a file cabinet. She catalogued everything in a neat and orderly fashion. The printouts of the "unsolved murders" were carefully stored in her two filing systems. She would try to access more information tomorrow. She would look for a "more info" icon, or something—anything—that could give her a clue. And she would try to access information on the wolf reintroduction program. She would go back to the website on "wolves in the Adirondacks" and check for other links. She might find newspaper articles, and other documents that could tell her who was behind this program, and reveal to her other important details of this project.

Bill and Marge Wilkes were at the hospital in just over half an hour. They raced to the entrance to the ER, and charged up to the information desk to get quick directions to Room 417.

"Hi. We're looking for Room 417."

"What's the name?"

"Jonathan Wilkes, our son."

"Yes, he is in there." She turned to the Security Guard. "Brad, would you please escort them to Room 417?"

"Sure." He turned to the Wilkeses. "Come this way, please."

Marge turned to Bill and said, "I'm surprised we didn't have to give all our information first."

"It's all been taken care of, Mrs. Wilkes," Brad responded.

They passed the Nurses' Station, and walked further down.

"He's in there," Brad said, pointing.

"Thank you," Bill said.

"My pleasure," Brad replied. Then, he turned, and briskly walked away.

Marge, and then Bill, peeked inside, nervous about what they would see. Their son was hooked up to a monitor that kept track of his heartbeat, breathing, and blood pressure. He was also hooked up to an IV, and was sleeping.

Bill hesitated; but Marge walked right up to Jon, placed her hand on his, and said,

"That's my boy. I love you so much."

Jon's eyes opened; and his heartbeat and blood pressure spiked suddenly.

"Mom!"

"Hi, Johnny. Your father and I have missed you. We love you."

"I love you, too!" Jon blurted out.

All of his emotions had been bottled up for twenty years; and now they welled up within him; and he thought he would burst with emotion. His mother leaned toward him; and they hugged each other as best they could. His broken arm throbbed with pain; but he ignored it. And bawled like a little baby.

Marie lay in bed thinking about all the good times she had enjoyed with her daughter, Elizabeth. She remembered how scared she was to go to Kindergarten. So she rode with her on the school bus, and went into the classroom with her. After two days, she was fine. Marie remembered "Lizzy" growing up, and how she loved to help with chores around the house. She loved to wash dishes, clean the house, and do the laundry. She especially loved to cook. And they would read books together. What a wonderful daughter! They were very close. They were that rare mother-daughter combination that never had a serious loss of communication, even in Lizzy's teenage years.

Marie remembered how excited Lizzy was about going up Sugar Loaf Mountain that day. She had asked if it was okay. And, of course, Marie had said it was. She trusted her Lizzy, and believed that everything was going to be just fine. If only she had told her No; but that was not Marie's personality. Marie believed in letting Lizzy make her own decisions.

She felt guilty, even though she knew it was not her's or Lizzy's fault that she was gone. And she felt the tears welling up inside of her. She could feel the depression: that awful feeling of emptiness and hopelessness.

"She's gone. Gone forever. I'll never see her again. My baby! Dear God, I can't stand it! I'm hurting so badly!"

She sobbed uncontrollably for several minutes; and then, mercifully, she fell asleep.

After a few minutes, Bill Wilkes walked up to his son.
"I'm sorry, Son. I treated you so badly. Will you forgive me?"
"Oh yes, Dad. I love you, too."
They hugged. Father and son wept together.
Suddenly, Marge said, "Where are the Billingses?"
"Right here," said Eamon. "We wanted to give you your space."
He and Julie walked through the entrance and joined them.
"Thank you so much, Mr. Billings," Marge said. "And Julie."
"You can call me Eamon."
"Thank you, Eamon."
Dr. Ben Watson entered the room.
"I see you have a family reunion," he said. He had no idea how true his statement was.

He continued. "Your son was mauled by a cougar. He is very lucky that it is cold outside, and that he had a lot of heavy clothing on. That probably saved his life. His chest is bruised and slightly lacerated; his arm is broken up badly; and his left cheek, as you can see, is torn up. From what I can see, your son is lucky the cat got distracted."

"Thank God for that," said Bill.

"Believe me, Dad. I did."

"Tell us more," Marge said.

"We're going to keep him a few days to make sure he is okay. We don't want him to get infected, if he's not already. And we need to talk with him about surgical repair to his arm."

"I'm all for it," Jon said.

"We will be through with our initial analyses and tests by tomorrow, and we will schedule an emergency surgery tomorrow around 2:00 in the afternoon. This one may take some extra time, because his arm is so severely damaged."

The doctor explained that they had Jon on Morphine to manage his pain level. He went over a few more technical details, and then left the room.

Dr. Watson was a very genuine person who sincerely cared for people. The Billingses and Wilkses, including Jonathan, were all very impressed. A lot of doctors had a lousy "bedside manner". Dr. Watson was not one of them.

"What a wonderful person!" Marge exclaimed.

"You're a very lucky young man," said Julie.

"Yeah, I could have gotten a real grouch for a doctor," Jon said.

Jon laughed. They all laughed. Jon's arm hurt when he laughed. But he didn't care. He needed some humor. It was therapeutic for him.

After they laughed a while, Bill suddenly got serious. He turned to Jonathan and said:

"Son, what happened out there?"

Eamon and Julie already knew; but they didn't interrupt the conversation, because they felt it was best for Jonathan to speak for himself.

"My car had a flat tire. I was hoping to surprise you. But I didn't quite make it."

"Oh, you surprised us all right," Marge said with a loving smile.

"So I stopped to change it. It was cold; and I was in a hurry. I was almost done when the cat jumped me. It was huge! And so strong!"

He paused, and looked up into his father's eyes.

"I didn't know a mountain lion was so strong."

He continued, "I was lucky the wolves came along, because the cat left me alone so it could fight the wolves. I got up; and that's when Mrs. Billings and Mr. Billings came by. They were just in time. I got in the car. A wolf banged against the car door, right after I closed it."

"That's really scary," Marge said.

"So there ARE wolves in the area," Bill said. "I keep telling people; but they just don't believe me."

"How many were there?" asked Marge.

"Looked like about ten or more."

"Did they kill that awful cat?" Marge sounded hopeful.

"No. The cat got away." He paused. "Looked like the cat killed a couple of the wolves."

"That must be one mean mountain lion," said Bill.

"How big?" said Marge.

"Felt like two hundred pounds. I could hardly move with him on top of me."

"Wow!" Bill said.

"Well, we're glad you're here," Marge said.

She paused, "Well, I mean—"

"I know what you mean, Mom. You're glad I'm safe."

"Thank you, Dear."

They continued talking; and then Bill asked, "Where's your car?"

"Just above the three turns of the Athol Road."

"Three turns?"

"Yeah, the straightaway before you get to the O'Neills' house."

"Oh, I see… You mean the Camaro?"

"Yeah."

"We wondered whose car that was."

"Now you know."

"A real hot rod."

"Yeah."

"Fun to drive?"

"Lots…. Except when it gets a flat."

They all laughed. They all looked at each other. And laughed some more.

Finally, Eamon said to Julie, "We'd better get going."

They said "Goodnight", said they would be back to visit tomorrow, and left.

"They're so nice," Marge said.

"Yes, they really are," said Bill.

"They saved my life," Jon said with a smile.

"We'll have to do something for them to show them how much we appreciate them," said Marge. She continued, "We could have them over for dinner."

"Better find out what they like to eat," Bill said.

"How about taking them out to a restaurant?" Jon suggested.

"Okay," said Marge.

"I'm paying," Jon said.

They talked for another twenty minutes. Jonathan gave some more details about what he was doing, and apologized for his bitterness and long twenty-year absence. He asked for their forgiveness.

They were glad to say, "We forgive you, Son."

By the time the conversation was over, Jon felt really clean inside. He had made things right with his parents; and he felt his guilt feelings disappear. And he sensed the warmth of God's love, and of his parents' love as well.

"We'd better let you get some rest," Bill said. "You've got a big day tomorrow."

"Have a good night, Dad."

"Goodnight, Son."

"Goodnight, Johnny."

"Goodnight, Mom."

They left him; and the thought came to him that they were like the Waltons when they said "Goodnight" so many times.

Jonathan proceeded to pray and thank God for His protection, His answer to prayer. And he told God that he would serve Him for the rest of his life. Then, he fell asleep.

CHAPTER NINE

December 21, 2025

When Jon woke up the next day, he made a decision that he would do some investigating into why there were so many wolves in the area. He was glad for himself that they had been there, because, ironically, they had saved his life; but he knew that something in the ecology was very wrong. He could hook up with a whole bunch of websites and perhaps find out what was going on. Yes, when he got to the house, he would begin to start working on that project. He would have plenty of time.

His cell phone rang at about 10:00 AM. It was his father.

"Hi, Son. Just wanted to let you know we towed your car to our garage. The keys are in the glove compartment."

"Thanks, Dad."

"Oh, yeah, your wheel is loose. Back right side."

"Oh, I forgot to tell you…"

"You lost the lugs."

"Yes."

"I'm going to the Chevy dealership today to get them. Don't worry. I'll put them on."

"Thanks."

"Hi, Dear."

"Hi, Mom. I'm doing fine. The nurses are taking good care of me."

"Is your surgery at 2:00 still?"

"Yes."

"We'll be there," Marge affirmed.

"Son, we'll be there around 1:00. We'll talk to you then," Bill said.

"Thanks, Dad. I'll see you then."

"Goodbye."

They said their Walton family goodbyes, and hung up.

Eamon and Julie walked in.

"We bought you a gift that you can enjoy for the next couple of days," Julie said.

They handed him a devotional book authored by Max Lucado.

"Thank you."

"And here's an 'Our Daily Bread' if you like. It's free," Eamon said.

"Thanks again."

"We can't stay," Julie said. "We're going to our daughter's house for lunch. But we will be back to visit you tonight."

Jonathan read a few pages of Max Lucado, and the December 21st Our Daily Bread article. Then he laid back and rested for awhile. When he awoke, his parents were there. It was just a little before 1:00.

"How do you feel?" Marge asked.

"Better. But my arm hurts; and I can't wait for surgery."

"It won't be long now," she said.

"I'm really tired," Jon said.

"I know. Lay back and rest if you like," she said.

He laid back and rested some more. At about 1:30, a nurse came in to prep him for surgery. Bill and Marge waited outside.

The aides came in, and lifted him onto a gurney to roll him down to surgery. Both parents followed them to the operating room. The doctor told them it would probably take a longer time, because of the extent of the damage. They waited outside for a while, and then went back to the waiting room. The doctor would call them when it was over.

Susan Morehouse had an hour she could use to surf the internet and print out information. She was so efficient that she could do in two hours what the average person would do in eight.

She logged in, and immediately decided to go to the DIAC website. She had tried to access records on the DIAC project of reintroducing wolves into the Adirondacks, but it looked like they had been deleted. She wondered if there was a back door to get to these files.

She didn't want anyone else to be privy to her web searches; so she didn't call in any of the DIAC computer experts. If the files were accessible, they were able to easily access them. If only she had a good friend who was a computer genius! She was unaware that the man she passed yesterday on her way home would end up being that good friend.

Jonathan came through the surgery, and was in the recovery room by 5:00 PM. The operation was a big success, but it had been quite a challenge for the doctors to make it so. They were very relieved that it was now over.

Jon's injuries would take a few months to heal. His forearm had been rebuilt, and his face had been repaired through a brand new "plastic surgery" technique using nano-technology coupled with a compound that stimulates the growth of new human tissue. In one-hundred percent of these facial "surgical procedures", there were no scars left at all. The tiny nano-robots were collectively pre-programmed with the image they were to create; and they would work together to create that projected image. Their job was completed in just a few hours, and they were then gathered up by the doctor in charge, and could be electronically programmed for another surgery after sterilization. The human tissue would always grow in the projected area set within the boundaries set by the nano-machines. In Jon's case, the face would be repaired within six days. It was quick, painless, and surprisingly inexpensive. All the doctors had to do was program the machines, place them at the scene of the surgery, and then remove them when the electronic signal indicated that they were finished. The cost was just under a thousand dollars: a very affordable price for a popular new medical procedure. This was good news for the insurance companies.

Jon had decided that, during his recovery period—mostly from the forearm surgery—that he would check out some information he felt he needed to know. He would start with "wolves in New York State", and then go from there. He knew about the DIAC website, and would access their files.

Marie was back on the internet, searching for more information. She was hopeful that someone would talk with her. So she decided to get into a private chat with someone if she could. She posted a question: "Anyone want to talk about unsolved murders?"

Almost immediately, she received an answer: "Antoinette, I invite you to a private conversation."

The name of the sender was "Shorty". Jim Ellenberger, a former DIAC executive, had information that no one else could know, because he had been on the committee which oversaw "Operation Wolf", the reintroduction of timber wolves into the Adirondack habitat. He kept a close watch on the DIAC chatroom, and had an alert system that picked up buzzwords like "wolves" and "murders". The alarm had sounded; and a surprised Jim Ellenberger had answered ASAP.

Antoinette accepted the invite, and the firewalls protected their conversation. However, there was one chatroom member who could hack into their conversation. His name was "Roamer". But Roamer had not been in the chatroom for a week. And if Antoinette and Shorty were lucky, Roamer wouldn't pick up the conversation later, once he returned.

Antoinette: "What do you know?"
Shorty: "I know plenty. We can't talk here too much. Better to meet somewhere."
Antoinette: "Some place easy. McDonald's."
Shorty: "Wolf Road, Albany."
Antoinette: "When?"
Shorty: "Today. Two hours from now."

Antoinette: "Okay. I'll do it."

Shorty: "Wear a name tag that says 'Antoinette'."

Antoinette: "How about you?"

Shorty: "I'll find you. Do you have a purple dress?"

Antoinette: "No. How about red?"

Shorty: "Okay. Good enough. When I find you, I'll say I'm Shorty. Then you hand me your name tag, and I'll throw it away."

Antoinette: "Then what?"

Shorty: "We meet somewhere else."

Antoinette: "Why?"

Shorty: "Trust me."

Antoinette: "All right."

Shorty: "I'm on your side."

Antoinette: "I'm on my way. I know where it is on Wolf Road. I'll go in for coffee."

Susan Morehouse e-mailed Marie: "Let's get together." Then, she logged off, and resumed her investigative activities. She felt the need to get in touch with a computer expert whom she could trust. Maybe Marie knew someone. And she remembered that Marie was going to do some research herself. Maybe she found something that she missed.

Susan went through the Yellow Pages, looking for computer technicians. She found several. But she had a worrisome feeling of distrust. If one of these advertised professionals found out her identity and her supervisory position in the DIAC, her cover could become compromised. She would be more comfortable trying a more person-to-person approach.

Marie pulled into the parking lot of the McDonald's on Wolf Road. She parked her 2023 Hybrid Honda Civic, and walked into the restaurant. It was 8:02 PM. She was thirteen minutes early. She had on her red dress, and a name tag identifying her as Antoinette.

"Are you coming from the conference across the street?" a young woman asked.

"What?"

"I see your name tag. I was going to go, but I didn't. How is it going?"

"Oh I see. My name tag." Then she added, "No, I'm on a blind date."

"I see. Well, I hope you're meeting Mr. Right."

"Me, too."

Marie chuckled. That was a hilarious conversation. It actually cheered her up. She wanted to thank the lady who initiated that dialogue, but she had left. Marie ordered a coffee, and then sat at a table facing the entrance. She made sure that she was conspicuous. Shorty should be coming soon.

Jim Ellenberger parked his 2025 BMW Hybrid. He was very nervous. He had not driven straight to McDonald's, but had taken an alternate route. During the longer drive, he had repeatedly checked his rear-view mirror to see if anyone was following him.

He was sure that someone might be onto him, or would be, shortly. He was seventy-nine years old: the youngest member of the committee that initiated and oversaw Operation Wolf. Some recent events had made him more and more afraid, even to the point of paranoia.

Five months ago, one of his fellow committee members had died in an automobile accident. His car was found driven off the road and into the river. The coroner declared that the cause of his death was drowning.

Then, a month later, a second committee member had driven across the road, and over a cliff. There was speculation that another car may have forced him off the road. The left side of the charred vehicle had evidence of being hit by another vehicle. But the authorities concluded that it was an accident. Then, the next month, a third committee member died in a similar-type accident, hitting a tree and rolling down a large bank with jagged rocks at the bottom.

But the last two deaths were more frightening. One was a supposed suicide. He was found in his home, hanging from a second-floor balustrade. Jim felt it was a very suspicious death; but the authorities declared it a suicide. Jim had known this man for over fifty years, and was certain he was not suicidal.

The fifth death was an explosive one. Literally. His country home exploded suddenly and mysteriously in the middle of the night. Again, the authorities called it an accident. Jim didn't believe it at all.

He believed that someone, or ones, had murdered all five of these committee members, beginning five months ago and continuing on up until the middle of last month. And now, he was one of only two surviving committee members. If the pattern was to continue, one of the two was on schedule to be killed any day now.

Jim was becoming more and more paranoid, but it was absolutely justifiable. He was literally expecting death at any moment. He didn't know exactly why someone wanted him dead, but he was expecting it at any time.

Jim stepped out of the car, and walked briskly toward the entrance of the restaurant. He could see a woman wearing a red dress, who was looking toward the entrance. She was blonde, beautiful, and looked like she was in her twenties. He walked in, and saw the name tag: Antoinette. Yes, it was her. What a relief!

"Hi, Antoinette. I'm Shorty."

"Hi, Shorty," Marie said, surprised that he was an elderly man.

She then put out her hand: "Marie Trombley."

They shook hands. "Jim Ellenberger."

"Thanks for meeting me here."

He nodded nervously. He began to speak in an urgent tone.

"We've got to talk. But let's go somewhere else."

"Where?"

"The Stewart's in Saratoga. Route 9."

"Okay. I know where that is."

"We will leave at different times."

"Okay."

She handed over her name tag. Jim Ellenberger took the tag, and threw it in the trash. He then walked back out, and looked around before he stepped into his car. He then headed for Saratoga. It was 8:20.

Marie took her time, and finished her coffee. Then, at 8:30, she stood up and left. At 9:15, she arrived at Stewart's. And Shorty wasn't there! She decided to wait, hoping he would show. At 9:20, Shorty arrived. He had taken a longer, round-about route to get there. Now they could talk. Finally.

"I have some information you need to have."

He handed her a manila folder. It was really thick.

"There is more information out in my car."

Marie began. "My daughter was killed. But I don't believe it was murder."

"What's her name?"

"Elizabeth Trombley."

"I remember that incident. Seven teens died."

"How?"

"It was not murder. At least, not directly."

"What do you mean?"

"The papers will tell you."

"These, or the ones in your car?"

"Both."

He added, "Keep this confidential. There are people who are looking for us on the internet, and our physical location, because they want to get to us and silence us. They don't know I'm revealing any information; but I fear they will eliminate me to be safe from prosecution."

He continued on. "I was twenty-three when the committee to start Operation Wolf was formed."

"Operation Wolf? What's that?"

"It was a DIAC program."

"Department of Indigenous Animal Control."

"Yes. Anyway, we drew up a plan in 1969 to reintroduce the endangered timber wolf to the Adirondack Park."

"Was that a good idea?"

"We thought so at the time. We expected to introduce one hundred wolves, tagged, and under constant supervision."

"Why?"

"We wanted to restore the ecological balance. The deer population was way too high; and we believed that a small population of predators would pare the population down to a normal level. The number of deer taken by hunters didn't seem sufficient at the time; so it seemed like a perfect plan."

"Why do so many people say there is no such thing as a wolf in upstate New York?"

"Because it was a closely-guarded secret. A few of the newspapers reported on it, but the DIAC downplayed it." He continued. "Anyway, around 1986, something changed. And others got involved. Powerful people. They wanted to increase the number of wolves; and they didn't tag them all. It was a formula for disaster. And it doesn't make sense. I don't know why; but I suspect there is a reason. A good reason."

"Why what?"

"Why they introduced more wolves into the Adirondacks. I don't know why they did it; but the order came from someone high up in the DIAC."

"How many wolves were placed in the Park?"

"About eight hundred."

"Wow!"

"That's way too many. And they have multiplied. I would estimate at least two or three thousand today. Or more!"

"What happens when the wolf population is too high?"

"They encroach on human territory. They eliminate their natural prey; and then they must invade human territory and seek new prey. Pets, livestock, and people."

Jim Ellenberger continued. "All of us on the committee objected to the change. It was crazy. So they removed us from the committee, and replaced us with DIAC members who would do their bidding. These were people who believed a larger wolf population was sustainable. In twenty-four years, they increased the number of wolves introduced into the Park from about sixty to about eight hundred."

"This is really scary," Marie said.

"Yes, it is. I was waiting to see how long it would take for the wolf population to move into human territory and pose a serious threat. It has finally happened this year."

He added, "I'm sorry about your daughter."

"May I show you a picture?"

"Sure."

"This is my Lizzy," she said as she pulled one of her many pictures out of her pocketbook.

"Wow! She's beautiful....And so young."

He began to weep. Quietly. He quickly forced himself to regain his composure, and began to speak some more.

"If I'd only known what was going to happen, I would not have—"

"It's not your fault, Mr. Ellenberger."

"It's okay to call me Jim."

"It's not your fault, Jim."

"Thank you, Marie. You're very kind." He paused, took a deep breath, and continued.

"I have to tell you that you must be careful. My life is in danger; and yours will be, too, if they find out what you are doing."

"Doing?"

"Investigating this project. Operation Wolf."

"Why would they want to kill me? Or you, for that matter?"

"Because they are hiding something."

"What are they hiding?"

"I don't know."

"Where do we go from here?"

"Read all the materials. And then chat with me again. I'll be under the name 'Sanhedrin'."

"San what?"

"Sanhedrin."

"You'd better write it down."

"If I do, memorize and destroy the note."

"Alright."

"And Marie?"

"Yes?"

"Change your internet chatroom name."

"To what?"

"How about 'Twiggy'?"

"Sounds great. 1961?"

"1962, I think. Maybe 1960."

"Twiggy it is," said Marie.

Jim looked at his watch. "I must go, Marie."

"We'll talk soon?"

"I'll chat with you tomorrow."

They walked out to their cars; and Jim gave her a briefcase packed full of information. She left for home, ready to stay up all night, and to do some serious homework.

CHAPTER TEN

December 22, 2025

Jonathan Wilkes was ready to leave the hospital. He was eager to get on with his original plan. He would find out what the payout cost of his parent's mortgage was, and write out a check to the mortgage holder, for that exact amount. He would present it as a Christmas present. He had well over a million dollars saved up, and he could easily afford to do that.

And he also wanted to reacquaint himself with his parents. Twenty years away from them was a long time; and he wanted to get to know them in the present time.

But the doctor said that he had to stay for one more day of observation and IV feeding.

"Okay," he sighed.

"Think of it this way," the doctor said. "You're lucky to be alive."

"You're right. I'm blessed by God to be alive."

Jon suddenly realized that, even though it appeared to be good luck that he was alive; in reality, it was an answer to prayer. It was God's plan.

He prayed in his thoughts: "Lord, please show me what to do. I need You."

Susan Morehouse called Marie, and set up an appointment to meet with her. They decided on 6:00 that night. Marie said that she had a lot to share; but it had to remain confidential.

Marie was tired, because she had stayed up until 3:00 in the morning reading the information that an "anonymous" source had given her. Actually, the source was not anonymous, but wished he was.

So, 6:00 PM would be perfect. She could sleep for a few more hours, then read some more, do some errands, and still have plenty of time to get ready to meet with Susan.

Actually, she would meet her at a local restaurant—Bill's Diner—and then she would show her the papers. She would see a wealth of information.

But one element was missing.

Why?

And some of the "Who?" were missing, too.

What, where, how, and when were present in abundance, though there seemed to be the possibility of more than the papers revealed.

Why? The question gnawed at her. Why would anyone do this? She couldn't make sense out of this. What could anyone possibly GAIN from this?

Matthew Hastings was a young man who lived in the Hague. He was driving home in his 2014 Dodge pickup truck, ready to chop some more wood. He had dozens of customers who bought the chopped wood; and his prices were definitely lower than his competitors. Fortunately for his competitors, Matthew was satisfied with serving only forty clients. That was all he wanted. He made plenty of money during the wintertime, operating this business. During the rest of the year, he mowed lawns and did landscaping.

He was on his way home when he noticed a group of pigs ahead, just wandering along the road. He called on his cell phone to report the sighting. He decided to investigate, so he parked the truck, stepped outside, and looked around. He knew who the nearest pig farmer was, and pulled up his cell's directory. He found the number, and gave him a call.

"Hello?"

"Mr. Granger?"

"Yes. Who's this?"

"This is Matthew Hastings."

"Hi, Matthew. Can you call me back in ten minutes? I'm really busy, right at the moment."

"I found your pigs."

"What?"

"Your pigs are wandering along the roadside."

"Boomer Road?"

"Yeah." He added, "I called the authorities, so they can help, also."

"Alright."

"I'm a mile or so south of your farm."

"Okay, Matt. I'm on my way."

"The pigs are staying together. They're off to the side now, in a big field. I'm walking towards them now."

Frank Granger had been busy repairing a broken water pipe. He was almost finished, when Matthew called him; but he left this unfinished project to recover his livestock.

Jonathan Wilkes was busy reading, reviewing his life, and pondering how he would live his life differently now. He would be more kind, more thoughtful of others, more forgiving. He wanted to live the rest of his life helping other people. He had already found redemption for his past, present, and future. But he wanted to do more than just "talk the talk". He wanted to "walk the walk". He needed his life to be right with God, and right with his fellow-man. He couldn't wait to start living his life, and doing things he had neglected for so long. There was a purpose for his survival; and he was determined to find and fulfill that purpose. He knew he was spared for a reason. He would spend the next few months seeking out that reason.

The wolves were traveling north inside the forest, alongside Boomer Road. They saw an occasional vehicle pass by, but they were looking for something they could catch. They passed by a small pond, and stopped to take a drink. After drinking, they continued on. And then, they spotted their prey.

Frank started up the truck that he used to transport livestock. He drove towards Boomer Road, and turned south. He continued on this route for about a mile and a half, looked towards the left, and saw his pigs in Rodney Preston's field. This was a large field, bordering on a thick forest in the background. He parked the truck, exited, thanked Matt Hastings, and then called his pigs. Matt watched as the hogs were slowly moving across the huge field towards Frank and his truck. "He's good," Matt thought.

Suddenly, the wolf pack came out of the forest, and charged towards the hogs. The predators were swift runners, and gained ground easily. The pigs squealed and scattered. Frank looked on in horror. At first, he was concerned for his animals. Then he saw Matt running towards the nearest tree.

"Hurry!" Frank wished him to safety.

Matt had at least twenty yards to go to reach the tree. He strained at the edge of his endurance. He could hear the pigs going down as the wolves caught them. He could feel his heart pounding, partly out of physical exertion, and partly out of fear. He could "feel" the pain of imminent death chasing him down. He felt that, at any moment, he would be dragged down by these vicious beasts. He didn't relish the idea of being alive and being eviscerated at the same time. He was straining to get to safety, and felt that he was about ready to pass out. When he reached the tree, he grabbed the nearest branch, and pulled himself up with "super-human" strength.

The wolves had closed in quickly from three different directions. The nearest predator snapped at him, just missing his right leg as he pulled himself up. A second wolf grazed his left foot. A third wolf leaped into the air from behind, almost catching a piece of his coat.

Matt hooked his legs over a second branch, and grabbed for a higher limb with his right hand. He moved higher up into the tree, and breathed a sigh of relief. He could hardly believe he was safe!

Frank climbed into his truck, and dialed 911. He gave his location, and described what was happening. He e-mailed some footage of the attack, and then sat there, waiting for help to arrive. He saw Matthew climbing higher up into the tree, safely out of reach of the pack. The wolves gathered around the dead pigs and feasted. Matt dialed 911, and showed them the footage of the horrifying scene below.

Jan Duvalier was the dispatcher who answered Frank Granger's 911 call. It reminded her of several other similar calls she had received in the past few months. She remembered that a couple of victims didn't make it; and so she had vowed that, no matter what the cost, she would not allow another victim to die on her watch. So she made sure she dispatched a rescue copter immediately.

Five minutes later, the chopper was on the way. Several squad cars were also dispatched. At this moment, they were racing at high speed, toward the Hague. Manuel Fernandez, the copter pilot, radioed the control tower.

"We're on our way. ETA in four minutes."

The GPS was counting down: 3:50, 3:49, 3:48,… The rescue team had been briefed on the tense situation; and they were ready and focused on their mission.

Matthew Hastings was talking with his wife, Sharon.

"Honey, I may be a little late. I'll be home as soon as I can."

"What's the matter?"

"Nothing that I can't handle."

"Did you get a flat tire?"

"No."

"Engine trouble?"

"No."

"What then?"

"Oh, I stopped to help someone. I'll be home probably in a half hour."

"Alright. I'll have lunch ready for you."

They said their "Goodbyes", and hung up.

Matthew could hear the rescue chopper in the distance. He had been up in the tree for about ten minutes. He wondered just how they were going to rescue him.

Manuel motioned to his co-pilot to dial Matthew's cell phone number.

"Mr. Hastings, we have spotted your location. We are prepared to rescue you by air, unless you want to wait for the squad cars."

"How will you rescue me by air?"

"We have a special ladder that curves, and gives a lot of slack to both yourself and this helicopter. It's a new invention; and we have already used it successfully."

"Okay, I'll take an air rescue. Thank you."

The rescue team lowered the curved ladder. It was designed to preserve the safety of both parties. It had a built-in extra fifty feet of slack that would come out if the end (the bottom) of the ladder was snagged. The slack would only come out if necessary, ten feet at a time, up to fifty feet.

Also, once the person being rescued touched the bottom of the ladder, it automatically would be slack, so that the person wouldn't be pulled prematurely from his place of peril. But it would not be slack once the person grabbed hold of it and was secure on it.

This curved ladder was an invention patented in 2020, just five years ago. And it was designed to save lives that were once considered impossible to rescue by helicopter.

Matthew grabbed hold of the bottom of the curved ladder, and stepped onto it. It was surprisingly easy. Once he was securely on it, the ladder sent a computerized message to the helicopter pilot that Matthew was secure, and that he could begin lifting him up to the chopper.

"This curved ladder is quite a machine," Matthew thought. "Safe, efficient, and very smooth. Really easy to step on and ride."

The squad cars arrived; and the police officers exited the cars with their guns drawn. The wolves, meanwhile, had eaten their full, and were not so aggressive at the moment. When the cops discharged some warning shots, the predators slowly moved away. This cleared the way for the chopper to lower Matthew down by his truck.

Matthew was relieved that his ordeal was over. He drove home to his wife, about thirty minutes later than he had originally planned. He then explained what happened; and she said he should report the incident. But he told her that the police would fill out a report. He reminded her that Frank Granger and his pigs were the real victims of these animals. Then he went outdoors to chop wood. But he was much more watchful of the nearby wooded area, aware that at any time, there could be danger lurking there. After a few more days, he would carry one of his pistols with him for protection whenever he went outside.

The police filled out a report; and arrangements were made to dispose of the pigs' remains.

Marie Trombley decided to leave early for Bill's Diner in Warrensburg. It would take her eight or nine minutes to get there. She left at 5:30, so that she could be twenty minutes early. She picked up the folder and briefcase, and carried them out to her Honda Civic. She wanted to be there early, so that she would have more time to prepare herself to be ready to present her findings to Susan.

Susan Morehouse was still wondering if Marie knew a computer technician they both could trust. Maybe that computer expert could find a link, or a name, or something, which they could follow up on, simply by pulling up these deleted files.

Well, Marie had some kind of information; and she was excited about finding out this new data. Maybe this new information would be what they needed, to put at least some of the pieces of the puzzle together. She hoped she could learn who was behind the accelerated wolf reintroduction into the Adirondack Park, and the reason why.

The question kept eating away at her: "Why?" And why was it so "hush-hush"? It didn't make sense to her.

She put on her coat and gloves, and walked out the door. It was 5:45; and she liked being early. She would walk into the eatery at about ten minutes before six.

Marie was sitting at a corner table. She let the waitress know she would be joined by a friend in just a few minutes. She took a piece of paper, and wrote down the outline of what she wanted to reveal. She had made copies of what was in the envelope; and she planned to copy all the rest. This was all confidential; but she would pass the confidence on to Susan. She was pondering how to proceed, when Susan walked through the door.

"You're early," Marie said.

"I always am," Susan replied.

"That's a good trait. Make yourself comfortable. I'm buying; so order whatever you want."

"Thank you; but you don't have to do that."

"I want to. I appreciate your help."

"It's my pleasure. Okay, I'll accept your offer. Thank you."

"Glad to do it."

The waitress came over. "May I get you something to drink?"

"Coffee, please," Marie said.

"I'll have Decaf please," said Susan.

"I'll give you a couple of minutes to look over the menu," the waitress said.

"Thank you," Marie said. Then she turned to Susan and began: "I know a lot about this DIAC project. It's called 'Operation Wolf'."

"That's a good name for it," Susan said.

"I talked with a member of the committee that started the whole project. He wants to keep it confidential for right now."

"I will do that," Susan said.

"Marie handed her the copies which she had made.

"These are for you. I'll give you some time to peruse them while we wait."

"Here's your coffee."

"Thank you."

"You're welcome, Marie."

"And here's your Decaf."

"Thank you very much, Joan."

"You're welcome, Susan."

"Are you ready to order?"

"Yes. I'll have the hot turkey sandwich," Susan said.

"I'll have the same, please," said Marie.

"Would you care for any soup or salad? Our soup is Cream of Potato."

"I'll have the soup, please," Marie said.

"Salad, please, with Italian vinaigrette," Susan said.

Joan thanked them for their order, picked up the menus, and walked away.

Then, Susan started to read the papers in front of her. As she did, her eyes widened.

"Wow! This is amazing!" she said.

"That's only part of it. I have more information to give you," Marie said.

They talked for a full hour, making sure that nobody was eavesdropping. They realized they didn't know why this DIAC program was taken over and accelerated; and they didn't know all of the "Who". The "How" was replacing the original committee, that was formed to start and oversee the program, with a committee of new and cooperative members. The "When" was 1986 to 2010. The "Who" were some powerful people in New York State, of whom one was now the Governor of the State. The New York State Police Commissioner, then the Albany County Sheriff, was also involved. But there were at least two other people involved—powerful people.

The "What" was the approximate ten-fold increase in growth of the wolf population in the Adirondack Park. And there was something else. It was suspected that there was possible chemical treatment of these animals: a treatment which altered the chemical balance of these creatures. It was believed that the altered wolves may have killed off some or all of the other wolves: namely, the ones that had not been chemically altered.

The "Where" was the Adirondack Park where at least seven hundred and fifty additional wolves were introduced into the wild, between 1986 and 2010.

What was missing was the "Why" and part of the "Who". If they could only put the rest of the pieces together, they might be able to come up with a plan to counteract this, and bring these conspirators to justice.

Marie and Susan had a serious problem with the whole situation. Their situation was comparable to being inside a computer game where there were invisible enemies to fight against; because there were powerful people involved in this conspiracy who were behind the scenes, invisible, and therefore much more dangerous than ordinary opponents. The visible enemies were dangerous enough; but the silent, unseen enemies were far more dangerous. These unseen enemies could see THEM, but they could not see the invisible enemies.

"So, where do we go from here?" Marie asked

"I don't know yet. I need to think about this. This may take some time."

"How long?"

"To do this right, probably several months."

"Why so long?"

"Because we have to find out WHO the enemy is, before we take action. We have to do this in a SAFE way. And we need to find out WHY."

"How?"

"By getting a computer expert to dig up information that has been deleted from the DIAC files; and by accessing any links where they might have left a clue that is missing right now."

They decided to keep looking for answers. The police could not be trusted; state workers—including DIAC—could not be trusted; and someone or ones unknown and unseen could not be trusted. But somehow, some way, they would get to the bottom of this. They agreed to keep in touch every day by phone, e-mail, or meeting together.

They were two women with different motivations, but the same goal. One was desperate to get closure on the death of her daughter. The other wanted simply to solve this case, and keep others in the Adirondack area from getting hurt or killed. If Susan was reading the situation correctly, a lot of people were in grave danger.

CHAPTER ELEVEN

December 22, 2025

Roamer began to scan the DIAC website. He had not been there for eight days. His last login had been December 14th at 4:03 PM. On the fourteenth of December, he began a "project" which kept him busy for a whole week, taking his focus away from the internet site.

This was his sixth "project" in five months. His projects were executions made to look like accidents, suicide, or sudden natural death. He enjoyed this last execution the best. He had gone into the Wilton Mall, walked up to his victim, and injected cyanide into one of his veins after he "bumped" into him. Then, he had called 911 on a "borrowed" cell phone. He remained anonymous, and said that the man was having a heart attack. The poison had killed him instantly; and the only evidence was a tiny pin-prick on his hand. He walked away after several people gathered around the corpse, and calmly disappeared into the crowd.

Roamer was looking to execute one more victim. He knew he was the last committee member. He had not even tried to locate the last member yet; but now he would focus his attention on him. He had found three of the victims on the DIAC website, and he was hoping that the last one would be here also. The other three had not even chatted on secure sites; and it took no effort to find them. Now, he would look deeper into the website and its links and chatrooms to see if he would catch the last surviving member of that ill-fated DIAC committee.

If that last member was there, he had done a good job of avoiding the other three members who had talked openly about the DIAC program. He was secretive and more cautious, perhaps even aware that someone was looking for him. He knew the name, because he had looked it up the night before. Now, he would focus solely on catching this man. The target victim had moved recently; and Roamer wasn't aware of his new location. He had not left a forwarding address, but used a PO box instead of a physical home address. The PO box was in the town of Argyle. But evidently, the man had never lived in that town. So Roamer had a goal. Find the seventh man, and eliminate him.

Roamer clicked onto the chatroom icon and logged in. He scrolled down the conversations looking for anyone who might be discussing Operation Wolf. He was trying to see if any of the people in the chatroom had been tipped off to vital information.

Roamer was the Governor's watchdog; and he could access places few people in the world even knew existed. He could go to secret chat spaces, and listen in without anyone even knowing he was there. He could crack any encrypted code he had tried. He was one of the world's best computer hackers.

He was looking for a clue. And then he saw it.

Sanhedrin entered the chatroom. It was 8:07PM. He greeted Toad and Sara, and talked with them for a while.

"C'mon, Twiggy! Log on," he thought to himself.

At 8:11, he saw the message: "Twiggy has entered the chatroom."
Sanhedrin: "Hi, Twiggy!"
Twiggy: "Hello, Sanhedrin."
Sanhedrin: "Want to talk? I'll invite."
Twiggy: "Okay."

They entered into a private chatroom.

Sanhedrin: "I'd love to meet with you. Twiggy is such a nice name."
Twiggy: "I like my other name better."

Sanhedrin: "Don't say it."
Sanhedrin: "I have an ex-wife with that name."
Twiggy: "Same place as before?"
Sanhedrin: "Sure."
Twiggy: "First or second place?"
Sanhedrin: "First, this time."
Twiggy: "When?"
Sanhedrin: "10:00,"
Twiggy: "Tonight?"
Sanhedrin: "Yes."
Twiggy: "Okay, bye."

Roamer read the words "unsolved murders". These were buzz-words for trouble. He then hacked into the private chatroom, and read their conversation. He then exited, and looked for Shorty and Antoinette. But no one by that name had been in there since that private encrypted conversation. But he was smart enough to check out other private conversations, because he knew they might have other chatroom names. He could check the registrations of Shorty and Antoinette. He would do that in another half hour. But first, he wanted to check the private conversations. He loved doing this. Sometimes, he would get side-tracked doing this, because he enjoyed it so much. But he would not be side-tracked for long, because he was still focused on the task at hand. But this was "profitable recreation" for him.

The seventeenth private chat was between Twiggy and Sanhedrin. Roamer had never seen them before. A red flag went up. Then, he saw a clue in the private conversation: "I like my other name better." Roamer connected the dots: "Antoinette?"

He decided to quickly check the registrations of Antoinette and Twiggy to see if they matched. They did. Now, Shorty and Sanhedrin. Another match!

He knew where they were meeting, and when. He would put on his special listening device, and breach their private conversation. Then, he would take whatever action he needed to take. He was aware of who Jim Ellenberger was. He would eliminate him, and then get Marie Trombley to tell him who else knew about Operation Wolf. Then, he would get rid of her, also.

At 9:45, Marie pulled into McDonald's on Wolf Road. She walked in, ordered a Filet of Fish meal, and waited for Jim. At exactly 10:00, a nervous Jim Ellenberger walked through the entrance. Marie could tell he was afraid. He didn't order anything, but simply walked over to Marie, and sat down across from her.

She said, "Are you afraid of someone?"

He said, "Yes."

"Who?"

"I don't know; but I think they are coming for me soon."

"Why not go to the authorities and take a chance?"

"The Police Commissioner is in with the Governor."

"What about his assistant? Maybe HE can help you."

"I didn't think about that."

"It's worth a try. If you have no chance with the Commissioner, maybe you would have a chance with his assistant."

"Maybe I'll try that."

Marie paused. "Have my French fries."

"Thanks."

He grabbed at them nervously. He kept looking out the window. He didn't realize that Roamer was outside in the parking lot listening in. He could hear every word they said. He continued listening.

"I have another folder to give you. If I am killed, please follow the instructions on the first page of this information."

"Killed?"

"Remember I told you my life is in danger. I need you to follow the instructions on the first page of the papers in this folder."

"Okay, I'll do it. Call me. Or leave your cell phone on, so I can reach you."

"Alright," he said. Then he added, "You must search for the WHY. We don't know why they accelerated the wolf population. If we could find the why, we might be able to stop this. But we also need to find out who else is involved in the plan, besides the Governor and Police Commissioner."

Then, he spoke in a slower and even more serious tone: "Marie, please read the first page now; and then, I have to go."

She pulled out the first page; and her eyes widened as she read it. She nodded in agreement. She understood.

"Thank you, Mr. Ellenberger."

"I hope to see you at least once more, Marie."

"Me, too."

"Take care of yourself."

He stood up, and walked towards the door. He looked back toward Marie. She could sense a genuine sadness in his face as he left. She watched him walk forlornly towards his car. He was partially stooped over, looking like a beaten man, defeated by his unfortunate circumstances. He got into his BMW, and drove away.

Out of the corner of her eye, she saw a set of headlights go on; and a black Ford Mustang accelerated and followed the BMW. She gasped.

The thought came: "Call his cell! Warn him!"

She dialed the cell. "Pick up, Jim, please!" she thought. One ring. Two rings. Three—

"Hello?"

"Jim, you're being followed. I'm sure of it. A black Mustang. Call 911, or stop by a squad car. Or run through a red light to get a cop's attention."

"Thanks. I will."

Marie figured she had better get to Jim's friend's house. She left quickly, and called Jim's friend from her cell as she was driving towards his house.

Jack Leland picked up the receiver to his home phone.

"Hello. This is Jack."

"Hi, Jack. This is Marie Trombley. I have something for you from your friend, Jim Ellenberger."

"Jim who?"

"Jim Ellenberger."

"Oh, Jim. I haven't seen him in years. I was his lawyer back several years ago."

"I'm on my way right now."

"I'll put my outside light on."

She had to drive to the town of Moreau, and out into the country. She was looking for the second house on the right: number 258. It was a large house at the end of a long driveway. She found it, and turned right onto the drive. The outside light was on. She parked. A door opened. A tall, thin man walked up to the car.

"Hello, Marie?"

"I have the information right here."

She handed him the envelope.

"Thank you."

"You're welcome, Mr. Leland." Then, she said, "It's a very urgent message, so I'd better leave so that you can take it inside and read it."

"Thank you, Marie. I'll read it right now. Take care of yourself."

She said, "Goodnight," and drove away.

Jack went back into the house, locked the front door, and went to his den. Then he put on his reading glasses, and took out page one. It read, "Don't say a word, Marie. You need to take this envelope over to Jack Leland in Moreau. On the back of this page is his phone number and the directions to his house. I will probably be killed in the next few days. So he needs to have this information to help my family members. I never made out a last will and testament. So I have included it in here.

"I also have given him the same information I gave you on Operation Wolf, so he can work with you if you need help. Inside this folder is a key and directions to a storage locker in Albany. Inside the locker is a briefcase with the information. Please give him a call, and go to his house right after you leave here."

Jack decided that he would help this woman. He was sad, though, about the fate of his old friend. And as he looked at the bottom of the page, he became even more sad. He wanted to contact Jim; but in front of him were the words in bold letters: "JACK, DON'T CONTACT ME!"

Jim Ellenberger was an old man; but he could drive like a teenager. He dialed 911, and then accelerated rapidly.

"Albany Police Department. What's your emergency?"

"I'm being pursued by a black Ford Mustang. I'm headed north towards Exit 8 East. Can you meet me at this exit? I'm in a silver 2025 BMW. I will make a move to let you know I'm there."
"What's your ETA?"
"I'm coming fast."
"Two minutes?"
"ASAP."

Suddenly, the BMW pulled away. Roamer wasn't ready for the move. He had put his listening device away; and so he hadn't heard Jim's latest cell phone conversation. He decided to continue his pursuit. He accelerated quickly, and chased the BMW. When he reached a hundred miles an hour and saw the BMW still way ahead and pulling away from him, he changed his mind, eased off, and exited at Exit 7.

Roamer knew he would need to trade in his Mustang for a different car—a blue 2025 Camaro he knew was for sale. The Mustang was fast; but he had been discovered somehow. He knew he needed a new car that was fast, but not known.

"Maybe Marie called him!" he thought. "Man! I should have kept listening!"

Roamer came up with an idea. He would get to Jim Ellenberger, using a "tried-and-true" method—a car bomb. It was simple. He just had to wait for the opportune time. He now had Jim's license plate number; and he could access his new address through internet files which held his updated personal information. It was just a matter of time, and Roamer would kill this last ex-member of the DIAC committee.

Jim Ellenberger saw the Mustang turn right behind him as he was racing towards Exit 8 East. Instantly, he slowed down. He redialed 911, and told them his pursuer gave up and left the highway at Exit 7. Then, he told them that he needed to talk with the New York State Assistant Police Commissioner. They gave him his office number. He programmed it into his cell phone so that he could call him at a later time. He wasn't sure when he would call, but he wanted to be ready at a moment's notice. He would take a chance on the Assistant PC; and maybe, just maybe, he'd live to "see another day".

Marie was afraid to go home. "Paranoid" was the word. She had visions of someone in a black Mustang coming to her house and pointing a gun at her. She checked into a motel room after parking her car in the back. She hoped she would be safe. She went into the room, locked the door, and dead-bolted it. Then she crawled into the bed and fell asleep.

CHAPTER TWELVE

December 23, 2025

Jonathan Wilkes woke up around 8:00AM. He was excited about leaving the hospital. He wanted to spend time with his parents, and to do things for them, showing them that he loved them. He knew that he could never make up for twenty lost years; but he could make the next twenty years a time of joy and reunion.

Dr. Lucas walked in. He told him that the nurses would be doing some more tests before he could leave—taking another blood sample, a urine sample, and his blood pressure. A few other details, and he would be out of there.

Bill and Marge walked in. So did Eamon and Julie. They had met out in the lobby, and had started talking about getting together on a weekly basis, at least for a while. Then, it might end up being once a month, or whatever they would decide.

"Hi, Son."

"Hi, Dear."

"Good to see you all again," Jonathan said.

"Good to see you, too," said Julie.

"Ditto," said Eamon.

They talked until all the tests were done; and they all walked out together.

Marie woke up at about 9:00. She had slept longer than usual. And it had been refreshing. She had dreamed about happier times: times when her Lizzy was just a young girl, so alive and so vibrant!

She was a very loquacious little girl, always wanting to show people what she had seen or done or written down on paper. She would do a Science project, and would tell all the parents who came to the "Open House" about how she made it, and what it was. She would stop and chat with complete strangers at the Mall. Even when she was eight years old, she could carry on an extended conversation with any adult, even if that adult didn't say a word. She was one big bundle of fun-filled energy.

Marie had also dreamed about her husband, Robby, who had left her a couple of years ago. She dreamed that he had returned, and that everything was back the way it was supposed to be. She felt a great feeling of joy and safety during these dreams; and it would have been fine for her if these dreams had continued on forever.

Then, she woke up; and the awful reality hit her like a freight train moving at full speed. She felt lonely, fearful, and sad. She felt like her life was over; that she would never laugh again, never feel the joys that she could remember so vividly just a few short years ago. She felt trapped—suffocated by her awful circumstances. And she didn't know where to turn.

She wept: silently and alone. And she wondered if her pain would ever end. She felt like she couldn't take it anymore. She wondered if there was a God, wondered if He would even care; and if He did, how could he ever put the broken pieces of her life back together? She had never been interested in what people called "religion". She had thought it was a waste of time. But now, in her despair, in her deepest emotional need, she felt she needed help from something, or Someone, beyond her. Maybe, just maybe, there was Someone, some Deity, some God out there Who would help her.

Her heart had been broken twice. First, Robby had left; and it had hurt her so deeply she had cried every day for six months. But she kept on going for Lizzy's sake. She continued her small internet business, continued cleaning houses, and continued to do everything she felt she could to provide for Lizzy's needs.

When Lizzy died, her heart was broken for the second time. It was by far the most traumatic experience of her forty years of life. She was in emotional freefall, because the whole foundation, the "bottom", of her world just fell away from underneath her. Her very life was ruined. Her whole "house of cards" had collapsed; and she was crushed under the burden of her own emotional pain. She felt her life had no more purpose; that it was meaningless, empty, and even hopeless.

Mechanically, she stood up. She felt she had to "pull herself together". She didn't know why: maybe it was just survival instinct. She HAD to survive. Somehow.

She slowly placed one foot ahead of the other, and walked to the bathroom. She looked in the mirror, and thought that she looked old. Then, she splashed her face, took a washcloth, and wiped away her tears.

She took a deep breath, and talked to herself.

"Get a grip, Marie. You have to keep going. Don't quit now."

She regained her composure, and took a shower. She felt a little better, a little refreshed. She didn't feel great; but she felt that she could cope, that she could "hang on" for a little while longer.

She gathered the courage to go home. She left the motel, and drove the thirty miles to Cameron Road. She parked, and scanned the house, moving her head to the left, and back to the right. It looked like no one had been there.

Roamer had covered his tracks well. He had gone to Marie's house, but had left no evidence of being there. He had originally thought of disposing of her first, but decided that he should wait until after he eliminated his primary target: Jim Ellenberger.

So Roamer had done the "next best thing". He had entered the house, checked out all the rooms, and then bugged the place. Being familiar with the interior of the house would make it easier for him to get Marie later on; and placing "bugs" all over the house would make it easier for him to pick up information from her if she used the phone to contact Jim or anyone else who had pertinent information, or if she invited someone over to talk about these things. All of the rooms in Marie's house were bugged; and so was her home phone.

Jonathan and Bill gathered Jon's gear out of the Camaro. They set Jon's office in the upstairs den. Jon would sleep in the adjacent bedroom. This was a great arrangement for him, because he would have his own private area for study and research, and yet could visit with his parents by simply walking downstairs.

The house was a large two-story ranch house with beautiful maple floors. The upstairs had three bedrooms, a family room, a bathroom, a kitchen, a dining room, a laundry room, and a den. And the downstairs had the exact same layout, except the downstairs family room was called a "living room".

Jon made a few calls, and set up his wireless internet service. His cell phone was also on the same wireless service. Then, he decided to give away his Christmas present sooner than he had originally planned.

He logged into one of his special search websites, clicked on to a few successive icons, and electronically transferred $312,052.96 from one of his accounts as a payoff for his parents' mortgage. Then he sat back, smiled, and pulled out his checkbook. He wrote out a check to his father for that same amount, wrote "Merry Christmas. Your mortgage is paid!" in the comment section, and dated it 12/25/25. Then he wrote "VOID" on both sides of the check, after he had signed it. He then placed it in a large manila folder, and labeled it "Dad and Mom 2025".

His arm was throbbing in pain; but he didn't care. He wanted to do this. He NEEDED to do this. And so he took the time to get it done. He felt a wonderful sense of satisfaction: a feeling of accomplishment so meaningful that he could hardly contain his joy.

"Thank You, Lord," he said. "Thank You for enabling me to do this. You know I love them very much. And Lord, please show me what to do with the rest of my life. I want to please You. I love You so much."

Jonathan's mind segued to his next move. He decided he would spend a couple of hours a day checking some things out. He wanted to know what was going on with so many wolves in the area. In all of his life, even hunting and fishing, he had never known of or seen a pack of wolves in this area. It made him uneasy to think that if the cougar had not been there, maybe the wolves would have taken him. If so, there would have been no chance of survival.

He would check out the search engines for wolves in New York State. Maybe he could find out what caused the wolf population in the area to be so excessive. He could see them heavily populated in Alaska or the Yukon. But upstate New York? This didn't seem right. Something was very wrong here. And he knew that if the population became too great, they would invade human territory on a regular basis. And that was not good.

He would be ready, from now on, for any confrontation with anomalous wildlife. He had several rifles and pistols down in the basement, with lots of ammunition. He couldn't use the rifles until his right forearm healed; and that would take two or three months. So he decided to always take a handgun with him. He had a pair of Glock 40's among others; and he brought them up from the cellar, and loaded them. He could shoot a pistol accurately even left-handed; and so he placed one semi-automatic in a holster on his person, for his left hand. Then he placed the other pistol in his glove compartment.

Jim Ellenberger decided to go into hiding. He was determined to survive. He had already given himself a false address to throw off anyone who was trying to get him. But he needed to get out of the area for a while. He had to keep in touch with his old friend and lawyer, Jack Leland, because he needed him to possibly contact the Assistant Police Commissioner. Also, he would need Jack to help him "disappear" for a time, until it was safe for him to return.

Jim would have to change his identity; and he needed Jack to help him do that. Jack used to work for the Albany Social Security Office, and had the means to give Jim a new identity. Jim would have a new car, and all new identity information, complete with a photo and fingerprints, and even DNA readings, all assigned to a new name. He would move out of state. Florida was great around this time of year; and so he would move to the Tampa-St. Petersburg area, on the Gulf of Mexico. He would be in a situation like the "witness protection program". All files of Jim Ellenberger's identity would be removed by friends of Jack Leland who worked for the FBI. And from now on, Jim would do all of his financial transactions with cash—no checks, credit cards, or debit cards, but cash only. Even a man like Roamer would not be able to locate Jim, unless he did something foolish to reveal his true identity.

Jim left Jack Leland with information about how to get secret messages to Marie. He would do it through UPS signature mail, with Jack as the middle-man. Jack would not be identified by Roamer, because his office was in a huge complex in Albany.

Jim would also have his special e-mail address, complete with the information taken from a deceased internet user, and so would be untraceable from the "identity" standpoint. He might have to gamble that anyone seeking to find him was not able to pinpoint the state, or city, or exact location, of his computer. If he felt it was safe, he would e-mail Marie. Or he could text her from a disposable cell phone, if he thought it was safe. Or better yet, he could find a "secure, hacker-free" chatroom. He wasn't sure if such a chatroom existed that was accessible to him, but wished there was. For now, he would limit his means of contact to UPS signature mail.

Jim Ellenberger successfully "disappeared" within twenty-four hours. Jack would have all of his information in a UPS package marked for "Jim Newman". He could pick it up at a contact's house in Philadelphia, PA, on the way down to Tampa, FL. He could stay at a nearby motel, and try out his new identity. He would find that everything was set up for "Jim Newman", and there were no "loose ends" as long as he stuck to cash-only transactions.

Jim had been given new license plates, based on his new iden-tity. And he traded in his BMW for a new Buick Park Avenue.

Roamer could not find Jim Ellenberger's BMW. He had located his residence; but Jim was not there. He waited awhile in his new car, the blue Camaro. He was a good distance from the house, on a hill overlooking the Ellenberger home in the town of Half Moon. This hill was a perfect place to set up a surveillance camera. After doing just that, he vacated the area and went home.

Roamer would not succeed in locating Jim Ellenberger, because he was gone—as if he had disappeared off the face of the earth.

Roamer decided to keep monitoring Marie's activities and phone calls. He had bugged every room in her house; and so he could get any information that she received or passed on over the phone, or by private in-house conversation. And, of course, he would watch her internet communications.

He wanted to find out what she knew, and who else knew it. He didn't want any "loose ends" out there. He would not strike out at her unless he needed to do so; but rather, he would use her as a source of information. Only when it became necessary would he dispose of her. He could do that easily, and at a moment's notice.

CHAPTER THIRTEEN

December 25, 2025

Jonathan Wilkes woke up at 8:00AM. He was excited about this special day for several reasons.

First, Christmas is a celebration of the birth of Jesus Christ. He loved to think about the amazing miracle—that God Himself would choose to become a Member of the human race, which He created. God had to become a mortal Man, so that He could die for the sins of the whole world, thus paying the penalty for all of mankind's sins.

But Jonathan knew that Jesus' death for the sins of the world did not guarantee automatic forgiveness for everyone in the world. Only those who believe and accept that forgiveness for themselves are truly forgiven. It involves the person admitting that he or she is a sinner deserving of Hell, but also believing that God has provided forgiveness for them through the sacrificial death of Christ, as in Romans 5:10 and Ephesians 1:7.

And the clincher is the resurrection of Christ, which millions of believers celebrate on Easter. The resurrection was confirmed by more than five hundred eye-witnesses (not of the resurrection itself, but seeing the resurrected Christ); and it proved that Jesus was indeed God the Son, and therefore has the power and authority to give to all who accept His forgiveness for themselves, that very forgiveness which they accept.

Jonathan was very thankful that God the Father cared enough about him to send His Son (God the Son) to be his Savior (Provider of forgiveness). He thanked God every day for his salvation (forgiveness of all of his sins).

Second, Jonathan was excited about the beauty of the season, with all the decorations and lights and the beautiful white clean snow of early winter.

Third, he loved the spirit of the season, where people tended to be more sociable and friendly, with strangers coming up to each other and saying, "Merry Christmas!" And he loved to hear the Christmas carolers sing the songs; and see them smile and wave, and walk from house to house. And people were in a more generous mood at this time of the year. Soup kitchens were at their best, giving to the less fortunate a free Christmas dinner. And he loved to be in church services at this time of the year. It was such a cheerful environment, where everyone sang the familiar Christmas songs, and listened to the Christmas story they had heard so many times before. And yet it never grew old, because it is such good news for all who choose to receive it.

And fourth, Jonathan was excited about Christmas, because it was a day where he could demonstrate his OWN generosity. He was planning to give that manila folder to his parents with the voided check, with "Merry Christmas. Your mortgage is paid!" written on the "memo" space. Then, he would tell them how well-off he was, and confirm what he had done for them. And he had "created" a special Christmas card for them on the computer, and printed it out.

Jonathan could hardly contain his excitement. And he took the time to start his day with prayer. He prayed that God would use the true story of Christmas to show people they needed Him, and that many would receive this forgiveness for themselves. He prayed for all those whom he knew, including his family and friends. And he prayed for the people in authority all over the world. And he thanked God for his salvation, and for all the other blessings that He had given him.

Then, he turned to his Bible, and opened it. He was reading in the book of Micah. He was at chapter four. And he continued into chapter five. He noticed something in verse two of chapter five that he had missed before. This verse was talking about Jesus Christ and how He existed "from everlasting". In other words, He had no beginning, but has always existed: in eternity past. The words "from everlasting" mean that Jesus has already lived FOREVER! And Jon was reminded of Isaiah 57:15, where the prophet wrote that "God... inhabits eternity". That means that God lives in eternity (forever) in the past, present, and future. He has no beginning or end. So when Jonathan compared the two verses, he thought to himself that since God has no beginning (also in Psalm 93:1-2), then Jesus is shown to be God, because He (Jesus) has no beginning.

Interesting!" Jon thought to himself.

At 9:00, Jon shaved, took his shower, and decided to have his Christmas breakfast with his parents. So he walked downstairs, and turned right, and passed the laundry room to his left as he walked down the hall towards the kitchen and dining room. He heard his mother's voice:

"Merry Christmas."

"Merry Christmas, Mom."

"Merry Christmas, Son."

"Merry Christmas, Dad."

"I brewed some coffee for you."

"Thanks, Mom."

He poured himself a cup, and sat down at the dining room table.

"I'm so glad you came back to us. Please feel free to say what's on your mind," Marge said.

"Well, I'm happy to be here. I love you both."

"We love you, too," said Bill.

"We have some presents for you," Marge said.

"And I have something for you also," Jon said with a smile.

"Let's eat breakfast first," Bill said.

The three had eggs, sausage, and toast, along with their coffee. Then, they proceeded to the living room, and opened their presents.

Then, Jon said, "I have something for the both of you. I'm going upstairs to get it. I'll be right back."

He got up, went upstairs, and picked up the manila folder. He came back downstairs, and entered the living room with the folder.

He said, "First, I want to tell you this is not a joke. I will explain to you what I did, after you see what's in the manila folder."

Jon waited as Bill opened the folder. Bill's eyes widened, and he turned to his son.

"What's this?"

He showed the voided check to Marge.

She said, "What's going on, Son?"

"I paid off the balance of your mortgage."

"You can't do that," Bill said.

"I already did."

"That's a lot of money," Marge objected. "We can't accept that."

Jon was offended. But he asked God to help him speak in a right manner to his parents.

"You know, the reason I left you for twenty years was an argument over money. Why do we have to argue about these things? I'm a millionaire; and I want to do this for you. And I can make that money back in a year! Don't let your pride get in the way of receiving this gift. It's Christmas! We should not be arguing over filthy lucre! Haven't we learned anything from twenty years ago?"

"I don't know about this," Marge said.

"I left you because I asked you for something that you wouldn't give me. It was a money issue. And now, I have given something to you because I CAN, and because I WANT to. And you don't want to receive it."

"We don't feel right about this," Bill replied.

"You're refusing me when I want to take and when I choose to give. I can't win!"

"We're not refusing you," Marge reasoned. "We just don't want to take all this money."

"Why? Because it hurts your pride? I'm not going to tell ANYBODY that I paid the balance off. That's none of anybody else's business! And I don't think any less of you than if you paid it all yourselves. But I will have a hard time NOT thinking less of you if you refuse this gift and spurn my love."

"But it's so much money!"

"Not to me," Jon replied. He added, "Do you know how much it hurts me when you say you won't accept my gift?"

"We're not trying to hurt you," Bill said.

"But you ARE!"

"I don't know what to say," Bill said.

"Just say YES, and stop arguing with me."

"Why are you really doing this? So we'll love you more?" Marge asked.

"I'm not doing this to buy your love. I already know you love me."

"I can't get past the amount of money this is," Bill said.

"It's only about one-fifth of what I have saved up. And I can make that much back in one year."

"It's still a lot of money," Marge said, quieter now.

"To you, maybe. But not to me. What's the point of making a beautiful Christmas gift a bone of contention?"

"I don't know, Son," said Bill.

"You're worth MORE than all this. God blessed me and gave me all this money; and I want to honor my father and mother like the Bible says to do. Why should I NOT pay off your mortgage? Should I be so greedy that I want to horde all my money when I see my own 'flesh and blood' parents struggling? It's not fair. And you will hurt me now worse than you hurt me, back twenty years ago. Yes, I'll deal with it, because I'm older now; but the hurt will still be there."

"Okay, I guess…" Bill started.

"All I want in return is your love. I'm not doing this for love; but it's all I want in return. Besides, I'm set to inherit part of this house anyway. Think of THAT as the payback if you want."

"Well…" Marge said.

"You know I've got a point here about your wills."

"You're right," Marge said.

"Okay," Bill said.

"Let's not fight him anymore," Marge said.

"Son, we don't want to lose you for another twenty years," Bill said.

"You wouldn't—no matter what. But you would have broken my heart if you had refused my gift."

"We want what's best for you, Dear," Marge said.

"Thank you. Thanks to both of you. So then, are we all okay with this now?"

"Yes, I'll accept your gift," Bill said.

"Me, too. It's just so soon. So quick," Marge added.

"You'll get used to this," Jon said.

"Thank you from the both of us," Bill said.

"You're very welcome," Jon said.

He decided to change the subject.

"Let's all have a second cup of coffee."

The tension began to dissipate from the room.

"Sure," Marge said. "I'll get it."

She brought the coffee pot in, and served the coffee.

"Now, that's a great cup of coffee," Jon said.

"Thank you."

"My pleasure."

Jon sent up a quick prayer: "Thank you, Lord."

Bill and Marge and Jonathan continued to talk for another hour: and none of them brought up the subject of the payout of over $300,000.00. In all three of their minds, it was a done deal: and that discussion was a thing of the past.

At about 10:45, the calls began to come in: Emily, Bill's and Marge's oldest daughter; and then Linda, the younger daughter.

Then at noon, Bill, Marge, and Jonathan went to the Sagamore Dining Room in Bolton Landing, for Christmas dinner. It was a wonderful experience for the three of them; and Jonathan let Bill and Marge pay, because he knew it would make them feel good to do that. Then, at about 2:00, Bill and Marge drove back home; And Jon drove around to a couple of friend's homes; and then later on, about 6:00, he returned to the house he had just paid off in its entirety. He talked with his parents some more, and then retired to his upstairs den to go on the internet for a while.

Susan Morehouse knew that Marie was feeling depressed; and so she invited her over to their Christmas dinner at her house on

Library Avenue. Marie accepted the invitation, and was there at noon. She told Susan that she would love to help her serve the meal; and she started out by helping Susan set the table and place the rolls and butter and olives and other food items on the table. Then, they sat down and ate.

There were six others besides Marie and Susan. Susan's two sisters, Leona and Mary, were there, along with their respective husbands, Josh and Daniel. Josh and Leona had two boys, Cory and Zack, ages nine and eleven.

Everyone had a great time, enjoying the food and, later on, the presents under the Christmas tree. Then, at the very end of the unwrapping of the presents, Leona spoke.

"And what's the greatest Gift of all time?"

The two boys answered in unison: "Jesus!"

"That's right!"

And she read Luke 2:10-11.

"And the angel said unto them, Fear not: for, behold, I bring you good tidings of great joy, which shall be to all people.

"For unto you is born this day in the city of David a Savior, which is Christ the Lord."

Marie was profoundly moved by the message; and somehow, she felt a glimmer of hope. Maybe, just maybe, her life was not over. Maybe there was still some purpose for her life, something to hold onto, something to live for.

The family chatted for a couple of hours, and played a couple of games of UNO, while the boys played some video games. At 5:00, they had a light supper with a delicious green salad and a baked ham, corn, and mashed potatoes.

"Turkey for lunch. Ham for dinner. This is great!" said Josh.

"Who could ask for anything more?" Leona said.

"Not me," said Daniel.

"Me neither," Mary chimed in.

Marie said, "I really appreciate you inviting me over. It would have been really hard for me to be alone today."

"We're happy to have you here," Susan said. "You are welcome in this house any time. I really mean that. Don't be a stranger."

"I won't," she replied.

Josh and Leona and the two boys left at 7:00, and headed for home in Clifton Park. Then, Daniel and Mary left for their home in Saratoga at 7:30. Marie and Susan were left alone. They began to talk.

"I know life has been hard for you," Susan said.

"It hurts a lot," Marie said, with tears in her eyes.

She let down her guard, believing that Susan understood her.

"I want to help you. Maybe finding out why your daughter was killed, and bringing these awful conspirators to justice, will help give you some relief."

"I hope it does. Right now, this is my reason for living."

"Oh, Marie! You are such a beautiful and loving person. You have a lot to offer this world. You have EVERYTHING to live for."

"I know I shouldn't keep feeling sorry for myself all the time."

"Don't sell yourself short, Marie. You are an important person. And you mean a lot to me, as a friend."

"Thank you." She paused. "Thanks for having me over."

They talked for another twenty-plus minutes; and then, Marie left. She was home by about 8:30. She parked her Civic, walked to the front door, and put the key in the lock.

She felt a sadness inside of her; and when she walked into the house, the crushing realization that her Lizzy was gone came crashing down on her again. Down the hallway to her right was Lizzy's room. She entered the room, feeling sad and empty inside. She picked up Lizzy's graduation photo, brought it to her chest, and cried. Then, she carefully placed it back.

She sat on the corner of Lizzy's bed. To the right was Lizzy's desk. She stood up and picked up the 2025 Warrensburg High School Yearbook. She looked over all the pictures of her daughter for the next twenty minutes. So many activities, so much life, so much to live for! And that life was suddenly, violently, needlessly, snuffed out. It was a tragedy impossible for her to cope with.

She closed the Yearbook, and dropped to her knees. She wept, closed her eyes, bowed her head; and for the second time in thirty years, spoke a prayer.

"Why?"

She was overwhelmed with sorrow.

"Why? Why Lizzy?"

She continued, "God, I don't know if You exist; but if You do, please tell me why. Please take my pain away. I can't take it any more."

She rose up, got ready for bed, and cried herself to sleep.

December 28, 2025

Marie Trombley received information from Jack Leland via UPS that Jim Ellenberger was okay. But there was a problem, because nobody could find the phantom enemy who had pursued him. They didn't even know his internet name: Roamer.

There was no way that they could find all of the "who", the people involved in the conspiracy. Without this knowledge, they could not safely proceed in their investigation. They would have to be very careful in their quest for more information, because someone very dangerous was out there, waiting for them, and possibly planning to kill them.

Marie and Susan hoped that they would find a computer expert whom they felt they could trust; and they hoped they would find this person soon. If that expert could hack the deleted files in the DIAC website and surf in areas that might point to the "why"; maybe this case could be solved. Marie wanted closure concerning the death of her daughter. And Susan wanted to see human lives spared from future wolf attacks.

The media had been virtually silent about the issue for the most part; and the authorities had also been "mum". Both the media and the authorities labeled the incidents, not as "wolf attacks", but as "unsolved murders".

Marie and Susan were at an impasse. They couldn't find the additional information which they needed. They would keep searching, surfing, and straining to find the rest of the pieces to this complicated puzzle. They needed a break: something or someone to help them to solve this mystery.

Jonathan Wilkes was able to access everything, and even more, than Roamer could. He was one of the most brilliant computer experts in the world. He wondered what the deleted DIAC files revealed; and so, he hacked into them, and discovered that the Governor of New York State had some secret files in a file cabinet to the left of his gubernatorial master bedroom in the Governor's mansion. These files described a program to reintroduce the wolf population in the Adirondacks. The deleted files in the DIAC website mentioned that the information about this program was in the Governor's personal files.

Jonathan wondered if there was anybody interested in solving this problem. He wanted to contact that person. Maybe someone in the DIAC? He wasn't sure WHOM he should try to contact.

Also, Jon was curious about why the Governor was in the middle of all this. And why was it so secretive? He concluded that the Governor had a skeleton in his closet, a secret which he didn't want brought out into the open.

Jon wanted to see the information in the Governor's personal files, but it would not be easy. They were locked away in an old-fashioned file cabinet in an obscure room next to where the Governor slept. Jon wanted to get to these secret files.

"Hmmm!" he mused. "Maybe I'll think of something."

He would be thinking for a long time, and would finally hatch a feasible plan by early May of 2026.

CHAPTER FOURTEEN

February 26, 2026

Jaime Woodrow and his sixteen-year-old son Cody were shoveling snow outside of their Lake Placid home. They had received over two feet of snow in a blizzard which had lasted for eight hours. They shoveled all around the huge two-story house.

It was a T-shaped house. The original part of the house—the bottom, or stem, of the T—was sixty feet long and thirty feet wide, with a breezeway and garage added on, for another thirty feet of length, making the size of this "stem" thirty feet by ninety feet. The top of the T was a bedroom-wing which was fifty feet long and twenty feet wide. This huge house was way out in the country, with only a few houses nearby. The driveway to the house was over four hundred feet long.

Jaime grabbed the snow rake, and raked the snow off of the roof of the bedroom-wing, as far up as the rake would go. Then, he began to rake the western part of the house. His back was to the woods, thirty yards away.

The pack was moving through the snow, searching for food. Prey was scarce, because so many of the rabbits, deer, and other prey, had already been killed by predators. The predatory population had grown too large to be supported by the Adirondack deer population, and by the other prey in the region. The ecology of the area was unbalanced now; and that meant that the predators were more likely to breach human territory. This pack of eight wolves was a lean and hungry pack. They were moving at a moderate pace, and would not stop until they found a target.

Jaime handed Cody the snow rake.

"Here, Son. Now it's your turn. You can rake the breezeway and the garage. Thank you."

"Okay, I'm all over it."

"I'm going to shovel around this side of the house again, and then around the bedroom-wing."

"Okay, Dad."

The pack was moving towards the Woodrows' house. They had killed human beings before, and would do so again if they could. They had about a half mile to go to reach the huge house.

Cody finished raking the garage and breezeway, and then began to rake the eastern part of the house, with his back to the woods, about fifty yards away. Jaime was shoveling on the southern side of the house, along the length of the bedroom-wing.

The wolves were almost to the edge of the wood line to the east of the house. Just seconds later, they came out of the forest, and saw their prey.

Jaime looked toward the east, and froze.

Cody kept on raking, oblivious to the imminent danger.

Jaime ran toward the eastern porch. It was a ten-by-ten area, bordering on the bedroom-wing and the eastern side of the house. There was a door to the house there, but it was locked. He fumbled for the keys in his panic. "Where are they?"

The wolves charged.

"Cody! Head for the breezeway!!!"

Cody turned, saw his Dad was not going to make it in time, and ran toward the porch to defend him.

"Nooooo! Codyyy!!!"

They both ran up the stairs to the porch, just a few yards ahead of the pack leader. The wolves gathered at the base of the stairs. Cody looked at the tools hanging on the wall. He grabbed an ice-chopper, believing it would make a good weapon. Jaime grabbed a baseball bat that one of the younger children had left out from the summertime. It was a short bat— a great weapon! Cody had a hunting knife on him; and he unsnapped the sheath, so he could get to it quickly if he needed to fight up close.

The lead wolf charged. Cody stabbed it with the ice-chopper; and Jaime clobbered it with the bat, dropping the beast. Father and son were cornered, but not dead yet. They were both tall and stocky: built like linebackers. Jaime checked his left pocket for the keys. He felt them, and inched toward the door.

"I've got the key, Son."

"Okay."

There was no time to escape just yet, because three more wolves charged. Cody stabbed the nearest one. Jaime swung the bat, hitting the second wolf in the head. The third wolf broke through, and knocked Jaime down, sinking his teeth into his left arm. Jaime winced in pain. Instinctively, Cody pulled out his knife and stabbed the wolf in the throat. The predator released its grip on Jaime's arm, retreated, and collapsed. Another wolf charged, while Jaime fumbled for the bat. Cody pierced it with the ice-chopper; and it retreated.

The wolves hesitated. Two were dead; three were wounded; and three had not yet joined the fight.

Jaime handed Cody the keys. Cody unlocked the door, which swung outward.

The last three wolves charged. Jaime swung the bat, and hit one of the wolves in the left shoulder, and then in the back, disabling it. Cody stabbed another wolf with the chopper with such force that it remained stuck in its side. He lost the weapon, because the wolf jumped off the porch. The third animal jumped Cody; but he pivoted to the right, and stabbed it in the side with his hunting knife. But the knife didn't penetrate far; and the wolf landed on its feet and ran through the door of the house. Jaime and Cody followed it. Cody turned around just in time to close the door; and he heard a loud thud, as a wolf crashed against it.

The wolves were hungry, and would eat their dead. The five would eat their full, and move on. But because they were wounded, they would eliminate each other, beginning with the weakest and most damaged. If any were left, it would fall prey to another wolf pack, or maybe even a mountain lion.

Jaime rushed to the entrance to the bedroom-wing, slipped and fell, and was knocked "out cold". Cody kneeled down, and checked his pulse. His father was alive, but not breathing. He began to do mouth-to-mouth resuscitation.

The wolf climbed the stairs in the center of the house. He headed toward the upstairs bedroom-wing. His nostrils were filled with the human scent. It was everywhere. The smell of prey! He entered the hallway of the bedroom-wing. The middle room door was ajar; and he entered the room, emitting a throaty growl.

He heard something crying. A baby was lying on the bed. He took the doll into his mouth, and shook it violently. It was not anything he wanted to eat; and so he dropped it. He walked out of the room, and headed left toward the western room.

Cody's grandmother, Irene Woodrow, was in the eastern room, sleeping. The door was partly open; and it would open up into the room, toward the left side. There was a six-foot mini-hallway beyond the opening of the door before it opened up into the bedroom. Above this area was a beautiful ten-by-ten-foot skylight.

The wolf could not enter the western room, because the door was closed. So he turned, and moved toward the eastern room. He passed the middle room, and approached the partially-open door straight ahead.

"Bbbbad to the bone! Bbbbbbbaad!"

The wolf turned, and grabbed the "Cool Catfish" plaque. It continued to sing.

Irene woke up.

A second plaque, also motion-activated, began to make noise. Big Mouth Billy Bass began to sing.

The plaque blurted out: "Take me to the water!"

The wolf dropped the first plaque, and grabbed the second one. "Put me in the river!"

The wolf was now in a frenzy, shaking the plaques, and tearing at them. The fish kept on singing.

Irene heard the noises, sensed the danger, and crept out of bed to see if she could close the door in time. She grabbed the first weapon she could find—an old tennis racket. The floor creaked under her feet. She stopped, and felt her heart leap into her throat.

The fish stopped making their noise. Then, the wolf's ears cocked straight up. A creaking sound! He sensed there was real food beyond the door. He crept towards the eastern room, and pressed against the door.

Irene saw the door open wider. She hid behind the corner of the wall, just out of sight of the wolf. She raised the racket, and crouched down.

The wolf pushed the door open, and saw an image of the woman in a mirror. It was the real thing to him; and he prepared to strike.

Irene saw the image of the wolf in the mirror. She could see the wolf creeping closer, with its ears laid back, the mouth gaped open, and the tongue hanging out. The wolf's lips curled back, as he bared his razor-sharp fangs and let out a low, throaty growl. The grandmother tensed up, waiting for the wolf's head to move into view in front of her, waiting for the right moment to strike. She could feel that "hair standing on end" tingling feeling all around her. She knew she was in a life-and-death situation; and she only had one chance to save her life.

The wolf surged forward a foot further. Now, Irene could see the wolf's head coming into view. She gripped the racket handle firmly, just like she used to in her younger years. She had played in a lot of local tournaments, and had even won a few of them. That was over thirty years ago. But even at age seventy, she could still handle a racket well. She was strong for her age; and she intended to kill this intruder.

The wolf saw the image move, and then saw that another image was to his right, and moving at the same time. He hesitated, not knowing which image to attack.

The arc of the racket came from behind her back, and over her right shoulder. She could feel the adrenaline rushing through her body as the racket face picked up speed. By the time it hit its mark, it was moving at over seventy miles an hour.

The side of the racket face hit him on the head with so much force that it broke a part of his skull, and entered into his brain. The wolf collapsed. As the dead wolf's nerves twitched post-mortem, Irene dropped to her knees, and thanked God for His help.

She heard footsteps coming up the stairs, and the voice of her grandson.

"Grandma! Are you okay?"

Cody helped her to her feet. They walked arm-in-arm to the bed, and sat down. Both were visibly shaken. Then, Jaime walked in. He looked at the wolf, and then at her.

"Mom, did you do this?"

He couldn't believe his eyes. His mother laughed nervously.

"Yes. And I hope I never have to do it again."

For the next half hour, the three huddled together, talking with and comforting each other, until they felt calm enough to function normally.

Jaime decided not to report the incident, because it was illegal to kill a wolf in New York State. He was afraid the DIAC would order him to pay a huge fine. So they hid the evidence.

Jaime and Cody both decided that they would have a gun on them at all times when they went outside of the house. They would not allow the younger children to play outside unsupervised. Jaime's wife, Mindy, would also keep a gun with her for protection whenever she went outdoors. Finally, they told Irene that she needed to keep her bedroom door closed and locked whenever she was sleeping.

Over the winter, a number of farmers lost livestock; and many of them shot one or more of the predators. They didn't report the incidents, because they feared paying large fines.

The Spring came, the snow melted, and the ground began to dry up. Soon the grass would become green again; and the trees and bushes would start to bud.

CHAPTER FIFTEEN

April 16, 2026

Jonathan Wilkes had recovered well from his injuries. His arm was completely healed, except for some pain which he still felt now and then. But even that pain was fading away.

He was beginning to become more physically active, going to the YMCA in Glens Falls, practicing some jump shots on the basketball court, and lifting weights: namely, light weights to rehabilitate. He had been exercising faithfully every other day for the last three weeks, and was beginning to feel healthier.

He had taken the last few months off of his investigation of Operation Wolf, because he felt that the next step for him would have to be accessing the information in the Governor's file cabinet. He was thinking up a plan, but he had not completely formulated it yet.

Jon woke up at about 8:00AM. He began the day with prayer and a personal Bible study. He was reading in Revelation 2 and 3. He noticed a part of a sentence in chapter 3. In verse 8, "behold, I have set before thee an open door, and no man can shut it:" hit him like a ton of bricks. In the context, Jesus was talking about an open door of opportunity to share the good news of salvation freely provided by the death and resurrection of Christ, to all who receive this gift of salvation (forgiveness of all sins—past, present, and future) by simple faith. But it was an interesting phrase, perhaps pointing to a principle—namely, that God can open a door of opportunity whenever it is needed.

"Dear God, please show me how to get to these files, if it is your will," he prayed.

Maybe, just maybe, God would provide him with the wisdom to come up with a plan to get to those secret files. Maybe God would open up the door, and make the way clear for him. He would continue to pray about this, and to brainstorm towards a solution—a detailed plan to gain access to these files.

Jon grabbed a quick breakfast, and talked with his parents for about half an hour. Then, he went back to his upstairs den, and went on the internet just to surf for a few minutes. Maybe an idea would strike him. After ten minutes, he decided it was time for a shave and a shower. By 11:00, he was heading out the door.

At 11:25, he turned off of the Adirondack Northway at Exit 19. Then, he turned right onto Aviation Road, then right again into the parking lot of the Aviation Mall. He stepped out of the Camaro, walked to the northeast entrance, and proceeded to the Radio Shack. He bought some computer equipment there; and then, he walked into Sears, and went to the automotive department. There, he purchased a flare gun, just in case he experienced another emergency on the road. Then, he walked into Jonathan Reid's store, and bought two suits. He liked the brand name, and the reasonable price. He put all of his purchased goods into his IROC-Z, and then decided he was hungry. So, he walked back into the Mall, and went over to the Aviation Mall Dining Center. He went to the Chinese restaurant, and bought a full and delicious meal at a very reasonable price.

Susan Morehouse was on her way to the Mall to buy an item at Sears. As she parked, she realized that she was hungry. So, she decided to go to the Dining Center in the Mall. She walked through the entrance.

Jonathan Wilkes had been looking around to see if anyone he knew was walking around nearby. He continued to eat, and to scan his surroundings with his eyes, searching for someone to talk with. All of a sudden, he recognized someone; and he stepped up out of his seat, and moved to his left. And bumped into Susan Morehouse.

Susan was caught completely off guard. She slipped and fell.

"I'm sorry," Jonathan said, his six-foot-two athletic body stooping down to help her up.

During their collision, Susan felt surprise, then anger, and then relief that she was okay.

"Are you hurt?" Jon asked.

"No."

"I am so sorry."

"That's okay." ("It'll have to be," she thought.).

"Let me make it up to you. I'll buy you lunch. Please. I'm so very sorry."

Jonathan felt really badly about this.

"No, I'm not hungry," she lied.

She just wanted to get out of there. She was embarrassed, because it seemed like everybody saw her fall; and she felt like they were all looking at her.

"Okay," Jon said.

Susan looked at him as he said that, and saw a handsome man over six feet tall, with an athletic build and a sad face. He looked familiar.

"Do I know you?" she asked.

"I don't think so."

"You look so familiar."

"I'm Jonathan. Jonathan Wilkes."

"Susan Morehouse."

Susan was a "Plain Jane", not a looker. But Jon noticed her look of determination and sincerity. Most people didn't impress him, but Susan did. She really looked "genuine", even though at the moment, she also looked frazzled.

"You know what?" she said. "I think I'll take you up on your offer."

She decided to get a Subway Club sandwich. When she returned to the table, she sat down across from Jon, and handed him the change.

"Thank you."

"You're very welcome, Susan."

She began to unwrap the sub.

"So what do you do for a living?" she asked.

"I'm a computer technologist. I worked in Washington D.C. for ten years. I am on temporary leave. I may decide not to go back. I have some other plans on my plate."

"A computer expert?"

"Yes."

"Interesting," she said. ("This is just who I'm looking for," she was thinking.).

"How about you?"

"What?"

"What do you do for a living?"

"Oh," she said, coming out of her daze. "I'm a supervisor at the DIAC, the Department of Indigenous Animal Control."

"Really." ("Wow! This is amazing," Jon thought. "Just who I'm looking for!").

"Tell me more about yourself," she asked, before taking her first bite of the Subway Club.

They talked in between bites; and continued talking long after they had finished eating. Along the way, they developed a genuine friendship. They needed each other; but more than that, they really liked each other.

Finally, Susan said, "I need to talk with you confidentially. Can I trust your confidence?"

"I'm a born-again Christian. You can trust me."

"Okay. I need somebody whom I can trust, that can do what you do."

"A computer expert?"

"Yes."

"You need me?"

"Yes, please. If you have time."

"Oh, I have the time. I'm on leave."

"Great! Thank you."

Jon smiled. "You know, I have something funny to tell you."

"Really? What?"

"I've been hoping to find a DIAC person whom I could talk to." He paused. "Are you familiar with 'Operation Wolf'?"

Susan suddenly went into a panic attack. Her pulse became rapid; and she had difficulty breathing. She took a deep breath, tried to calm herself, and spoke nervously.

"How do you know about that?"

Jon sensed her fear. "I did some research," he said.

"Why?" she said fearfully.

"Because I had a close call several months ago."

"Close call?"

"I was attacked by a mountain lion; but I also saw a pack of about ten wolves. I'm lucky to be alive."

Susan began to calm down. Her fear gave way to sheer curiosity.

"How did you escape?" she asked.

"The cougar actually let go of me, and attacked the pack."

"Was it crazy?"

"Must have been. The cat killed a few of the wolves, and took off."

"But how did you get away?"

"Mrs. Billings and her husband. She was my Math teacher."

"Yes?"

"They were driving down the roadway; and they let me in their car. They saved my life."

"So, the wolves maybe saved your life?"

"Yeah," he said. "That's true, yeah, you're right. They distracted the cat; and my life was spared." ("This woman is pretty smart," he thought.).

"You really were lucky," she said.

"For sure."

"Then what happened?"

"I spent a few days in the hospital. My arm was crushed when the cat bit me. It was huge! Must have been two hundred pounds!"

"Now that IS unusual," said Susan. "But cougars are like people. They come in all different sizes: small, medium, and large. The largest mountain lion I think ever weighed was over two hundred and fifty pounds."

"I know one thing for sure."

"What?"

"I never want to meet this beast again, unless I'm walking on it, and it's a rug."

They laughed.

They had a great rapport. And that day, they agreed that they would work together as a team, and try to solve this puzzling case. So, they needed to come up with a plan.

Jonathan warned Susan that there were hackers out there who could access ANYTHING they say, even in private chatrooms. He told her that he was able to do this; and that there were many others who could, as well. So, they would have to arrange their meetings in a way that was not accessible to a hacker.

Jonathan asked her who else knew about Operation Wolf; and, at the same time, warned her that she had to be very careful about divulging any information. She told him about Marie; and he listened intently.

"I'm sorry about Lizzy," he remarked. "That's really sad."

Then, Jon told Susan that Marie's security might be compromised. He would look over the chatroom conversations to check. He said he wanted to meet Marie, and let her know how careful she needed to be, in light of the possible presence of hackers.

But first, he wanted to go to Susan's house to check her computer, and to make sure her place was not bugged. Once he did that, he told her that she was not compromised, as far as he could tell.

While he was there, he checked the private conversations at lightning speed, using methods only a world-class hacker could utilize. After just a few minutes, he knew that Marie was compromised, because he could see what others could not see, in a private chatroom.

They went over to Marie's house on Cameron Road; and he used his advanced GPS to spot any listening devices that might be present in her house. Sure enough, he found eight "bugs" in her house: one in each of seven rooms, and one in her home-based phone. He quickly removed and destroyed them. Then, he said that Marie needed to be very careful. Someone had been in her house; and that "someone" could be very dangerous.

Then, he told Marie and Susan that he had a way to contact people that could evade any hacker, because it would plug the private chatroom into his "impossible-to-hack" matrix.

Marie then asked if they could contact Jim Ellenberger. He told her that he could contact Jim through their present method via UPS, and give him a website he could go to—a website which had a secret chatroom, firewalled by the advanced matrix. Jon could tie Jim's computer into the secure chatroom, using Jim's personal information, and the model and serial number of Jim's computer. Jon would bring Mr. Ellenberger "up-to-speed" about everything that was going on. And he would warn him that he could not contact anyone other than him or Susan or Marie, through this secure chatroom.

Then, Marie told Jon about Jack Leland. Jon replied that Jack would also be included in the "inner circle", and kept "in the loop".

So, Susan, Marie, Jim, and Jack would all be allowed into this secure, secret chatroom. There, they would be safe, protected by the world's most secure firewall—one that could not be hacked in a hundred years.

They needed to come up with a plan. Jon invited them to come up with ideas; and they were welcome to suggest those ideas inside the secure chatroom. But in fact, Jon had almost finished formulating a plan. It would be a risky plan; but then again, they were already in a risky position.

CHAPTER SIXTEEN

April 30, 2026

Roamer was to report to the Governor in a couple of days. He was preparing his presentation. All committee members taken care of, except one: Jim Ellenberger. Jim was "off the radar" at the moment. But he would mention a possible link: Marie Trombley.

Roamer had Marie under surveillance for the fourth day. He had set up his GPS surveillance apparatus three days ago. His GPS was not nearly as sophisticated as Jonathan's; but he could watch Marie's car by satellite, because it could spot her license plate from outer space. Since he knew her license plate number, he could keep track of where she was driving, and therefore with whom she could be associating. He could make note of all the locations where she went. One place she liked to frequent was the Richard's Library in Warrensburg.

He couldn't follow her communications anymore, unless he was within a hundred yards of her proximity; but he could keep track of her locations from a distance. He was sure that he would find her associates, because he believed she would unwittingly lead him to them. Then, when the time was right, he would be ready to strike.

He needed to get these pesky people out of the way. But first, he needed to know who they were. He knew about Jim, and about Marie. And he had detected a Susan Morehouse. He was sure there was someone else; and that "someone else" might be the one who could bring his whole world down.

Susan entered the secret website. There, she found a note from "Phantom", the code name for Jonathan Wilkes: "Meet me in this room at 3:30."

This was a safe way to communicate. Jonathan made sure that he remained a phantom to the hacker or hackers, by instructing Jim, Jack, Susan, and Marie to never mention him outside of this secret chatroom. They could post messages here to meet at different times. And Jonathan had instructed them to go to the secret chatroom at least twice a day, so that he could keep them informed of all the latest developments. Constant and undetected communication was a high priority, to keep them as informed and safe as possible.

There was one other glitch he had to deal with. What if the hacker came into this chatroom from Susan's or Marie's computer? How could he know if that was happening? There were three safeguards. First, anyone who tried to access the secret chatroom was first quarantined, and placed alone into a cybervestibule. While he was in there, he would be asked a series of questions which only the owner of the computer (Susan, Marie, Jim, or Jack) would know, unless the hacker had the information "at his fingertips". But even if the hacker had acquired that private information, he would most likely be slower to answer than the person he was trying to impersonate. The system had a time limit attached to it.

The second safeguard was detected imagery from Jon's GPS. He could literally see the user of the computer electronically. If he saw someone other than the user of the computer (Susan, Marie, Jim, or Jack), then he would know that a hacker was trying to breach the chatroom. The electronic imagery came from two sources: satellite detection, and a hidden camera inside the website. Jon could easily see the person inside the cybervestibule.

The third safeguard was the automatic ejection system. When the chatroom detection system identified a hacker, it would "sound" a silent alarm, and then automatically boot the hacker off. The hacker would not be able to get past the cybervestibule's security system to get into the chatroom and access information.

Jonathan also had his own computers protected. If someone else tried to use his computer, he would be rejected by a fingerprint detection system, and a DNA detector. There was also a specific access number combination that he would press with specific fingers, making it virtually impossible for a hacker to "trick" the computer.

Besides all this, Jonathan had a three-computer setup. He would access first on a computer set up in a "secret" room behind the den. Then, he would go to either of his other two computers—one in the den, the other in his bedroom. A hacker would not know about the correct order of access; and he would not know where the first computer was located, or that it was even necessary.

At 3:30, Jonathan was going to reveal his plan. He went into the secret chatroom at 3:20. Jim Ellenberger was the first to join him. Then Jack, Susan, and Marie entered in that order. All of them easily passed the security system. They were all safely inside the chatroom.

Roamer tried to get in, but couldn't. He had more than met his match in Jonathan Wilkes. Only, he didn't know about Jonathan Wilkes. The invisibility of this phantom was frustrating for Roamer, because he had never had a secret chatroom or computer he couldn't hack. Until now.

Phantom: "Hi, Sanhedrin."
Sanhedrin: "Hello, Phantom."
Phantom: "Don't go anywhere. I have a plan. It could be done in just a few days."
Sanhedrin: "Great."
Legal Eagle: "Hello, Phantom. This is Jack."
Phantom: "Hi, Legal Eagle. I have a plan I think you will enjoy."
Legal Eagle: "I can't wait to hear it."
Phantom: "Here comes Susan. Hi, Super Decade."
Super Decade: "Hi, Phantom. I bet you have a plan."
Phantom: "I do. Hi, Twiggy."
Twiggy: "Hi, Phantom."
Phantom: "I have a plan."
Twiggy: "Can't wait to hear it."

They all greeted each other for the next couple of minutes. Then at 3:30, Jonathan began.

Phantom: "I call this meeting to order. Here is my plan. Governor Devane has crucial information in his files; but they are not in any computer file, or I would have it by now. His files may contain the rest of the 'who' involved in this plot. And it may tell us the 'why'. We know what, when, how, and where. But I believe the rest of the pieces of the puzzle are probably in these files."

The four listened intently, all of them deeply curious. Jonathan continued:

Phantom: "I have thought of a way to get to those files. I have some friends who will help me do this. One of them has been in the Governor's mansion before. He and I will go into his bedroom, and then proceed to his files. We will take pictures of the files. If we have to, we will simply take the files with us."
Super Decade: "How long will it take to take the pictures?"
Phantom: "About two to three seconds per page. But we don't know if there are five pages or five thousand pages. If there are more than one hundred pages, we may just take the files, and maybe put a dummy file in there."
Legal Eagle: "I have a question, Phantom."
Phantom: "I'm all ears."
Legal Eagle: "How are you going to get in there?"
Phantom: "I'll tell you how. I have already talked to a few of my friends; and they are going to collect…"
Twiggy: "That's disgusting!" Marie paused.
Twiggy: "But brilliant."
Legal Eagle: "I agree. Go for it."
Sanhedrin: "When is this going to happen?"
Phantom: "In two days."
Super Decade: "Start the countdown."

CHAPTER SEVENTEEN

May 2, 2026

Philip Rivers was wondering why he had ever said 'Yes' to this project. He had been told that he was gathering samples for a scientific project. In a way it was, because it would be interesting to observe how these creatures would adapt to their new environment. It took him a while to find a good population. He had rubber gloves on; and he had a small battery-operated vacuum cleaner with a bag to collect dirt, and these nasty creatures.

He would try to collect as many of them as he could. Three other people were doing the same thing. Together, they wanted to get a thousand of these. Looking at the numbers here, he was sure that they would get a lot more than that number. One of the creatures crawled up his arm; and he quickly brushed it off.

"Cockroaches!" he said. "So disgusting!"

Once the roaches were collected, the next job was deliverance. Jonathan had an idea. He had hacked into the financial statements of the Governor's mansion; and in there, he had found a number of private contractors who provided all sorts of services for the property. Deliveries of food to the kitchen area might be a consideration as a vehicle to plant the roaches into the mansion. Several maintenance services, including a window-cleaning service, were also good possibilities that could be used to deliver these awful creatures.

Jon had checked all the names of the staff, to see if anyone he knew worked there. He found one; and he was a Security officer. Jon read the name, and smiled. He and Fred Ransom had played sports together, and were good friends back in their high school days. But he had not kept in contact with him since graduation. Now, he felt regret. He hoped that Fred would still be the friend he used to be: not just because it would make it easier to divert his attention to effect the "plan", but because he really wanted to renew their friendship, and maybe even play some basketball with him again.

Jon felt badly that he was planning to deceive his old friend; but he was doing it to save lives and to bring the perpetrators to justice. And if he was successful, Fred would never know; and there would be no harm done to their friendship. He hoped that everything in the plan would go well. He prayed that it would.

Jon's homemade GPS had located all the security cameras in and around the Governor's mansion; and Jonathan marked their locations on a blueprint of the complex. He mapped the easiest route to the file room. Indeed, it was on the back side of the mansion: the south side.

He had studied the Security officers' routines for months. He saw that there was no break in the action. The Security officers watched every entrance to the Governor's mansion like a hawk.

But there was one weakness. One of the entrances was a little more obscure, and more separate from the other entrances. It was guarded; but only one Security officer could see it at any given time, while on routine patrol. Jon calculated that if the Security officer guarding this entrance could be distracted from his duty for even thirty seconds, someone could sneak into the mansion while his back was turned. The traffic of people was not as busy inside the area or vestibule past this entrance, because of its location away from most of the activity inside the mansion.

Jon studied to see if the Security officer he knew ever guarded this entrance, and if his scheduled routine showed a pattern. He learned that every fourteenth day, Fred Ransom was the guard for that entrance from 4:00PM until 12:00 midnight. And every third day following, he guarded it from 12:00 midnight until 8:00AM.

Jon could track Fred's routine through the satellite eyes of his GPS, activated directly from the Camaro parked in his parents' garage. His laptops were connected to the GPS, and were protected by the GPS's security firewalls, which could not be hacked in a hundred years.

He had to figure out how he could cause a thirty-second diversion. He would be more comfortable with a one-minute diversion. He decided that he would strike up a conversation with his old friend, and get him to turn his back on the entrance. And he figured that a "delivery man" and a "maintenance worker" would be the best candidates to go in through this entrance carrying the vials of cockroaches.

He would disarm the security cameras for several minutes, by planting a virus into their computer system through a back door on the website for the Governor's mansion. The virus would not permanently damage their security camera system, but just shut it down for about twenty minutes. This would give Philip Rivers, Stan Rounds, Jeb Woods, and Ted Lackey enough time to release the roaches from the vials.

Philip Rivers would be a "delivery man" talking with a "maintenance employee" (Stan Rounds) about the "need" for additional supplies. Jeb Woods was a "salesman" coming in the front door, selling accident insurance to the employees. He was a great talker, and could sell ice cubes to an Eskimo. Finally, Ted Lackey was a "private contractor" who had actually interviewed and procured a "job" there. His "job" was to clean the bathrooms.

All four would have vials of cockroaches. Philip and Stan would come in through the back door during Jon's friendly-chat diversion with Fred. The security cameras would be disabled at that time; and they would nonchalantly walk in through the temporarily unguarded back door. They would mingle with anyone in the vestibule area, and then proceed to walk into certain specified areas of the mansion, and release the filthy beetles. The vials were automated machines which would release all of its contents by air pressure. It was a process that took just about five seconds per vial. The roaches would be automatically catapulted out of the vials, and would become the newest residents of the Governor's mansion: soon to be the most unwanted residents.

Jeb the "salesman" would come through the front door much earlier and mingle with the managers and employees of the mansion.

He would then go to specified areas and secretly release the scary insects.

Ted Lackey would come in and do his "job", and release the roaches into all twelve bathrooms, except for the Governor's private bathroom.

All four of these men had twelve vials of fifty-plus roaches each. They would infest the place so badly, that the women in the mansion would scream, and run out of the nearest exits. Jonathan chuckled as he thought about the plan. He was sure it would work.

Once the assignments were completed, the four would carefully leave the mansion with their empty vials. These vials were immune to normal security detection, and were very small and compact. Twelve of these vials could be dispersed into various pockets—suit pockets, shirt pockets, and khaki pockets, for example. And the vials were shaped in such a way that they could pass for ultra-thick pens. And each vial had a special hand-grip on it, with a manual trigger to use, in case the automatic button didn't work.

Jonathan had one more hurdle to jump, in this master plan. He had to figure out exactly what time-slot would be the best, in which to carry out this action.

Roamer walked into the Governor's office. It was exactly 3:25PM. He and the Governor then went into another room which was completely bug-free and camera-free. Whenever Governor Devane wanted to talk in private with complete confidentiality, he would use this room. Now was definitely one of those times.

"Hi, Todd. What's up?"

"I've got problems, Bruce."

"What do you mean?"

"Real problems."

"Okay, just tell me."

"There is an invisible person out there who knows about our plan. I don't know how much he knows, but I'm sure he knows too much."

"Then, eliminate him."

"I can't find him."

"What?"

"Whoever he is, he's very smart. He has firewall protection so complex, it makes my eyes water."

The Governor was getting a bit nervous.

"You mean he's evading YOU? One of the world's best hackers?"

"Yes. He's so good, I don't know if I'm even in his league."

"Are you saying you've met your match?"

"I'm afraid he's MORE than my match."

"Can you find anything about him?"

"No."

"Not even a trace? Some computer footprints?"

"Nothing."

"Okay. If you find him, get rid of him." He added, "What about Jim Ellenberger? Do you have any news for me about him?"

"He's in hiding." Roamer paused. "I think he's out-of-state."

"Why?"

"Because he would be out of our jurisdiction."

The Governor began to look really worried. Roamer hated it when the Governor showed signs of stress, because he inevitably became the recipient of his anger. He could see Bruce Devane's veins begin to bulge around his temples, and in his neck. Then, his eyes began to narrow, and his face became taut.

"Here it comes," thought Roamer.

Governor Devane pointed a shaky finger at Roamer, and spoke angrily.

"I'm paying you ten percent of my fortune. All I can say is, you had better come up with a way to find these two!"

"I'm trying."

"That's not good enough!" the Governor said in a raspy voice.

"But—"

"No buts. Do your job! If those people spoil everything, we have too much to lose! I have my plan set up to happen this fall."

"Okay. You're the boss."

"What are you going to do about this invisible man and Jim?"

"I'll come up with a plan."

"Okay."

The Governor seemed to be regaining his composure. He was beginning to calm down. He had "made his point" to Roamer; and now, he was about to "shift gears".

The Governor began to pace back and forth.

"Now—what about Susan and Marie?" he asked.

"I bugged Marie's house. But I think she found the bugs, and removed them. Or someone else did. Maybe the invisible man."

"Go on."

"I'm keeping track of both Marie and Susan. But I lose them in that super-encrypted secret chatroom. They can come and go as they please; but I can't even get past the cybervestibule."

Governor Devane thought for a while on these problems.

"Just follow their cars if you can't follow them on the internet. They might just lead you to their invisible friend."

"Okay."

"Maybe you'll find this phantom's car with theirs."

"Good thinking!" Roamer said. "Anyone you want eliminated?"

"No. Not yet."

"When?"

"I'm thinking that Marie and Susan may physically lead you to this phantom, this computer genius, and maybe even to Mr. Ellenberger."

"So, hold off for now?"

"Yes."

"Alright."

The Governor was in his planning mode, his problem-solving thought-processes firing on all eight cylinders.

"If you find this man, our good friend, the Police Commissioner, can give us added manpower to chase him down and liquidate him. That holds true about Jim Ellenberger, also."

"Thanks. I could use the help. That Jim Ellenberger is some stunt driver, for an old man!" Then he said, "Marie and Susan will be easy to catch and kill, but Jim's a different story—at least, while he's driving. And if this invisible ghost-man is as good a driver as he is a computer expert, I'll never catch him by myself."

"A point well taken," the Governor said.

"That's all I have. I did eliminate the next-to-last committee member; and that's all I've got for you at the moment."

"Thanks, Todd, for all of your hard work and dedication. I really appreciate it. You deserve every bit of that ten percent I'm giving you."

"Thanks. I must go."

"I understand. Goodbye for now."

"I'll keep in touch."

Roamer left the Governor's mansion. He hoped that he would get a "break" soon: that one of the women would lead him to the others. Then' he could "safely" eliminate all of them, one-by-one. "The dead tell no tales," he thought to himself. He stepped into his new blue Camaro, and drove away.

CHAPTER EIGHTEEN

May 2, 2026

Jeb Woods was the first of the four to arrive at the Governor's mansion on Eagle Street. He was "selling insurance". He chatted with the Security officers as they checked his briefcase and sent him through the Security detector. He was sure the officers wouldn't bother to check his pockets; but if they did, he had the vials carefully hidden in a couple of really deep, secret pockets, designed in such a way as to obfuscate the view of anyone looking for hidden substance. The fabric of his suit pants was surprisingly thick; but the secret pockets were made of a very thin fabric, making them, and their contents, difficult to detect.

The Security detector found no weapons or harmful substances; and his suit really did look normal. He did not arouse any suspicion. In fact, he was a very likeable guy: cheerful, and fun to listen to. So, they let him in.

Jeb enjoyed playing the part of a salesman. He was so skillfully loquacious, that he could talk about someone's interests, and then automatically transition into the sales pitch. He had no problem getting to his assigned areas, and emptying the vials.

Ted Lackey came in about ten minutes later. He showed the guards his "special contractor" card, then went through the "weapon-detector booth", or WDB; and he was in. He proceeded to do the "preliminary checks" of each restroom, as a private contractor, with the agreement that he would begin the cleaning "job", starting in a couple of days. He went to each restroom, and quickly released the disgusting insects. He smirked as he thought about the two-thousand dollar check they were mailing today to his newly-set-up Post Office box. "Our tax dollars at work," he thought to himself. Ted worked quickly at his "job", and would be "long gone" before women began screaming at the sight of the cockroaches.

Outside, in the back area of the mansion, Philip and Stan waited, all dressed up in their respective uniforms, while Jonathan walked up to distract the Security guard he knew so well.

"Hi, Fred. It's Johnny, your old basketball buddy."

"Wow! Is it really you?"

"Well, I'm a bit older now."

Fred laughed. "It's working," Jon thought to himself.

"Me, too," Fred replied. "And some days, I really do feel my age."

Jon tried not to look at the two men walking about twenty feet behind the guard and gingerly opening the door.

"How long have you been here?" he asked.

"Oh, about six months."

"Well, I hope it works out for you." He paused, and said, "Hey! Remember that time we both collided on court?"

"I'll never forget it."

"I couldn't walk for two days."

"Me neither."

They laughed. The men were in. Time to leave.

"Well, it's so good to see you. Give me a call some time. We can reminisce some more."

Oddly enough, he really wanted to get together with Fred. They really WERE old friends; and to his delight, they were STILL friends.

The two talked for a few more seconds, exchanged phone numbers; and then Jonathan left.

Fred resumed his patrolling of the area; and the thought crossed his mind that this whole meeting with Jon was a rather odd experience. But he dismissed the idea that the experience was suspicious, because Jon had always been a really good friend of his. And he had really enjoyed the conversation.

Philip and Stan really looked like they belonged there; and so, nobody even noticed them. They went to their rehearsed places, each of them guided by a mini-GPS. The mini-GPS knew the entire layout, or blueprint, of the building, and guided them easily. They released the roaches, and walked out another back entrance. They had also left behind two other items, each with a tracking device.

All four of the men had left the mansion, and were driving away, by the time the security cameras were back online. The virus had come and gone. The guards had not panicked, because their computer analyst reported that it was a low-level virus that would last no more than half an hour. So they had stayed alert, made sure the Governor was well-guarded, and waited for the virus to run its course and clear out. The bomb-detectors had not been affected, and indicated that there was no threat. It had been a tense twenty minutes for the guards; but they got through it with no one getting harmed. So, they all figured that they would still have their jobs tomorrow.

"Wow, we did it!" Susan said in the secret chatroom.
"Yes, we did," said Jon. "Now comes phase two."
They continued their conversation.

Super Decade: "I'm all ears, Phantom. Tell me more."
Phantom: "We'll use Mr. Congeniality: the one who can talk your ear off."
Super Decade: "Who's that?"
Phantom: "Jeb Woods. We're having him shave off his nice, neat little beard and mustache, and giving him a new hairstyle. We'll give him a cool hairstyle: a Mohawk."
Super Decade: "Great idea!"
Phantom: "Here's the plan. Our friend Jeb will pose as an exterminating contractor. He will sell his 'company's' services, and then call for the evacuation of the mansion for several hours. Then, he will call an exterminator company to send some exterminators up to literally do the job."
Super Decade: "Interesting."

Phantom: "Jeb will literally broker the deal. He will actually get paid for doing this. Our tax dollars at work."

Super Decade: "Amazing! Then you move in?"

Phantom: "Exactly. Once the mansion is evacuated, for safety and insurance reasons, we move in."

Super Decade: "Is it that easy?"

Phantom: "I think so. We should be able to walk through the main front entrance with easy clearance."

Super Decade: "We?"

Phantom: "Jeb and me. Anyway, we will be going in to 'check out the infested areas'; and we'll have gas masks on; and we'll go right to the back, and access the files."

Super Decade: "What about the security cameras?"

Phantom: "We're okay, because we're supposed to be there. And, for some reason, the Governor chose to not put security cameras in his bedroom and secret file room."

Super Decade: "Great!"

Phantom: "But there is one glitch."

Super Decade: "Oh?"

Phantom; "He has a laser silent alarm system in both rooms."

Super Decade: "So, what are you going to do?"

Phantom: "We could disable it; but that might arouse suspicion. So, my plan is to bypass it, using my infrared gear."

Super Decade: "So, you can see the laser beams, and avoid touching them and avoid activating the silent alarm?"

Phantom: "Exactly right. Just like we were in the movies."

CHAPTER NINETEEN

May 3, 2026

Steve Raines was walking through the woods in back of his new country home in the town of Blue Mountain Lake. His wife, Evie, was thawing out some Sirloin steaks for lunch. The property was over three hundred acres; so Steve had a lot of space to explore. He and Evie had moved up recently from New Jersey to take possession of his inheritance. Now, he was exploring the area.

His dog, Buford, was by his side. He was a two-year-old Great Dane, with lots of youthful energy. Sometimes Evie got a little jealous of all the attention Steve gave to the dog.

The pack was traveling southward at a furious pace. They had not detected any large prey for three days. They needed to satisfy their voracious appetites. It was a small pack of six members. They were a mile north of Steve Raines, and approaching fast.

"Hey, Buford. You like this stream?" said Steve.

He liked talking to his dog. He'd sometimes forget that Buford was not human.

"That's it. Take a drink. I think I will, too."

He got down on his knees, cupped his hands, scooped up some water, and drank.

"What a nice piece of property!" he thought. "Probably some good fishing a ways downstream."

After a few minutes, they continued west. They came to a large clearing with a few trees near a small pond. There were a lot of bushes growing up here. "The place has been logged," he reasoned. "That's why there is young growth here." They spent a few minutes surveying the area, and then moved west towards the next stretch of woods. Steve decided not to enter the forest here, but instead turned back, and moved eastward towards Evie and their new house.

Predator eyes were watching a deer grazing in a small meadow. The deer sensed the danger, and bounded away. The wolves gave chase. Prey and predators moved through the forest, and quickly advanced towards a large clearing with a small pond.

Buford's right ear stood straight up. The deer was half a mile away; and Steve couldn't hear it. But Buford could. He let out a whining sound, and then started barking. He could hear other noises now. The noise of danger. They were coming, and Buford knew it. Steve was still unaware, oblivious to what was fast approaching. Buford's lips pulled back; and he let out a throaty growl.

The deer crashed through the forest, snapping limbs, and staying just ahead of the pursuers. Steve could hear the deer now; and he turned his head to the right. Seconds later, the deer burst out of the forest, and bore down on Steve. Steve ran to get out of the way, and then he saw the pack moving out of the trees. He ran towards the nearest tree. A wolf knocked him down; but Buford ripped into it. The big dog gripped its neck, and shook it with all of his might. Three of the wolves kept pursuing the deer. Buford released the wolf, and faced the last two invaders. Steve stood up, and saw the tree was nearby. He crept toward it. Buford kept the two wolves at bay, barking loudly.

The wolves bared their fangs, and charged the dog. Buford evaded the first attacker, and met the second one head-on. As Steve climbed the tree to safety, he could hear the horrific struggle. The other wolf joined in; but Buford broke free. His master was safe; so he could run now.

The three wolves brought the deer down in a flanked attack: from the right, left, and rear. The struggle was over in a couple of minutes; and the deer lay still and silent, ready to be eaten. The rapacious victors began their bountiful feast. They wasted no time in gorging themselves.

Buford ran towards the forest, then to the right, and back towards the small pond. He headed towards a clump of bushes that formed a huge semi-circle, and stopped.

Steve saw the injured wolf slowly rise up and limp away. Weakened and badly hurt, it was trying to escape from the rest of the pack. Steve watched the wolf go back the way from which it came.

Buford charged the first wolf from its right, and bit into its jugular vein, inflicting a mortal wound. He instinctively sensed that the second wolf was near. He released the first wolf, steeled himself, and prepared for the imminent clash.

The three wolves ate ravenously. Then, one of them stopped, and howled loudly. It was a chilling sound that reverberated through the forest.

Buford felt the full force of the wolf crashing into him from his left. He rolled with the wolf, his mouth gaping open and shut. The wolf bit into Buford's leg, and then tried to grip his neck. Buford broke free from the wolf, shook his head, and let out a huge growl. The two nemeses came together in a loud and furious death-clash; and the battle lasted for several minutes.

Steve could hear the fight from where he was. He waited, hoping and praying. Then he heard a silence, interrupted by howling in the distance, coming from the south. A couple of tense minutes passed; and he heard the sound of an animal limping towards the tree, and then a quiet whimpering sound as Buford approached. Steve climbed down off of the big maple tree, and greeted the big dog.

"Buford, am I glad to see you! Are you okay?"

He still talked to him like he was human.

Buford whimpered, and turned toward the east, towards home. Steve walked alongside him, looking around nervously. He could hear three distinct howling sounds in the distance, to the south, from behind the tree line, and deep inside the forest. He hoped that the predatory beasts would stay a distance away, so that he and Buford could make it safely home. The two didn't waste any time, and were back home in ten minutes.

CHAPTER TWENTY

May 3, 2026

Jeb and Jonathan went right through the front main entrance of the Governor's mansion. They were the "broker" and his "assistant". They had passed Security easily. And now, Jonathan got to see what he had only seen on a computer blueprint. The mansion was spacious and beautiful. But its beauty was marred by the presence of thousands of creepy cockroaches.

The front of the mansion had a huge banquet room with a three-story ceiling. Huge chandeliers hung from the high ceiling. A couple of large, elegant stairways led up to the second and third floors. The Governor's office, and the Attorney General's office were on opposite ends of the mansion; but both were on the second floor.

Jeb's and Jonathan's goal was on the third floor. They headed for the nearest stairwell, being careful to not converse with each other, in case someone was listening electronically. They "inspected" an area on the first floor, and then started up the stairs, moving closer to their goal.

Three Security officers were watching the computerized screens. They noted the two "brokers" going up the stairway, but were not suspicious, because they had been informed that they were just doing their job.

Jon turned on his cell phone, and followed the tracking device. He had to go down the second-floor hallway, and move to the left. He then went to the restroom at the end of the hallway. There was a vent in there which was not covered by a working security camera.

He removed the vent cover, reached inside the vent, and grabbed the two sets of pocket-sized day-and-night-vision infrared goggles. He put them into one of his pockets, and then replaced the vent cover. Then, he exited the restroom, and joined Jeb at a planned meeting-point on the third floor. They then proceeded to the Governor's bedroom, and then to the adjoining file room. Fortunately, there was no security camera watching the Governor's bedroom door and interior, because he wanted his privacy. Rumor had it that, once in a while, he would entertain a mistress or two. Jon knew that the Governor was an evil man; and so this rumor didn't surprise him at all. With no camera watching them, Jeb and Jonathan could enter the room with impunity.

The two easily avoided the laser security, because it was a simple combination of laser beams. Wearing their infrared goggles, they lifted their feet a couple of times, and bent down four times. They were safely inside the bedroom. And the file room was easier to navigate, because there were only two laser beams near the floor.

Once inside the file room, they electronically unlocked the file cabinet, and rifled through its contents. Most of the files were non-essential to them; but a couple of folders caught their attention. One was labeled "Family History"; another labeled "Operation Wolf". Fortunately, there were only a total of forty-eight pages in these two files.

They took pictures of all forty-eight pages, and then returned the files to their proper places in the file cabinet. They then locked the cabinet electronically.

"Time to leave," Jon thought to himself.

He put the infrared goggles back on. Jeb "followed suit". They stepped over the two laser beams in the file room, and carefully evaded the six laser beams in the bedroom; and they both breathed out a sigh of relief as they stepped out of the bedroom and into the hallway. They "kept their cool" and acted casually as they traversed the hallway and moved down the stairwell. They had been successful: in and out of the file room in less than five minutes. That was fast!

The exterminators had been told by Security that they had to announce when they were ready to enter the Governor's bedroom, bath, file room, and living room, all of which had laser security. When they did, Security turned off the lasers; and the exterminators fulfilled their contract.

Jeb and Jonathan left in Jeb's truck, a rare 2023 Lincoln Blackwood. Jeb drove Jonathan to his Z-28, which was parked in an underground parking lot.

"Great job today, Jeb. Thank you so much."

"You're very welcome, my friend. Any time."

"I owe you one."

"Nah. It was my pleasure. An adrenaline rush."

"Thanks. Your favor will not go unrewarded."

"I'll keep in touch."

Jon opened the car door, sat down, and waved to his good friend as he began to drive away. Jeb gave him a "thumbs-up", and drove away.

Jonathan looked at the mini-camera with the pictured files, and smiled. He was so excited about this new information that he almost backed into an oncoming car. He checked himself in time, and stopped. Then he came down from "cloud nine". He drove home, and went online immediately.

He e-mailed the file pictures to his secure chatroom, which had a port for pictures. He thought about printing them out, but decided not to do it at this time. He would have his four cohorts read the information on the secure site.

Sanhedrin entered the chatroom. "Did you get the information?"

"Take a look," said Phantom. Jon showed him the pictures of the files. The conversation continued.

Twiggy: "Wow!"

Legal Eagle: "I see."

Twiggy: "Where's Super Decade?"

Susan was later than she expected. She had forgotten to put gas in her car; so she had turned off at Exit 21. She had to wait longer than expected, because the gas station was unusually busy. After her ten-minute delay, she drove home. She knew she would be a couple of minutes late for the chatroom meeting.

Phantom: "She'll be here."
Sanhedrin: "So now we get to see if we have all the pieces of the puzzle."
Twiggy: "I hope it's all there."
Phantom: "I've read through some of it; and it does give us valuable information."
Legal Eagle: "Let's take some time to read this."

Super Decade entered the room.

Twiggy: "Hi, Super."
Phantom: "Good to have you here, Super."
Sanhedrin: "Hello, Super."
Legal Eagle: "Hi, Super."
Super Decade: "Hi, everybody. Sorry."
Phantom: "What happened?"
Super Decade: "Forgot I needed gas. Took longer than I expected."
Twiggy: "I understand. I hate when I do that."
Phantom: "I'd like to call a quick meeting."

Jon continued.

Phantom: "I believe the first thing we need to do is read these forty-eight pages. Does everyone have time to stay on here for a while?"
All said "Yes"; and they all began to read the files. Susan, a speed-reader, was first to finish. Then, Jack Leland finished; then Marie, Jim, and Jonathan. The faster readers conversed among themselves, waiting for the others to finish. Finally, everyone was back from the cyber library. That library was accessible

through a back door, and was as secure as the chatroom, because it was an extension of the room. When Jonathan entered the chatroom-proper, everybody wrote "Yay!"

Phantom: "lolol—The reason I took so long was to analyze where we are and what we need to do."

He paused briefly, and then continued on.

Phantom: "We have five powerful people involved. The Governor, the Police Commissioner, a lawyer, a campaign manager, and a computer expert named 'Roamer'."

All five of them had read the forty-eight pages, and understood that this was a serious situation. It was more than serious. It was downright scary.

Phantom: "I can tell you that Roamer is the one I fear the most, because he has eyes that can see almost anywhere. The lawyer, campaign manager, and Governor are easy compared to Roamer. Roamer is by far the most dangerous; but he cannot penetrate our security here. But outside of this chatroom, we are vulnerable. So, we must be very careful outside of this secure site."

Sanhedrin: "It must have been Roamer that followed me that night."

Twiggy: "That makes sense."

Super Decade: "We all have to be VERY careful."

Legal Eagle: "Keep watching your back."

Phantom: "We ALL have to be on the lookout. And we need to continue our secure communication."

Jon paused, and then continued his informational agenda. The other four needed to know more about what he knew, concerning this situation.

Phantom: "I can tell you that Roamer has tried repeatedly to get into this chatroom; but he can't do it. I don't want to scare you; but he was in our cybervestibule just a few minutes ago. I can see him now, trying again to get in; but he can't."

There was a moment of cyber silence; and then Jonathan continued his discourse.

Phantom: "The next person we have to be concerned with is the Police Commissioner. Not as scary, but almost. We have to be very careful. But I have already hacked into his files; and I have an idea."
Sanhedrin: "What?"
Phantom: "We have to trust somebody. I think the Commissioner's assistant is trustworthy."

Marie was fascinated at this idea—one that she had suggested to Jim. Jim was also interested in this idea; but was cautiously optimistic.

Legal Eagle: "Are you sure?"
Phantom: "Yes. I hacked his files; and he has a history of being a man of honor. He lives transparently, and is an officer of a church— one that really believes the Bible. He's a believer, according to his testimony. If he is, we can trust him. I think we have to take the chance.

Jon switched gears.

Phantom: "We also know the WHY. Because Bruce Devane is look- ing to evacuate the town of Mountain Meadow, and get the gold artifacts."
Sanhedrin: "Why did he have to populate the whole Adirondack Park with wolves just to evacuate one small town?"
Phantom: "Because Operation Wolf was for the whole Adirondack Park. But it ALSO provides perfect COVER!"
Sanhedrin: "How?"
Phantom: "Do you remember the Tylenol murders?"
Sanhedrin: "Yes."

Phantom: "A number of innocent people were murdered for apparently no reason—just randomly. But the reason WHY they were murdered was to cover up the FIRST murder. And infesting the WHOLE Adirondack mountain range provides great cover for the REAL intention—to evacuate that small town. The very size of the Adirondack Park obscures the small town."
Legal Eagle: "Very clever."

Roamer knew two of the cars he tracked. One was Marie's Honda Civic. The other was Susan's Toyota Prius. But he needed to find out what car the "invisible one" drove. His patience finally paid off. He got a satellite image of the car. Once he had the license plate number, he could pick up the vehicle's location whenever observable by satellite.

"Got it!" he said to himself. "Finally."

Jonathan, Susan, Marie, Jim, and Jack talked about the situation further. They all agreed to take some time to think about what to do next, and how to do it.

Then, Jon adjourned the meeting. Jim, Jack, and Marie logged off. Then, Jon spoke to Susan.

Phantom: "There's something I have to do."
Super Decade: "What's that?"
Phantom: "I have to go to the Bolton Landing library tomorrow morning; and I'll drive you there, Susan."
Super Decade: "Okay, I'll go. I'll get someone to fill in for me at work. What do you need to do?"
Phantom: "I have to fulfill a promise."

Roamer called the Governor, who then talked with the Police Commissioner. Could they have men ready to help Roamer at a moment's notice? Yes. Once he received the answer, Roamer pumped his fist into the air. He was so excited! He couldn't wait to put a bullet in this "invisible" guy's head. He wanted to kill this annoying guy more than he wanted to waste Jim Ellenberger.

CHAPTER TWENTY-ONE

May 4. 2026

Jonathan Wilkes really wanted to get this duty over with. He was a man of his word, but was a bit nervous about picking up Susan at her house. He wasn't sure if the hacker had a GPS that could spot cars; and he feared that Roamer might physically spot them by lying in wait at a distance, like a private investigator doing routine surveillance. He was getting a bit paranoid about this secret enemy. He feared that Roamer was getting closer, and that he was very dangerous. He had better keep alert. "Watch your back!" he thought.

Roamer tracked the Camaro from Athol to Warrensburg. He then saw him stop at Susan's house and proceed towards Bolton Landing. He dialed the Police Commissioner at his secret extension number.

"This is Roamer."

"Todd! How are you?"

"Good, Mr. Reynolds. Two major targets are headed toward Bolton Landing. I have reason to believe that one of them is our second most important target, our phantom enemy."

"Do you need four of my not-so-nice, plain-clothes associates?" He added, "I hear the Governor has given you the green light."

"That's right."

"Let's do it. Where to?"

"Bolton Landing. Probably the library. Susan goes in there quite often. I don't know why. But at least twice a week."

The Bolton Free Library was a pleasant sanctuary for avid readers, researchers, and "computer buffs" who wanted a quiet place to function. The librarian, Jenny Hall, had a strict rule: "No excessive talking in the library." And her corollary was, "Keep the noise down!" She had received an incoming call:

"Hi, Jen. This is Jonathan Wilkes. I'm on my way."

"Well, it's about time."

"I know. Sorry about that."

"What happened?"

"Some things came up that took away my time. I'm really sorry, Jen."

"It's been a whole month since you promised."

"Sorry, sorry, sorry."

"Alright, I've flogged you enough. I forgive you."

They laughed.

Jon continued. "Would you like to speak to your favorite cousin?"

"Susan? You know Susan?"

"Yes, I do. And here she is."

Susan greeted her cousin. The two relatives would talk incessantly for the rest of the trip to the library.

The Police Commissioner, Harry Reynolds, personally dispatched four of his "goons". They were a part of a shadow group which was "off the radar", and willing to do the "dirty jobs". This shadow group had made several people disappear. And they were being employed to do that today.

Jonathan parked his IROC-Z across the street behind an apartment building with a circular drive going around the back of the building. He had a paranoia of being trapped: of having his car boxed in by multiple cars. He also calculated that hiding the car would confuse anyone trying to find them.

Roamer wondered why the Z-28 was parked across the street; but he still decided to proceed with his plan. He would drive past the library, park, and walk back toward the library. He would wait outside the library, somewhere out of sight of the "targets", until his new associates arrived. He called the lead driver on his cell phone.

"What's your ETA?"

"About thirty minutes."

"That long?"

"We were in Saratoga."

"I see."

"We're coming fast; but we don't want to get stopped for speeding."

"Bruiser makes sense," Roamer thought.

"Thank you, Bruiser. See you soon, at the library."

"Bruiser", "Smash", "Big John", and "Striker" were following GPS guidance towards the Bolton Free Library.

Jon and Susan crossed the street, and entered the library. Jon walked over to the librarian's office. Jen was not there. In fact, he didn't see anyone in the whole place.

"Hello, Jen?"

"I'm back here."

"Oh, okay."

"Make yourself at home."

"Thank you."

Susan watched as Jonathan accessed a special website from all the computers, and started to download a myriad of programs into them. She had already calculated that he had the ability to do great things on a computer; but she was still surprised at the dexterity and speed he employed in his work.

Twenty-five minutes passed. Roamer was hoping that Jon and Susan would not leave before his cohorts arrived. His cell rang.

"We're three minutes away."

"Bring it on, Bruiser."

"Over and out."

Roamer pumped his fist into the air again. He was regaining his energy and excitement. Three minutes! Yes! He couldn't wait to "off" this guy.

Jonathan was just finishing up.
"What do we owe you?"
"Nothing. It's free."
"No, really. How much?"
"It's free. I'm well off. I don't need the money."
"Okay."

Roamer could see the three cars approaching. Just one more minute!

"Hey, check out our new addition. It's back this way," said Jenny.
Susan smiled and said, "Come on, Jon. You're going to like this." She turned to Jenny:
"Okay, Jen, lead the way."
For some reason, Jonathan was getting a bad feeling. He didn't know why, but he felt a surge of anxiety.

The men parked, and moved out of their cars. Bruiser was first.
"Let's go!" he said to Roamer.
He and Roamer walked to the front entrance of the library. "Smash" was next, then "Striker", and then "Big John".

Jon heard the front door open.
"I've got to go," Jenny said.
"Wait." Jon stopped her.
"Why?" Jenny asked.
"I want you to come with us."
"Why? What's going on?" said Susan.

The men were all gathered at the front entrance. Roamer and Bruiser scanned the front of the library. They didn't see anyone.
"Is he here?" said Bruiser.

"Yes, I'm sure he is."

"I'm really scared. I think someone is here to get us," Jon said.
Jenny answered, "Well, let's use this back exit."
"Let's go," Susan said.
"Let's hurry," Jon said.
They exited from the back of the library. Jon's heart pounded. Three newly-parked cars! We've got to get away fast!
He said to the others quietly, "Run!"
They ran.

CHAPTER TWENTY-TWO

The five men walked to the back of the library.
"Hello? We want to check out some books," Roamer said.
No answer.
"Hello?"

The three briskly crossed the street, and ran up the circular driveway. Jon and Susan got into the Camaro.
"See you later. Good luck," said Jenny.
She ran behind some large bushes, and hid. Jon turned the ignition key; and the muscle car roared to life.

"There's nobody here," said Bruiser.
"That doesn't make sense," Smash said.
"Yes it does. They left," Roamer said.
"Maybe they saw us," said Striker.
"Let's get 'em," said Big John.
They reached the front door, and watched as the red Camaro screeched down the driveway and turned right onto the main road. They scrambled for their cars. Roamer got into the nearest car, with Bruiser. His 2026 Mustang had a sunroof, and a great weapon in the back, on the floor. Roamer thought, "Cooool!" Blowing up Jon and Susan would be great fun!

"Don't even think about it! Use the rifle," said Bruiser. "The explosives are the last resort. I'm doing a little marketing on the side; and this is my sample."

He had forgotten to put it in his garage last night. He had been distracted by some friends of his who wanted to party. When he drove home from the party, he was drunk and tired. But when he saw Roamer scan the back of the car, he suddenly remembered. "Oops!" he thought. "Good thing it was Roamer seeing it, and not a police officer." Even the Police Commissioner wouldn't be able to save him from a prison term.

Jon turned right onto Mohican Road. It was a long straight-away, ending in a huge steep hill. He pushed the pedal to the floor; and the car accelerated rapidly.

Roamer stood up through the sunroof, and almost lost his grip on the rifle when Bruiser turned onto Mohican Road. The target was already three hundred yards ahead of them, and pulling away. He regained his balance, aimed the rifle, and fired. It was an automatic weapon, and sprayed bullets like the rain.

Jon hit the base of the hill at ninety miles an hour. He heard the sound of glass breaking behind him, and felt a breeze as bullets whizzed past him and hit the dashboard. A couple of bullets rico-cheted off of the top of the car. And then, a second hail of bullets hit.

"I can't believe it!" Jon said.

"What?"

"I put my two pistols and my rifle in the back of the car; and now we can't use them."

"Why did you do that?"

"I do it whenever I have a passenger. I'm responsible for the usage of any firearms I own; and so I move them all out of sight. Including the one on my person."

"I'll go back there and get them."

"No. I put them down under the panel where the spare tire is. It would take too long. And you would be a sitting duck back there. You're much safer here, up front."

Roamer was blocked by a huge tree branch, from firing a third round. He swore profusely as the Z-28 turned left onto Potter Hill Road. Then he sat down in frustration. Bruiser's Mustang lurched forward to reach ninety, and climbed the hill. Once they reached the top of the hill, they could see the Camaro on the next stretch of road; and Roamer stood up and fired again.

"Keep your head down!" Jon said, as another fusillade of bullets smashed through glass, and into the seatbacks and dashboard.

"The back windshield is shot out!" Susan said.

"I see that," Jon said. Then he added, "But the seats we're sitting in are bullet-proof. So are the tires."

"Really?"

"I worked for the Pentagon. I know about armor in a vehicle."

"Why not the back windshield?"

"I was going to bulletproof it, but I didn't. I'm sorry."

Jon began to slow down, because there were a lot of turns ahead; and these turns were not easy to navigate at high speed. He decided to activate the advanced GPS. At the moment, they were descending a hill and turning right, temporarily out of sight of their pursuers. He pushed the numbers; and the hologram suddenly appeared.

"What's this?" Susan asked, staring in amazement at the hologram.

"It's the most advanced Global Positioning System in the world."

"What can it do?"

"It's multi-functional. I set up the secure chatroom with it. And it can take control of this car, if we need it to."

"It drives the car?"

"Yes. It's a perfect driver. It could save our lives in a tight situation." He added, "It can even calculate survivability."

He saw a red flash to the left, and the letters RPGL.

"It can detect weapons, also."

He didn't tell her that the GPS indicated that their pursuers had a rocket-propelled grenade launcher ready to fire at a moment's notice.

They went around corners, and up and down hills at breakneck speed, pursued by their relentless enemies. Three cars were following them. First was Bruiser, with Roamer as his passenger. Next was Smash. And last was Big John, with Striker riding with him.

Jon turned right onto Trout Lake Road, and narrowly missed a young woman walking along the side of the road. The Camaro took the next turn, a right turn, at sixty miles an hour; and their bodies swayed to the left, like riders on a roller coaster. They began to speed around Trout Lake; and the GPS spotted another pedestrian. Jon avoided him by veering into the opposite lane, causing Susan to tense up. But they were safe. The GPS indicated no cars ahead for the next mile, and three cars behind them in the preceeding mile.

As the Z-28 hugged the road and soared around the lake, they were pulling away from Bruiser and Roamer. It was a wild ride at seventy miles an hour; and Susan was terrified. They turned right, climbed another steep hill, turned left, and motored down and then up, and turned right again, and raced down Lamb Hill Road.

The base of Lamb Hill Road formed a "T" with East Schroon River Road. On the other side of East Schroon River Road, Helen McCormick was wrapping up an agreement to sell an old house that had been on the market for two years. Her client, Jill Knowles, was walking toward the side door, and talking with Helen.

"I agree that we have to fix the kitchen and dining room area. I'll have a contractor repair it later on this week," Helen said.

"Okay, it's a deal, as long as it passes my inspection," said Jill.

"I'm willing to do whatever I can, Jill."

"Thanks, Helen. I appreciate that."

Thirty yards in back of the old house was a Day Care Center. The operator of the Center, Judy Kramer, and her assistant, Joan Mansfield, were directing the children outside to sit in a semi-circle.

Jon picked up speed going downhill, but was careful to stay controlled. He sped under the Adirondack Northway overpass; and he could see the intersection ahead. He knew there was a STOP sign at the base of the big hill. Bruiser, Smash, and Big John were all driv-ing recklessly, and inching closer to their target. Bruiser was now on

Lamb Hill Road, and speeding furiously downhill. The Z-28 came into view a quarter of a mile away. Roamer stood up with the rifle, prepared to fire, and suddenly was rocked to the right as Bruiser ran over a pot-hole. The rifle, which was already hard to hold onto at their present speed, literally flew out of his hands, and landed on the shoulder of the road. Then he was rocked to the left. He sat down, and picked up the grenade launcher.

"What are you doing?" Bruiser asked.

"I lost the rifle."

Reluctantly, Bruiser said, "I guess this is more important than getting my sale."

Bruiser was fuming inside, because it had taken him over six weeks to get this weapon sample and arrange a meeting with a potential buyer; and he was certain to make well over one hundred thousand dollars on the deal if it materialized.

"Careful. Don't lose this one, too," Bruiser said.

"I won't. Just drive slower for a second. Please."

"Alright," Bruiser said, and eased down to a slow sixty miles an hour.

Roamer got up and carefully raised the terrible weapon, and felt tremendous wind resistance. But then he saw how easy it was to operate, and simply aimed it forward and fired.

Jon knew that the RPG had been fired; and he prepared to do a quick deceleration and left turn onto East Schroon River Road.

Joan Mansfield stood in front of the semi-circle of children; and Judy Kramer, her boss, was to her right. She motioned to the kids to close their eyes.

Then, she said, "Now children: Think of the most peaceful, quiet thing you did today, before you came out here."

The IROC-Z made a terrific screeching noise as it grinded to a halt, skidded past the STOP sign and across East Schroon River Road, and faced left.

The children at the Day Care Center opened their eyes at the loud noise; and some of them screamed.

Helen and Jill stopped talking, and turned around in surprise at the sudden interruption to their otherwise normal routine.

The RPG picked up speed as it approached the Northway overpass.

The Camaro stalled.

Roamer sat down.

Jonathan spoke a special series of fourteen code numbers to activate the GPS car-control function.

Then he said, "Land Traffic Controller, take control!"

Susan said, "Look! To the left!" She screamed in absolute terror.

The heat-seeking missile was only a few seconds away, its deadly cargo heading straight for the Camaro's engine. Jon and Susan stared in horror at the sight of this motorized killer. They could see the front of the missile, and the trail of fuel behind it, looking like a comet-shaped protrusion.

Bruiser could see the Camaro in the distance.

"We got him!" Roamer shouted.

"Yes!" said Bruiser.

The Land Traffic Controller instantly fixed the mechanical problem; and the big engine roared to life again. Jon and Susan felt a terrific G-force as the Camaro lurched forward with instant acceleration.

The missile's heat-sensor was confused. Its original target had suddenly moved. And now there were multiple targets ahead. It sensed the body heat of the two women: Helen the real estate agent, and Jill, her client, who were talking excitedly outside the house, and pointing at the Camaro as it sped away. It also sensed the heat generated by a furnace inside the old house. The missile veered off-course.

The two women saw the missile in time, and jumped off the front porch, diving to get out of the way. The missile vacillated between the women, the furnace, and the Z-28. It split the difference, and hit squarely in the center of the house.

The children at the Day Care Center screamed in alarm at the horrific explosion.

"Everyone back in the Center!" Judy said.

They all hurried inside; and Joan dialed 911.

Helen and Jill ducked as flying debris fell all around them.

"Helen, I'm sorry. Your contractor will have to fix the whole house."

"No need to worry. The insurance will cover the expense."

Roamer couldn't believe his eyes. He let out a tirade of expletives. Bruiser wasn't happy about it, either. "What a waste!" he thought.

Bruiser turned onto East Schroon River Road, just as Smash was moving under the Northway overpass. Big John and Striker were now speeding down Lamb Hill Road.

Roamer raised the missile launcher, and fired again.

CHAPTER TWENTY-THREE

"Oh no! Look, Jon!"

Susan was so frightened, her whole body was shaking. Jon was busy watching the hologram. The Land Traffic Controller's threat alert system picked up the missile on its radar. Instantly, the LTC steadied the Camaro at sixty miles an hour. The missile, traveling at over one hundred and twenty miles an hour, would hit in five seconds.

The LTC waited: six seconds, five, four, three—. Suddenly, it made the Camaro veer sharply to the left, and then make a sharp right. Jon's and Susan's bodies were shaken like rag dolls, even though they were strapped in by their seatbelts. The Z-28 accelerated rapidly; and the missile missed the Camaro's spoiler by less than three feet, and crashed into a tree, cutting it down as it detonated. The tree began to fall towards the road, but was stopped by other trees in its path, and ended up falling the other way.

Roamer was livid. He stood up and fired again.

The Camaro made a left turn, and accelerated onto a long straight stretch of road, known as "Dead Man's Run".

"Oh God, I don't want to die!" Susan said.

Jon looked at her, knowing the LTC was in control. He could see her sobbing uncontrollably. He felt powerless to help her. And then he realized he had the answer.

"Susan, has anyone ever told you the gospel: how to be saved?"

"Yes. A long time ago."

"Just talk to God."

Instantly, she began to pray.

"O God, I'm sorry. Please save me. Please forgive me, for Jesus' sake, because He died for me."

Immediately, she sensed that she was now safe. She felt a peace in knowing she had God's forgiveness.

"Thank You, Lord," she said. "Thank You."

The Peregrine Falcon was circling overhead at twenty thousand feet. It spotted a small rabbit nibbling flowers along the roadside. The falcon folded its wings, and went into a dive towards earth.

"The LTC will try to outrun the missile. Hang on to the 'Oh No!' bar to your right."

"How long can it do that?"

"Until we reach the end of this stretch. It's about six miles long."

"So we ARE going to die. Well, at least I'm ready now."

Jon could see that she was no longer afraid. She was in God's hands now; and she was willing to accept the possibility of an imminent death.

"How fast can the car go?"

"About one-eighty."

"What are we doing now?"

"One-twenty, one-thirty; we're getting there."

He added, "Close your eyes, Susan."

She closed her eyes, and thought about what it would be like to open her eyes and be in Heaven with her Savior. Meanwhile, Jon decided to pray:

"Lord, please, if there's a way, please deliver us. If we're meant to die now, we're ready. But if You have something You want us to do yet, some reason in Your eternal plan for us to live, then I pray for a miracle. Please send an ANSWER from Heaven."

The falcon began to pick up speed. It passed the twelve-thousand-foot mark at just over a hundred and twenty miles an hour.

The Z-28 streaked along the road at a hundred and eighty-six miles per hour, its deadly pursuer inching ever closer. Jon figured they had about sixty seconds left, and then looked at the GPS counter: "sixty-three, sixty-two, sixty-one..." One minute to impact!

Thousands of miles above the earth, satellites were tracking the whole chase. The matrix had been continuously revising the survivability chance, but right now the percentage was hovering close to zero.

Jon and Susan were not sure what to do except wait and pray. They had, as far as they knew, only one chance: to make it through the straightaway, and outmaneuver the missile at the turn. But there was one big problem: the missile would catch them before that could happen. The missile was traveling at one-ninety, and literally crawling towards them through the air.

Suddenly, the satellite matrix survivability meter jumped to ten percent, then twenty, thirty, and all the way to ninety percent.

"If I'm going to die, I'm glad I met you."

"Me too, Susan."

"I'm glad we know where we're going."

"You're not afraid to die now, are you Susan?"

"No."

She moved her left hand, and gripped his right hand firmly, knowing that they were about to leave this world behind.

There was a break in the forest, a straight line where trees had been cut down. It was a quarter-mile straight line, and forty feet wide. The falcon was rapidly approaching this area.

"We got him!" yelled Roamer.

Bruiser wasn't so sure. He wanted to see them blown up before his eyes: to see the proof.

All of a sudden, the GPS showed a dot moving from the top left of the hologram screen. It indicated something above them was moving rapidly towards the road ahead.

"Susan, do you see this dot? Something is falling out of the sky."

"What is it?"

Jon suddenly had an epiphany, a light-bulb moment. The thought crossed his mind: maybe, just maybe, this was God's answer.

"I don't know," Jon said. "But I think maybe it is God's answer to my prayer."

"What did you pray?"

"That God would send an answer from Heaven."

Susan processed this quickly.

"I think you may be right."

Both Jon and Susan began to sense that there was hope yet that they might escape this danger and live to see another day.

The falcon was at seven thousand feet now, falling at one hundred and eighty miles an hour. The rabbit below was unaware of the impending danger.

Jon was staring at the LTC counter: "forty-four, forty-three, forty-two,..."

Suddenly, the LTC began to slow the car; and the counter began to tick rapidly: so fast he could hardly read the numbers.

"LTC, why are you slowing the car down?" he asked.

The LTC flashed an answer onto the hologram screen: "Preserving engine performance."

Then it said, "Brace yourselves."

The falcon was approaching three thousand feet. It lined up with the break in the woods, and glided at two-hundred and ten miles an hour.

A few more seconds passed. The meter kept counting as the missile closed in: "twelve, eleven,..." Ten seconds to impact!

The survivability meter was at one hundred percent. Jon didn't understand. Susan closed her eyes, her lips moving in prayer.

Bruiser and Roamer were half a mile away, waiting to see the impact. Smash gained on them; and Big Jon and Striker were also closing in.

Jon froze, waiting for certain death, and staring at the meter: "seven, six, five…"

The rabbit heard the car approaching, and hopped away. The falcon saw its prey move, but was distracted in that same moment by the Camaro passing the break in the woods, three hundred feet below. Then the falcon's radar picked up something small and to the right. It identified it as prey. The bird's radar calculated in a fraction of a second that this new prey would end up directly in its line of attack.

Jon closed his eyes, and squeezed Susan's hand.

The bird of prey descended below the treetops and into the break in the woods. The falcon's peripheral vision sensed the missile just before the impact. Falcon and missile collided in mid-air.

The countdown meter stopped.

The momentum of the falcon pushed the missile to the right, and downward toward the ground to the right of the shoulder of the road. The missile detonated. The ground shook at the force of the explosion.

Jon and Susan heard the explosion, and realized that they were still alive. They both opened their eyes, and wondered just how they had evaded this inescapable danger.

Roamer couldn't believe his eyes. He was too angry to curse.

"That was a close call," Jon said.
"That was God's answer to your prayer," Susan replied.

"I sure wish I knew how He did it."

"I have to admit. I'm curious too. But I think it was that dot falling from the sky."

"Maybe—"

"It took it out?"

Jon thought about that.

"Whatever God did: He is amazing," Jon said.

"I concur."

"Well," Jon said, "we had better pray again. He has one more missile to fire."

"What can we do?" She looked back and downward.

And saw the answer.

CHAPTER TWENTY-FOUR

"I don't…" Jon began.

She interrupted him.

"The flare gun!" she exclaimed.

The Z-28 reached the corner and turned left.

Susan unbuckled her seatbelt and said, "I'll fire the flare gun, so you can keep track of your invention."

"Okay."

She grabbed the flare gun, and loaded it.

Jon said, "You ever shot a flare gun?"

"A couple of times. Early in my career."

"Careful; we're moving fast."

Jon ordered the LTC to slow the car to sixty miles per hour.

"When they come around the corner, they will fire again," Jon said. "When they do, just fire out the back."

Susan crawled into the back, did her best to avoid the broken glass, and steadied herself. She had a solid grip on the flare gun; and she prepared to fire.

Bruiser and Roamer raced around the corner.

"Here they come," said Susan. "Tell me when."

"Not yet."

Roamer muttered, "These people must have nine lives."

He stood up and fired the last missile. "This had better work," he thought.

"Now, Susan! NOW!"

Susan fired the flare.

The heat-seeking missile sensor picked up a second target, approaching at nearly four hundred miles an hour.

Bruiser's eyes opened wide as he went into shock. He could see the terror of death coming for him; and he knew there was no escape. His appointment with death was NOW; and there was nothing he could do to stop it. Roamer saw it coming, too; and he cursed God for the last time this side of death.

Susan saw the drama unfold before her very eyes.

Missile and flare clashed together. The windshield of Bruiser's car imploded; and shards of glass pierced through Bruiser's skull, impaling his brain and killing him instantly. Roamer had sat down and ducked; but he would die anyway. The car reeled to the right at eighty miles an hour, and rolled alongside the roadway and off to the right. Then it slammed into a huge tree, and exploded.

The LTC's threat-detection system deleted the letters RPGL. Jon and Susan felt a surge of relief.

Smash came around the corner.

"It's not over yet," said Jon.

Then he spoke to the hologram: "Land Traffic Controller, take control."

The LTC again took command of the car. It surged forward, picking up speed. Smash was gaining fast, but the LTC would give him a "run for his money". Jon thought to himself, "Can a Camaro outrun a Corvette?"

The Camaro turned left, then right, then up the hill. Then it leveled off, and turned right onto the arterial. The decision-making system of the LTC took a nano-second to make the choice: "North or South?" It chose Route 87 South, towards Saratoga and Albany.

Smash turned onto the arterial; and Big John and Striker headed up the hill. Jon and Susan passed the North entrance ramp, and headed for the South ramp.

The LTC picked up two threats: a Colt 45 and a nine-millimeter Glock Model Thirty-Seven. The Camaro slowed, turned left onto the South ramp, and entered the Adirondack Northway heading south towards Albany.

Smash accelerated on the arterial, then slowed, and turned left onto the south ramp.

Big John and Striker turned right onto the arterial.

"What do we do now?" Susan asked.

"I don't know. I hope the LTC does."

With so many vehicles on the highway, the LTC had to balance the speed of the car with the safety of the passengers. The Z-28 was moving at over one hundred and ten miles an hour, passing cars on the left and right, and making moves which a normal driver wouldn't even dare to consider trying. With pinpoint accuracy, the LTC was making the Camaro extremely hard to catch.

But Smash was no ordinary driver. He was known among his circle of friends as a guy who loved to take chances. He had a rule he loved to follow. He liked to drive twice as fast as the speed limit. He would go sixty instead of thirty, eighty instead of forty; and if the speed limit was fifty-five, he would drive at a hundred and ten. The only people who dared to get into a car with him were those who had a "death-wish", or a hapless person who had never ridden with him before. Striker rode with Smash once; and he learned to close his eyes. He remembered going airborne at a corner at the top of a big hill. He was curled up in a fetal position, expecting to die; and all he could hear was Smash's hysterical laughter. When the wild ride was over, Smash asked him if he would like to drive around again soon. Striker was shaking like a leaf; and his face was white as a sheet. He wanted to tell him he was a nut-case, but decided on saying, "Thanks, but no thanks."

And that was exactly the reason why Striker rode with Big John. He believed he had a much better chance of survival riding with Big John.

Smash was moving fast and deftly in and through traffic, keeping up with the LTC, and even gaining a little ground. The 2026 Corvette was a faster car, and hugged the road slightly better than the Z-28; but the LTC was driving the Camaro so well that the Corvette's advantage would normally be nullified. But Smash was not normal; and the faster car gained ground.

"Land Traffic Controller, come up with a plan and do it," Jonathan ordered.

The satellite-based matrix began calculating an enormous amount of computerized data every second. It scanned twenty miles in every direction; and it submitted hundreds of plans to the decision-making system (DMS) of the brain of the LTC. In less than five seconds, the LTC's DMS narrowed it down to one. The car continued on its way, winding in and out of traffic, and headed for the next exit.

The Land Traffic Controller had calculated that Jon and Susan would survive a dangerous stunt; but that their closest pursuer would not. It had already calculated that only the driver of the Corvette would die. The drama would play itself out; and the LTC would eliminate one of the pursuers.

Jon and Susan were not afraid to die; but they were about to experience the most frightening ten seconds of their lives. They did not expect what was going to happen next.

Neither did Smash, Big John, or Striker.

Suddenly, the Camaro veered to the right, and entered the right side of the down-ramp exit at a hundred and ten miles an hour.

Jon had a severe attack of anxiety, closed his eyes, and instinctively put his arms in front of his face. Susan screamed in fright, and felt like she was going to have a heart attack. This experience was like going down a roller-coaster and not knowing whether or not they were going to crash. Would they hit traffic moving east or west? What made it more frightening was that the light they were approaching was still red.

The Camaro barreled toward the red light and what appeared to be certain death. Yet the survivability meter was at one hundred percent. Susan watched in disbelief as the light turned green; and the car sped through the green light at a hundred miles an hour, and up the entrance ramp straight ahead.

Smash had decided to follow them, and entered the exit downslope. He was only four seconds behind the Z-28. The Corvette practically flew down the ramp, and went through the green light at a hundred and five miles an hour, and accelerated up the entrance ramp.

A double-length truck carrying lumber was traveling on the Northway between the exit ramp and the ensuing entrance ramp. The driver was going seventy miles an hour in the right lane.

A half-mile back, Big John was watching the chase on his GPS, and decided he was not going down the exit ramp. He was shocked when he saw what happened next.

The Camaro barely cleared a black SUV as it raced out of the entrance ramp at the top of the incline. Jon and Susan both felt a rush of adrenaline as the LTC-controlled Camaro weaved safely in and out of traffic.

Smash was not so fortunate. His Corvette was cut off by the huge truck. He tried to avoid the crash, but was moving way too fast. He crashed at an angle into the truck at a hundred and twenty miles an hour, and was deflected to the right. The Corvette rolled over to the right, off the road, and into the nearby trees. The car and driver were destroyed in a spectacular explosion. Twenty seconds later, Big John and Striker saw the fire as they sped past the scene of the accident. They decided they were going to catch up to the Camaro and knock it off the road with their 2025 Impala.

"Let's get 'em," Striker said.

"I will," Big John replied.

He pushed the pedal to the floor.

Then Striker pulled out his lethal Glock Thirty-Seven and said, "Maybe I can shoot them."

CHAPTER TWENTY-FIVE

Susan breathed a sigh of relief.

"Jon. Jon!"

"What?"

"You can open your eyes now."

"Oh, yeah. I just had to close them for a second."

"More like a minute."

Jon opened his eyes, and relaxed. He felt safe, at least for the moment.

But it was only a short moment.

"We're slowing down," Susan said. "Look! Up ahead!"

"I see. A traffic jam."

Jon felt a surge of worry. He wondered where the third car was.

He knew they had to be close. The Colt 45 and the Glock Thirty-Seven were plainly visible on the LTC threat alert system.

Suddenly, the Camaro veered to the left and lurched forward with tremendous acceleration. The traffic jam was opening up! Just in time.

"There they are! Let's hurry!" Striker said. He gripped the semi-automatic weapon, and tensed up.

"They're gaining on us!" Susan said.

"We're almost out of the traffic jam now."

"Time to pray again."

"Believe me," said Jon, "I have been."

Jon looked in the rear-view mirror, and saw the white Impala creeping up on them, and moving slightly to the left. He saw an arm with a gun reaching out of the right rear window. It was supported with his other hand, keeping it as steady as possible at ninety miles an hour.

"Get down, Susan!"

A hail of bullets rang out, as Susan put her head down. Bullets went into the dashboard and front windshield, zinging by Susan's and Jon's heads, and lodging in both of the front seats. The layer of Kevlar in the seatbacks protected them from harm.

"The front windshield bullet-proof too?" Susan inquired.

"Yes."

"Is it safe now?"

"Not yet. Stay down."

"No argument from me," Susan said.

"Careful," Striker said. "Not too close. They can knock us off the highway by braking suddenly."

Striker fired at the tires and the gas tank area. But nothing happened.

"Must be bullet-proof," he said.

He added, "We're out of the heavy traffic. Let's get to his side, and knock him off the road."

Both cars had been accelerating after clearing the traffic jam. Striker couldn't hold the gun outside the window anymore, because the wind-resistance was now too great. But if he got the chance, he could fire at the driver and passenger from inside his open window. He wasn't sure if the driver's window was bullet-proof or not, but he was willing to put it to the test.

Jon and Susan passed a police observation and radio position.

"We have a speeder...no, two speeders," officer Jim Ridley radioed.

"Can you catch them?"

"I don't think so."

"How fast?"

"One-thirty."

"A hundred and thirty?!!"

"Yes."

"Okay; I'm five miles ahead of you in the fast lane. I'll call in the cavalry."

He radioed four more squad cars, and told them to be ready for pursuit.

"Cop car! What do we do, Jon?"

"Let the LTC decide."

The LTC ignored the car, and moved on.

Striker had opened the left rear window a few inches, and stuck the barrel of his semi-automatic on top of the glass. He sprayed bullets at the cop car as they soared by.

Officer Larry Oswald felt a bullet rip through his right arm. A second bullet went into his right leg. He slowed the car down considerably before he lost control. He veered to the left at sixty, rolled over the guard rail and down a small hill. He was surprised to discover he was still alive, and radioed for help.

The squad cars up ahead were immediately made aware of what was coming.

"He's armed and dangerous!"

"We hear you. We see him coming," Officer Bailey said.

The LTC directed the car past the next exit, passed the patrolling squad cars, and slowed down. It detected a lack of traffic ahead.

"We're slowing down," said Susan.

"I know," Jon said. Then he said, "Land Traffic Controller, do you have a plan?"

The word "Yes" flashed onto the hologram.

"Okay," said Jon.

"It's in God's hands," Susan said.

Jon added, "And the LTC's," as he watched the Impala approach, in his rear-view mirror.

"Let's lay back," Officer Bailey said. "We can't stop this."

"Okay, we're following your lead," Officer Kelly replied.

The four squad cars stayed back, following at a safe distance.

The Impala came up to the left of the Z-28. Striker shot point-blank at Jon. Jon winced, but knew that the bullets would not reach him. He knocked on the window.

"Bullet-proof," he said.

Suddenly, the Impala swerved to the right. The LTC skillfully moved the Z-28 to the right, and accelerated.

"Look out!" Striker said.

Big John accelerated just in time. The LTC suddenly decelerated, and swerved to the left. Big John accelerated just in time again. The LTC quickly recovered, moved to the right, and accelerated so fast, Jon and Susan felt their heads snap back onto the neck rests. The LTC then veered right, decelerated, veered left, and smashed into the Impala.

The Impala lost its stability, and began to swerve wildly. Big John was desperately trying to recover. He was breathing heavily, and sweating profusely. A surge of fear welled up inside of him. He could not change speed quickly now, because his car was almost totally out of control. Then he and Striker saw the Camaro close the gap for the second time, and felt the terrible impact from the right. To the left was a huge drop in elevation. They were about to die; and they knew it.

Jon looked at the survivability meter. It was at ninety percent. The Camaro recovered from the collision in just a few seconds. He and Susan saw the Impala roll over the guard rails and disappear over the edge of the cliff.

Big John and Striker screamed in fear, and put their arms up in front of their faces. The car rolled violently down the huge incline; and the air bags inflated. They could not see now; but they could feel the terror as their bodies were jerked mercilessly from side to side; and they drew closer and closer to their violent end. The speed of the car's descent reached over a hundred miles an hour, and ended up in a huge ball of fire as the car slammed into the rocks below and exploded.

Jon and Susan were relieved. It was over; and they started to relax. The LTC began to decelerate the car slowly and safely; and the survivability meter registered now at one hundred percent. And then the unexpected happened.

CHAPTER TWENTY-SIX

The LTC saw it immediately. The Camaro was down to a hundred and six miles an hour. A collision up ahead!

Suddenly, the Camaro veered to the right, and avoided a fatal crash. The survivability meter went down into the low twenties as the car began to swerve out of control. The LTC kept pointing the wheels forward; and the car kept veering back and forth. The Camaro was all over the highway at this point, still traveling at over a hundred miles an hour. Jon and Susan realized that they were in a dangerous situation. The LTC had to maneuver the car past the sparse traffic and simultaneously regain control of the car. It was unable to brake, as it would then lose total control of the vehicle.

Officer Bailey had watched the whole drama unfold. He had dispatched Officers Hayden and Flewelling to the crash site below, while he and Officer Kelly pursued the Camaro. He was about to call for backup when the collision occurred. The chaos which followed caused the two squad cars to stop the pursuit. Officer Kelly was amazed at the maneuvers of the Z-28.

"That driver must be a Daytona champion!" he said.

"It's an IROC-Z," Officer Bailey replied. "International Racing of Champions! I feel bad that I had to radio ahead for a roadblock."

Jon's and Susan's bodies were rocked left to right, and back again. They couldn't do anything to save their lives. All they could rely on was their faith—in God, and in the LTC's ability to bring the car back into a position of safety. The survivability meter had been all over the charts, from one hundred percent to near zero, and everywhere in between. The car veered way to the left; and Jon and Susan thought they were going to fall over the precipice. They could see the steep drop directly ahead of them; and then suddenly they were moving straight ahead on the highway, and then toward the right. They could see the huge wall of rock ledge to the right; and it looked like they would crash into it. Then the car swerved back the other way. Then the wild arc of the wild back-and-forth movements of the car began to narrow; and the centrifugal force began to lessen; and suddenly the Z-28 was heading straight down the highway. Finally, the LTC began to ratchet down the car's velocity safely. The survivability meter climbed to one hundred percent by the time the speedometer reached sixty-five. They were safe at last!

The LTC saw the patrol cars a couple of miles up ahead, and "wisely" turned off at the next exit, and then drove the car to a gas station. The squad cars were waiting to intercept a car that never came. By the time they realized the car had turned off at the previous exit and then consequently went to investigate and search for the car, it was gone.

"I'm afraid I'm going to have to park the car in a garage somewhere and purchase something else," Jon said.

"I don't think so," Susan said. "Talk to the authorities. You were the intended victim."

"What about the Police Commissioner?"

"Yeah, you're right. He probably already knows what you're driving."

Jon thought for a moment.

"Wait just a minute. Maybe not," he said.

"What?"

"Roamer may not have divulged his information to the Commissioner."

"But he will get the information from him eventually. Unless..." Susan was thinking.

"What?" Jon said.

"He was with those guys, right?"

"Well…" He paused. Then his eyes lit up. "Yes, that could be right."

"I'm sure of it!" Susan said.

"Interesting," Jon mused, scratching his sore head.

"What if we get the information first, and erase it from his computer?"

"Great idea, Susan!"

"Can you do that?"

"Yes, I can do a trace. My GPS knows all three of those cars and the license numbers."

"How soon can you do it?"

"As soon as I drop you off and go home."

An hour later, Jon was home. He parked the Camaro in the garage, feeling very fortunate that his parents, Bill and Marge, were gone for a two-week vacation. They had left a couple of days ago, and wouldn't be back until the middle of the month. He didn't want them to worry: he knew they would be very worried if they saw the damage to the Camaro. So he called a friend of his who owned a Garage, and asked him to come over to the house, tow the car away, and fix it. He also asked him to paint the car black. He would have the car back in three days. Meanwhile, he would go to Motor Vehicles and get a new license plate number, to be safer from electronic detection.

With that business taken care of, Jon would concentrate on the business at hand. He set his cell phone down, and went on the internet. He did a trace on the three cars using the GPS technology connected with his computer-setup. He found nothing.

Then he thought, "What if the computer expert pooled cars, and was a passenger with one of the pursuers? Could his car be…?"

"Yes," he thought. "Maybe it was…"

He dialed Susan.

"Come and get me!"

"So soon?"

"I've got an idea, Susan."

"I'm all ears."

"Let's see if there are any abandoned cars near the Bolton Free Library."

"Can't you just get the GPS to find it for you?"

"Yes, maybe, but I'm hoping he left some paperwork in there."

"I see." She paused. "I'll be right over."

Susan picked him up, and drove him to Bolton Landing in the Prius. They found the blue Camaro easily, and checked it out. Jon's GPS was able to unlock the car electronically, and simultaneously block the vehicle's security alarm system. They found papers in the glove compartment, and a laptop in the back seat. They took them, and left the area. Fortunately, nobody nearby seemed to be paying any attention; and anyone watching them probably thought the blue Camaro was Jon's or Susan's car. That was good. This whole affair was messy enough; and they didn't need any more complications. The last thing they wanted was for someone to call the cops on his cell phone, because that would tip off the Police Commissioner.

Jon had a hunch. He was sure that Roamer had the information, but had not communicated it to anybody except the ones who had pursued them. So all he had to do was find the necessary files and remove the information. So he worked on it, and checked it out as soon as possible. By about 5:30 PM, he had deleted all the traces of his Z-28 and of his identity, from Roamer's laptop files. He then traced the other computers that Roamer used, and deleted the information in them through a back-door remote connectivity-deletion device, a tool which he had placed in the GPS. By 6:00 PM, he was done.

While deleting those files, Jonathan took the time to download Roamer's personal and contacts information into his three laptops, with the lightning speed of the GPS. He figured he might need it later.

Susan, Marie, Jim, and Jack were all on the secure website. They were waiting for Jon to get there. While they waited, Susan filled them in on what had happened. And then they gave their input.

Sanhedrin: "You're lucky to be alive."

Legal Eagle: "That's pretty amazing."
Twiggy: "Wow! That was like—a miracle."

At 6:05, Phantom entered the chatroom.

Sanhedrin: "Where have you been, Phantom?"
Phantom: "Covering my bases. It took a little longer than I thought. Sorry about that."
Sanhedrin: "That's okay. I was just a little worried about you."
Twiggy: "So was I. Especially after what Susan told us."
Phantom: "Oh, she told you everything?"
Legal Eagle: "I hope so."
Phantom: "Well, so much happened that I'm glad I didn't have to tell you. I'm glad she filled you in." Then he added, "I have a plan."
Super Decade: "I can't wait to hear it."
Phantom: "I plan to take a nice long shower and go to bed. My car is in the Garage for a couple of days; so I'm going to have plenty of time here to think. I need my brain to be firing on all eight cylinders; so a good night's sleep is imperative."
Legal Eagle: "I understand."
Twiggy: "Do you have a plan for our investigation?"
Phantom: "I'm working on something. I may need as much as two days to formulate a plan. But keep logging into this secure site; and I'll post a time to meet once I'm ready with a plan."
Sanhedrin: "Okay."
Legal Eagle: "Sounds good."
Twiggy: "Thank you."
Super Decade: "Luv ya."

Jon didn't know what to think about that last entry. He felt a surge of emotion, but kept it in check. He typed in his next entry.

Phantom: "Thank you all. Have a good night. Please check in at your regular AND irregular times."

Police Commissioner Harry Reynolds was pacing back and forth in his office. He had invited the Governor over for an urgent meeting. The Governor walked in with two of his bodyguards. Once inside, he dismissed the guards to the outside of the office. The Commissioner spoke first.

"We have a problem."

"I know," Governor Devane said.

"What do you want to do?"

The Governor thought for a second. They had tried to eliminate these pesky people. Should they try again? The Governor spoke.

"Do we know who this phantom person is?"

"No. Unfortunately, we don't know."

"Surely Roamer had some information."

"He must have, but he didn't share it with us."

"What about his computers?"

"If it was on there, it's been deleted. There's no way to bring it back. It's completely gone." Harry continued: "I wish Roamer had shared more information with us. But whatever he had, it's gone now."

"Untraceable?"

"Completely."

The Governor sighed.

The Police Commissioner's cell phone rang.

"Hold on, Bruce. I need to answer this call….Hello?"

"This is Officer Bailey."

"Do you have the information?"

"No, none of us had on our surveillance equipment."

"What?"

"It all happened so quickly; and then we had the two accidents."

"But they called you ahead of time."

"I'm sorry, Sir."

Harry turned to the Governor. "No luck," he said.

"The Northway used to have surveillance on all of their entrances and exits. Too bad the last administration eliminated that. We could have benefited from that equipment."

"I know."

"Well," the Governor said, "we DO know about three people: Marie Trombley, Susan Morehouse, and Jim Ellenberger."

"We still can't find Jim."

"What about Susan and Marie?" the Governor asked.

"They've got to have some connection with Jim, even now."

"I agree."

"Should we bring them in for questioning?"

"We have to."

CHAPTER TWENTY-SEVEN

May 5, 2026

Assistant Police Commissioner Charles Daley had been suspicious of his boss for a long time. But it was only recently, a week ago, that he had a friend of his, a repairman, place a couple of "bugs" in the Commissioner's office. One was in his phone; another behind a painting which he had that was hanging in his office behind his desk.

Finally, it paid off. He had two recorded conversations: one between the Police Commissioner and the Governor, and the other between the Police Commissioner and Roamer. He listened intently to the first conversation, and wondered what the Governor meant when he asked the Commissioner if he could "have men ready to help Roamer at a moment's notice". Then, he listened to the second conversation. And he wondered what Roamer, or Todd James, meant when he used the word "targets". That sounded ominous.

He put the two conversations together and thought, "Were they sending men to kill these 'targets'?" And, "Was this some kind of clandestine operation: part of a larger conspiracy?" And, "Who were the 'four of [his]…not-so-nice plain-clothes associates'?" He needed to know.

And then he listened to a third conversation. He thought, "Why can't they find Jim Ellenberger? Is he hiding? Is he in danger?"

And he pondered about Susan and Marie. "What did they have to do with all of this?" And, "Who is this 'phantom'? Someone else they've marked as a target?"

Charles Daley knew there was something going on: something sinister. He didn't know what it was; but it was something he needed to deal with. He wondered who Jim Ellenberger was; and he was very curious about the identity of the "phantom person", the invisible man. This was intriguing. And he wondered what connection these two women, Susan and Marie, had with Jim Ellenberger. He had to keep an eye on all of this, and find the answers to all of these questions.

He had witnessed several cover-ups since the Governor had first won political office in 2022. There was a lot of money not accounted for, and buried by the Police Commissioner and some of his associates. They seemed to think that they could get away with anything; but Charles Daley was determined that he would somehow get to the bottom of this.

Jon, Susan, Marie, Jim, and Jack were all in the secure chatroom.

Super Decade: "You got a new car?"
Phantom: "I decided to splurge a little."
Twiggy: "What did you get?"
Phantom: "A 2026 Nissan Maxima."
Legal Eagle: "Great choice, Phantom."
Sanhedrin: "A quality car."
Phantom: "It's fun to drive. And for now, I have the GPS inside the Maxima."
Super Decade: "Congratulations, but I hope you keep the Camaro, too."
Phantom: "I'm planning on it. But I may keep it hidden until this caper is over."
Legal Eagle: "I understand."
Phantom: "Thank you all. Now, I'm ready to get down to business."

Jon continued.

Phantom: "I called you here today, because I have a plan. I am calling Charles Daley as soon as we get off of here. I am going to meet with him today ASAP."
Legal Eagle: "Will you tell him everything?"
Phantom: "It's all or nothing. By the way, I think we got Roamer. He's not trying to log in; and he didn't try last night."
Twiggy: "That's great. And I think you should see Charles Daley right away."
Super Decade: "I agree."

Susan looked out her window.

Super Decade: "Wait!"
Phantom: "What?"
Super Decade: "Cops outside my house. Coming to my door!"
Phantom: "Log off, Susan! Quick!"

Susan heard a knock at the door.
"Police! Open up!"
"Just a minute!" Susan said. She finished logging off.

Phantom: "Let's all log off. Be back here sometime tonight. I'll try to post a time."

Marie heard a knock at her door.
"Police!..."

Twiggy: "They've got me too, Phantom."
Phantom: "Okay. Don't offer them any information."
Twiggy: "Alright."
Phantom: "Good luck. We're with you."

Marie logged off, opened her front door, and was led to a squad car. She would be rejoined with Susan at an undisclosed location.

Jonathan Wilkes dialed the Assistant Police Commissioner.

"Assistant Police Commissioner Charles Daley here."

"Hello, Mr. Daley. This is Jonathan Wilkes. I'm calling on a secure line. What I'm going to say is confidential; but I have reason to believe you are a man of Christian principles of honesty and integrity. Are you?"

"What's this all about?"

"Can we trust you?"

"Who's we?"

"I'm sorry. We're not starting off well here. We just had an attempt on two of our lives; and we need to know if we can trust you."

"I don't know who you are."

"Okay, I'm going to lay it on the line. We believe that you are honest, but your boss is not."

"What's this all about?"

"Somebody was sent to eliminate us. I believe it was because of our investigation."

"Investigation of what?"

"A plan the Governor has."

Suddenly, the Assistant Police Commissioner connected the dots. The Governor had given the Police Commissioner and Roamer "the green light"! He paused. "So the word 'target' DID mean someone they wanted to kill!" he thought.

"Are you there?"

Charles snapped back to the conversation.

"Yes," he said.

"Can we trust you?"

"Yes. I now see what you're talking about."

"You do?"

"Yes. I have been suspicious of Harry Reynolds for some time now. He's been involved in some serious cover-ups. So I recently bugged his office and learned some information. It all fits now. Sorry I was so abrupt with you."

"That's okay. I'm a Christian, too." Then he added, "You're not bugged, are you?"

"No. I'm more cautious than Harry. I use a bug-sweeper every day."

"Excellent."

"Also, my office is on the back side of the New York State police headquarters building, away from everybody else. I'm like the outcast; and they think I'm 'out of the loop' and don't know what's going on."

Jon said, "I have a lot of information to show you; and we have to act fast. Two of my associates have been arrested, probably for questioning. They might break under interrogation; and that could expose the rest of us to great harm."

"They tried to kill you already."

"That's right. They would love to see us dead. There is a fortune in gold artifacts involved."

Charles raised his eyebrows in palpable surprise. "Gold artifacts?"

"Yes."

"How valuable?"

"Maybe in the billions." Jon added, "We need to get to a federal judge and arrest our Police Commissioner."

"And our Governor," Charles said. He added, "Do you have a good case?"

Jon said, "You wouldn't believe how much dirt we have on these two. And I have been digging into even more information—about two other associates: a lawyer and a campaign manager."

"We have to make sure we don't make a false arrest. These are powerful people here, Jon."

"No false arrest. Guaranteed."

"Okay, e-mail me the information."

"Roamer's gone. I guess it's safe."

Jon pushed some keys and pressed SEND.

"Okay, I'm sending it now."

"I'll print them out," Charles said.

"Okay."

Charles scanned the e-mails and printed them out. He was amazed at the Governor's plan.

"How did you get this information?"

"A little sleight of hand."
"Where was it?"
"Can't tell you that."
"I see. You had to sneak in and get it. I won't arrest you for that."
"It was in the Governor's file room."
"You got in there?"
"You'd be surprised what I can do."
"I'll bet."

CHAPTER TWENTY-EIGHT

Jim Ellenberger decided to come out of hiding. He had to, if he was going to find Marie. A couple of months earlier, he had sent her a necklace by way of UPS with a letter that read:

"I cannot tell you how much you remind me of my daughter, Phoebe, who passed away from melanoma back in 2021. She was only fifty years old. I know that I may have placed your life in danger; and so I am giving you this necklace with a tracking device inside. If you are ever in danger, turn it on. It will send out an alert to a device I own, no matter how far away I am. It's in my cell phone; and I will be alerted immediately. Please don't turn it on unless you need help. To turn it on, press the two sides of the locket of the necklace at the same time, and you'll hear a light click, and a whirring sound, like the sound of a DVD turning around in rotation. Then, don't touch it again until you've been rescued. I'm giving you this gift, because I don't want to lose you. If I think you're in danger and you forget to turn it on, I will send you a quiet reminder using my cell phone. You will feel a prick and a vibration that only you will be able to detect. Activate the necklace before your hands are tied. I'll talk with you further about all of this in successive letters.

Please destroy this letter after you read it. I care about you very much."

Love,
Jim Ellenberger

Jon wanted to kick himself for not having a way to track Susan's and Marie's locations. He had not placed a function for randomly finding individual people into his GPS tracking system. He could track a car once he had the license plate number; but tracking a human being was more complicated. To do it properly, he would have to install an electromagnetic tracer into the GPS, and program it into the satellite matrix by transmitting the electromagnetic tracer program from his GPS directly to the eyes of the satellites. Then, the distinctive electromagnetic field surrounding the person being sought had to be submitted to the GPS's tracer, and from there to the satellite eyes. The satellites would also need an image of the person. Then, the satellite eyes could scan worldwide to find the lost person.

But Jon had not installed this function. And it was too late now. So he had to find another way to locate them. He wondered just what he could do. And then his cell phone rang.

Jon felt safe answering the call, because he was confident that Roamer was gone.

"Jon Wilkes here."

"This is Jim Ellenberger."

"Jim?"

"Yes." Then he said, "I'm flying up to Albany Airport. Can you pick me up?"

"I'm not going to be able to, because I'm meeting with the Assistant Police Commissioner. He's on our side; and we are going to arrest the top people."

"Bruce and Harry?" he said, deliberately not mentioning their positions in case someone was monitoring the call.

"Yes." Then he said, "We'll have to coordinate. Can Jack pick you up?"

"Sure."

"Okay, I'll text or call you when I get to the Assistant Police Commissioner. Let me know when you are going to get into Albany so we can all get together on this."

"We need to get to Marie and Susan. They could be in great danger."

"How are we going to do that?"

"I have a tracking device planted on Marie."

Jon's heart began to pound heavily as he felt a new surge of hope.

"You do?"

"Yes."

Susan and Marie had been taken to a special facility near Albany. The police officers involved were all under the Governor's and Police Commissioner's special payroll. They did whatever the Governor and Police Commissioner wanted, caring only about the extra money they made rather than the ethical implications of what they were being told to do. This facility near Albany was in reality an old warehouse: a place where the Police Commissioner could do things in a clandestine manner. This place was obscure: separate from the standard facilities in Albany.

Police Commissioner Harry Reynolds was there, waiting. He wanted to get to Jim Ellenberger and the invisible "phantom" through Marie and Susan. Harry Reynolds would let his officers interrogate them, to see if they would volunteer information on their whereabouts.

The reality was that Susan and Marie knew where the Phantom lived, but not where Jim Ellenberger was staying. They knew where Jack Leland lived; but his name would never come up, because their interrogators were not even aware of his existence.

Susan and Marie had tried to encourage one another, once they were brought together at the warehouse. They were determined to stay strong and not give out any important information.

Harry Reynolds ordered his officers to interrogate them separately. So once they separated them, Officer David Hale began to question Susan.

"I'm Officer Hale. I have a job to do; and that is to find out who and where this Phantom friend of yours is. We don't want to harm him. We just want to question him."

Susan noticed two things about this man. First, he appeared to be a very pleasant person. He was using a gentle demeanor and smooth speech. He could have been a great salesman. He could have sold ice cubes to Eskimos; and woodstoves to Hawaiians.

Second, he had a physical feature that revealed his true character: his eyes. They were dark and ominous. She could see hatred emanating from his very inner being. She picked up a frightening message from his eyes. She dared not give him any information. She determined in her mind that she would die before giving up Jon or Jim or even Jack, if his name ever came up.

"I'm not giving you any answers," Susan said.

"We have a real problem, Susan, because we have five people who are dead; and we need to find out why."

"Those five people tried to kill us. They shot at us, and even fired explosives at us."

"Really?" he said, feigning surprise. "Can you take us to the car so we can see the damages?"

"I don't know where he took it."

Officer Hale cupped his left hand under his chin and pursed his lips in "controlled" exasperation. Then he stared directly into Susan's eyes and smiled pleasantly.

"What a fake!" Susan thought.

"If you want, Susan, we can lend you a cell phone; and you can call your friend and talk with him. Maybe we can find out where the car is."

"He won't answer."

Officer Hale paused, obviously trying to figure out what to say next. Ten seconds passed. Then he continued.

"Would he answer if we let you use your phone?"

"No," she said tersely.

"Can we try?"

"No, it wouldn't do any good. He's very secretive."

Officer Hale decided that this conversation was going nowhere. He decided to end it.

"Okay, Susan. That's all for now."

Officer Fresnon interrogated Marie in a similar fashion. She didn't give in, either. This was the first round. They would resume questioning in a few hours, in a more intense manner.

Jim Ellenberger's flight out of Tampa, Florida was just taking off. He would arrive at Albany Airport in about two hours. Jack Leland said he would be there to pick him up.

Jonathan Wilkes took a taxi to the McDonald's on Wolf Road in Albany. He was going to meet Charles Daley, the Assistant Police Commissioner, and formulate a plan to apprehend the Governor and the Police Commissioner. They would need an order from a federal judge; and Charles had said that with the evidence they had, there would be no problem getting the judge to sign the order of arrest.

But Jonathan had to ask Mr. Daley for help with his other perplexing problem. He needed his help to rescue Susan and Marie.

"Certainly I can help," Mr. Daley said. "I'll use some of my most trusted men. They are loyal to me, and will do what I ask without question. I have always given them an explanation for everything I do; but they would follow my lead anyway."

"Jim Ellenberger will be at Albany Airport in two hours. We could have them meet us here; and then we can track Susan and Marie."

"Maybe we'll find someone else there."

"Who?"

"Our friend Harry Reynolds."

"Can we get to a judge quickly?"

"I'm glad you asked. We have an appointment with my friend, Judge Gainer."

"When?"

"Right now."

"Okay, thank you. Let's go for it."

Judge Derek Gainer was a member of the Second Circuit. He was known as a very stern judge, but was good friends with Charles Daley. He had been a federal judge for twelve years. When Charles and John came to his office, he greeted them warmly.

"Great to see you, Charles."

"Likewise, Derek."

"Who's this young man?"

"Jonathan Wilkes, a computer technician," said Charles.

"Well, well. Maybe he could help me with something."

"Sure, I'd be glad to," Jonathan said.

"We need your help," Charles said.

"I know," said Derek. "Let me see the papers."

"Here they are," Jon said.

Judge Gainer perused the papers quietly for a few minutes. He said nothing while he was reading.

Then he looked up and said, "I'll gladly issue the order."

After he signed the federal order of arrest, he said, "Now Jon, may I borrow you for a while?"

"Sure, we have time before Jim arrives at the airport," Jon said, looking more at Charles than Judge Gainer.

"Here's what I need…"

Jon uploaded some programs into the judge's computer. It didn't take him long. He finished granting the judge's request in about eight minutes.

The judge thanked him and said, "I know you're in a hurry. Get out of here."

They all laughed. Judge Gainer pointed toward the office door and said, "Go get them."

Jon called Jim Ellenberger, and asked him if he and Jack could drive to the Wolf Road McDonald's. He said "Yes," and that he was flying over Pennsylvania now. It wouldn't be much longer.

Jon and Charles traveled back to the Wolf Road McDonald's. As Charles drove, he called his trusted officers.

"Meet me at Wolf Road McDonald's, all six of you. Bring your unmarked cars."

"I'll tell the others," Jake said. "Over and out."

Charles turned to Jon.

"These six are like family to me. They would follow me off a cliff if I asked them. But they know I always have a good reason when I call them for a special mission."

A few minutes later, Jon's cell phone rang. It was Jim.

"Hi, Jon. I'm about ready to land. Jack is already at the airport, waiting for me."

Charles answered into Jon's cell phone speaker: "Great! Reinforcements are just a few minutes away. We'll all leave from Mc Donald's—but carefully, so we don't look too conspicuous. The last thing we want is to be noticed by a lot of people. But we'll be in constant radio contact."

"How will we stay inconspicuous?" Jim asked.

"We all know Albany like the backs of our hands. We'll travel in separate groups: no more than two cars together. We'll tell each other our locations by radio. That way we won't be a parade."

"Won't Harry Reynolds intercept your messages on the radio?"

"Oh no. We use a secret channel: one that Harry doesn't even know exists."

"I see."

Charles turned into the McDonald's parking lot. Six unmarked cars with six officers were waiting for them.

Jack Leland looked at the clock. It was 6:50PM. He was watching the plane land. Soon it taxied to a stop; and several minutes later, the passengers were walking down the stairs. He saw Jim coming towards him. He was wearing a gray suit and red tie, just like he said. Jack opened the door of his BMW, stepped out, and waved. Jim acknowledged him by waving back, and walked briskly towards the car. When he got there, they shook hands.

"Glad to see you back, Jim."

"Thank you, my good friend. Great to be back."

They got into the BMW and headed towards Wolf Road.

As they were moving, Jim said, "I'm a little worried. Marie hasn't activated her tracking device. I'm going to send her a reminder."

He pressed a few buttons on his cell phone, and pressed SEND.

"There," he said, "If she is able, she'll turn the tracking device on."

CHAPTER TWENTY-NINE

Marie and Susan were in separate rooms. Their hands were tied to the backs of their chairs; and they were being closely guarded. It was about 7:20; and one of the officers came in with some boxes full of fast food. There was a Burger King nearby; and he had gone out to get food for everyone in the old warehouse. Marie and Susan were invited to eat; and their hands were untied.

Marie had just begun to eat when she felt a pricking sensation and a vibration from the locket on her necklace. She looked around the room. The guards were not paying attention to her, because they were busy eating their full. She quietly pulled out her locket and activated the tracking device. Then she continued eating.

"Good girl!" said Jim. He turned to Jack. "She just activated her necklace."

"Just in time," Jack said.

"I just hope the bad guys don't discover it."

"Is that likely?"

"No, but I still worry about it."

Jim's tracking GPS told him that he was over twenty-five miles away from the tracking device on Marie's necklace. The GPS would give him directions to the place where she was being held; so she would be easy to find.

Jack Leland turned into the Wolf Road McDonald's parking lot. They met with Jon and Charles inside the restaurant; and they talked for several minutes to discuss how they were going to proceed with the rescue operation. Once they discussed the logistics of the mission, they proceeded to leave the restaurant: not all together, but a couple of cars at a time.

The signal directed them southeast of Albany, onto Route 20. After another ten minutes, the GPS told them to turn east toward East Schodack. They traveled east on this road for a mile, and then were guided to turn north onto an obscure road. They were a quarter of a mile away from their destination; and Charles Daley was looking for a place to park. Suddenly, the road turned sharply to the right, in an eastward direction.

"We're on Deer Walk Road, number one-fifty-two," said Charles. He continued. "Do not proceed further than 152 Deer Walk Road."

All six officers responded in the affirmative. They all found places to park, and waited for the next order. Charles and Jon got out of the car, and walked behind Jim Ellenberger and Jack Leland. They walked forward, and moved closer to Marie's position.

"There it is!" said Jim. "The warehouse! On the left."

"Alright," said Charles.

He gave the order from his portable radio.

"Everybody out, but quietly, two by two. Larsen and Davey, you two will go around the back of the warehouse: the north side. Bill and Norris, take the east side; Bob and Jack, take the west. The rest of us will take the front of the building, the south side."

Then he added emphatically, "And all of you, quietly take out any guards patrolling outside the building. Shoot to kill."

Susan and Marie had just gone through phase two of their series of interrogations. Phase one was the "nice guy" approach, followed by a two-hour intermission. Phase two was a "verbal threatening" approach, designed to frighten them into talking. The interrogating officers made all sorts of threats, including, "We can make you disappear." That threat really scared Marie; and she said, "Let me think about this." She was beginning to break under the pressure.

The third phase of questioning would begin in about two minutes; and it would be the phase where they would use deception. If the deception didn't work, they would begin to use physical violence.

In at least half of their previous interrogative sessions over the past several years, the deceptive phase worked. This was an effective means of getting at least one of the prisoners to talk. The officers would try to convince one of the prisoners that the other prisoner had talked, so he might as well "come clean". They said that they would compare the two stories of the two prisoners if they both talked. If anyone gave out false information, that person would be punished. And if a prisoner refused to talk, he would be punished. Police Commissioner Harry Reynolds would personally interrogate Susan first, and then Marie. He liked doing this type of interrogation, because he was such a convincing liar.

Harry was a sociopath who enjoyed hurting people. So if these two women refused to give him the information he wanted, he would begin to use physical violence. This was the part of interrogation that he liked the best.

He also loved to see his officers hurt people, too. Under his watchful eye, he had seen some of his officers beat several prisoners to death. He enjoyed hearing them scream and cry and beg for their lives. He was incurably sadistic. Susan and Marie had not seen Harry yet. They had not looked into his cold, dark, murderous eyes. To look at Harry, once he took off his sunglasses, was to look almost into the face of the Devil himself.

Larsen and Davey carefully approached the north side of the warehouse. They saw two guards patrolling the area. They were in position, looking really bored, but walking back and forth, looking around to see if anyone who was not welcome came into view. Larsen and Davey were well-hidden. From their safe position, the two marksmen fired simultaneously from twenty yards away. "Aim for the head," Larsen had whispered. All the guards heard was, "Pffft! Pffft!" They were both dead before they hit the ground.

Charles signaled Bill and Norris; and they took out the two guards in front of the warehouse. They dragged them out of sight, and then went to the east side of the building. Bob and Jack stayed near the west side.

Charles and Jon found a stairwell leading up to the second level of the warehouse. There was a window there; and they looked in. The place was dimly lit. They could see several guards posted. And they could see a bright light near the northeast side.

"That must be the interrogation room," Jon said.

"Good observation," Charles said.

The door opened, and a tall, stocky man walked out. He looked toward the west side of the building, gave a hand-signal, and then went back inside the room and closed the door.

"That's the Police Commissioner," said Charles.

"Nice shades!" Jon said.

Quietly, Charles Daley radioed the six.

"Deploy your infrared goggles. Draw your weapons. Get ready to go in quietly. Four guards inside: one at each corner. Be alert."

The old deserted warehouse was not locked.

Larsen and Davey found a way in. They had seen the infrared signature of a guard through the outside wall of the warehouse. But a Teflon-coated bullet traveling through the wall would make noise; so they silently entered the building and waited for a chance to sneak up behind him. The guard turned away and yawned. Quickly, Larsen approached him. The guard suddenly turned and saw him; but before he could make a sound, Larsen's bullet found its mark.

Bill and Norris took out another guard; Bob and Jack the third; and Charles hit his mark on the fourth. It all happened at the same time: a quiet and well-coordinated attack.

Bob could see five infrared signatures in the northeast room. He and Jack, and the rest of the six, approached slowly. Their plan was to break through the door, shoot the officers, and take the Police Commissioner alive.

Susan was on the left side of the room, in a ten-foot-by-ten-foot cubicle area surrounded by a thick partition wall. Marie was in the main part of the interrogation room.

Susan was groaning in pain from the physical violence she had just endured, because she would not break under the pressure of the threats and deception. Her nose was broken, and her lips were badly cut.

Marie was not hurt, but shaking terribly. And she was sobbing uncontrollably. She couldn't hear the words that were spoken in the ten-by-ten cubicle; but she had heard the sound of Susan screaming.

"Larsen, Davey, take out the left guard through the wall. We'll gamble he's not the Police Commissioner."

Davey took him out; and at the same time, Charles burst through the door and shot the second guard.

"Hands up, Harry!"

Harry had one hand behind him, with a gun ready to fire.

"I said hands up, Harry!"

Harry pulled the gun out of his back holster.

"Don't make me shoot you!"

Harry drew the gun, and Charles fired. The Teflon-coated bullet tore through his vest and into his heart. Harry collapsed.

"Why did you make me do it, Harry?"

"Nothing left to live for, now that I'm caught," he gasped.

His body convulsed, then went limp; and his eyes closed in death.

"Are you okay, Susan?" Jon blurted out.

"Now that you're here, yes," she said weakly. She smiled, despite the pain. "I was waiting to be rescued. I knew you'd find me." Then she passed out with exhaustion.

"She's fine," Charles said. "Post-traumatic reaction, a stress reliever. She'll wake up in a few minutes."

Marie watched as Susan was being carried out of the cubicle. When she saw Susan, she began to mumble incoherently. Then she said, "I'm sorry. I'm sorry. I'm sorry."

"For what?" Jon asked.

"I gave you up."

"They're all dead, Marie. They can't hurt us anymore."

"Is Susan okay? Please let her be okay."

"She's going to be just fine."

Jon noticed that Marie was starting to relax, to come out of her anxiety attack. He was glad to be able to comfort her.

"Marie, I want to thank you for saving Susan's life."

"I saved her life?" she said, incredulously. "How did I do that?"

"You activated your tracking device."

"Oh yeah."

"We couldn't have done it without you."

"Thank you. I feel much better now."

She began to laugh nervously. "Imagine that. I saved her life!"

Charles Daley motioned to Jonathan. It was 8:30. He gave the order to his men:

"Call the cleanup crew! And let's get out of here. The Governor is next!"

CHAPTER THIRTY

New York State Governor Bruce Devane was in his file room, looking over some of his papers on Operation Wolf. He had left some information on one of the pages, next to his planned evacuation date of August 14, 2026. That was the date he planned to order the Adirondack Park residents to be evacuated, temporarily. One town, Mountain Meadow, would be permanently evacuated. The Governor was going to condemn that town, citing numerous environmental infractions, and declaring it off-limits to human habitation.

The information that he had written next to the evacuation date was nothing new. It was a reminder of who he was going to use as a "scapegoat".

When he signed the order of evacuation, he would go to a federal judge, and get an order to arrest the Police Commissioner for instituting and initiating a massive cover-up of the many wolf attacks in the Adirondacks, having labeled them as "unsolved murders". He also had proof of a number of brutal actions which he had committed. He even had videos showing him and other rogue officers beating people to death.

He had a plan of arrest. It would be without warning. And while Harry was being held, a prison guard "on the take" from the Governor would see to it that several inmates would attack and kill the incarcerated Police Commissioner. This attack would happen so quickly that he would not have the opportunity to implicate the Governor.

The Governor had a powerful man in the police force on his side: a former federal agent he was going to pay a million dollars to do his bidding. He would carry out the Governor's plan: the arrest and subsequent death of Harry Reynolds, and would be promoted to a higher position, as an administrator in the force.

After the Commissioner's death, the news media would report what the Governor wanted it to: that the Police Commissioner was the villain, and the Governor was cleaning up the whole mess left by the Commissioner. The motive for the cover-up would remain a mystery, and be buried, because he was dead.

The Governor didn't like Harry Reynolds at all. He made him sick. He had only used him so he could get to the gold artifacts. To the Governor, Harry Reynolds was an "animal", a "low-life"—not at all sophisticated like Sam Lowell or Scott Franklin. On the other hand, the Governor HAD liked Todd James, despite all the murders HE had committed. Todd, even with all his "faults", was more cultured, and much more intelligent, than Harry Reynolds. However twisted Governor Devane's likes and dislikes were, things just seemed to work out to his advantage. Because with Roamer gone, and the Police Commissioner out of the picture, Mr. Devane would get to keep eighty percent of this new fortune he was about to acquire.

The frequency of the wolf attacks would give him good reason to declare the Adirondack Park unsafe and to evacuate the residents until the predators were destroyed.

The Governor would use "eminent domain" on Mountain Meadow, the one town which stood in his way, citing many environmental infractions and also introducing and allowing a mining company (secretly owned by himself) to come in and mine the area. The business contracts had been signed, giving his company the mining rights to the mountain area that surrounded the town of Mountain Meadow. With the town permanently evacuated, his company could secretly acquire the artifacts and then quietly dissolve.

His mining company was based and set up in Nicaragua with the stolen identity information of a deceased person. Once the company acquired the fortune, Governor Devane would dissolve the company by declaring Chapter Seven bankruptcy; and once the debts were discharged and the company's assets sold, then all the stolen identity information would be destroyed and deleted. The Nicaraguan-based company would quietly disappear, along with its deceased "owner". All links between the stolen identity and the Governor were already virtually untraceable. But once the treasure was all extracted from the "mining site", the stolen information itself would be destroyed, deleted, and virtually untraceable.

The Governor had a storage plan for the artifacts, which he would store in boxes labeled as something else. Once the artifacts were sold, he would dissolve the two shadow companies which he had created to secretly market the treasures to the highest pre-screened bidders. These shadow companies' transactions were already well-hidden; but once all the business was completed, these companies would also disappear virtually without a trace.

If somehow New York State discovered that the treasures being mined were historical artifacts, the bill signed into law by the Governor in December of 2023 would prohibit and prevent the state from confiscating them from the Nicaraguan-based company. But even though the law was a safety-net, the Governor preferred to not have anyone in authority know about the golden artifacts. The people who were going to do the mining were only those he was willing to allow in on the secret. He and his oldest son Jim, along with his two co-conspirators, and a few "trusted" contractors he would pay handsomely to provide equipment and labor, and who were friends of his whom he could trust to keep a secret: these were the ones who would be involved in the "mining" of the gold artifacts.

And there were probably other treasures inside that huge chasmotic area. The Governor licked his lips at the thought of finding additional treasures in there. He let his mind wander a little while longer; and then he placed the file folder back in its place and locked the drawer.

Sam Lowell, the lawyer who had worked out all the details of the "mining" contract, was relaxing with his family at his spacious home in Clifton Park, on Gingham Avenue. He lived in a beautiful area: where a lot of rich people lived. Clifton Park was the upstate version of New Rochelle: a miniature of that affluent community.

Sam's wife, Janet, was doing the laundry and perusing through the family albums with her daughter and son-in-law, Terry and Jackie Nelson. They were reminiscing about all the good times they had experienced, including how they enjoyed vacationing up in the Adirondacks, and in other resort areas such as Orlando, the Bahamas, Cape Cod, and Hawaii.

Janet was not aware of Sam's involvement in the Governor's plot; and she would not have approved of it if she knew. She was a traditional housewife, and not interested in legal work at all. Yet she was one hundred percent supportive of her husband. She had a deep love for him and for all of their children. All of their sons and daughters were grown up and had families of their own. And all of them had college degrees and successful careers.

Janet would appear for photo ops with her husband, and she would speak out for causes she believed in; but she would never think of being involved in his legal and political affairs. She knew that Sam and the Governor were friends; and she had met the Governor on several occasions. But she had never liked him. He had been unfaithful to his wife Emily, and had courted a number of lady friends before and after her death two years ago. Emily had had breast cancer which she fought for nine tortuous years; and through it all she had tried to keep the family together. Her two daughters and two of their three sons had been upset with their father for his infidelity; but she would not leave him. She was a devout Christian, and refused to become bitter. Rather, she showed him unconditional love all the way up to her death. Janet could not comprehend how Emily could be so forgiving, but respected her for it, and believed that there was something about her faith in Christ that enabled her to love, even when others could not love. Her love was supernatural, beyond normal human capacity.

While Janet was with her daughter and son-in-law, her husband Sam received a call on his cell phone.

"Hello, Sam?"

"This is he."

"This is Bruce. I've been arrested."

"What?"

"I'm at the Albany County Jail. Can you meet me right away?"

"I'll be right over." He paused. "What are the charges?"

"Some really wild accusations."

"What accusations?"

"That I am guilty of a plan to do harm to the people in the Adirondack Park; and to confiscate property that belongs to the State of New York—certain gold artifacts."

"Don't volunteer any information, Bruce. I'll be right over; and we can talk in private."

Neither Sam Lowell nor Governor Devane were yet aware that Harry Reynolds was dead. The Governor had been told that the Police Commissioner was called away to a family-related emergency, but that he would turn his cell phone back on in a day or so and fill him in on all the news. The Governor thought that either Harry Reynolds had decided to betray him, or that Charles Daley and his arresting officers were telling the truth about Harry. He wasn't sure. But he chose to believe that Harry had not turned against him; and that once he returned from his family-related emergency, he would make all of this police-business go away. And Sam Lowell would also come to his aid. With both the Police Commissioner and Sam Lowell on his side, he was sure he could beat this "rap".

Sam Lowell figured that information had leaked out, and that Harry might have been forced to make an arrest to keep from looking suspicious. He would need Sam's expert advice to get out of this difficult situation. He, along with Scott Franklin, would go to work to discredit anyone who had brought such "unwarranted and preposterous" accusations against a sitting Governor.

When Sam arrived at the County jail, he and Governor Devane went into the "Private Conference Room" where lawyers and clients routinely talk in private, without fear of being heard by anyone. They had no idea that Charles Daley and Jonathan Wilkes had bugged the room and were taping every single word. To Sam, it would be illegal, and therefore would never be done. But Charles and Jon had already worked through the legalities in question.

Once the session was over, Sam was arrested as a co-conspirator. Sam and Bruce had talked about the "files" and other aspects of the case, believing that the private room was indeed private.

"Entrapment! Inadmissible in court!" Sam said.

"We'll see," said Charles.

Charles didn't tell the Governor and Sam that he already had the original files and several copies of those files. The Governor was not aware of any search warrant the police had to search his living quarters. But after the arrest, Charles Daley ordered a search authorized by a search warrant signed by Federal Judge Derek Gainer. This federal judge informed Charles that there were a couple of loopholes in the New York State law books that had been added in 2018, but were so obscure that many lawyers were not even aware of their existence. These loopholes stated that if the security of a large number of American citizens was compromised by the laws prohibiting both "entrapment" and "illegal search and seizure", then those two laws "could be deemed null and void in that particular case, if and only if a federal judge so ruled". Since Derek Gainer was a federal judge who wanted the Governor, and whoever else was involved in this illegal plot, to be brought to justice, he signed a waiver for Jonathan Wilkes and Jeb Woods retroactive to the date they acquired the information, and also signed a waiver allowing the Governor and Sam to be secretly recorded in the private conversation conference room. The security of a large number of American citizens—over 300,000 residents of the Adirondacks and millions of visiting vacationers—was already compromised, and would be compromised further if Derek Gainer had not signed the citizen-security waivers.

The beauty of this waiver provision was that the recording was now actually admissible in court. But for now, Charles did not give Sam Lowell and Governor Devane that information. They would find out before the court dates, because their defense attorneys had the right to know, but not quite yet. Sam Lowell, and the Governor, were "going down", and they didn't fully understand it yet. They were unaware that they had no legal recourse: not a legal "leg to stand on".

CHAPTER THIRTY-ONE

May 7, 2026

The campaign manager, Scott Franklin, was the last co-conspirator. He and his wife Sally were vacationing in Jamaica; and he was not planning to talk with the Governor or anyone else about their plans until the first week of August. But on the sixth of May, Charles Daley and a group of his police officers received the "green light" to arrest Scott. The Jamaican authorities were very cooperative, and stood back the following day while Police Commissioner Daley had him arrested and Mirandhized.

Once back in Albany, New York, Commissioner Daley had his best officers begin to interrogate the three defendants separately to get as much information as they could. The files provided a lot of data; but they wanted to see if they could get even more information before they set out to solve the ecological problem that had been created. And they wanted to know everything they could about this case so that they could prosecute these three felons as effectively and severely as possible.

Would they talk? Would one of them "rat out" the other two for a plea-bargain?

The Governor was tight-lipped. He refused to talk. He knew that even if he was finished, he would not give up the one thing he didn't have in his files: namely, the exact location of the gold artifacts. He kept that in another place in the mansion—behind a heating vent grill in his private bedroom. He wasn't about to give that up.

"You'll never get any information out of me," he said.

He added, "I'm the only one who knows where the gold is."

He was lying about that, because his oldest son Jim had the exact location in his file cabinet. He was aware of the plot; and his father had told him that if he (the Governor) could not get to the location and retrieve the artifacts, then he (Jim) should go and recover this treasure. Jim would be on his own when it came to retrieving the gold sculptures; and he could share with his brothers and sisters as he chose. But Jim was the only one in the family that Bruce told about the gold artifacts. So if he shared with his brothers and sisters, it would be in a way that would not reveal the secret source of this income.

Sam Lowell wouldn't talk, either. As a lawyer, he knew better than to volunteer any information. He was an accessory; and he knew he could probably plea-bargain his way out of serious prison time. But if he spoke out against the Governor, he would lose any chance of sharing in the Governor's fortune. Besides, he was sure that he would be able to at least save himself by supporting the Governor and getting them both out on technicalities. He still felt that the case against them was weak.

On the other hand, Sam was sure that, even if they were convicted, he would be out of prison first; and he could get to the artifacts somehow. He was almost certain that Bruce had told his oldest son Jim where the artifacts were. He would work with Jim and get his ten percent.

Scott Franklin, the campaign manager, was the weak link. He was not connected to the plan, except for the political machine he created to sweep Bruce Devane into the Governor's seat, giving him the unique authority to issue an Executive order of evacuation, clearing the way for him to implement his plan. As Governor, he would be able to follow through with his shadowy takeover of the mountains that surrounded the town of Mountain Meadow. And he would be able to extract the gold artifacts, those ancient Huron sculptures that were now buried under tons of mountainous rubble. As Scott contemplated his options, he asked himself, "What guarantee do I really have that the Governor will really share any of that fortune?" It was not a written contract—only verbal—and Scott was not at all sure that an unscrupulous man like Bruce Devane would even think of honoring a verbal agreement.

The truth was that the Governor DID plan to give Scott his ten percent. But Scott had always felt some skepticism about the whole deal; and he was sure he didn't want to serve serious prison time. So he agreed to testify against the other conspirators in exchange for leniency. Charles Daley was elated! He told Scott he would only get a two-year sentence and five years' probation.

Yes, Scott would cooperate with the authorities. Even if the Governor DID plan to pay him the ten percent, Scott concluded that it was a losers' game; and he would rather be on the winning side.

"He must have a map of the area stashed somewhere. We've looked all over his living quarters and haven't found it," Charles Daley confessed to Jon.

"You checked the files, his desk, and all over his living space?"

"Yes. It's like trying to find something in the dark."

The last three words triggered Jon's mind: "in the dark".

"Lord, what are You trying to tell me?" he prayed.

He visualized being "in the dark". In his vision, he could see. He wondered why he could see in the dark; and he realized he was wearing night-vision goggles in his imagination. "What did that have to do with anything?"

Then, he remembered the infrared goggles he took out of the heating vent on his way to the Governor's file room. These goggles had night-vision capability! Finally, he connected the dots. The heating vent! You can hide things there!

"Are you there?" Charles Daley asked for the third time.

Jon snapped back to the present time.

"Yes."

"I thought your phone went dead for a second."

"The heating vent!" Jon blurted out, excitedly.

"What?"

"Check the heating vent!"

Charles Daley thought for a few seconds. "I don't think we checked the heating vents." He paused for another few seconds. "It's a possibility….Let me get back to you, Jon. And thank you. This could be the answer."

He ended the call, and dialed one of his officers.

"Larsen, did you check the heating vents?"

"No, I didn't."

"Let's check the vents in the bedroom and file room; and then in the rest of his living quarters."

"Right away. I'll call you if we find any information."

Larsen and Davey drove back to the Governor's mansion and rushed up to the living quarters. They had the screwdrivers ready to remove the heating vent covers. Larsen removed the first vent cover. Nothing! Davey removed the next cover. And his eyes grew wide with surprise. "Bingo!" he thought.

A black cylinder with a cap lay inside the heating vent. He removed the cap and took out the rolled papers. The first page was instructions and written directions to the treasure site. The second page was a map of the area. The third page was a detailed description of the inside of the collapsed cave-area, with the nearly exact locations of both the wooden and golden artifacts. And the fourth page suggested an additional search deeper into the cavernous area. It also included a warning that the area could collapse very easily; so whoever was doing the exploring needed to be very careful and walk lightly.

"Larsen, take a look at this!"

"You found it?"

"Yes. Can you believe it?"

"Wow! The map of the treasure site!"

"Do you think we should keep it for ourselves?"

They laughed.

Then they called Police Commissioner Daley.

"We got it!" Larsen exclaimed.

Mr. Daley's heart skipped a beat. "Great job, guys!" he said, gasping for breath.

"We'll bring it to you, with copies."

"A half hour?"

"Roger that."

"See you then."

Charles Daley was elated. He now had the Governor right where he wanted him. But he decided to not tell him what he knew until the mining-contract investigation was complete. He was trying to find out what the legal implications of this contract were. He would locate and interview the man who authorized it with his signature: Glen Hastings, on February 15, 2023.

CHAPTER THIRTY-TWO

May 8, 2026

Jerry and Millie Butler and their two daughters were on their second day of vacation in the Eagle Nest Lake area. They had enjoyed fishing, barbecuing, and hiking up and down the trails in the area.

The lead wolf picked up a scent: one which the pack had known before. They had already killed human prey, and would kill again. Although they had left evidence of their rampages, their kills had been placed under the category of "unsolved murders".

A group of fourteen hikers were going up the north side of the old Eagle Nest trail. Jon and Helen Slokum were the leaders of the group; and they had a dozen teenage hikers with them. At the top of Eagle Nest Mountain was an observation point, where one could see for forty miles to the north, east, and west. And there was another observation point a quarter of a mile away where one could see forty miles to the south, as well as to the east and west.

This group of hikers came up every year from Newark, New Jersey. They were not aware of the ecological changes in the area. When they reached the top of the mountain, they saw nobody else at the observation point. They walked up the steps to the floor of the observation facility. To the right was a pair of restrooms, fully operational, both with a small window at the back, at eye-level for an average-sized adult.

Ellie, Mary, Elena, Marianne, Elizabeth, Karen, Cory, Michael, Jim, Robert, Bruce, and George were all there. Jon and Helen had them line up by fours at the three observation points. After they finished their observation activity, they were ready to eat their rations. They had dried fruit, mixed nuts, beef jerky, and candy bars. They were unaware of what was about to happen below.

The pack was nearing the edge of the wooded area. The trail they were following was a mile north of Eagle Nest Mountain. Half a mile ahead of them was the Butler family, vacationing at the campground near the base of the mountain. The camp was open, but not attended by anyone else. It was a place open to the public, and owned by the State of New York. Eagle Nest Lake was just a short walk away from the picnic tables; and there was a dock in the middle of the lake where people could dive off, or just lie down and take in the sun's rays. There was a ladder on the side of the dock; and the depth of the water there was ten to twelve feet. The family could see the lake from the picnic area.

The fourteen hikers were enjoying the rations, and talking happily about their times here. They had memories of so many good times! And they were enjoying the great outdoors once again. They all loved the beauty of the Adirondack Mountains in contrast to the big city. Sure, there were a lot of things to do in the city; but there was not the expanse of valleys, mountains, lakes, and rivers. The hikers were thinking of how invigorating and healthy the environment was here, unaware that there was danger lurking just two and a half miles away.

Jerry Butler saw them first. They were a half mile away, across the lake. And they were moving fast. His wife, Millie, was taking pictures with her cell phone, of some birds perched in the nearby trees; and her daughters were playing "Hide and Seek" nearer the lake.

Jerry decided to call the girls first. He ran toward them and yelled.

"Jillie! Emily! Come on!"

He yelled again. "Emily! Jillie!"

The girls stopped playing. Their Dad sounded serious.

"Come here! Run!"

Fortunately, the girls obeyed.

His wife turned, saw the wolves a quarter of a mile away, and let out a terrified scream.

"What was that?" Helen said. She heard it again. "That sounded like a scream."

The wolves bounded towards their prey with relentless determination. They could see the prey running away, heading towards the camper.

"What's going on down there?" Helen said.

"I heard it too," Jon said.

Some of the teenage hikers also heard it; and they were getting nervous. One of them, Cory, went to one of the observation points and looked towards the lake.

"Wolves!" Cory said excitedly. "Wolves! Down by the lake!"

He looked again at the scene below.

"There are people down there, running!" he added.

Jon and Helen didn't want anyone to panic, even though they themselves were getting really scared.

"What are we going to do?" Marianne asked.

"I don't know. I need to think," Jon said.

He knew they could not go down the mountain. The wolves were too close to their vehicle.

"They made it!" Cory said happily. "They made it!"

Jerry slammed the door of the cab just in time. The two girls were sandwiched between him and Millie. They could hear the terrifying growls and the sounds of scraping and pounding against the sides of the cab. Jerry backed up, turned the camper around, and sped away. The pack followed them for a while, and then gave up. They were riled up, and were moving in a widening arc, seeking for another prey. Then they reached the mountain path, a half mile south of the lake. They reached the parking area and sniffed the dirt. A couple of the wolves started up the mile-and-a-half trail; and the rest of the pack followed.

"Where did they go?" Helen asked Cory.
"Heading this way!" Cory replied. "Just now!"
There was only one option that made sense.
"To the restrooms!" Jon ordered.
"You girls, go with Helen! Guys, come with me!"

The wolves were halfway up the trail and racing towards the top. They had not eaten in three days; and they were ravenous. And there was food up ahead.

All six of the girls followed Helen; and they shut the door. They were in a spacious restroom with a couple of benches to sit on. There was a shower stall and a large supply of soap and towels in a cabinet.
"At least we can all be nice and clean," thought Helen. The girls caught on, and decided they would each take a shower, since they were locked safely inside.
Five boys followed Jon into the men's room. Jon counted. "Where's Bruce?" He felt a panic attack, and then opened the restroom door. He didn't see any wolves yet. He stepped outside and looked around. Then he texted Bruce.
"Where are you, Bruce?"
The text came back. "In a field, just out of the woods."
"How far?"
"About a hundred yards south of you."
"We're in danger. Climb a tree. Any tree. And don't come down until we say."
"Okay."
"Do it NOW!"
"Okay."
Jon turned back towards the restroom and opened the door. As he walked in, he saw two wolves behind him running towards him

from twenty yards away. He froze for a moment; and the boys pulled him in and began to shut the door. The lead wolf crashed against the door; and it shook. For one tense moment, the door opened an inch. One of the boys, Michael, saw a mouthful of teeth as the stunned wolf turned back towards the opening.

Marianne texted Bruce.
"You're not with the others? Where are you?"
"Up a tree."
"Stay there. Don't come down."
"I can hear the wolves from here."
"They're all around us."
"You sure you're safe?"
"Yeah, the door is locked."
"Windows?"
"Only one; and it's small and way up high."
"Okay."

Michael grabbed the door handle, closed the door, and locked it. He could hear the claws of wolves scraping the door and the adjacent wall. Everyone inside the restroom was real quiet. Then George said, "Where's Bruce?"
"He's safe," Jon said.
"Where is he?" Jim asked.
"Up a tree," Jon answered.

"Let's stay calm, everybody," Helen said.
"We're safe here. Don't be afraid. I'm going to call Jon; and he will call 911." She dialed Jon.
"Jon, is everybody there?"
"Yes, except for Bruce."
"What?"
"He's safe. Outdoors, but safely up a tree."
"Okay. Tell him to stay there."
"I did."
"Have you dialed 911?"

"I'm about to, right now."
"Okay. Call me back when you're done."

"Eagle Nest Police Department. What's your emergency?"
"We're at Eagle Nest lookout point. Fourteen of us. We're locked in the restrooms, and surrounded by a pack of wolves. Can you help us?"
"What is your name. Sir?"
"Jon Slokum. I'm here with my wife and twelve teenage hikers."
"We'll send a couple of rescue choppers."
"Can you shoot the wolves from the air?"
"It's illegal to kill wolves."
"Even if people are in danger?"
"Yes."
"How can you rescue us then?"
"We can tranquilize them."
"Okay. Please hurry."
"Two choppers are being dispatched right now."
"What's the ETA?"
"About fifteen minutes."
"That long?"
"The choppers are way south of here."
"Okay. Thank you."

Jim Dwyer began: "This is a Fox News special report. We have some breaking news. We are just hearing that a daring rescue is about to take place at Eagle Nest Point, in upstate New York, way up in the northern tip of the Adirondacks. We are getting information right now from one of our reporters on the scene."
"Hey Mom! Listen to this," ten-year-old Mary Harding said.
Her mother, Irene, came into the living room.
"What, Dear?"
"There's a rescue going on."
"Where?"
"I think it's where Jimmy is."
"Eagle Nest Mountain?"

"Yes."

Irene felt her heart pounding. She could see the images coming from a Fox News reporter who happened to be in the area and was riding in one of the rescue choppers. She listened to the special report, her eyes glued to the set.

Jim Dwyer spoke: "We have our own Bill Hanes right at the scene of the rescue. Bill, what's happening out there?"

"Jim, it appears that an entire pack of wolves, about twenty, have surrounded some hikers; and they are locked inside the two restrooms, waiting to be rescued."

"How many hikers are there?"

"Fourteen."

"How are they going to rescue them?"

"They have shooters who have to tranquilize the wolves; and then they can rescue the hikers."

"How long before the tranquilizers wear off?"

"I'm told that this particular tranquilizer will put out a one-hundred-twenty-pound wolf for twenty minutes."

"That's cutting it close, isn't it?"

"Any higher potency endangers the wolf."

"What about the hikers? They're in danger. Why don't they just kill the wolves?"

"New York State law. It's illegal to kill a wolf in this state."

"Okay. Any new news to report?"

"They've shot about six of the wolves. Here goes another shot. Got him!"

"How long before the actual rescue?"

"They're saying about five more minutes."

"Does that leave enough time?"

"They think so," Bill said.

"Thank you, Bill."

During this news flash, Irene Harding dialed her son, Jimmy.

"Are you okay, Dear?"

"Yes, Mom. They're coming to rescue us."

"How long before you're safe?"

"We're safe now."

"I mean, how long before they rescue you?"
"I don't know. Should be soon."
"Okay, son. I love you."
"I love you, too."

In a few minutes, the gunners shot tranquilizer darts into a dozen more wolves. Then one chopper hovered while the other began to land. The rescuers were in constant phone contact with Jon and Helen.

"Let's go," Helen said. "They want us to open the door. The chopper is ready."

The girls were fearful, but ready to go.

Bill Hanes reported: "They're opening the door. We can see the girls coming out.

They're leading them to the first chopper." A few seconds passed. "They're pulling them up into the helicopter. One…two…three. It won't take long."

"Get ready, guys," Jon said. "When I open the door, you be ready to get in the chopper."

"The first chopper is taking off," Jim Dwyer said. "It's going to look for the last survivor: one of the hikers who is stranded in a tree. They will locate him, and try to rescue him with the second chopper."

Bruce could see the helicopter coming his way. He would wait for the call to come down from the tree. He wasn't about to come down early. He was afraid there were some wolves still around that may not have been immobilized.

The text came: "Bruce, can you see us?"
"Yes."
"Where are you?"
"In a pine tree ahead of you and to your left."
"We are looking. Can you wave safely?"
"Yes." He waved.

"We see you."

"Thanks."

"Don't come down yet. The other chopper is on its way."

"OK."

"The boys are coming out," Bill Hanes reported. "They are heading this way, towards the rescue chopper."

A few seconds passed. "They're climbing into the chopper. One…two…three. They're coming in fast."

A few more seconds passed. Jon climbed inside and gave the crew a "thumbs up" signal.

"Okay, we've got them," Jeb Thompson said. "Let's take off."

Bruce received another text message. "The other chopper is coming now. Get ready. We'll tell you when to make your move."

The first chopper moved out of its hovering position facing the pine tree. The second chopper landed as close to the tree as possible, about twenty yards away.

The wolves were just behind the tree line, to the east of Bruce's position, fifty yards away. They had retreated from the oncoming rescue helicopters. They were hungry, and waiting for the food to come down from the tree.

"We're about to rescue the last hiker," Bill Hanes said. "He got separated from the group. And climbed up a pine tree for safety."

"Okay, you can tell Bruce we're ready," Jeb said.

The text came through: "We're ready, Bruce. You may climb down and get into the chopper."

"The boy is climbing down the tree," reported Bill.

"Come on, Bruce!" shouted Cory. Some of the other boys joined in.

"His name is Bruce," continued Bill, "and he—"

Suddenly, Jeb Thompson leapt out of the chopper: his six-foot-six three-hundred-pound frame hitting the ground and rolling.

The wolves were charging at Bruce. Bruce ran towards the chopper, terrified. Jeb fired off a shot; but the wolf didn't go down right away. Jeb drew his knife, and prepared for the impact.

"Get in! Quick!" Bill said, and pulled Bruce into the chopper. The six boys watched in horror as the wolves attacked Jeb.

Jeb raised his left arm to diffuse the force of the first wolf. He was crouched down, knife ready. He took the blow; and the wolf sank its teeth into Jeb's forearm, crazy with hunger. Jeb stabbed it through the heart, pulled the knife back out, and prepared for the second attack.

He felt jaws close on his right ankle. Fortunately, he had his army boots on; and he kicked at the wolf with his left leg. Then he rolled to the left. The wolf released its grip, circled, and attacked him from the other side. Jeb felt the pain as the beast bit into his left calf. He struck the wolf in the snout with his knife, and the wolf backed away. Prey and predator circled around, each one prepared for a battle to the death.

The first chopper spotted the action and moved in. "Shoot him if you can," the pilot said. But the gunner knew if he missed the wolf and hit Jeb, the tranquilizer dart could be fatal to him. So he told the pilot he'd have to wait for a clear shot.

Jeb held out his left arm, not looking forward to the pain of being bitten again. When the wolf clamped down, Jeb sank his knife through the wolf's left lung. Instantly, the wolf let go of Jeb's forearm and thrashed about on the ground, the knife still embedded in its chest. Jeb retreated to the chopper; and Bill Hanes helped pull him in.

"Are you okay?"

"No, Bill. But I'll live."

"You were live on national TV. Millions of people just saw what you did!"

The other chopper began to pull away. "They got him. We're all clear. Let's get them out of here."

The wolves began waking up; and so the rescuers decided to allow only Jon to exit the chopper and enter the mini tour bus. He would then drive it home. The first chopper served as a lookout, and gave the okay. Jon descended from the chopper and ran to the bus. He quickly opened the door and climbed in. Once he started the engine and shifted into gear, he gave the pilot a "thumbs up" sign. The chopper turned, ascended to two hundred feet, and flew away.

Jim Dwyer, the Fox newscaster, continued his report: "Thank you, Bill. So all of the hikers are safe. And we saw extraordinary heroism demonstrated by one of the rescuers, risking his life to save someone else. We will continue to follow this story as we get more information. This is a live Fox News exclusive."

Irene and Mary Harding were relieved that the hikers all got out safely. As they hugged each other in mutual relief, they heard the TV reporter, Jim Dwyer, say:
"And now we have more information on the recent arrest of Bruce Devane, the Governor of New York State. Authorities have been tight-lipped about the whole affair, stating that there is an ongoing investigation of a number of powerful people in the state. We will continue to follow this story as it unfolds."

CHAPTER THIRTY-THREE

May 10, 2026

Jonathan Wilkes and Susan Morehouse were eating lunch at the Luck-E-Star restaurant in Warrensburg, and talking about the ecological balance of the Adirondacks.

Jon sipped his soda and asked, "How soon will the wolf population run out of prey?"

"Any time now. We have DEC and EPA investigators all saying that there has been a steep decline in the deer population in the past few months. In fact, all of them agree that at this rate the deer population will be reduced to zero in less than a month."

"EPA. That's Environmental Protection Agency, right?"

"Yes."

"How soon before the danger to humans accelerates out of control?"

"Anytime now, because some of the wolf packs are going to run out of food sooner than others. Whenever they run out, they will move out of their normal hunting range and encroach into human territory. We've seen a lot of that already, but the media downplayed it. They didn't report the livestock that had been killed last winter. And they reported human fatalities as 'unsolved murders'."

"I hope we can stop the wolves before the area goes into complete chaos."

"Me too," Susan said. "It scares me just to think about what thousands of starving wolves could do to people in the area."

"You know, the tragedy is that it is not the wolves' fault. They are only doing what is natural. They are predators that will go after anything or anyone they identify as prey. The real fault lies with all the people who altered Operation Wolf and injected them with that dangerous chemical photonygenol."

"It's too bad ALL the wolves have to be killed," Susan remarked.

"Yes, it is. But we can replace them with NORMAL wolves—maybe a dozen—and monitor them closely."

"It's interesting that you say that, because we are considering that very option at the DIAC."

"Really," Jon said. "That's good."

"The key is that we have to keep their population in check so they don't pose a serious threat to human life by invading human territory."

Jon smiled, and nodded in agreement. Then he said, "I wolf-proofed my parents' house."

"You did?"

"Just in case. I don't want to lose them."

"So how do you wolf-proof a house?"

"I had a contractor put temporary bars on all the vulnerable windows that are low enough for these super-aggressive animals to break through."

"You really think they would break through a window?"

"I don't know; but I'm not taking the chance."

"It IS possible; but that's more like something a grizzly bear would do. But these wolves ARE three times as aggressive as normal; and if they're hungry enough, they just might do it."

"Their garage doors are automatic; so they can safely drive in and out of the garage. But I had to wolf-proof the breezeway, because all there was between them and the outdoors were flimsy screens."

"Well, I hope the wolf packs never try to attack your Mom and Dad. Or you."

"Or any of us."

"I'm very watchful, even in Warrensburg. And I know Marie is, too."

"I have been watching your houses, too."

"You have?"

"Yes." He paused. Then he explained. Susan listened attentively, curious. "I programmed my GPS to set off an alarm on my cell phone if wolves get within a mile of any of our houses—yours, Marie's, and where I live. I can then warn them, or you, to get to safety."

"When did you do that?"

"A couple of days ago."

Susan looked at her watch. It was 11:25AM. Almost time to leave.

"Are you ready for the interrogations?" she asked.

"I've BEEN ready."

"It's almost time to go."

Jon turned towards the waitress.

"Check please."

Marie Trombley had driven down to Jim Ellenberger's house to wait for Jack Leland. The three of them would be driven by taxi to the New York State Capitol Building.

Jon and Susan were scheduled to testify at a New York State Senate hearing from 1:30PM to 3:00PM. Then they were scheduled for a subsequent hearing with the New York State Assembly, the state's one-hundred-fifty-member House of Representatives from 4:00 to 6:00PM. Marie, Jim, and Jack would be there to observe the hearings and to offer whatever support they could. The acting Police Commissioner, Charles Daley, would also be there to testify.

Jon had decided to drive the Maxima. It was a 2026 model with all the extra options. He activated the LTC, and ordered it to drive him and Susan to the Capitol Building's best available visitor parking space, and to get there by or before 12:30PM.

The LTC drove them there in fifty-eight minutes, getting them to their parking space at exactly 12:30. From there, it was a three-minute walk to the State Capitol Building; and they were greeted by Security and quickly ushered in. Then they signed in, and waited to be briefed on what would happen, and what they would be doing.

During the briefing session, Marie and Jim had to wait outside the briefing room. Jack Leland, the lawyer, was allowed to stay with them during this session. And Commissioner Daley was also present in the room.

Once the briefing was over, Jon and Susan took their places in the Senate Hearing Room; and Jack Leland was beside them as their legal counsel in case they needed him. Marie and Jim were seated nearby.

Senate Majority Leader Mark Weinberg entered the Hearing Room at exactly 1:20. All the other Senators were already there. The mood in the room was very serious. Marie felt very intimidated, but still believed that Jon and Susan would do well at this hearing.

There were also moods of curiosity, hopefulness, and expectation. The Senators were curious about the plight of the people living in the Adirondack region. They were hopeful that there was a way to solve the problem; and they were curious about what the plan to solve it would be. And they had a sense of expectation: that the problem would be solved.

The meeting began with the Senate Majority Leader presiding. He had Jon, Susan, and Charles sworn in; and then he allowed Jon and Susan to give brief presentations of the situation, with facts, figures, and estimates. Then the questioning began. Senators Reid, Hannah, and Warren questioned them until 2:15. Then everyone took a break. At 2:30, the hearing continued; and this time, Senator Weinberg himself was asking the questions.

A few minutes into this part of the session, Senator Weinberg asked Susan Morehouse point-blank:

"How long before the Adirondack Park will be in a state of emergency?"

Susan answered, "In my opinion, the Park is already in a state of emergency. The clock is ticking; and the wolf population is already invading human territory. Anyone going outside of his or her home is in danger of being hunted down by rogue wolf packs. Unless they have a lot of fire-power, or unless they can get to a safe place, they will not survive."

"Are there human fatalities happening right now?"

"Yes. And I believe there are some that we don't even know about. Undocumented hiker disappearances. Vacationers are at serious risk. It's not summer yet; but there are some early vacationers who come up to this area."

"Should we close down the Adirondack Park?"

"Yes. I believe we should."

"Evacuation?"

"Yes. We should consider it."

"There are six million acres and maybe a half-million people in the area right now, including early vacationers and 140,000 permanent residents."

"It will not be easy."

"Where would they stay?"

"I don't know entirely. With relatives and friends outside the area. New York State temporary housing and relocation. Homeless centers. Churches. We're talking about a two-week relocation: maybe three or four weeks, if necessary."

"Can you outline a plan?"

"I would like to defer to my colleague, Jonathan Wilkes."

"Okay, just a couple more questions, Susan...."

After a few more minutes of Susan's testimony, Senator Weinberg began to question Jon.

"Mr. Wilkes, what is your plan to restore the Adirondacks to its former state?"

"Senator Weinberg, my plan is four-fold."

"Go on."

"First, we must evacuate and relocate as many people as we can. Then, secondly, we must destroy the wolf population. Our investigation suggests that the wolves were injected with a chemical called 'photonygenol', technically 'Photonygenol 4', which increased the aggressiveness of lab rats by two hundred percent, and had lasting effects on the animals, and on their offspring. These chemically-altered predators must be eliminated. Third, we must reintroduce a deer population and rabbit population into the area. Other indigenous animals will need to be reintroduced into the area, also."

Jonathan stopped, paused for emphasis, and took a deep breath. Then he continued.

"And fourth, we need to form a special Commission overseen by the DIAC to make sure that something like this never happens again."

"How do you suggest we destroy all of the wolves?"

"Military technology."

"Like fighting a war?"

"Yes. We have to consider this as a war."

"Can we get them all?"

"Probably not; but the more we get, the less danger we will see in the future. We can moniter the wolf population; and we will probably see the offspring several generations down the line becoming less and less aggressive. If there are still problems with the few remaining wolves, we can consider a second and much smaller campaign to eliminate them as well."

"What is your plan for using military technology?"

"Senator Weinberg, I worked in the Pentagon for ten years. I am familiar with how effective our technology can be. I suggest that New York State request the President of the United States to allow and authorize deployment of the National Guard to do the job. They are organized for the security of the homeland, and would work alongside the New York State Guard; and so they are the logical and smartest choice to eliminate the wolf population."

"How soon can we implement this plan?"

"I would defer to my colleague, Charles Daley, the acting Police Commissioner of New York State."

Senator Weinberg turned to Charles Daley.

"Commissioner Daley, you have heard and, I believe, agree with Mr. Wilkes: that deploying the New York State National Guard is the best plan?"

"I do, Senator Weinberg."

"How soon could that be done?"

"It would take a couple of weeks, because we have to evacuate and relocate the majority of the people living in the Adirondacks. Those who refuse to leave must stay in their homes, and not interfere by getting in the National Guard's way."

"What else?"

"It will take time to deploy the National Guard; and we have to establish a starting point of entry into the Adirondacks, and a finishing point. The logistics of this operation are massive, covering six million acres. But we have the technology to succeed, including state-of-the-art infrared day-and-night-vision helmet screens, laser-guided automatic weapons, and super-light body armor."

"How many in our New York State National Guard?"

"About sixty thousand."

"How many do we need?"

"Depends on how quickly we want the job done."

"Wouldn't sixty thousand people accidentally shoot each other?"

"We have the technology that can prevent that."

Jon had asked Charles and Susan not to reveal that he was secretly helping the National Guard by programming another feature into his matrix numerical locator system, which is a part of his advanced GPS. He would tie this locator system, with its added new feature, into the computer main frame at the New York State National Guard Headquarters in Latham; and only the top two officials of the New York State National Guard would know about it. And not even THEY would know how he was doing it, or what his GPS really was.

"We do?" the Senator asked.

"Yes. They will be able to mark the wolves with infrared and satellite technology. And it will be electronically tied to their weapons. A warning light will flash if they are aiming at 'friendlies'."

"By 'friendlies', you mean 'people'?"

"Yes."

General Red Logan, the head of the New York State National Guard, was already aware of the plan and the technology to be installed. He wasn't sure if it would work; but he was a fan of modern technology, and was willing to cooperate in this coordinated effort.

"How will they do that?" the Senator asked.

"I'm sorry. I have been told that's classified information," Charles answered.

Jonathan nodded in approval.

The hearing continued for another forty minutes, going a half hour overtime, with other state Senators expressing their concerns and doubts, and asking questions. All in all, it was a favorable hearing. The Senate was scheduled to review some documents on the case, and then call for a vote. The voting would take place within two business days.

Once Senator Weinberg adjourned the hearing, Jon, Susan, and Charles were ushered over to the House Chamber, where they would testify at the second hearing, set to begin at 4:00. After a half hour of testimony, the Speaker of the House, Greg Nemire, declared an hour break for dinner, but to be back at 5:30. There was a huge cafeteria there, which served better food than most commercial restaurants. And it was free, compliments of the New York State taxpayers. So Jon, Susan, Charles, Marie, Jim, and Jack all sat down together and enjoyed their meal and discussed how things were going.

"In your professional opinion, Jack, how did we do at the Senate hearing?" Jon asked.

"Great. I didn't have to lift a finger or say a word to help you. You said it all: and maybe better than I could." He laughed.

"Do you think the Senate will vote 'Yes'?" Marie asked.

"No doubt in my mind," Jack said.

"I sure hope so," Susan said. "And soon, before too many more people die."

"Even one more is too many," Marie said.

"You are so right, Marie," Jim said.

"Well, we're here, and doing all we can," Jon said. "My conscience is clear. I know we're doing the right thing. And—"

"God knows, too," Susan said.

"You read my mind," Jon replied.

"Well," Jack said. "A half hour of questions to go."

The six continued talking and eating. At 5:20, they stood up, and began walking back to the House Chamber.

Speaker of the House, Greg Nemire, began to question Susan, then Jim, and then Charles. He was very precise, like Senator Weinberg. In twenty minutes, he finished his questioning. And called for an immediate vote.

"Wow!" Marie said to Jim. "They don't waste any time, do they?"

"This is amazing!" Jim said.

All over the Chamber, one by one, they could hear the voices of the Representatives as they gave their names and spoke their votes.

"Representative Fitzgerald. Yea."

"Representative Beecher. Yea."

"Representative Girard. Yea."

Jonathan and Susan practically held their breath as the voting continued. They were in awe of what was happening. It was surreal.

Jack Leland was fired up; and Charles Daley was elated.

The electricity in the Chamber was infectious. So far, the vote had been unanimous. Then it came down to the last Representative. He was an Independent; and his vote was almost always unpredictable. He opened his mouth to speak.

"Representative Katzman."

He paused and smiled. He loved the attention which he received as a contrarian. Then he took a deep breath as all eyes were locked onto him. He let out his deep breath and said:

"Yea."

At that moment, the electricity of the Chamber was "over the top". The entire House of Representatives stood up and gave Representative Katzman, and the unanimous vote, a standing ovation. So did Jon, Susan, Charles, Jack, Marie, and Jim. After two full minutes of clapping and cheering, Speaker Nemire spoke:

"Please be seated!" He paused and looked around. "Everyone! Please be seated!"

People began to sit down. "Thank you!"

"Mr. Speaker, the vote is unanimous. The 'Yeas' have it," the clerk said.

"Thank you very much, Mr. Snyder."

There was a quiet buzz all around the Chamber. Then the Speaker began his summary:

"Today, May 10, 2026, is a day to remember. It is one of the few days that the House has voted on a bill unanimously."

He paused. There was some laughter as Representative Katzman stood up and bowed.

"Thank you, Mr. Katzman." The Speaker said.

More laughter erupted. The Speaker paused. Once the laughter died down, he turned serious, and spoke again.

"Just two days ago, a bill was placed on my desk, by our new acting Governor Paul Atkins. It was drawn up by two of the men who gave testimony today: Mr. Jonathan Wilkes and Police Commissioner Charles Daley. It began with some very sobering statistics: three deaths in 2024, forty deaths in 2025—." His voice began to crack up—"And it could be over two hundred in the first four months of this year, most of these happening in April. And in this month alone, we are getting reports daily of people being killed and more being injured, by packs of ravenous wolves, every single day now."

He paused and looked around, left to right and back again. It was so quiet, one "could hear a pin drop". Some of the Representatives were in tears. Some were audibly crying. Everyone—even Representative Bill Katzman—was dead-serious.

Speaker Nemire continued.

"I did not and do not believe we can afford to wait. And that's why I called for an immediate vote. The people in the Adirondacks are in danger. Great danger. We must act. We must act NOW! So we are returning this bill to Governor Atkins with a unanimous vote; and we URGE the Senate to do the same. I implore Senate Majority Leader Mark Weinberg to speed up the process and take a vote TODAY, before the Senate dismisses. Let us give the new Governor the bill he needs, so that he can sign it into law, and call the President of the United States to order the New York State National Guard—fifty thousand of them—into the Adirondack Park."

Senator Weinberg was about to dismiss the Senate for the day when he heard about the House vote. And the Speaker's plea. And he made a quick decision. He called for a quick vote on the bill.

It was unanimous. All sixty-three of the Senators voted 'Yea'; and the vote was over in five minutes. The Senators were still dismissed almost on time; and the bill was on the Governor's desk that same day.

After signing the bill, Governor Atkins placed a call to the Oval Office. President Allen James Westcott took the call immediately.

"Mr. President?"

"This is he."

"This is Governor Atkins."

"Good evening, Governor."

"Good evening, Mr. President."

"I've been waiting for your call. I've already been briefed. One of our computer specialists is assisting you, I see. A Mr. Jonathan Wilkes."

"Yes, he is."

"He's a good man. Best the Pentagon ever had."

"That's quite a recommendation coming from the President of the United States."

"Feel free to give Jon the message. And he has a job with us anytime he wants to come back."

"I'll tell him, Mr. President."

"You can call me A.J."

"I'll tell him, A.J."

"And I will tell the Secretary of the Army, Joseph Fielder, to order fifty thousand New York State National Guard troops to save the Adirondack Park."

"Thank you, Mr. Pre—I mean A.J."

"You're welcome. And if you want to, you CAN call me Mr. President. Whatever makes you comfortable."

"Thank you, Sir."

After the conversation, the President buzzed his secretary.

"Get me the Secretary of the Army. Please."

"Right away, Mr. President."

"Thank you, Marlene."

In thirty seconds, the President heard a voice:

"SA Joseph Fielder here."

"Hi, Joe. This is the President."

"I've been waiting for your call. And I'm waiting for you to order me to give out the orders to fifty thousand men and women."

"I'm issuing the order to send fifty thousand New York State National Guard troops into the Adirondack Park and authorize them to destroy the rogue wolf population that is killing American citizens even as I speak. And also, you may use Air Force firepower as well: any and all means at your disposal. All branches of the military are members of the same team. We will work TOGETHER, and get this done."

After concluding his conversation with Secretary Fielder, the President looked down at the last sentence of the bill signed by the Governor of New York. He read it again:

"We authorize the National Guard to work in conjunction with any of the other branches of the United States armed forces: to utilize any and all means at their disposal, to carry out this mission."

At 7:15 that night, Robin Hayward at CNN reported some "breaking news".

"This is Robin Hayward at CNN. We have breaking news of a deadly attack by wolves in the New York State Adirondack Mountain region. Authorities there have just recovered three cell phones with pictures of the attack, taken by the victims. You may not want your children to see this, for it is really graphic."

Millions of viewers watched the horrifying scene play out. Many could hardly believe their eyes. The cell pictures were downright frightening. It started out with a happy family picnicking in a large field. It went on; and they were eating and talking happily. Then someone pointed to the right. The phone camera moved to the right and picked up a group of wolves coming out of the forest about a hundred yards away. They were gathering; and a couple of them were howling, calling the rest of the pack.

The phone camera turned the other way as the owner of the phone began to run. A blur of ground could be seen for the next fifteen seconds. Suddenly, the ground was seen close-up as a wolf grabs the phone. The viewers saw the wolf's mouth up close, with the razor-sharp teeth and slobbering tongue. The camera then went dark as the phone dropped, and landed face-down in the dirt.

The second phone was up in a tree where the owner was safely viewing the wolves. People were seen running and being chased down by wolves. It was such a horrible thing to watch that the camera was turned away and moved on towards the left. There, the last survivor on the ground was running away; and he jumped over the edge of a cliff. Then the phone went blank.

The third phone had been found at the bottom of the cliff. It started with the initial charge of the wolves; but the person holding the cell camera was already running away. Then the phone camera turned forward and followed the ground ahead towards a cliff. Then it dislocated and showed the person beside it falling; then it turned towards the ground below, and went dark as it hit the dirt.

All of these three cell phone videos together took less than one minute to show.

Robin Hayward reported, "We have been told by authorities that one person survived the attack and was rescued. The rest did not survive."

The reporter went on to say that this was one of many predatory attacks on humans in the last five months, and that New York State authorities were forming a plan to solve the problem. There was talk about evacuating the Adirondack Park and using the National Guard to go in and eliminate the wolf population. President Allen Westcott would be addressing the nation in just a few minutes. Millions of people in the U.S., and throughout the world, were now intensely focusing on the Adirondack region of upstate New York, and wondering what was going to happen next.

CHAPTER THIRTY-FOUR

May 11, 2026

Jonathan Wilkes was up by 8:00AM. He thanked God for helping him and Susan, and the other four, get through the hearings. And he was thankful that the House and Senate unanimously passed the bill to allow the Governor to sign into law the authorization needed to set in motion the chain of command for deployment of the National Guard.

By mid-afternoon, Jon could already see the results of the bill being passed. People all over the Adirondacks were already preparing for a one-month leave of absence. Many were boarding up their windows and removing their valued possessions to take with them wherever they moved.

Jon had already found a nice place to relocate his parents. Bill and Marge would get a nice vacation in the Bahamas for a one-month stay, bought and paid for by their millionaire son.

Jon had made arrangements for himself to stay at a Holiday Inn in Glens Falls, starting in a few days; and had arranged for Susan and Marie to stay in a couple of rooms down the hall about fifty feet from his room. He already had moved one of his three computers into the Holiday Inn. The other two would remain at his parent's house and would protect it from any burglars looting deserted homes. There was a security system that used a human voice to warn looters to back away. If they refused to back away, the house would "defend itself". To avoid chance of prosecution, Jon made sure everything was on audio-tape and video-tape; and he also would know about any attempt of burglary through his GPS detector system, which would send an alarm to his cell phone. He could then "talk audibly" to the looter and report him to the police with satellite images of the offender. Jon figured that most looters would move on and leave the house alone. It would just be too much trouble for the would-be thief to deal with the super-advanced security system. They would move to some place easier to loot.

While thousands of people were leaving their Adirondack homes and businesses, hundreds of squad cars were patrolling the area looking for looters. And the New York State National Guard was beginning to mobilize, setting up checkpoints where they would form a perimeter from which they would advance into the Adirondack Park in their effort to exterminate the deadly wolf population.

At 4:00PM, Jim Dwyer the Fox newscaster spoke:

"Top officials in New York State are working together to deal with the crisis in upstate New York. Numerous reports of wolf attacks have been coming in. They are no longer being suppressed as 'unsolved murders'; and so the truth is now beginning to come out. Yesterday, the New York State House and Senate unanimously passed a bill authorizing the deployment of the National Guard to save the Adirondack Park area from the rogue wolf packs which are roaming, and terrorizing the people in the area.

"New York Governor Paul Atkins called President Allen Westcott last night, and requested him to authorize the Secretary of the Army Joseph Fielder to order fifty thousand New York State National Guard troops to deploy to the Adirondack Park area and destroy the wolf population."

Jonathan decided to call Susan and invite her to go out for dinner to celebrate the victory they won yesterday. They were very happy to be a part of the solution to this serious problem.

He picked her up; and they went to the Olive Garden restaurant in Glens Falls. They decided they would spend some serious time there, eating and talking about how Jon was going to help the National Guard implement the plan. After about an hour of eating and conversation, Jon said:

"I need a few hours to program my GPS like I said I would. This is confidential between you and me."

"My lips are sealed, Jon."

"Then we get to watch the military do their job. They know best how to carry out the plan. I'm just providing them some extra tools to use."

"I'm glad I met you, Jon. I believe it was God's will."

"Me too. You're an inspiration to me."

"When this is all over, what are you going to do?"

"I would like to develop my GPS even more, and market it to the Pentagon to keep our country safe from our domestic and foreign enemies."

"Where do you want to live?"

"I don't know."

"I want to be your best friend."

"You can't."

"Why?" she asked nervously, fearing rejection and feeling vulnerable.

"Because God is my best Friend."

"Oh, yeah." She breathed a sigh of relief. "That's true. Same here." Then she added, "How about your second best friend?"

"I think you are," Jon said. He saw where this conversation was going. He said, "You never married, did you?"

"No," she said, and looked down at her plate.

She felt sad, lonely, and very vulnerable. She regretted that she never started a family because she was pursuing her career. She was seriously thinking about giving up her career for a family. "It's not too late," she thought. "If only—"

Jon interrupted her thoughts. He said, "Would you like to go out with me?"

She felt a wave of joy engulf her. "Yes, I would. I love you, Jon."

"Why?" Jon wanted to be sure her love was genuine.

"Because you are a caring person. And you have the qualities in your life that I am looking for in a companion."

"I see. Do you want to talk about it?"

They talked; and from that dinner date and on, their relationship was different. Jon was a little slow to admit that he loved her; but finally, he did.

May 12, 2026

Jon was up the next morning at 8:00. He always started the day with prayer and a Bible reading. He asked God to help him to successfully program his GPS with an added special feature to the matrix locator system. It would allow the GPS to hook into the mainframe of the National Guard computer system and exchange data between satellites and the National Guard computer mainframe. This new added feature could locate anyone in the world and identify him or her as human. It could not identify the names of the people it located—that feature would be added later, before he sold the GPS to the Pentagon—, but it COULD differentiate between humans and non-humans. He programmed this feature to specifically identify three entities: "Y" for humans, "X" for wolves (including coyotes and packs of wild dogs), and "Z" for other creatures. The infrared signatures would determine "X", "Y", or "Z".

Then Jon added another feature to the matrix locator system, a program he called Deep Sight Infrared, or DSI, which enabled it to see through solid matter and identify the depth of the object observed. It was a feature which he enhanced through a laser-based eye that was on all the newer satellites. This eye could be enhanced electronically from his GPS to see with far greater vision capability than anyone in the Pentagon suspected. This eye, enhanced by the GPS, could see through a thousand feet of solid rock and still identify what the object was: in this case, X, Y, or Z. One could correctly say that the GPS was seeing all of this through the satellite eyes which it enhanced.

Once Jonathan hooked the matrix locator system to the National Guard computer mainframe, the National Guard could watch all of the Adirondack Park in sections—or sectors—on a huge screen, and a series of related observational surveillance screens. The National

Guard would be able to monitor the positions of all their troops as they advanced through the Adirondack Park. And their computer system would be able to identify any danger and its proximity to their troops. Those keeping watch through the computer system could then warn the troops which were in jeopardy. If a dozen wolves were headed for their troops in Sector Forty-One, for example, they could instantly be warned and would have time to get ready to fight the interlopers. In addition to that, troops from other nearby sectors could be called in to help the ones in that "danger-zone" sector. The ones calling them could give them exact directions and coordinates through their radio connection system. It was a tremendous communication system, which would help keep the entire group of fifty thousand National Guardsmen as a unified whole, moving in near-perfect coordination step-by-step through the Adirondacks.

It took Jon all of four hours to complete this enhancement and hookup between the GPS, the satellites, and the National Guard computer-system mainframe. Then he put the entire enhancement and hookup system to the test. He studied sections of the Adirondack Park through his own computer using the same hookup, and identified sector numbers and objects within those sectors. He then communicated with the National Guardsmen who were now watching the Adirondack Park on their large screens. They confirmed that they were beginning to identify people, wolves, and other animals. And they found out something curious. Near the town of Mountain Meadow in the northern Adirondack region, there was a huge concentration of wolves. The town, oddly enough, was not normally bothered by wolves, because the one opening to the side of the mountain range facing them was caved in, and because the wolves were INSIDE the miniature mountain range! That meant that this particular group of mountains which engulfed Mountain Meadow to the west, east, and north, were all CAVERNOUS!

There were several openings to this cavernous group of mountains; but they were all on the sides of the mountains facing AWAY from the town of Mountain Meadow. Whenever the wolves exited the cavernous area inside the mountains, they would be on the other side of the mountains, and therefore, a safe distance AWAY from the residents of this small town. And since the mountains were treacherous to climb and traverse, it was very rare for a wolf or pack of wolves to cross over the mountains and invade the town. It had only happened once in the last six months; and some Mountain Meadow residents with rifles killed the six wolves that entered the area before they did any serious damage. A few livestock were lost; but there were no human casualties.

Wolves coming out of the cavernous mountains normally traveled away from the town.

"How ironic!" Jon thought. "The one town the Governor wanted to be evacuated just happens to be one of the safest in the whole area."

A map of the entire Adirondack Park was generated, magnified, and printed out in sections, or sectors. It showed the date, and the number of wolves, people, and non-wolf animals, using the letters X, Y, and Z. It kept a running total sector by sector, and a grand total. Jon looked at the figures: one hundred and eighty-three packs averaging about fourteen per pack. The largest pack had thirty-four members, and the smallest only three. There were over two thousand and five hundred wolves roaming the area! Other animals were identified: about three thousand large animals and over eight thousand small animals going down to the size of a rabbit. And there were a surprisingly small number of animals smaller than a rabbit: just over a hundred thousand.

The statistics were scary. The larger prey was not there in sustainable numbers. Their population was diminished to the point where the deer population would run out in a short period of time. This prey would only sustain twenty-five hundred wolves for a few weeks. And the smaller prey would not last long, either.

But there was something else that was curious. There was that huge population of wolves concentrated around Mountain Meadow, inside the cavernous miniature mountain range. The locator system feature identified these two-thousand-plus wolves, which also needed prey. It appeared that they were residing in a huge lair. Packs of wolves were flowing in and out of this lair constantly. Sometimes there were three thousand predators in the lair; sometimes only fifteen hundred. But there was always a huge number in the lair. So the leadership at the New York State National Guard Headquarters had made a decision. Their soldiers would start their advance in the southern Adirondacks, move north, eliminating all the roaming packs; and then they would coordinate with the Air Force and detonate the entire lair, collapsing it, killing the wolves inside.

May 21, 2026

The evacuation was almost completed. Whole communities had moved. Schools were closed. Evacuated towns were being patrolled by police and National Guardsmen to prevent looting. About ten percent of the population refused to leave. Vacationers were warned to leave, because the area was under New York State and federal Martial Law, a state of emergency. The National Guard was continuing to set up for their initial offensive, set to begin in three days.

CHAPTER THIRTY-FIVE

May 23, 2026

It was a day of great expectation, and yet fear. The fifty thousand National Guard troops were enough to fight a war. But the enemy they were about to engage was a different kind of enemy: an enemy that would not just kill you, but eat you alive if it could. This enemy was fast-moving and deadly: one that would stalk you as prey and swarm you like bees attacking a hapless invader. From the Division leaders down to the squad leaders, the message was the same: be alert, be ready, be fast, and shoot to kill. This was a serious enemy that must be destroyed. They were told to call for backup if they were outnumbered. These predators were targets which you had to kill at a distance; because if they got too close, you would be in serious trouble.

"Do not, I repeat: do not deactivate your helmet screen capabilities. They are designed to be used day and night, and will keep you up-to-date with the enemy's position at close range. But be alert, because your infrared setting will only identify the heat signatures up to three hundred meters away. This short range is the one weakness of the setting. It will warn you; but you will not have a lot of time to prepare for battle.

"If you get lost, use your GPS and head north. If you are alone and surrounded by unfriendlies, climb a tree and call for help."

These were just some of the warnings and commands given out by all the leaders. This was a serious mission; and some of the leaders, including First Lieutenant Simon Martin, were certain that some of their troops were going to die.

Simon Martin, leader of Second Platoon in Company B, was a decorated war hero. He had fought in the Iranian War, and served military time in Yemen as well. He had been shot in Iran and placed in a prison camp for nine months. He survived the torture and starvation, and was rescued when Tehran was taken. His captors were taken by surprise by a Special Forces unit; and Simon considered himself to be very fortunate to be alive. He knew that in any war, you must take the enemy seriously. He would do everything in his power to kill the enemy and keep his platoon members unharmed.

All the soldiers were to form a line one hundred miles long, and move from south to north. Each soldier was to have a partner with him at all times. The platoon leader would move back and forth and coordinate with the squads in his own platoon and with the company commander. The troops were to move quickly, but carefully. There would be scheduled stops along the way for necessary reasons. Nobody was to lag behind or get too far ahead. If they were engaging the enemy, they needed to coordinate together, and not fight the enemy by themselves.

Simon Martin would operate mostly with First Squad, but would skillfully coordinate with Second, Third, and Fourth Squad. Operating with First Squad placed him into close proximity to First Platoon with its leader, Lieutenant Larry Rice. Larry operated mostly with his Fourth Squad, which was directly to the left of Simon's First Squad, to the west of Simon. The company commander, Captain Bobby Montero, would be in constant contact with the four platoon leaders.

Alex Warfield, a staff sergeant, and leader of Simon's First Squad, had nine good men: Max, Patrick, Al, Jose, Bill, Mike, Donovan, Mark, and Joe. They obeyed him without hesitation, because they believed that he would never make a decision that would be wrong or detrimental to any of them. He teamed up with Max Williams, a supremely talented African-American sharp-shooter.

The other three squads were very efficient, and as well-prepared for this war as First Squad. These three squad leaders were in constant contact with Simon via their communication system.

Each member of the National Guard were issued ceramic helmets equipped with a screen which automatically showed and identified infrared images within three hundred meters in every direction, a communication system, and a GPS guidance system directed by satellite-based technology, compliments of Jonathan Wilkes and his advanced GPS. The Guard was equipped to fight with M-16 automatic rifles and nine-millimeter pistols. They were also issued two knives apiece for hand-to-hand combat. The squad leaders and other officers: lieutenants, captains, etcetera, had the added but optional usage of "smart ammunition", which were bullets with computerized infrared-detector chips that would calculate the exact distance to their target and explode when it reached that target spot rather than exploding early if it passed through something else along the way. This smart ammunition worked great when the target was stationary and hiding behind a thin cover, because it would spot the target, travel through the thin cover, and only explode once it hit the target. But the problem with smart bullets in this campaign was that wolf packs were usually not stationary. Consequently, most of these officers chose to use the ordinary bullets, believing that they would be more effective most of the time. Once again, individual shooting capability would trump so-called superior or "smart" technology.

But there was a third choice: to use mixed ammunition. In a three-round blast, one smart bullet and two conventional bullets would discharge. Simon decided to try the mix. He figured that if wolves were charging him, he might get two of them with a three-round blast. The conventional rounds would drop the closest attacker, and the smart bullet might travel clean through that first wolf and hit a second one and explode. He thought it was worth a try, but understood why only a few officers—none of his four staff sergeants—chose to try the mix. It was an unknown in this particular type of warfare, because this was a fast-moving enemy which was not the ordinary stationary one hiding behind cover and firing back at you. This was an enemy that charged at you at a rapid pace and would kill you up-close with fearsome predatory powers.

The Guard would not use artillery in its advance, because of the possibility of killing civilians and destroying people's properties. Enough damage could be done with ordinary weaponry. An M-16 three-round blast would easily kill a wolf at a distance, and a nine-millimeter handgun could drop a wolf up-close when properly aimed. All but the newest recruits had logged sufficient hours of shooting practice to be adept at using all of their "ordinary" weapons, including the knives issued to them. The new recruits were disbursed among the many companies of the Guard, and would get crash-course "on-the-job" training. About five hundred "newbies" were placed near the edges of the National Guard line, watched and reinforced by veteran warriors.

About fifty cameramen were embedded into the fighting force; and each was granted a handgun and knife for extra personal protection. A cameraman was to use them only when he had to: to save his life or the life of someone else. All fifty observers were given uniforms, complete with the ceramic helmets which would help them to avoid danger and allow them to communicate with the soldiers, the officers, and their TV stations. Bernie Stansford was a cameraman who was chosen to accompany Simon Martin's Second Platoon.

The company that they were in was part of the 3rd Brigade, made famous from the Iranian War of 2024. As part of the 42nd Infantry Division, they had a history which demanded great valor and strength. This particular company they were in was the foremost sub-unit of the brigade, and even of the entire 42nd Division, known for its skill and marksmanship. Second Platoon was the most talented of the four platoons in this company. And First Squad was the best-rated squad. Staff Sergeant Alex Warfield, who led the squad, teamed with Max Williams, a highly-talented sharp-shooter. Both of them had sniper-quality precision. Yet on fast-moving targets, their abilities—although way above average—were sometimes blunted. They both could easily hit a stationary target at five hundred meters, and a slow-moving target at that range most of the time. But a fast-moving target at three hundred meters or closer took extraordinary skill and concentration. Some of their kill shots would become disabling shots or even near-misses. They never missed by much, but they would have to be at their best, in timing and concentration.

Simon Martin, their platoon leader, was a great leader; and he inspired confidence in his group. He believed in following the basics; and so he repeated the basic instructions again and again so that it became a part of their mindset. He drilled their minds until the basics became a part of their lives. A thought became an action; an action became a habit; and a habit became a way of life. These soldiers ate, slept, and breathed the basics; and that's why they were so efficient in all of the training exercises; and now they were in a real-life battle with an enemy they never imagined they would have to face. One that was not human. One that sparked fear in the hearts of many who are afraid to go into the woods. But these brave soldiers were going into the woods to fight this fearsome enemy: one that frequently visits people's nightmares.

A one-hundred-mile line of fifty thousand soldiers would mean a soldier every ten feet. They would pair up for protection so that each pair would be twenty feet apart. But in a mountainous region, that ideal formation would be broken; and order would inevitably turn into chaos.

What made the mission even more difficult was the fact that there were hundreds of lakes and ponds, and rivers that would have to be crossed. And some mountains were impossible to climb in certain areas; so the tightly-held line of the National Guard would have to break up and come together again to regain continuity. Each squad was equipped with an inflatable boat with a small, lightweight motor which was strong enough to carry the entire unit. And there were two designated soldiers in each squad who had mountain-climbing gear. And each soldier had gear designed for climbing trees in the middle of the forest with no lower branches still alive.

Simon spoke to his Platoon: "The Adirondacks is the largest state park in the United States of America. We have over a hundred and ten miles to cover. The enemy we face will kill you; they will not take prisoners. They will eat you alive if they can. Do not hesitate to shoot to kill. And do not get separated from this group. If you are called to help someone: once you're done, return to your original formation. I will be with you all the way to the end, God willing."

When he said, "God willing", all forty of his platoon members knew that he meant it. Simon was a Christian who believed that God was in control of everything; and so whatever happened would be in the scope of God's will. They knew that Simon was for real. He was a man who didn't just "talk the talk"; he "walked the walk". One could describe him using lots of words; but the words "hypocrite" and "phony" would not be among them. "Genuine", "honest", "transparent", and "fair" would be some of the words that would describe their leader, Simon Martin. And all forty members of the platoon knew that their leader would not hesitate to die for them.

At 6:00 the following morning, they would begin the advance. They would advance quickly, yet carefully. Their goal was to cover the one hundred and ten miles in six days: about fifteen to twenty miles a day. On the sixth day, they would circle around the top of the Adirondack Park and approach and surround the cavernous mountain range which surrounded the town of Mountain Meadow. That would cover an extra ten miles for the soldiers on the outer parts of the hundred-mile line. Then, on Day Seven, they would destroy the wolf lair inside the mountain range by setting explosive charges inside the cavernous mountains, then backing off, and collapsing the lair by detonating the charges in tandem with an Air Force strike.

The fifty thousand foot-soldiers would not be alone. There were about six hundred military vehicles with armed men patrolling the highways and roads in the Adirondack region. In addition to that, state and local police were also on patrol throughout the area.

Jonathan Wilkes, Susan, Marie, Jim, and Jack all got together in the secure chatroom. Even though they were sure they were safe elsewhere, they figured it couldn't hurt to continue using this secure website.

Twiggy: "So they start tomorrow morning. I'm so glad. I hate to think of anyone else being hurt by these merciless creatures."
Super Decade: "They're starting early in the morning."

Phantom: "You're right, Super Decade. 6AM. It will take about six days. The Adirondack Park is huge! Six million acres."

Sanhedrin: "That's a lot of square miles."

Phantom: "About 9400 square miles, shaped like an oval."

Legal Eagle: "There may be some wolves that migrated outside of the Park. Could they endanger the military operation by coming at them from out of 'nowhere'?"

Phantom: "I thought about that. I think they will be on the alert for unexpected contingencies. That's how the military operates."

Legal Eagle: "We could have some unexpected contingencies ourselves. We cannot allow anyone to know how the stage was set to get our information from the Governor's mansion. If we do, there could be legal complications."

Twiggy: "I am amazed at the way the justice system works. So much of the system is upside-down and broken. I wish it could be fixed."

Legal Eagle: "I know there is that same contingency rule, a back door in the system that gives us an 'out' on the problem."

Sanhedrin: "Like for the entrapment situation? And the illegal search and seizure?"

Legal Eagle: "Yes. The 'Extenuating Circumstance Clause' would even cover this action. It says if there is a danger to the security of a large number of American citizens, then otherwise unlawful means of obtaining information that could save lives may be considered a contingently-lawful means of attaining information."

Phantom: "But you think there may be a problem?"

Legal Eagle: "Only that it could make the trial a lot longer."

Phantom: "Why?"

Legal Eagle: "Because the defense lawyers might make a big deal about endangering people's health."

Twiggy: "But they can't win. Right?"

Legal Eagle: "No; but they can spend some time presenting their case, tying us up in court for a lot of extra time. They might try to come up with an exception to the exception, because of the high office of the person whose living quarters were infested. And if our whole scheme comes out, which it probably won't, there could be individual lawsuits from anyone who was in the mansion when it was infested."

Phantom: "I have to admit: infesting the Governor's mansion with cockroaches was a really filthy and dirty trick. Lolol."

Legal Eagle: "A very SMART dirty trick, lol. We just would be better off if we keep it all our dirty little secret."

Phantom: "Thanks for the compliment. And yes, our lips are sealed. Right, everyone?"

Twiggy: "Yes."

Sanhedrin: "No problem here."

Super Decade: "My lips are sealed. But if they ask us, we can't lie."

Phantom: "True, but just don't volunteer any information. If they ask you a 'Yes-or-No' question, then you may have to invoke the Fifth Amendment. And don't answer a 'new-information' question. Don't volunteer any information."

Legal Eagle: "If you're not sure, I'll be your legal counsel. You have the right to have a lawyer present when you are being questioned."

Super Decade: "Okay."

Legal Eagle: "The main point is: Don't volunteer ANY information."

Phantom: "He who keeps his mouth keeps his life, but he who opens wide his lips shall have destruction."

Sanhedrin: "Sounds like Proverbs."

Phantom: "It is. So you know the Bible?"

Sanhedrin: "Yes. I'm a Christian, Phantom."

Phantom: "You are? That's great."

Twiggy: "What do you mean by 'Christian'?"

Phantom: "We'll get together, Twiggy: you, me, Super Decade, and Sanhedrin if he wants. And if Legal Eagle wants to join us, he is welcome. We'll describe what the word 'Christian' really means."

Legal Eagle: "I'll take you up on that."

Phantom: "Okay, let's all get together the day after tomorrow."

Super Decade: "How about breakfast at Denny's?"

Twiggy: "I love it."

Phantom: "In Saratoga?"

Sanhedrin: "Sure. I love pancakes."

Legal Eagle: "Okay, let's do it. 10AM. Day after tomorrow."

CHAPTER THIRTY-SIX

May 24, 2026—DAY ONE

It was dawn. A beautiful medley of colors was rising over the mountains to the east. Birds had been chirping for about an hour, their minor-note music stimulating the stomata on the leaves to open up and receive the carbon dioxide needed to effect the process of photosynthesis. One could hear robins, mourning doves, chickadees, and other birds indigenous to the area. The National Guardsmen and women were already awake and ready for action. They were talking excitedly about the mission. They were anxious to get started. Most of them had never seen any active duty before; and they were eager to begin. Some of the soldiers who had seen active duty were excited, but also cautious. They knew the gravity of war. They had seen comrades die. They also knew that anyone who underestimates the enemy puts himself in extreme peril. And the enemy the National Guard was soon to face was fearsome, vicious, and hunted in packs. They were the most dangerous predators one could face because of their speed and their numbers.

Lieutenant Simon Martin had his troops up and ready by 5:45AM. He began with a prayer and a quick reading of Scripture: Psalm 121. He read it from the King James Version:

"I will lift up mine eyes unto the hills, from whence cometh my help.

"My help cometh from the LORD, which made heaven and earth.

"He will not suffer thy foot to be moved: He that keepeth thee will not slumber.

"Behold, He that keepeth Israel shall neither slumber nor sleep.

"The LORD is thy Keeper: the LORD is thy Shade upon thy right hand.

"The sun shall not smite thee by day, nor the moon by night.

"The LORD shall preserve thee from all evil: He shall preserve thy soul.

"The LORD shall preserve thy going out and thy coming in from this time forth, and even for evermore."

Their leader closed the Book and said another prayer, asking God to protect them and bless them, and help them to fulfill this mission. And he thanked God for all He had done for all of them.

All forty of the Platoon members respected Simon's faith; and they paid attention to all of the words read and spoken. Three of the ten men in First Squad were also Christians: Alex, Jose, and Joe. The other seven were favorable to the message of God's love, but had not yet taken the step of receiving the free gift of salvation, namely, the forgiveness of all their sins: past, present, and future—eternal life. Some of them would receive Christ as their Savior during this mission, because it was going to get scary, and they would be forced to think seriously about their own mortality. Death was a definite possibility, because the enemy they were about to face was a mortal enemy.

At 6AM, the entire National Guard as a unit began to move forward. Alex was looking around and saw a lot of Y's and a few Z's in motion. No X's yet. About fifteen minutes into the advance, he could hear gunfire in the distance.

Alex was paired with Max. They were both from Albany; and they had similar backgrounds. Both had lost their fathers at a young age; and both had to become really responsible and help support the family. They were both surprisingly mature; and both were deeply patriotic. And they related to each other as good friends. They understood each other, and could anticipate each other's next move in a complex situation. In training, they were a nearly perfect two-man team, working in tandem almost like one person living in two bodies. Their minds were so well-connected that they worked together almost "as one man". If one of them moved in one direction, the other would automatically cover him. If one needed backup, the other would be right there to help. What one couldn't see, the other would.

The infrared screens which they had, attached to their helmets, were electronic and surprisingly inobtrusive to normal vision. They could see their surroundings clearly, and yet still see the infrared heat signatures of every warm-blooded creature. What they had to watch out for were cold-blooded snakes. Up in the northern Adirondacks especially, there were rattlesnakes. The platoon leaders carried snake-bite kits. The boots the soldiers wore would normally protect them from a poisonous rattlesnake; but a snake could on occasion strike above the top of an army boot. So the soldiers had to be careful.

First Squad consisted of five pairs of soldiers: Alex and Max, Patrick and Al, Jose and Bill, Mike and Donovan, and Mark and Joe. Lieutenant Martin was back and forth, leading them. A half hour into the advance, Simon identified some X's. They had appeared suddenly, out of the west. They were moving at a fast pace, heading towards them. To the left, he heard gunfire. He saw some X's stop; but some others were closing in on some Y's. He realized that there was an entire wolf pack bearing down on just a handful of soldiers.

Larry Rice, the leader of the platoon to the left, was calling Simon for help. Immediately, he ordered his western four, Alex and Max, and Patrick and Al, over towards the action. As he was giving out orders, he saw a couple of Y's get swarmed by at least a dozen X's. "Dear God, please help us!" he prayed.

Alex and Max moved in tandem. They could physically see the wolves moving, they were so close. Alex raised his M-16 and fired, killing a wolf with a quick three-round blast. Max took out his pistol and fired, killing a wolf just fifteen yards away. Patrick fired at a predator which was coming at them from behind, from the south.

"We're being flanked," Alex said to Max.

"Yeah, I know," Max replied.

The four soldiers formed a circle, looking outward and covering every direction. They came across a couple of dead soldiers and warily moved on. They could all see a lot of X's in all directions.

A hail of gunfire was heard in the distant left as other platoons were being attacked by a second wolf pack.

"This is not going well," said Max.

"Just stick with me," Alex said.

Al shouted out, "Wolves coming from the south!"

Jose and Bill, and Mike and Donovan, were running towards them. They planted themselves, and sprayed the forest with gunfire. Mark and Joe and Simon were fifty feet to the right; and they were firing at the pack. The wolves attacked from the south, north, and west simultaneously; and Alex and Max continued firing at them.

"There's so many of them!" Max exclaimed.

Patrick and Al were still firing towards the south, when several wolves broke through and were approaching their red-zone, a ten-yard perimeter.

"Patrick! Al! Turn around!" yelled Alex.

They turned, saw the predators, and reacted with lightning speed. Both fired in unison, killing two of the wolves. But a third broke through, biting Patrick in the right forearm. Another wolf knocked Al down, and ripped into his left thigh. Both soldiers lost the grip on their guns, and were now engaged in hand-to-hand combat. Patrick punched the wolf with his left hand, and Al reached for his knife. Patrick felt the pain as his left hand was being mauled; and Al stabbed his attacker in the eye. The wolf released his grip; and Al impaled him in the neck, killing him. Then he heard Patrick scream; and he fumbled for his pistol. He picked it up and fired at the wolf's chest cavity.

Alex and Max were too busy to help Patrick and Al as they were also under attack. One wolf had broken through; but Alex rolled and dodged the attack, giving Max the time and space to shoot it. Then they shot two more of the creatures at point-blank range. By the time they finished fighting, the damage to Patrick and Al had already been inflicted. Both were wounded, and would have to be sent to a hospital. Alex and Max checked on all sides. No more X's.

Alex called in a Medivac chopper, giving the precise coordinates of their location, and describing as best he could the nature and extent of the injuries. And he also gave them the approximate locations of the dead soldiers in the area. Lieutenant Rice and Staff Sergeant Gregg Winslow had both died defending Fourth Squad, because the squad had been overrun. Second Lieutenant Dan Wells would replace Larry Rice as platoon leader. And the five survivors of the Fourth would remain in the advancing Guard line. One of its members would act as squad leader: Sergeant Robbie Bennett.

Alex thought, "If it's this dangerous only a half hour into the Park, how much worse will it get when we go deeper into this expansive mountain region?"

As the Guard penetrated deeper into the area, gunfire was heard from varied distances. For now, there was no immediate danger nearby for Simon, Alex, Max, and the other thirty-six men left in their platoon.

The rest of the day was mostly uneventful for the Guard. Medivac helicopters removed the dead and injured; and there were DIAC choppers which removed over two hundred dead wolves from the first eighteen miles of the southern Adirondacks. At 9:00PM, the National Guard promptly stopped their advance, and began to set up camp. They had covered eighteen miles in fifteen hours. Their one-hundred-mile-long camp was guarded by sentries all along the line. The leaders teamed up with other leaders; and they used members of their respective squads to stand watch. Two out of each squad, plus a leader, kept watch for three hours. Then another three would keep watch for three hours while the leader slept. Finally, a third group of three would complete the job as sentinels. At any given moment, nearly twelve thousand soldiers were patrolling the wooded areas; and they kept alert, continually watchful for sudden danger.

At the National Guard computer mainframe, Lieutenant General Andre Warner, the Assistant Commander of the New York State National Guard, saw packs of wolves moving towards sectors four-hundred ninety-six through five-hundred and ten. He sounded a warning to the leaders in the area. Simon and his thirty-eight platoon members soon heard the sound of gunfire a half-mile away. All the platoons within a quarter-mile of the breached sectors were on alert. Simon, Alex, and Max were all awake and alert. Then the call came in. Some packs were headed their way. Over a hundred predators. They were only a mile away; and their ETA was about three minutes. Quickly, the Platoons all over the area were getting ready for the incoming attack.

The packs were coming from the northwest. They were hungry and moving fast, about twenty miles an hour. Their night vision was excellent; and they were looking for prey. They were coming, and would destroy everything in their path.

It was a terrifying three-minute wait. They were coming—a group of packs banding together for the purpose of destruction. Suddenly, they appeared on their night-vision-activated screens. Simon commanded his men to climb the nearest trees as fast as they could. They had only seconds left; but they all made it to safety. Now they could pick off the predators from a safe position. Other soldiers climbed trees just in time. But some didn't make it; and they were swarmed. The wolves slaughtered a number of soldiers, because they couldn't shoot them all before they reached them.

Simon, Alex and Max, Jose and Bill, Mike and Donovan, and Mark and Joe, all fired at the super-pack as it approached, passed them, and moved away. A lot of the animals fell; but many of them inevitably made it through the gunfire. Once the animals passed by, Simon ordered First Squad to pursue the surviving animals. It was time to flank the enemy.

"Stay alert! Don't hesitate. And watch your back!" Simon said.

The nine moved south and then eastward, led by Simon and Alex. They swept through the area, eliminating unfriendlies as they went. The whole area looked like the fourth of July as soldiers from every corner fired at the enemy. The predators attacked with reckless abandon, killing more soldiers as they moved eastward. Finally, the number of wolves were diminished enough to effectively manage. A few were left; and they were easily shot down. Once the battle was over, First Squad returned to their original position.

The hundred-mile line of the National Guard had been decimated by roving packs at more than a dozen points. Even the 69th Regiment—a battalion—, the most famous unit in the 27th Brigade, had lost a soldier. And the New York Guard, had lost some soldiers in their 88th and 14th Brigades. Other places in the Guard line had been breached. They were still strong; but they had felt how powerful and dangerous their enemy could be. They had gained a deep respect for, and would not again underestimate, this enemy. They knew they would have to face them for at least five more days. They kept a sharp lookout for the rest of the night, and longed for the sunrise.

CHAPTER THIRTY-SEVEN

May 25, 2026—DAY TWO

Daybreak began; and a weary National Guard began to get ready to move. They could see the devastation of last night's battle. Dozens of soldiers were dead; and hundreds had been wounded. The hundred-mile line would be more sparse as the Adirondack area widened. They were about to be swallowed up by the mountainous area. The line of foot-soldiers resumed their advance.

Jonathan Wilkes, Susan, Marie, Jim, and Jack Leland all met at Denny's restaurant in Saratoga. All were present by 10AM. They exchanged pleasantries; and then Jon said that he wanted to inform them about what was going on.

"As you know," he said, "the National Guard is now about twenty-to-thirty miles north of here, and now about twenty-five miles inside the Adirondack Park. I have good news and bad news."

"Good news first, please," Marie said.

"They killed over seven hundred wolves already. That's about one-seventh of the entire population, and one-fourth of the roaming population."

"About five thousand total?" Jack recapped.

"Yes. If you include wolves just outside the Park area that come and go as they please."

"How many do that?" Marie asked.

"About five hundred," Jon said.

"So, forty-five hundred in the Park, and five hundred just out-side the Park," Jim mused.

"That's correct," Jon said.

"So what…what's the bad news?" Susan asked.

"There has been loss of human life." He paused, and then continued: "Sixty-four bodies of our soldiers have been transported out of there; and two are missing. And there are over four hundred wounded."

All four of them gasped at the numbers. The mood was somber.

"I have to tell you," Jon said in a lugubrious tone, "that this is sickening to me. To see all these men die because of one man's selfish greed. A man who was ALREADY rich to begin with!"

"It shows you just how evil human nature is," Susan agreed.

"I wonder how many more will have to die?" Marie said.

"I hope, none," Susan interjected.

"There's more bad news. The bodies of at least a dozen local residents were discovered, also, during yesterday's military advance."

Jon had to stop and take a drink of water before he could con-tinue. He was losing his composure. He took a big gulp of water, and continued.

"I have to tell you: I don't know how people still staying in the Adirondacks can survive. We all moved out just in time."

Don Krysinski and his wife Debbie had elected to stay in their home about five miles south of Fourth Lake in the southwestern area of the Adirondack Park, way out in the wilderness. In the past two weeks, during the evacuation, they had managed to buy and store a lot of food so they could "hunker down" until this ordeal was over. Their two children were not allowed to go outside. Don figured that the National Guard would easily kill all the wolves in the area, and pass them by about three o'clock in the afternoon. In addition, there were squad cars and military vehicles patrolling the areas. So the Krysinskis felt a false sense of security, a misplaced confidence that they were safe. What they didn't understand was how dangerous the wolves really were, and how vulnerable the house was to attack.

They were eating lunch in the living room, with the curtains to their large picture window wide open. They were watching a gray fox in the distance, through the picture window, walking along through their huge field. All of a sudden, a deer came running out of the forest, heading straight for the fox. The fox bolted out of the way; the deer passed the fox, and continued towards the house.

"Wow!" said Lori. "The deer is running straight for us."

"I'm sure he'll stop," Debbie said.

"Stop, deer. Stop!" Lori ordered.

Her twin-brother Tony just stared at the animal, with his mouth open and his eyes real wide. He didn't know what to think.

The deer was just eighty feet away and still coming.

Don gasped and pulled Tony away from the picture window. Debbie grabbed Lori, and started to carry her towards the hallway.

The deer leapt. Debbie screamed as she watched the doe crash through the glass. It was amazing and frightening at the same time. But it was nothing compared to what happened next.

The deer stood up and looked confused. It was stunned, and didn't know where to go.

"Keep away from the deer, Tony," Don warned.

Suddenly, a large pack of wolves emerged out of the forest. The Krysinskis all watched, frozen for a few seconds.

Then Don said, "To the cellar! Quick!"

They scrambled past the deer, and went down into the cellar. The wolves invaded the house, and killed the stunned doe right in the living room. Then they ate ravenously.

"What do we do now?" Debbie asked.

"We're safe here," Don said.

"Shouldn't we call for help?"

"We're not supposed to be here. I think we should just wait for the National Guard. They should pass this way in a few hours."

"Well, we have everything we need down here. Even video-games for the kids."

"We sure have plenty of food," Don said.

"We're safe here. Right?" Debbie said, looking for confirmation.

"Yes, we're very safe."

"We have to watch that Lori and Tony don't unlock the cellar door and let the wolves down here. We've got to watch them at all times."

"It's okay. I have a special dead-bolt at the top of the door. And believe me, I bolted it. And it's a really strong door."

The wolves were roaming all over the house. Some of them tried to get into the cellar; but they could not break through the cellar door to get to the human prey.

The Krysinskis hoped that the National Guard would get there soon.

Jonathan Wilkes and the other four all placed their orders for breakfast. Then Jon took another sip of coffee and began.

"I told you, Marie—and Jack—that I would tell you what a Christian is."

"I'm all ears, Jonathan," Marie said.

"I'm listening, too," said Jack.

"A Christian is simply someone who has accepted the only Answer to his sin-problem," Jon said.

"What do you mean?" Marie asked.

"To be a Christian, one must first see that he—or she—is a sinner with a serious need for forgiveness. Without forgiveness, we only have one option—to end up in Hell forever. And I have to say: Who in his right mind would want to burn eternally?"

"If Hell is real, that's really scary," Marie said.

"If Hell is real," Jack said, "then I'm in a lot of trouble."

"We were ALL in a lot of trouble," Jon said. "But God loves us, and provided a way out: a way to escape Hell."

"I was taught that Jesus died for the whole world," said Marie.

"So was I," said Jack. "But you're saying that we are not automatically saved by that. Right?"

"Right. Our sins were placed on Jesus—so many sins that the Bible says that Jesus BECAME sin. Sin is what God judges. If my sin is still connected to me, I will be judged with and for my sin. So I needed to have my sins taken away. That's why they were placed on Christ. God ALWAYS judges sin. Sin was connected to Christ and judged. Christ experienced suffering and death, being under and experiencing the judgment for sin. If we accept Jesus as our Savior, then the judgment for our sin is already experienced FOR US by Jesus Christ when He suffered and died for our sins.

"So we have the choice. Will we stay connected to our sins and be judged with and for our sins, or will we accept and believe the fact that Jesus became connected to our sins when they were placed on Him, and that He was judged with and for our sins?"

"What do you mean when you say that we need to have our sins taken away?" Marie asked.

"Sin is either connected to us, or we accept it as having been connected to Christ. If it is connected to Christ, then it is disconnected or removed from us. It is then judged with Christ at His death; and once our sin is judged, WE cannot be judged by God, because our sin is GONE: disconnected, removed, taken away forever.

"Another way to describe it is that when we are connected to our sins, we have to pay the price, an infinite DEBT, for all those sins. Romans 6:23 says, 'For the wages of [or payment for] sin is death, but the gift of God is eternal life through Jesus Christ our Lord.'

"There is no such thing as DOUBLE JEOPARDY with God. Either WE pay the debt, or CHRIST does. If we refuse to accept HIS payment (death on the cross) for our sins, then we will have to accept OUR payment (an eternity in Hell) for our sins. The death of Christ is the gift of God, the payment for our sins, reducing our debt to ZERO."

"So how do we get our debt to zero?" Marie asked.

"I know I've been wordy, but I wanted to really explain what a Christian really is," Jon said.

"Okay, I understand," said Marie.

"We get our debt to zero by accepting His payment for our sins and reaching out and receiving it by faith. At that point, we are forgiven of (released from) our debt. We no longer will have to pay for our sins, because the payment is made FOR US. We no longer are going to HELL, because our debt is FORGIVEN. That's what forgiveness of sins is: forgiveness of our debt of all our sins—past, present, and future."

"I want that forgiveness," said Marie, with tears welling up in her eyes.

"I have never heard it explained like that before," said Jack. "So if I get it right, Jesus SUBSTITUTED His payment for ours."

"Exactly right. He suffered, bled, and died as our SUBSTITUTE—punished IN OUR PLACE. That's why the Bible says, 'Christ died for our sins'."

"Now," Jon continued, "you know that He rose from the dead. Right?"

"Yes, I believe that," Jack said.

"So do I," said Marie.

"Are you enjoying everything?" the waitress asked.

"Yes, very much," Jon said. "Thank you."

Jon continued, "Jesus had to be God if He was going to be our Savior. Jesus said He had the POWER to lay down His life, and the POWER to raise Himself up from the dead. Only GOD has power over death. Jesus also said He had the POWER to forgive sins. Only GOD has that power."

"I see," Marie said. "So Jesus is not just a man. He's GOD, too."

"That's right, Marie," Jon said. "John 1 says that Jesus was and is God. And that He became a man. He became a man so He could have a mortal body to suffer and die for us."

"That makes sense to me," Jack said.

"I see it," Marie said.

"Now that you have heard and understood this, I'd like to lead you both in a prayer that you can say to God. Would you like to talk to God and receive His free gift of forgiveness?"

"Sure. I want to go to Heaven," Marie said.

"I sure don't want to go to Hell," said Jack.

"Let's pray," Jon said. "Feel free to pray with me. Remember, this is YOUR prayer to God."

He began slowly, so that they could pray with understanding, and not just be repeating words mindlessly:

"Dear Jesus, I'm sorry for all of my sins. Please forgive me for all of my sins—past, present, and future. I believe You suffered and died for me. You were judged and punished for MY sins. And I believe You rose from the dead. I pray that You will save me from eternal punishment in Hell. Lord Jesus, I invite You to come into my life. Please give me that free gift of forgiveness and a future in Heaven forever. Thank You for forgiving all my sins—past, present, and future. Amen."

Marie could feel a joy she had never known, flooding inside of her. She was ecstatic. "Wow! I just feel so happy! I can see that He is in my life forever."

Jack said, "I feel different, too."

"Did you receive the gift of forgiveness?" Jon asked.

"Yes," Marie said.

"Yes, I did," said Jack.

"The Bible says, 'For whosoever shall call upon the name of the Lord shall be saved.' Romans 10:13. You called on Jesus' name; and therefore you are saved."

"I believe it," Jack said.

"So do I," said Marie.

"I'm so happy for you both," Susan said.

"Me too," said Jim.

The waitress cleared the table and refilled their coffee cups. Then she asked them if they wanted to order anything else. They said 'No thanks'; and she left to get their check.

"Let's take a moment to pray for the safety of all of the National Guardsmen and police officers in the Adirondacks," said Marie.

"Great idea, Marie," Susan said. "And let's pray for all of the people who are still in their homes up there."

They all bowed their heads, and Jon prayed out loud.

Don and Debbie Krysinski and their two children had been trapped for over two hours in their cellar. The pack of wolves was still roaming around the house, while the trapped family huddled together. They could see the wolves outside the miniature cellar windows, which were at ground level. These windows were too small for a wolf to crawl through. But watching them try to get through these windows was still a scary sight. Other wolves were pounding on the cellar door, but it wouldn't give. Even though the Krysinskis were safe, they were still terrified. Suddenly, they heard the sound of gunfire.

Simon, Alex, and Max fired with pinpoint accuracy at the wolves outside the southern mini-windows. They then trained their guns through the picture window. Jose and Bill advanced to the right, towards the eastern side of the house.

Simon, Alex, and Max advanced left to the western side of the house. No wolves there. They continued their advance, pistols ready to fire, and approached the northern side of the house. They turned the corner and saw some wolves gathered near the tiny ground-level basement windows. They were trying to dig under them, but all they met with was a cement wall. The three soldiers opened fire and quickly eliminated them. Then they prepared to enter the house, while Jose and Bill stood watch outside. Simon opened the western door; and a wolf charged towards him. He fired his pistol and hit it in the left shoulder, and also right inside its snout and out the back of its throat. It collapsed with a gurgling sound.

They could hear the sound of another wolf inside the house somewhere.

"There he is," said Simon. "I'll get him."

He could see the wolf—one which had survived the shooting earlier through the picture window—walking around, disoriented. Simon put him down with a shot to the brain.

Alex and Max went through the house, making sure there were no more wolves left alive. They killed two wolves which were near the cellar door. All unfriendlies were now dead, according to their infrared-activated screens. No more X's in sight.

"Is it safe yet?" Don Krysinski asked.

"Yes, for now," Alex said.

"I suggest you leave this house," Simon said. "Dangerous animals are roaming the area."

"But I thought you were killing them all."

"It's a lot harder than you think. I would leave if I were you."

"Oh…Alright," he said.

The soldiers escorted him and his family to his Chevy truck, and then headed north.

The National Guard troops continued their advance north, fighting valiantly as they went. By 9:00PM, they were thirty-eight miles into the Adirondack Park. They were sixty-two miles south of Mountain Meadow. And now they were stationary and on the alert for sudden danger. They knew that they could be in for another nightmare.

Staff Sergeant Mark O'Connell was the leader of Third Squad, in the Fourth Platoon, near the western edge of 3rd Brigade. They were about eight miles west of Simon Martin's Platoon. Mark was a courageous leader. He and his squad had fought off a pack of thirty-plus wolves. They had been in an area that isolated them from the other squads. Quickly, they climbed on trees and a couple of houses, and kept firing until they killed them all. Like Simon, Mark knew that they had to attack such a large pack from a position of safety.

They had also fought off a couple of other wolf attacks; and in both of these cases, they literally pursued the wolves on foot. And Mark O'Connell personally led the charge both times. Twice, he risked his life to save some of his squad, killing several wolves at close-range and fighting off a wolf that charged him by sidestepping it, rolling left, kicking it in the chest, and then throwing his knife into its heart. Then he quickly reloaded a clip into his empty pistol in time to shoot two more predators. In all of these incidents, nobody in the squad, including Mark O'Connell, received even a scratch.

Eight of the squad were sleeping while three were on guard. All of a sudden, two Z's appeared: two large Z's. They were coming from the north and moving in a circular motion. They would move next to each other and then separate. Over and over again, this happened. Staff Sergeant O'Connell thought to himself, "A fight. A good one." This was going to be a sight to behold. Soon, the growls, the roars, and the crashing of branches became audible as the fight moved closer. The noise got louder and louder as the ferocious battle continued.

Jeremy and Terence were on guard with Sergeant O'Connell. As the mini-battle came closer, they could identify the roars of a mountain lion and a black bear. The soldiers were not under orders to kill these animals; so they moved to safety and let the battle pass through their camp. The lion was massive! "It must be over two hundred pounds!" thought Mark. And the black bear was a small adult, about two hundred and fifty pounds. The combatants were evenly matched; so finally, after another five minutes, both animals gave up and went their separate ways. Neither animal had posed a threat to the soldiers during the fight. And once they separated, they simply moved on, southward.

Suddenly, Jeremy and Terence and their NCO detected a group of X's. O'Connell ordered his troops to rise up and get ready. It was another super-pack. It looked like at least sixty wolves; and so NCO O'Connell ordered his men to climb the nearby trees and wait. The other nearby squads were alerted and also prepared for battle, taking positions of safety. This time, the National Guard was ready. In three minutes, there were fusillades of bullets raining down on the hapless predators, picking them off like ducks in a shooting gallery. The National Guard was winning!

During the rest of the night, there were other attacks. O'Connell's squad could hear gunfire in the distance. So could Simon Martin's Platoon.

Some parts of the line were not attacked; other parts were. Also, patrols of squad cars and military vehicles eliminated some of the wolves as they encroached on or near the roadways, whenever they came within range of their gunfire.

CHAPTER THIRTY-EIGHT

May 26, 2026—DAY THREE

The National Guard had faced an enemy for forty-eight hours now, had eliminated fourteen hundred of them, and was preparing for the third day's advance. All over the hundred-mile line, soldiers were gathering up their equipment, eating rations, talking with their partners, and getting psyched-up for the next leg of their perilous journey. Never before in recorded history had an army of 50,000 been deployed for such a purpose as theirs was: to eliminate a huge predatory population which was threatening the lives of millions of civilians. This task was proving to be a daunting one; and many of the soldiers were praying for God's hand of protection. They had seen on the first day how devastating the enemy was, and had adjusted well on the second day; but they had acquired a healthy fear towards this foe, knowing that any hesitation in this epic battle could mean the difference between life and death.

The embedded reporters had all survived so far. The soldiers had protected them from danger, sometimes putting their own lives at risk in the process.

Bernie Stansford, the cameraman assigned to Simon's Second Platoon, had been busily talking with the soldiers whenever there was time. He recorded the conversations so that he would be able to use them in a documentary planned for the first week in July. There would be special reports and many interviews on national TV from the present-day and through the month of June. The documentary would be scheduled as a summary of the entire operation—one which was fundamentally unique: a seven-day war against an enemy which consisted, not of elements of humanity, but of the animal kingdom. This would be a documentary which would consist of the entire panorama of events, and of the participants in those events. It would give an account of the thoughts, words, and actions of the soldiers, and even their emotions, their attitudes, their motivation and drive to continue on to complete the mission: to "see this thing through".

He had discovered that most of Second Platoon was comprised of "city boys"—thirty of them. The rest were from rural areas: eleven of them, including Lieutenant Simon Martin. As they were setting up the perimeter, before they had begun the advance, Bernie had interviewed all forty-one members of the platoon. He had started with Lieutenant Martin, then Alex Warfield and his partner Max Williams, then Patrick and Al, and had continued on, moving through all four squads systematically. Then, once the advance into the wilderness began, he reported on the events of the first two days. He reported that Day One was filled with a lot of danger, while Day Two had relative calm, because they were more prepared.

Now Day Three had arrived; and with it came uncertainty. Would it turn out to be tragic like Day One, or victorious like Day Two?

They were thirty-eight miles into this massive wilderness known as the Adirondack Park. They were able to travel about twenty miles a day, because they could navigate around the mountains which were difficult or impossible to climb. And some mountains were partly navigable; and so the soldiers would normally traverse the lower parts of these mountains rather than the higher elevations located at or near the peaks. The advanced GPS would scan the higher elevations and alert the National Guard of any wolves detected in those areas. Most of the wolves stayed on the lower and easily accessible parts of the mountains, and at ground-level. In many cases, mountains were shown by the advanced GPS to be completely devoid of wolves; and the Guard could simply walk around these mountains if it was quicker to do so. Most of the time, the Guard would walk around the mountains or trek over the lower parts of the mountains, avoiding the higher elevations altogether.

Yet sometimes wolves were detected on a mountain. Then the Guard would have to "sweep the area" and destroy them. Since the wolves were abnormally aggressive, they would invariably attack the soldiers, and consequently become targets of their guns. Once the "sweep" was completed, the soldiers would reform their part of the hundred-mile line. The GPS assigned to each one of the soldiers helped keep that line from total chaos by reuniting them after they took separate detours over and around mountains. The advanced GPS would instruct the soldiers' individually-issued GPS's to guide each soldier back into their proper relative positions within that hundred-mile line. The advanced GPS was constantly scanning and tracking all of the soldiers in relation to one another, tying together the locations of the soldiers in "real-time" with the sectors of the Adirondack Park through its satellite imagery.

The National Guard had covered eighteen miles on Day One because their GPS capability was tied in with Jonathan Wilkes' advanced GPS. The advanced GPS literally instructed the soldiers "step-by-step" where to go, based on the continually-updated surveillance system of the National Guard computer mainframe. Then on Day Two, the Guard advanced twenty miles.

Now on Day Three, they were about to advance another twenty-two miles, because they would not meet with much resistance by wolf packs rampaging through their advancing units. A few small skirmishes occurred; and the small number of wolves involved were quickly destroyed. It was an eerily quiet day; and some of the soldiers wondered if they were in the "calm before the storm", like the eye of a hurricane. Some wondered if maybe the wolf population was regrouping. Would there be a sudden "all-out attack"? Other soldiers were just happy to not have to face danger like they had done during the first two days. And the most optimistic of the National Guardsmen and women took the time to actually enjoy the sights and sounds of this peripatetic adventure. They could hear frogs croaking, crickets chirping, and grasshoppers making their constant musical sound. An occasional woodpecker could be heard drumming away on a tree in the distance, looking for insects inside the tree-trunk. Various species of birds perched in the branches of trees above them. Occasionally, one could hear the scream of a bobcat or the hooting of a black bear in the distance. Military vehicles and squad cars could be seen and heard at various times throughout the day. The sporadic wind made a gentle noise as it rustled the leaves of trees and brush. And the scent of flowers was in the air.

A few deer could be seen in fields, grazing. Chipmunks, squirrels, ducks, and wild turkeys were seen, as well as other small wildlife. It was a beautiful day to be alive and hiking through the Adirondacks.

Bernie was enjoying the intrinsic beauty of this wilderness expanse. He had grown up in Queens, and then lived most of his adult life in Manhattan. He had longed for this journalistic assignment for two reasons. He loved adventure. He craved a life of action. In the city, he felt boxed-in. But outdoors, he felt free!

Secondly, he loved the beauty of the outdoors. In the city, there was so much ugliness. Life was insipid to him in such a setting. In fact, it was downright depressing! So when he could get into a serious outdoor setting, his mood would change from miasmic to cheerful as quickly as a Porsche can go from zero to sixty miles an hour. This was a welcome metamorphosis, a psychological boost which gave him more energy than a whole case of Red Bull energy drinks. He would happily interview people for the rest of his life in this kind of environment. While he was here, he totally immersed himself into these surroundings and refused to think about the city and all the drugs, violence, immorality, and other filth that resided there. He blotted them out like a distant memory, and replaced them with the beauty of God's creation.

He took a few minutes to review that first interview with Lieutenant Simon Martin.

Bernie: "Please state your name and rank."
Simon: "Simon A. Martin, First Lieutenant..."
Bernie: "How old are you, Lieutenant, and how long have you been in the National Guard?"

Simon: "I am thirty-one, and I have been in the National Guard for thirteen years."

Bernie: "I have been told you are a decorated war hero. Can you tell me about that?"

Simon: "I really don't think of myself as a hero, although I have been awarded such things as the Purple Heart and the Congressional Medal of Honor."

Bernie: "How did you become what many consider a war hero?"

Simon: "I was a Staff Sergeant leading my squad into a strategic area of northern Iran, on the outskirts of Hamadan. I was shot in the left arm and captured by their version of the Republican Guard."

Bernie: "So you were advancing towards Tehran?"

Simon: "Yes."

Bernie: "So what happened next?"

Simon: "I saw unbelievable tortures. Some prisoners they left alone. But others they tortured without mercy. I don't even want to describe to you what they did to some of our brothers-and-sisters-in-arms."

Bernie: "Did they torture you?"

Simon: "Yes; and I have the scars to prove it."

Bernie: "I know this must be upsetting to you, but I just feel the need to ask. How many people did you see tortured?"

Simon: "Hundreds. It was awful." (Sobs uncontrollably for a full minute) "They even tortured their own people—torturing them, and using them as human shields. Some of them they killed, and placed them at the scenes of Allied bombing sorties to make it look like they were killed by the Allied forces."

Bernie: "Like in Libya back in 2011?"

Simon: "Yes."

Bernie: "Do you want to continue this interview now, or would you like to wait a while?"

Simon: "I want to do it now. The world needs to hear the truth."

Bernie: "I heard they starved you. Is that true?"

Simon: "From day one they starved us. By the time the Special Forces unit rescued us, in October of 2024, there was not one of us who weighed even a hundred pounds. It was like a German World War Two concentration camp."

Bernie: "How many soldiers were imprisoned with you?"

Simon: "About eighty. But by October of that year, after nine months of starvation and torture, twenty-six of us were still alive."

Bernie: "How did you survive?"

Simon: "By the grace of God. I prayed literally all the time I was awake. I will not lie: I was scared to death that at any moment they would take me and torture me. And sometimes they did. And I prayed to God to keep me from screaming; and somehow my body endured the awful pain they inflicted."

Bernie: "Did you scream?"

Simon: "A few times, but not much."

Bernie: "How about the others?"

Simon: "Most of them a lot. And when they did, they would hurt them even worse."

Bernie: "You're a brave man: a true patriot. And you ARE a hero!"

Simon: "I am who I am: no more, no less."

Bernie: "How would you compare this war? Humans versus wolves?"

Simon: "Much different, because the enemy is so different."

Bernie: "In what way?"

Simon: "This enemy takes no prisoners and acts by instinct rather than hatred."

Bernie: "Anything else?"

Simon: "This war will be quicker. But we have to be alert. In some ways this enemy is more dangerous; in other ways, less. They have no weapons outside of their own predatory powers. But their predatory powers are so great, we must kill them before they can reach us and inflict damage."

Bernie: "Can you assess any advantage they have?"

Simon: "They are much faster than we are. We cannot outrun them. They are very powerful. And they hunt mostly in packs, making them even more deadly. They will attack us from all different directions at once if they can."

Bernie: "Please describe your advantages over them?"

Simon: "We can detect them on our infrared helmet screens as far away as three hundred yards. This gives us a little extra time to prepare. But we also have a surveillance setup that warns us of their approach while they are still miles away. If we use both of these tools wisely, we have a good chance of killing them without casualties on our side."

Bernie: "What other advantages?"

Simon: "We have the long-range weapons. They don't. But if they get too close and get through our gunfire, then we are in for some real trouble."

Bernie: "Hand-to-hand combat?"

Simon: "That's right. An up-close encounter with wolves could be disastrous."

Bernie: "Do you think that will happen?"

Simon: "Yes, absolutely. And way more often than people expect or think."

Bernie: "Why do you say that?"

Simon: "Because that's the way war is. War plays out on ITS terms, not ours. War is ugly. There is nothing pretty about war. I hate war. I'd rather avoid war. But sometimes it is necessary."

Bernie: "So you consider this a war, just like the Iranian and Yemeni wars?"

Simon: "Yes."

Bernie: "Thank you, Lieutenant, for your time. Any other comments or thoughts you want to add?"

Simon: "I am a believer in Christ. My prayer is that God will protect our military units, and that many of our soldiers will be challenged in the next seven days to consider their own mortality and their need to receive God's gift of salvation, of total forgiveness."

Bernie: "Well-said. Thank you very much, Lieutenant Martin."

Simon: "Thank you."

Bernie had been profoundly affected by this interview. He was amazed at the utter transparency and sincerity of this seasoned veteran. He was not ashamed to say he believed in Jesus Christ. He was not a coward by any stretch of the imagination; and Bernie respected that. In fact, he would look into this issue further, because he knew this man's faith was REAL! He would talk with him again and ask him about it. He felt a conviction, a need to know more. He knew that something was missing in his own life; and maybe—just maybe—he had stumbled onto it in this interview.

But for now, he would continue to interview other soldiers. He interviewed Alex for the second time. During this second interview, he chose to concentrate on his past experiences rather than on the war at hand.

Bernie: "Please state your name and rank."

Alex: "Alex Warfield, Staff Sergeant, First Squad, Second Platoon, Company B, Fifth Battalion, Third Brigade, 42nd Division, New York National Guard."

Bernie: "Please tell me about your past. Where did you live as a child growing up, and what was it like?"

Alex: "I grew up in Albany. My mother worked at the Marriott Hotel on Wolf Road, and my father worked on a construction crew. They were both hard workers; and for the first ten years of my life, our family of eight was well-fed."

Bernie: "Then what happened?"

Alex: "My father, after twelve years of not drinking, came home stone-drunk one night and started beating us. We loved our father and asked him to stop. We did not fight back. Finally, he stopped and passed out."

Bernie: "Go on."

Alex: "My dad continued to drink, and kept being violent towards us. So one day my mom, Chrissie, picked us all up from school and took us all south to her aunt's house in Poughkeepsie. We lived there for a year; and then my father begged her to return."

Bernie: "Did she?"

Alex: "Yes."

Bernie: "Was everything okay?"

Alex: "For a while, Dad stayed sober. But after a few months he began coming home drunk again. And he was always really mean when he was wasted."

Bernie: "What happened?"

Alex: "After a couple of month's abuse, my mother couldn't take it anymore."

Bernie: "What did she do?"

Alex: "She said she was going to stand up to him."

Bernie: "How so?"

Alex: "When he came home that night, she confronted him. She told him, 'Don't you dare lay a hand on me or any of our children!'"

Bernie: "How did he react to that?"

Alex: "He said, 'Oh yeah? And what are you going to do about it?' And he went into the kitchen and grabbed a sharp knife."

Bernie: "Then what did he do?"

Alex: "He grabbed me and put the blade of the knife across my throat."

Bernie: "This sounds like a stupid question. Were you scared?"

Alex: "Terrified. I thought I was going to die. And I knew I wasn't ready to die."

Bernie: "Why do you say that?"

Alex: "I knew I would go straight to Hell."

Bernie: "So—what happened next?"

Alex: "My father said, 'You can't stop me! I can kill every one of you if I want!' Then he laughed, and threw me down on the floor to his left."

Bernie: "Then what?"

Alex: "He came towards Mom."

Bernie: "Yes?"

Alex: "She backed away, and told us all to go to our rooms, and lock ourselves in. And she asked me to call 911."

Bernie: "I have to ask you why you didn't report the abuse earlier."

Alex: "Dad threatened to kill us if we ever ratted on him. He said the minute he got out of prison he would hunt us down."

Bernie: "What about your teachers? Didn't they see bruises on you and your siblings?"

Alex: "In the two months he abused us, he made sure he hurt us in places the authorities wouldn't see."
Bernie: "He never punched you in the face?"
Alex: "Never."
Bernie: "Getting back to the story, what happened next?"
Alex: (breathing heavily) "I dialed 911 and watched my mom. She backed up to the fireplace, and grabbed the poker."
Bernie: "I can see this is upsetting you. Do you want me to stop?"
Alex: "No, I'll continue."
Bernie: "Okay."
Alex: "She asked him to put the knife down."
Bernie: "Did he?"
Alex: "No."
Bernie: "What did he do?"
Alex: (breathing heavily) "He lunged at her with the knife."
Bernie: "What did your mother do?"
Alex: "She swung at him with the poker."
Bernie: "Did she hit him?"
Alex: "Yes. She hit him on the left side of the head, and he went down."
Bernie: "Was he dead?"
Alex: "No. I thought he was, but he got up."
Bernie: "Then what?"
Alex: "He was enraged. I had never seen my father this angry before."
Bernie: "Yes?"
Alex: "He charged at my mother, and pushed her so violently into the hearth of the fireplace that she fell down, unconscious."
Bernie: "Then what?"
Alex: "He picked up the knife he had dropped, and raised it up above my mother. Then he said, 'I'm going to enjoy doing this, Chrissie.'"

Bernie could see that Alex was reliving what was probably the most traumatic experience he had ever had in his life. Alex was breathing heavily, and in rapid succession, and shaking like a leaf. But he continued the interview, believing that Alex needed to tell his story.

Bernie: "Please continue, Sergeant."

Alex: "I ran to where the poker had fallen out of my mom's hand. I picked it up. And I raised it up to hit Dad. He didn't see me behind him."

Bernie: "What happened, Alex?"

Alex: (in a nervous, tight voice, and with tears in his eyes) "I killed him….I killed him."

Bernie: "I'm at a loss for words. I am so sorry."

Alex: "I know I did the right thing, but it still hurts. I had to save my mother."

Bernie: "I'm sure she is grateful."

Alex: "She is. She woke up and she hugged me. That's when the police officers arrived."

Bernie: "They must have questioned the both of you."

Alex: "For over an hour, they questioned everyone but my one-year-old youngest brother, Zach."

Bernie: "I won't ask about all the details, and what your father's side of the family did, unless you want to divulge any information."

Alex: "Most of them knew what my father was like when he drank, and understood we were defending ourselves. But a few of his relatives were angry and bitter, and wanted to take us to court."

Bernie: "You and your mother?"

Alex: "Yes. Both our prints were on that poker."

Bernie: "So, what happened?"

Alex: "There were separate trials for each of us, and we were acquitted of all charges."

Bernie: "I'm glad about that, but sorry to hear that you had to suffer the indignity of a trial."

Alex: "I'm over it, because God has replaced the sorrow, and all the anger and hatred with a love I never knew before. A year after my father's death, I found the Answer, and it is Jesus Christ my Lord and Savior."

Bernie continued to interview Alex, and found out that he had continued to go to a public school in Albany, and had to be tough and motivated to endure all the bad kids, drugs, gangs, and immorality that were prevalent there. He survived all of those bad influences, and joined the National Guard. He said he loved his country, and would die for the freedoms it provides for its citizens.

When Bernie interviewed Max, he discovered that Max had the luxury of having two loving parents who spent time with him, and motivated him to do well in school and stay away from all the bad kids, drugs, gangs, and immorality. His mother was a full-time "stay-at-home mom", and his dad was an investment-firm manager.

Two weeks after Max's fourteenth birthday, his father died in an airplane crash on a routine business trip. Max was devastated; but his mother was a strong woman, and helped him get through the emotional trauma. The very next year, she remarried. Her new husband, Derek Howard, was a very understanding and compassionate man: very much like Max's real father. He showed Max love and support. And when Max threw a tantrum and screamed at his "replacement Dad", he calmly sat down with Max and told him he knew he could never replace his father. He only wanted to show love and respect to the both of them. Max understood then that this man was genuine. And from that day on, they were close. Derek did a lot of things with his new "son", and supported Max in his activities.

Max loved playing sports; and he was good at it. He really excelled in basketball, with a seventy-five percent accuracy from the "field". He led his high school team to a state championship in his Junior year, and to the State Finals the next year. But he became really sick, and couldn't play in the final game. The team lost the Final by three points.

During his illness he decided to join the National Guard. A few months later, a fully-recovered Max Williams signed up. And both of his parents fully supported him, and told him they were proud to have "such a fine son".

Max met Alex at "boot camp", and they "hit it off" really well. They had both grown up in Albany, but had had very different childhoods. As best friends, they complemented each other. They worked so well together in the training exercises that the instructors joked that they must be "sharing the same brain". And now here they were, on a mission that would test them, and HAD tested them already.

So far, they had passed the test; but there were still four days left to complete this mission.

Bernie continued his interviews. Suddenly, he received the electronic warning. A pack of wolves was heading their way.

Jose and Bill pointed to a large rock formation which they could climb and defend. Bernie was with them; and they headed to the rocks, which were to the north and slightly east of them. They had been told they had about eight minutes to get ready for the encounter, which was plenty of time. They saw a place where they could easily climb: a narrow path in between two huge rocks. A few trees grew on top of this big rocky hill; and they could see that this was a great lookout spot. It would be easy to pick off anything that came into view from there. The three of them quickly climbed it, and waited. Soon, the X's appeared on their screens.

It was business as usual. Jose and Bill shot and killed eight out of twenty wolves that came into their sight. Bernie marveled at how they aimed slightly ahead of their targets and made kill-shots almost every time.

Mike and Donovan were stationed southeast of them, and thinned out the pack numbers, eliminating several of them. Then Mark and Joe shot several more, leaving only a couple of predators still alive.

That small skirmish was all that Second Platoon would face on this day. A few other small incidents took place along the hundred-mile line of soldiers, but nothing serious. There were no human casualties on this third day.

At 9:00, the National Guard stopped the advance. They were now sixty miles into the Adirondacks, past the midpoint of this massive state park. They were forty miles south of Mountain Meadow.

The night was a peaceful one. Only four sections of the hundred-mile line were attacked. And none of the attacks were large in scale. They were easily put down; and for most of the night, things were peaceful and quiet. The Guard slept well on night three.

CHAPTER THIRTY-NINE

May 27, 2026—DAY FOUR

At 6:00 AM, an energized National Guard resumed the advance. The soldiers had received their "second wind", and were ready for action. But there would be more talk and interviews again today than action. Some of the soldiers began to wonder again, as they did yesterday, what was going on. Were the wolves retreating? Were they drawing them into a trap? Were they regrouping? What would happen next?

Bernie continued his incessant interviews; and on a boring day like this—an uneventful day—the soldiers of Second Platoon were happy to comply. He decided to ask them a little about their hopes and dreams, what they thought about this war, and what they had experienced so far in this military campaign.

Bernie: "Please state your name and rank."

Lashaun: "Lashaun Michaels, Private First Class, Second Squad, Second Platoon..."

Bernie: "What do you want to accomplish in your life?"

Lashaun: "I want to make a difference in the world. I want to show people that they do not need to get involved in drugs and gangs and all the bad things out there."

Bernie: "How do you plan to do that?"

Lashaun: "I plan to tell my story. I plan to write a book; and I will tell them about the forces of good and the forces of evil. People need to choose the good."

Bernie: "Have you started writing yet?"

Lashaun: "Yes, I have. I have written over a hundred pages of my story; and I write whenever something comes to mind."

Bernie: "Any other plans?"

Lashaun: "I am planning to go to St. John's University and get a degree in Counseling. I want to be a high school Guidance Counselor, and help as many lives as I can."

Bernie: "Anything else?"

Lashaun: "I plan to work with the parents of those kids I counsel: to get them to see their kids in a realistic way, and get them to set goals and build relationships with their children. Most parents I know don't have a clue about their own kids. It's pathetic."

Bernie: "You are very thoughtful and wise for a person your age."

Lashaun: "I don't think I'm wise. I just believe in plain old-fashioned common sense. If people used it, the world in which we live would be a much better place."

Bernie: "Thank you very much. You are so right, Lashaun."

Lashaun: "Thank you."

Bernie: "So what do you think about this war?"

Lashaun: "It's a job we have to do. It's not pretty; but we are here to save lives."

Bernie: "What have been your experiences so far?"

Lashaun: "We've been attacked several times. The first hour of Day One was pretty intense. Wolves were everywhere; and we were not used to the enemy; and some of us were caught off-guard. But we adjusted well after that."

Bernie: "Any close calls for you?"

Lashaun: "I got up a tree just in time on Day One."

Bernie: "Can you elaborate?"

Lashaun: "Yes. We got the warning suddenly. We heard gunfire to the west of us, and got an electronic warning from Lieutenant Martin. Being the first hour, we didn't expect such a sudden and immediate attack out of the north. After that happened, we were much more prepared and vigilant; but that first attack slipped through the cracks in the system."

Bernie: "Tell me more."

Lashaun: "We had been advancing for about half an hour when we suddenly heard rounds of gunfire and got a warning from our platoon leader. At the same time, our screens suddenly filled up with X's. They were numerous, and moving quickly. We were in the middle of a huge field, and the nearest trees were in front of us, to the north. We ran towards these trees. We knew time was running out."

Bernie: "And your whole squad made it."

Lashaun: "Yes."

Bernie: "Please continue."

Lashaun: "We were almost to the trees when we saw the wolves coming at us. They came out of the woods about a hundred and fifty yards north of us. We were still about thirty yards away from the trees, and we strained to get there before the wolves did."

Bernie: "Yes?"

Lashaun: "One of our guys got stuck on the sharp edge of a dead branch, and I quickly freed him. He scurried up that tree and yelled, 'Look out!' I pulled myself up that tree so fast I thought I was flying. When I looked down, I saw a half-dozen wolves looking up at me. And they looked really hungry!"

Bernie: "That was close!"

Lashaun: "I was THAT close to death!"

Bernie: "What happened next?"

Lashaun: "We began shooting them."

Bernie: "Did you get them all?"

Lashaun: "No, but we got a lot of them."

Bernie: "Then what happened?"

Lashaun: "Once it was safe to come down, we left our position and continued north. And we heard that two of our First Squad had been injured. And we heard that the platoon to our left had taken a tragic hit."

Bernie: "I felt badly when some of your comrades were killed."

Lashaun: "It made me angry. Very angry!"

Bernie: "I'm with you on that one."

Lashaun: "We're going to beat these creatures!"

Bernie: "Yes, we are."

Lashaun: "This is a real war; and we're going to win it!"
Bernie: "I'm with you, Lashaun. I'm with you. Thank you for your
time."

Bernie could see the flash of anger in Lashaun's eyes. He could
see how much he wanted to fight. And he had seen anger in the eyes
of several other soldiers when the subject of casualties came up. They
would make this enemy—these chemically-altered, non-human
combatants—pay the price; and that price would be extermination.
The National Guard was more motivated than ever to eliminate this
predatory threat, this ecological nightmare. They were all looking
forward to Day Seven, when the very heart of this invasive wolf population would be blasted into oblivion.

Bernie interviewed more of the Second Squad, and then moved
on to Third Squad. The third soldier he interviewed was Jason Pierce.
Of all the interviews, this was the most fascinating to him.

Bernie: "Please state your name and rank."
Jason: "Jason Pierce, Private First Class, Third Squad..."
Bernie: "How do you feel about this war, this military operation?"
Jason: "God is good, man. He is so good! His angels are all around
me, man. We can't see them; but I know they're there."
Bernie: "How do you know?"
Jason: "God's word, man. The angel of the Lord encamps around
those who fear Him, and delivers them."
Bernie: "I'm not sure how to respond to that. Have angels protected
you?"
Jason: "Yeah. I was a dead man on Day One, surrounded by wolves.
They just looked at me and passed me by."
Bernie: "That's pretty amazing. Did anyone else see that?"
Jason: "My squad leader, Lance Rowland, saw it. He couldn't believe
his eyes. I had lost my rifle and my handgun; and so I reached
for my knife and prayed."
Bernie: "I'll be interested to hear Lance's story."
Jason: "Most people won't believe me. That's okay. I know what I
know."

Bernie: "Any other witnesses?"

Jason: "Two more, at least. My partner, Egypt Rashad, and Andrew Pratt. They both talked with me afterward, and asked me what I did to repel those animals. They thought I was dead for sure."

Bernie: "So you got separated from Egypt?"

Jason: "It was so intense, man. We were fighting for our lives. We were trying to stay together, but I tripped, and rolled down a huge hill. It was pretty steep; and I lost my pistol out of my hand, and I lost my M-16 in the fall."

Bernie: "I see."

Jason: "I lay there, stunned, but only for a moment. Then I staggered away from the base of the hill, disoriented, and separated from my comrades. That's when the wolves charged at me."

Bernie: "So you were unarmed and helpless?"

Jason: "I was as helpless as a little baby."

Bernie: "Your comrades saw you, but couldn't help you?"

Jason: "They were still fighting for their lives. It was open territory. No trees nearby. Must have been logged heavily in recent years."

Bernie: "But they saw you?"

Jason: "My squad leader, Sergeant Lance, came running to the place where I fell, and shouted at me. I saw him pointing, turned around, and saw the pack. He shot a couple of them, but had to stop and fight for his OWN life."

Bernie: "He knew he couldn't save you, didn't he?"

Jason: "Yes."

Bernie: "So he had to save the rest of his squad?"

Jason: "Yes."

Bernie: "This is an interesting story. Please don't be offended that I'm going to talk to the others about it."

Jason: "I won't."

Bernie: "Do you have any more comments?"

Jason: "I think something amazing is going to happen on Day Seven. Just wait and see. Something unexpected is going to happen inside the hollow mountains. An act of heroism that will touch the hearts of millions of people: a story that will make us laugh and cry at the same time."

Bernie continued to talk with Jason, and then interviewed Lance Rowland for the third time.

Bernie: "Please state your name and rank."
Lance: "Staff Sergeant Lance Rowland,…"
Bernie: "I interviewed Jason Pierce a few minutes ago."
Lance: "Did he tell you his story?"
Bernie: "Yes. I find it hard to believe."
Lance: "If I hadn't seen it with my own eyes, I wouldn't believe it, either."
Bernie: "Are you saying it DID happen?"
Lance: "Yes, it did."
Bernie: "Did anyone else see it?"
Lance: "Egypt and Andrew. Maybe more."
Bernie: "Jason said that he was rescued by angels. What do you think?"
Lance: "If you believe in angels, it is possible."
Bernie: "Do you?"
Lance: "Actually, yes. I do."
Bernie: "Do you believe Jason is right?"
Lance: "I don't know. Perhaps. Or it could be that the sun was in the wolves' eyes. Or maybe a strange noise deterred them. Or maybe they just were not in attack mode right then."
Bernie: "That's very interesting. Any more thoughts?"
Lance: "Whatever the reason, I DO consider it a miracle: a miracle from God. Whether He used angels or some other means, I don't know. But I DO believe that God miraculously protected him. It is, I believe, the most logical explanation I can give you."
Bernie: "Thank you, Sergeant Rowland. I appreciate your candor."

Bernie then interviewed Egypt and Andrew. Both of them confirmed Jason's story. One of them then gave Bernie a good piece of advice:

Andrew: "I believe that the Guard Headquarters is recording all of the satellite images. If that's true, this whole event can be seen

on the screen. Just look for about twenty X's moving towards
and passing a lone Y."
Bernie: "That's right! We could DO that! I'll call General Warner."

Bernie called General Warner; and the event was absolutely
confirmed as true. They narrowed it down to sector and time, and
watched the amazing sight. Bernie would show this incident on his
exclusive report, and include it in his upcoming documentary. He
would pose the question: "Was it chance or the hand of God?"

Bernie decided to interview Lieutenant Martin, and see what
his view of this would be. Simon pointed out that Hebrews 1:14 says
that angels do a service to believers. And in Luke 22:43, an angel
strengthened Jesus in the garden where He was praying. 2Kings 6:17
even revealed an army of angels protecting a couple of people. And
Ephesians 6:12 says there is an unseen spiritual war going on. Daniel
10:13 and 20 talk of angels warring against other angels in a struggle
between good and evil. And 1 Corinthians 4:9 and 11:10 indicate
that angels watch people, and are present where believers congregate.
Then Simon turned to Bernie, looked him in the eye, and spoke.

"Someone was certainly looking after Jason. The odds against
that many wolves passing up a meal is astronomical! It is virtually
impossible from the standpoint of mathematical probability. Not
even one wolf attacked him. This is not a one-in-a-million scenario.
It's more like one in an octillion."

Bernie thanked Simon, and then thought about what he would
say about these fighting men and women. Two of the members of
Second Platoon were women. Both of them had shown tremendous
valor, especially on Day One, standing their ground and fighting
alongside their male counterparts. Rebekah had actually saved the
life of her partner during that first hour of the advance of Day One,
and Katelyn had held her own during that same time, fending off a
furious attack without backing down.

Bernie decided he would mix all of the many interviews together
to get a summary of the experiences, the values, the wisdom, and the
collective courage of these brave warriors. He would reveal them as
ordinary people who were, in fact, extraordinary American patriots.

He would show the world a documentary that they would never forget. He began to speak into the microphone:

"What makes the heart of a hero? These are men and women of war, people from different backgrounds, different ethnicities, different childhoods: people who mostly had never met each other until they began training and working together in the National Guard. But though they are so different, they are all alike in some ways. They all love our great country. They are willing to fight for it. And here in the Adirondack Mountains, they are willing to fight an enemy that is threatening the lives of millions of civilians. The heart of a hero puts the lives of others ahead of his own life.

"I am proud of our men and women in uniform. They are amazing to me. These are people with hopes and dreams, like you and me: normal everyday people with families, friends, and vocational skills. Some love the Yankees, some the Mets; but all of them love our country and the freedoms we possess. And one of these freedoms is the freedom to live in safety. This is the freedom they are fighting for: the freedom of millions of people to live and vacation in safety within the Adirondack Park.

"And I have to say this. Many of them rely on a Higher Power for their strength, direction, and safety. Some of them have a deep faith in God, and in His Son Jesus Christ. Out of forty-one soldiers interviewed, twelve of them freely volunteered that they were believers. Perhaps there is a lesson in here for all of us. The closer we come to facing death, the more we think about facing our Creator. We wish all of our fighting men and women well; and we hope and pray that no one else will be hurt in this battle for the Adirondacks. This is Bernie Stansford, reporting for Fox News."

At about 4:00 in the afternoon, the National Guard faced several small attacks on its positions. Like Day Three, the attackers were small in numbers and easily defeated. The questions loomed in the minds of many of the soldiers: "Why has it been so quiet? What are the wolves waiting for?"

These questions would linger in their minds long into the night. Darkness fell upon the Adirondacks; and the Guard would have another good, but watchful, night of sleep. Many believed, correctly, that soon their circumstances would change; and the peaceful vacation they had enjoyed for two days would come to a sudden and violent end.

CHAPTER FORTY

May 28, 2026—DAY FIVE

The sun rose on a well-rested National Guard. They were still vigilant, and prepared for battle. They were eighty-three miles into the Adirondack Park. Fifteen hundred wolves had been destroyed. Crows and other scavengers were making meals out of some of them. The southern and central Adirondacks in the last four days had become a huge fast-food restaurant for scavengers. Many of the wolves had been removed, but more of them remained.

The Guard was on the move; and they knew they had to be watchful. They were only seventeen miles south of Mountain Meadow. Over two-thirds of the wolf population lay ahead of them. They were approaching the most dangerous part of the Adirondack Park. Most of the soldiers had mixed emotions. They were fired-up, but also nervous. They were happy about their success the last three days and nights. Their casualties were much less than those of the first fateful day. They only lost eight people in the last three days, compared with the sixty-four dead from the first day and night. The total dead was now up to seventy-two; and the number of wounded was tallied at over four hundred and fifty. The Guard, as a unified whole, had already been through the fire, and tested. They were a closer unit now, because they were in survival mode as well as attack mode; and they realized that they needed each other now more than ever. This tried-and-tested National Guard began to surge forward into new Adirondack territory.

Jonathan Wilkes, Susan, Marie, Jim, and Jack Leland all entered the secure chatroom. Jon initiated the conversation.

Phantom: "I have more good news today."
Super Decade: "What's that?"
Phantom: "Not one soldier was killed last night. And only two wounded. That makes three days of low casualties."
Legal Eagle: "I can't argue with that."
Sanhedrin: "That's encouraging."
Super Decade: "It's a lot better than the first day: that's for sure!"
Twiggy: "I'll be glad when they've eliminated every one of those awful creatures."
Super Decade: "The whole ecosystem will have to be reconstructed."
Phantom: "I'm going to file a report of the population of different animals like deer, bobcats, lynx, rabbits, foxes, and mountain lions. This will help the DIAC in calculating a plan to reconstruct the ecology of the area."
Then Jon continued.
Phantom: "But for now, we have a few days to go."
Sanhedrin: "And it ends with a bang."
Phantom: "Yes. The Guard plans to detonate at 4PM the day after tomorrow."
Legal Eagle: "D-Day at sixteen hundred."
Twiggy: "Can't wait!"
Super Decade: "Yeah! Me neither!"
Phantom: "We'll keep in touch on all of this."
Super Decade: "All the way to the exciting conclusion."

Lieutenant Simon Martin could hear the inevitable gunfire in the distance. Alex, Max, Jose, and Bill were advancing, guns always ready. They were always aware of the nearest trees, in case they needed to climb to safety in a hurry.

About 12:00 noon, the warning was sounded to the Platoon leaders. Several large packs were "heading this way". The nearest one was about five miles north, spotted by military patrol vehicles and the National Guard Command Center.

Major Bob Garrett couldn't believe his eyes. He had never seen so many wolves in attack mode in one general area, so close together. He had seen three different packs, all of which were huge. He and his driving partner, Major Jim Hughes, reported the packs as they found them, and fired at them to try to eliminate as many of them as they could. But the wolves were moving so fast that they were difficult targets. And besides that, they were spotted moving through fields at a great distance away.

"Wow, Bob! You should see this!" Jim had said, handing him his binoculars.

When Bob looked, he gasped, "Call the Command Station right away!"

Bob dialed the Command Center.

"National Guard Command Center. General Andre Warner speaking."

"General Warner, this is Major Bob Garrett. We are seeing a multiple attack headed for our troops. Do you see the super-packs on your screen?"

"Yes, and we are in the process of alerting the Guard troops even as I speak. We see hundreds of wolves converging towards 3rd Brigade, 5th Battalion, approximately. And possibly beyond that, as well. We are alerting ALL of the 4th, 5th, and 6th battalions of the 3rd Brigade at this very moment."

"Thank you, General. Over and out."

He turned to Major Hughes and said, "They did it. They are sending out the warning to the Guard right now."

"That's a relief," Jim Hughes replied.

"This is a real nightmare," Major Garrett said.

"Be glad when it's over."

"Roger that."

"What's the ETA?" asked Jose.

"About ten minutes," Simon said into his speaker. "Let's get the others to station themselves up those trees in the distance. We have great visibility, and we can gun them down as they move through the area. We have to be careful about pursuing them, because there are more huge packs coming this way. We don't want to get caught on the ground."

Alex, Max, Jose, and Bill moved to the group of trees straight ahead of them to the north, about a half-mile away. Mike, Donovan, Mark, and Joe moved more to the east, and climbed into a group of trees a tenth of a mile south, and fifty yards east, of Simon's first four: Alex, Max, Jose, and Bill. Simon stayed with his first four, and communicated with the other three squad leaders from his position there. Once the four squads were set, the pack was only a few minutes away.

"About two minutes to go," Donovan said.

"We're ready," said Mike.

Mark and Joe were in a super-serious mode. They both had talked about how dangerous this whole operation was, and had not been the light-hearted duo they usually were. They had been all business, and had kept a running total of personal kills as best they could calculate. Mark had twelve; and Joe had eight. Not bad for a couple of city boys.

Second Platoon waited with nervous expectation. So did the nearby platoons. Five miles of fighting men and women were up trees and large rocks and ledges, and even on top of some buildings, waiting for the enemy to appear.

Suddenly, the X's began showing up on the infrared screens of their helmets. The soldiers tensed up as they were swept up into a rush of adrenaline that moved from left to right as more and more soldiers detected the enemy.

Staff Sergeant O'Connell knew about the super-packs, but they were about eight miles east of his squad. But he still kept his group in a ready-to-strike mode. The Command Center had warned them that another separate pack was nearby; and they were anticipating their imminent arrival. Jeremy saw the X's first. He motioned to Terence as he called Mark O'Connell. The Staff Sergeant then sent out the warning signal to Lieutenant Charles Cooper, his platoon leader, who alerted the entire company. The predetermined electronic alarm warned the entire company, from the captain on down to the individual soldiers, in a matter of seconds. The signal meant only one thing: "Get to safety and get ready, for the battle is about to begin."

Simon Martin saw the dark, ominous forms of the super-pack emerging from the northern tree line and racing across the field. He joined in on the gunfire. The wolves came in droves, seeking to destroy and devour anything that was unfortunate enough to be in their way.

But the wolves were the unfortunate ones this time, because it was broad daylight. They were easy targets in plain sight of the shooters.

Mark O'Connell was experiencing a tense moment. A woman came out of the forest, looking disoriented. She was calling for someone. Was she in shock? Was she mentally challenged? He didn't know. But he did know one thing: she shouldn't be here. She was in one of the most dangerous places on the planet right now—in the wrong place at the wrong time.

He had not noticed her earlier, because his attention was focused on the X's headed this way. In truth, he HAD seen a few Y's, but they appeared to all be together in their respective homes. So he had not noticed this stray Y coming towards them, because his mind had been fixated on the approaching wolf pack.

Instantly he made his decision. He had to save her. He called for Jeremy and Terence to join him in the rescue attempt. The three of them left the safety of the trees, and headed for the woman. Jeremy and Terence fanned out to the left and right, while Mark went straight towards the woman. They could see the X's getting closer. Quickly, O'Connell warned the woman; but she did not respond. There was no time for discussion. He picked up the woman with a "fireman's carry". As he began to carry her toward the nearest tree, Jeremy and Terence began spraying the trees ahead with bullets.

Mark and Joe were having a serious shooting competition. Like the elf and the dwarf in "Lord of the Rings", they were keeping score of the numbers of their kills. Mark was up to eighteen; Joe was at fifteen. This was turning out to be a real massacre; and every time they killed a wolf, they were elated, thinking that "revenge is sweet". They were avenging their fallen comrades, including Patrick and Al who had to leave the fight because of their injuries.

"Take that!" Joe said as he fired. "This one's for Patrick."

"Here's one for you, Al!" Mark said as he made his next kill.

Joe fired again. "Seventeen," he said, proudly smiling.

"I'd better work harder," Mark said.

"I'm catching up. Oh, look; here's another one," Joe said.

Mark scanned the area and fired quickly. "Got one!" he said. "Twenty!"

Staff Sergeant O'Connell pulled out his pistol and hid behind a large rock. He had not had enough time to make it to the nearest tree and hoist the woman up to safety with the help of the other two. So this was his second-best option. "Get down, lady!" he ordered. She saw a wolf and ducked down quickly. She began to tremble and whimper in fear.

Wolves began to run past them at breakneck speed, and became the targets in a literal shooting gallery. They were falling left and right. Jeremy and Terence were crouched down, and firing their pistols at close range.

O'Connell took careful aim at the nearest predator and fired. One down. He fired again. Two down. Then he noticed some wolves coming from the west, flanking them. He turned in that direction, and prepared to defend himself and the woman.

Simon, Alex, and Max felt like they were in the eye of a hurricane. The last wolves were being eliminated; and there were no more in sight. But they knew that more were on the way. They were coming; and another fight would ensue. The three soldiers were tired, but ready.

Jeremy and Terence slowly advanced toward their leader. O'Connell and Jeremy both fired at the oncoming beasts attacking from the west. Terence covered their backs, killing a wolf that was coming from the east. The four were hunkered down for another five minutes; and then finally, the last of the pack was eliminated.

O'Connell called for a rescue helicopter; and the woman was evacuated from the war zone.

Simon, Alex, Max, and the rest of the platoon waited for the next wave of attack. But it never came to them. They saw the X's at a distance away; but the super-pack headed eastward more than southward. About five minutes later, they heard gunfire in the distance, a couple of miles to their right.

They expected a third wave, but to their relief, the third mega-pack passed them, too. Again, about ten minutes later, they heard faint gunfire about three or four miles to their right.

The National Guard line began to advance again. They were about twelve miles south of the town of Mountain Meadow. Fortunately, there was very little activity for the rest of the day. By nightfall, the line had advanced another ten miles. They were nearing the area of greatest danger. They had all been warned that the main lair was the most crucial target area of the entire Adirondack Park.

Once the Guard reached the parallel of Mountain Meadow, the hundred-mile line would hold its position to the south of Mountain Meadow, while the rest of the line would then cover the northernmost part of the Adirondacks, and then move inward towards the town to form a circle around the hollow mountains surrounding the town. Since the outer parts of the line had much further to travel, they moved farther north, stretching the line and making it more of a V-shaped structure. They would be traveling northwest from the eastern side of the line, and northeast from the western side of the line, would meet at the top of the Park, forming a rough circle, hopefully by nightfall of Day Six. They would be moving as fast as they could, and might not stop until 10:00 or even later, to meet at the top. If they had to, they could move effectively in the dark of night. Then they would rest until 6:00AM, and then move southward towards the town and the hollow mountains. They would still be moving on Day Seven, and would be in position by 3:00PM—1500 hours—on that fateful day.

Darkness fell over the Adirondacks; and so the fifth night of the military campaign had begun. There were about 49,000 soldiers left; and they were going through the scariest night of all. They were in uncharted territory, not knowing what would happen next. They knew that at any given moment, they could face relentless attack from this vicious, man-eating enemy. Many of the soldiers prayed for protection and help from God. And some of them prayed for their own personal salvation, knowing that there might not be another day for them here in this life. Over one hundred soldiers were dead; and nearly eight hundred had been wounded. And there was still almost two days to go. At 4:00 in the afternoon on DAY SEVEN, there would be a reckoning; and the "year of the wolf" in the Adirondacks would be over.

This fifth night was the most nerve-wracking for the soldiers, because there was much anticipation of a repeat of the first two nights. The Guard was exhausted, but wary. They could fall asleep easily, but could also wake up instantly, and be ready to fight in just a few seconds. They were a war-toughened line of soldiers now. They had been on the "front lines", and had experienced real war.

They knew that they still had a lot of work to do. It was a tough road ahead. Over two thousand wolves had been destroyed; but that left another twenty-five hundred to three thousand which were still alive, active, and very dangerous.

The first several hours of the night were very quiet. Then, all over the northern Adirondacks, the piercing howls of wolves could be heard. All 49,000 of these heroic fighting men and women heard the eerie sounds. It was enough to set even the most confident of these valiant warriors on edge.

CHAPTER FORTY-ONE

Several large Z's were seen moving south. Some of these were Whitetail deer fleeing the danger-zone. The National Guard let them pass. There were a few roaming bears and cougars that the soldiers also ignored. They had been ordered to "stand down" on everything but wolves, or coyotes or coydogs, unless human life was being threatened by one or more non-wolf animal.

There had been a few clashes with coyotes and coydogs; and a number of soldiers had been wounded by them. But the main danger was, and would continue to be, the wolf population. The coyotes and coydogs were classified as X's, only smaller. They were harder to aim at with a rifle or pistol, but were not as big and dangerous as wolves. They did injure a number of soldiers, but were not nearly as big a threat as their larger cousins. A one-hundred-thirty-pound wolf could do a lot more damage than a seventy-five-pound coyote or coydog.

Another danger was the rattlesnake population, especially during this last day, DAY FIVE. There had been several rattlesnake bites, but no fatalities. There were plenty of snake-bite kits around; and the bite-victims were treated right away.

Around 3:00AM, the howling stopped. The wolves from the north were ready to hunt. They were about to begin moving southward towards the Guard. Man and beast would clash once again.

The rampaging predators came from the south. Some of them were survivors of the National Guard's advance. And some had come from nearby areas outside of the Adirondack Park. They joined with each other to form a super-pack. They could smell the human scent on the ground. Many of them had eaten human flesh before; and they were driven by their ravenous hunger. They moved northward, eagerly approaching their prey.

A huge clump of X's appeared on the National Guard Headquarters computer mainframe screen. Major General Joshua Wilder saw it first. Initially, he squinted, not believing what he saw. Then it registered.

"We have a red alert, General."

"What?" Lieutenant General Andre Warner said.

"Take a look!" General Wilder said, excitedly.

General Warner looked intently at the screen. In sectors 1,285 to 1,312, they could see a huge number of X's moving north. They were an hour away from the National Guard line at the moment. But they needed to take action now. Packs were invading from the north; and so the super-pack from the south could create a firestorm of catastrophe.

"Send the warning to our men on the ground!"

"Right away, General," Major General Wilder said.

Quickly, the alert went down the chain of command. The hundred-mile National Guard line was already on full alert, and then they received this second alert. The eastern half of 3rd Brigade was in the worst position, because packs from the north were headed their way; and the super-pack from the south was also moving towards them. Fortunately, supply choppers had given them plenty of ammunition to replenish their dwindling supply. Thousands of National Guardsmen were scrambling up trees, houses, and large rock formations, getting ready for an attack from the north, and also aware of an attack from the south in less than an hour.

"Here they come!" yelled Max.

"I see them," Simon said. "There must be sixty or seventy X's headed this way."

"About two minutes away," said Max.

"Maybe less," Alex said.

"Bill, are you okay?" asked Jose.

"Yes, I think so. I feel a little sick."

"Take care of yourself. If you can't fight, just keep yourself safe up in the tree."

"I will."

"I'm praying for you."

"Jose, it's time for me to get saved."

"You remember I told you how?"

"Yes."

"Just talk to God."

"I will. And then I'll talk with you again."

Jose kept silent so that Bill could pray. Bill prayed and received the free gift of salvation: forgiveness for all of his sins—past, present, and future—trusting in the death and resurrection of Jesus Christ for his salvation.

Bill was amazed at the joy and peace that he felt. A great sense of relief swept over him, as if the weight of the whole world had just rolled off of his shoulders. In fact, the weight of the guilt of all his sin was completely gone. He felt a true release from guilt and fear. He was beside himself with joy and relief.

"Wow! Jose, I did it!"

"I'm so happy for you, Bill. You just made the most important decision you could ever make in your entire lifetime."

"I know I did," Bill said happily.

"Believe me, I couldn't be happier for you. We'll talk soon. But right now, I have to get ready to fire at the enemy."

"Okay, I'll rest a while."

"Don't forget to fasten yourself to the tree. We don't want to lose you. You're important to us."

"Thank you."

Bill fastened himself to the tree with his harness. He double-checked to make sure it was tight. Then he took the time to reflect on his wife and children. He loved them all very much; and he missed them, and could hardly wait to get back to them. And he was now a changed man. He would be more understanding towards his family now. He would be the kind of husband and father he knew he should be. And he would tell them what God had done in his life. He felt a surge of anticipation, excitement, and joy. He could hardly wait to get back home. But right now, he felt it was time to relax; and his body began to shut down in exhaustion. Amid the noise of gunfire, he fell asleep for a full fifteen minutes.

Jose was firing at a sea of infrared signatures which were moving past his position. He dropped a few of them; but most of them passed him by. He hoped Mike and Donovan and Mark and Joe were doing better than he was. And he knew the first three, Simon, Alex, and Max, were doing well. They were three of the ten best shooters in the entire hundred-mile line of Guard troops.

Jonathan Wilkes couldn't sleep. He felt burdened for the troops, who had been placed in harm's way. He climbed out of bed, went to the bedroom sink, and splashed his face with cold water. He found himself in a melancholy moment. He had a feeling of sadness take over his emotional state. "Lord, they need You. Please protect them. Please, Lord." He continued his prayer; and he couldn't stop the outburst of tears. He wept quietly for a couple of minutes. Then he regained his composure. He dried his face and his tears, and went back to bed. His digital clock said 3:37AM.

"They're coming. Any time now," Simon said.
"Our break will be over soon," Alex remarked.
"I wish I could get down out of this tree and stretch," Max said.
"Go ahead," Alex joked.
"No thanks. I want to live to see daylight."
All three of them laughed.

The storm came in unexpectedly, from the west. In the distance, the soldiers could see the flashes of light. A few minutes later, they could hear distant thunder.
"This is not good," Lieutenant Martin said.
"This is a very dangerous situation," said Max.
"A good time to pray," Alex said.
"Put in a good word for all of us," Simon said.

"Okay, Roger that."

They could feel the cool wind blowing through the trees. This was the sign that the rain was approaching.

"Get out your umbrellas," Simon said.

"Yeah, and I wish we could have lightning rods on the tops of the trees," Max said.

"Unfortunately, WE are the lightning rods," Simon observed.

Suddenly, they heard a loud thunder clap.

"I'll put in a good word for us all, right now," Alex said. He began to pray.

In just seconds, they found themselves in the middle of a huge torrent of rain, and surrounded by flashes of light and deafening crashes of thunder. They were in a frightening situation. If they stayed in the trees, they risked death by lightning. If they left the trees, they risked death by wolves. Both dangers were close; and nobody knew who would live and who would die. But they chose the safer option. Risk the lightning bolt rather than a raging super-pack of hungry wolves.

"Wolves coming from the north!" Simon said.

They were only a couple of minutes away.

Suddenly, a lightning bolt struck Simon's tree. But miraculously, it didn't hit Simon, but went down the other side of the tree, splitting it almost in half, shaking the tree, and making a terrible noise. Alex and Max heard the booming thunder and the ear-shattering cracking sound as the tree split apart. Then they saw their leader fall. The Y moved to the ground quickly, and lay there, stunned. The X's were moving closer.

"Lieutenant! Get up!" yelled Alex. Simon didn't move. Max was already down his tree. Alex followed suit; and they approached Simon. Quickly, they picked him up and moved him towards the nearest tree. Simon grunted.

"He's coming to," Alex said.

"That's good," Max said. "We need to get to safety. Fast."

The X's were dangerously close. Alex and Max got Simon walking; and the three of them moved towards the nearest tree as fast as Simon could move.

Sergeant O'Connell was talking to Jeremy and Terence, his two best shooters.

"You okay, Jeremy?"

"Yes. That was close! It split the tree right next to me."

"My ears are still ringing," Terence said.

"We've been lucky so far," Sergeant O'Connell said. "I just hope our good luck continues."

"This is a good time to pray," Jeremy said.

"Roger that," Terence agreed.

"Can't argue with your logic. Go to it," said the Sergeant.

"Can you climb, Simon?" Alex asked.

"I think so," Simon replied.

"I suggest we hurry," Max said.

Alex and Max turned simultaneously and fired several shots, dropping a couple of wolves. Simon strained to get up on the first branch.

"Max, stay with Simon. I'll go to the next tree."

"Be careful, Alex. I don't want to lose you, my friend."

Alex rushed away while Max climbed. A wolf charged at Alex, but he turned and fired just in time. The predator collapsed, just inches away. A flash of lightning lit up the sky. Fortunately, the night-vision screen had a light-sensitive protective shield which earlier models never had. It used to be that a lightning flash would blind anyone wearing night-vision apparatus. But no longer. The technology of these activated screens was astounding. Quickly, Alex climbed a maple tree and sat about fifteen feet up from the ground level.

The super-pack from the south had slowed when the storm hit. They stopped to lap up water off of the ground. Once satisfied, they resumed their northerly direction. Meanwhile, more packs of wolves from the north were entering the area occupied by the line of soldiers. The Guard opened fire, along several miles of the line, as the wolves approached. Several hundred wolves were killed; and sixteen brave soldiers lost their lives. The battle was over in fifteen minutes, but it had been a furious one.

And there was no time to rest.

"They're here! Coming from the south!" shouted Simon.

They could already hear gunfire to their right, about a half-mile away.

"At least the storm is subsiding," Max said.

"Yeah, I'm glad about that," Alex said.

"Let the games begin. Again," said Max. He added. "You okay, Lieutenant?"

"Yeah, I'm doing just fine, thank you," Simon replied.

The gunfire got louder as the wolves moved in a northwesterly direction. To the right, Mark and Joe could see the flashes of light from the rifles of their nearest comrades. And they saw infrared signatures heading their way.

"Here we go again," Mark said.

"I'm surprised I still have ammunition left," said Joe.

"I'm sure glad we do," Mark responded.

"Hand-to-hand combat would not be pretty," Joe said.

"That's for sure. They're like sharks with legs."

"More like piranhas," said Joe.

"Ready, aim, fire!" said Alex to himself as he dropped another wolf.

"How many of those have you got?" asked Max.

"Lost count," Alex said. "Maybe forty-five or fifty. A lot."

"Keep up the good work."

"I eat lots of blueberries."

"Oh yeah. Good for your vision. Right?"

"Yeah. I have the eyes of a hawk. Hold on." He fired at a wolf, but it kept moving.

"Missed it!" he said.

"Well," Max said, "We have to leave some for the rest of our company to shoot." They laughed.

"I'm up to twenty-eight," Mark said. "How about you?"

"Twenty-six," said Joe.

"Busy night tonight."

"Can't wait till sunrise."
"Can't wait till 4PM on DAY SEVEN."
"Kaboom!"

The battle was finally over; and the soldiers could rest for an hour before sunrise. An average of three from each squad watched for danger while the rest slept. When the dawn came, a hundred-mile line of war-weary soldiers would prepare to advance once again.

CHAPTER FORTY-TWO

May 29, 2026—DAY SIX

The sixth day of the offensive was uneventful compared to the previous day. There were small skirmishes, but surprisingly, the main wolf population which was left, stayed in or near their gigantic lair.

Lieutenant General Andre Warner, second in command to Four-Star General Red Logan, was trying to figure out the best way to cave in the huge lair located inside the mountains surrounding the town of Mountain Meadow. Major General Joshua Wilder was examining the satellite blueprint. A staff of computer experts had been mapping the area. To the west, north, and east were several large ground-level entrances. There were also some entrances up above, where evidently only humans and flying creatures could enter.

"What do you make of this, Doctor?" asked General Wilder.

"This is an old Huron tunnel system," said Doctor Mishael Romanov.

Although Dr. Romanov was a Russian immigrant, he was very familiar with Native American history. The Hurons, it was believed, had been eliminated by the Mohawk Indians centuries ago. But the pictures of the four gold artifacts found in the Devane files indicated Huron craftsmanship. If that was so, then these sculptures were priceless! Artifacts of an extinct civilization! It appeared to Romanov that a small part of the Huron tribe lived in seclusion inside this cavernous mountain area: an area which the Iroquois Indians, their mortal enemies, evidently avoided for reasons of superstition. Old Iroquois pictorial writings described a certain area which they believed was controlled by evil spirits; and the Indians would not normally enter that area. The Hurons, knowing that they were safe in this area, took sanctuary in the tunneled area, and lived there until they died out.

Millennia ago, right after the great Flood during Noah's day, a group of mountains was formed: now known as the Adirondacks. Most of these mountains were all solid and full; but there was a ring of mountains that formed and came up hollow inside. There were ledges and natural walkways formed within this hollow mountain ring. When Indians dug some caves, they found that it was hollow. And it was huge! They dug from three sides of the mountains, on the outer sides of the ring: west, north, and east. The inner part of the ring was dug for a backward entrance or exit towards the south, in case of attack by another tribe. It was hidden by a clump of bushes and a few small trees on the edge of the valley at the base of the mountain. It was a small entrance, with room for only one man at a time to pass through. It was guarded by several Huron warriors; and they successfully guarded it for over a century.

After the last of the Hurons died off, the cavernous hollow mountain area became a sanctuary for animals, and finally for the new wolf population. There was an underground river running through the area; and there were spots of sunlight that broke through the area, through the cracks between the mountains, which were all connected. Anyone who climbed this mini-mountain range had to be careful not to fall through the cracks between the mountains or through the holes in the tops of the mountains.

Dr. Romanov was examining the structure of the inside of this inter-connected cavernous area. He spoke to General Wilder.

"I can see a lot of weak points in the structure," he said.

"I'm glad YOU can see them, Doctor. I can hardly even understand the satellite picture data that I'm looking at."

"Do you see these areas here?" He pointed to what looked like an indecipherable maze to the General.

"Yes," General Wilder said.

"These areas are fault lines."

"Yes?"

"Now, you will notice that there are different densities in the rocks—different densities OF rock."

"I'll take your word for it."

"Where the fault lines and lower densities combine are where the maximum damage can be done by explosives."

General Wilder thought for a moment. He was obviously confused.

"I thought fault lines were subterranean," he said.

"Yes, yes, they are. But this is an exception to the rule. An anomaly. These fault lines ARE subterranean; but here they also extend several hundred feet above the earth's surface."

"So you are able to mark these weak areas?" he said, incredulously.

"Yes. And I will mark enough places to collapse the entire area."

"We are going to use our jets to ensure the collapse of all the entrances and to enhance the effect of the inside detonations."

"Yes. And that is a very good idea. It is better to use too much explosive power than not enough." The Doctor added, "And how are you going to place the explosives in these areas?"

"From the top, we will use secured ropes. These mountains are over a thousand feet high; and we have ropes that are that long."

"And can you avoid danger?"

"All of them have their infrared capability to locate danger, and should have time to climb to safety. The ropes they are climbing on are literally rope-ladders. And they are far more advanced today than they were even fifteen years ago."

"Could a wolf pull down the rope?"

"Yes, but it can be released in sections."

"So you can climb above the lowest section, and then release it?"

"Yes."

"How?"

"There are straps that are a quarter of an inch thick which are several times stronger than steel, which hold the sections together every twenty feet. They are light, and can be released easily from eight feet above the top of the section being released."

"It can't be released accidentally, can it?"

"It has been extensively tested; and there have been no accidental releases of rope sections."

"Okay, I'm convinced," said Dr. Romanov.

He started marking spots in the satellite map of the area to show the weaknesses. He had to indicate the area from the top, and then also indicate the depth of each spot. It was a formidable task, which only a few people in the world could handle. Dr. Romanov was one of those select few.

The plan was to secure ropes to trees, slide the rope-ladders down the holes and cracks at the top of the cavernous mountain area, and have the members of the demolition crew climb down these ladders. They would use mountain-climbing apparatus, including a harpoon-like gun used to fire a hook into a mountain wall to connect a rope to the wall. The "hook" would not open up until it penetrated into the rock wall. Once the hook opened up, securing the rope, it would send back an electronic message indicating how secure the connection was. It had been tested extensively; and the failure rate was about one in ten thousand. The soldier could then move laterally once the lateral rope was secured to the vertical rope. The lateral ropes were not ladder-like, but regular, ropes; and they were made of a material several times stronger than steel. A lateral rope can be traversed by a hanging rope-chair, connected to the rope by a motorized pulley system. This pulley system had a special ring that was attached to a wheel device powered electronically, and easy to attach and operate. The lateral rope, made of a super-strong high-tech substance, was practically frictionless, making it easy for the wheel-device pulley-ring attachment to slide on. The trick was to get the lateral rope fairly level so that the pulley system could slide easily back and forth. An electronic sensor that measured how level the rope was, came with the "hook". This particular invention was patented just a year ago, in May of 2025.

Dr. Romanov made over two hundred marks for detonation. He said that each explosion would need to be extremely powerful. There was a new substance that was a thousand times more potent than C-4, and just as easy to set and to detonate. They called it CZ-14. It was great stuff; and the military loved it for its effectiveness. General Red Logan, in conjunction with General Andre Warner, had made the decision. Two hundred and fifteen explosions of CZ-14 would be detonated simultaneously with the powerful sidewinder missiles shot from twenty F-18's.

"Wow! This has been one easy day," said Alex. "I feel like I'm on vacation."

"It's a nice break. That's for sure," Max replied.

"Don't get too settled," Simon said. "Things can change in a hurry."

"Heard," said Max.

"Heard," Alex said.

"Man! I can't get my count up, because there's nothing out there to shoot today," Joe said.

"That's okay," Mark said. "I like being ahead."

Sergeant O'Connell said, "What a great day this is."

"I hope tonight is like today," said Jeremy.

"Me too," Terence agreed.

"We can only hope," said Sergeant O'Connell. "We can only hope."

The hundred-mile line of troops was now stationary in the center, and V-shaped, with the eastern and western lines moving towards each other. Both lines had to close the gap, which required them to cover more miles than any of the previous days. The soldiers had moved strategically all the way up to the top edge of the Adirondacks; and they would join together as an unbroken circle at about 10:00PM, if possible, then sleep until 6:00AM, and would continue moving back towards the northern end of the cavernous wolf lair on Day Seven. And the circular line would ultimately be about forty miles long, giving the Guard more than twice the concentration of fire-power to fight anything that might emerge from the lair, on the afternoon of Day Seven. But they had to get through this next night first; and they were not in as safe a position, because they would not have the circle tightened until the afternoon of that next day. So they would have to be vigilant for this one last night: Night Six. 49,000 members of the Guard hoped that it would be an easy night.

Jonathan Wilkes, Susan, Marie, Jim, and Jack Leland were back in the secure chatroom.

Phantom: "This is it. The last night."
Sanhedrin: "Then it's detonation time."
Legal Eagle: "The year of the wolf will be over."
Twiggy: "It can't be too soon."
Super Decade: "I agree. I'll be glad when it's over."

DAY SIX ended with a relieved National Guard ready to take a much-needed rest. They hoped that the wolf population would stay in their lair tonight.

Tom Crandall was one of the minority of people who stayed in the Adirondack Park rather than evacuate. His brother Tripp was visiting, and was on vacation with his wife and young daughter. They had been in the town of Union Falls for the last month, and had been hiking and camping virtually non-stop, despite the danger. They slept in a camper, and were well-armed and alert. They stubbornly refused to leave the area. And on this particular day, they had driven up to the base of the northern-most area of the cavernous mini mountain range. They had avoided the National Guard and police patrols by using the back roads before the line of soldiers completely surrounded the area. They were now inside the Guard perimeter, and were asleep in their camper.

Just before dawn on this quiet night, little four-year-old Sally Crandall snuck out of the camper and wandered off, leaving the camper door open.

CHAPTER FORTY-THREE

May 30, 2026—DAY SEVEN

The National Guard was pleasantly pleased and relieved at the first rays of sunlight. Those already in position were to remain stationary while the demolition crew members were selected and removed from the Guard line and transported to the top of the mini mountain range, with the last-minute instructions and directions. They would be given all of the equipment they would need to set the detonators. All of them would synchronize their watches at 11:00AM when they were all to begin. The plan was to be done with the CZ-14 setup by 3:00PM. Once set, they would give the Air Force the okay. All the detonators set by the Guard would be set for 4:00PM. They would automatically detonate simultaneously. The Air Force would fire their Sidewinder missiles to hit at exactly 4:00PM to enhance the devastation. Twenty F-18's were cleared to take off from the newly-rebuilt Air Force base in Plattsburg, New York; and they would only need a few minutes to reach the target site. Eight war planes would circle in from the north at just over the top of the mountains, at 2,000 feet; four from the east at 3,000 feet; four from the west at 4,000 feet; and four from the south at 5,000 feet. All twenty of the fighter planes would fire their missiles, and then veer to the right, maintaining their altitude. The National Guard, meanwhile, would remain stationed in a circle at a safe distance, miles away from the target site.

Mountain Meadow was one-hundred-percent evacuated. The military did not want the town to be destroyed by the collapse of the cavernous mountains. Dr. Romanov had set the detonation plan to favor a collapse of the cavernous mountains towards the northward direction, to avoid destroying Mountain Meadow. A few houses on the north side of the mountains were in danger of being destroyed; but that was a small price to pay for the eradication of the chemically-altered wolf population.

Generals Red Logan and Andre Warner had considered other means to destroy the wolves in the lair. The two other main options were cyanide gas and the use of fire-spewing torches. It was argued that these two options were better ways to destroy the animals. But both Logan and Warner saw the cyanide gas option as more difficult logistically, afraid that some of their men would become trapped in the maze of walkways and tunnels, and that there might be a mass-exodus of wolves prematurely from the lair, before the soldiers could finish the job.

Burning the wolves out would be even more dangerous and difficult logistically; and PETA would object to that method as the absolutely worst method to use. A cruel and inhumane way to kill animals, they would say. And rightly so. Other "animal rights" groups would join in and protest.

Using explosives to collapse the mountains remained the best and safest move; and the choice of the military was to preserve the most human life over preserving a historical Huron site. Better to destroy the danger to human life than preserve the Huron site and lose lives unnecessarily. The two generals believed their men could safely drop down by ropes into the cavernous mountains and set the explosives. And coupled with the F-18 Sidewinders, the devastation of the area would be complete, trapping and killing ALL the wolves in the lair.

New York State could later seek to collect the gold sculptures and other historical artifacts buried in the rubble. The excavation would cost many millions of dollars; but the potential yield was in the billions.

Alex, Max, Jose, and Bill were all chosen to take part in setting the CZ-14 charges. So were Jeremy and Terence. Out of 49,000 soldiers, five hundred were chosen. They would divide up into teams and move to their respective sites.

There would be fifty teams of ten. One of the ten would go through the entrance while the others would stand by and guard the security of the rope system. The one soldier would set the charges, protected from above by the other nine.

Security of the ones setting the charges was paramount. Not only were they guarded by the other nine; they were secured to a rope around their waists, attached like a parachute would be attached, making the rope inseparable from the men and women descending into the cavernous areas. A release system was available to them if necessary; but the rope could not be accidentally released.

Then there was the rope ladder. It was several times stronger than steel, and was secured at the top of the mountain. If there was a weakness in any section of the rope ladder, an electronic security-breach message would be emitted. The extensive testing of the ladder proved nearly perfect security. Only once in ten thousand times was there a serious malfunction. And even in that case, one side of the ladder held the weight of the person below the breach. The person below was dangling under the half-broken ladder breach, but surprisingly, was still safe.

By 11:05, the fifty teams of ten would be already in motion. All times were set for 4:00PM exactly. Fourteen teams would each send a soldier through the vertical tunnels into the cavernous interior of the mountains. The other thirty-six teams would each send a soldier through the cracks in the mountain range. The fifty soldiers would set the explosives with their detonators as close as possible to the designated area and depth. The GPS designed by Jonathan Wilkes was a guiding factor in setting the explosives. The GPS guidance systems would be in the hands of the fifty soldiers who were setting the explosives. These systems would give accurate and complete instructions as to where to set the CZ-14.

"Sally!—She's gone!" screamed Missie.

"What are you talking about, Dear?" Tripp asked.

"Sally's gone!"

"What?" Tom said.

The three of them rushed out of the camper and started calling for Sally.

Sally had climbed up the mountain and crawled through a hole that was too small for an adult to enter. She was about five hundred feet above ground level. She crawled into the darkness; and the passageway became wider. She could stand up now, and carefully walked forward. Then she felt a wall, and kept moving alongside that wall. She walked along that wall for a couple of minutes, and came out into a small cavern. Now she could see a small streak of light shining from somewhere up above. She detected a small pool of water, glimmering in the light. But when she walked up to the edge of the pool, she realized it was filled with dirty water. She shied away from it. Then she suddenly realized that she was lost; and she began to cry.

Tripp and Missie and Tom were desperately looking for Sally. She had a two-hour lead on them, a significant head-start. And they knew that this little toddler could move really quickly when she wanted to. It was about 7:30AM; and they had a lot of ground to cover.

Jonathan Wilkes, Susan, Marie, Jim, and Jack Leland were all in the secure chatroom.

Phantom: "This is it."

Sanhedrin: "The endgame."

Twiggy: "Less than nine hours. I am SO happy!"

Super Decade: "Yeah!"

Legal Eagle: "Judgment Day!"

Twiggy: "I think we should tell our story."

Phantom: "There are certain classified things we cannot reveal. But yes—we CAN tell our story."

Super Decade: "But the story is not over yet."

Phantom: "You're right. We have to watch the last nine hours, and
see how it goes."
Super Decade: "We need to pray for the National Guard, the police,
and the people who are still staying in the Adirondack Park."
Phantom: "Let's all agree we will pray for their safety once we log off
this website."

Everyone agreed. And when they logged off, they all followed
through with that agreement. All of them prayed, earnestly and fer-
vently. The lives of these people were in God's sovereign hands.

Sally kept moving deeper and deeper into the chasm. She was
walking, crawling, stopping to rest. At first she had been sad when
she realized she was lost. But now she was filled with fear. She began
to scream, "Mommy! Daddy! Mommy!" and "Where are you?!" She
was confused, and trying to find a way back to her parents and her
Uncle Tom.

Missie was getting frantic. She kept screaming, "Sally! Sally!
Where are you?!" Her voice broke. She began to sob. She sat down
on a rock and buried her head in her hands. Tripp and Tom tried to
comfort her.

Tripp turned to his brother, and spoke.

"Shouldn't we dial 911?"

"They won't help, Tripp. They will order us out of the area.
We're not supposed to be here."

"So, we're on our own, then."

"Yes."

"I really wish they would help us."

"I know. But they will do just the opposite. They will make us
leave and then—"

"We would never find Sally."

"That's right."

"We're on our own. And so is my little girl." Tripp choked on
his words. He felt like he was losing his composure.

Sally wandered into another cavernous area, and saw a ray of light, and more dirty water. She was very thirsty; but she had been trained not to eat, drink, or even touch dirty food or water. She saw a loose rock; and she picked it up and threw it in her frustration. Suddenly, a large group of bats began to squeal and flutter about. This terrified Sally; and she screamed and shielded her face. She tried to run away, and hit a wall, and fell down, unconscious.

Another half-hour passed. Missie, Tripp, and Tom were all feeling desperate. They were halfway up the mountain now; and their voices were becoming hoarse from yelling out, "Sally! Sally! Where are you?!"

Sally woke up, still stunned. Her head was hurting; and her right arm was bleeding. She began to cry again. She started to move towards a tunnel entrance. She began to speak in a trembling voice, "Help. Help me. Somebody help me." Then she began to speak louder, "Help me! HELP MEEEEEE!!!"

At 11:00AM, Alex and forty-nine other brave soldiers descended into the abyss. He was walking down the rope-ladder. The electronic eye of his GPS locator said there were six hundred and fifty-three feet before he could step onto a rock floor. But he didn't have to go that far yet. He needed to go down only three hundred and twelve feet to get to a raised-up fault line. He carefully and slowly descended the rope-ladder. He also had a rope tied to his waist, securing him in case he slipped and fell. This rope was constantly tight, but automatically extended as he moved lower. Up above, this rope's winding apparatus was secured to a sturdy set of trees. The winding apparatus of the rope-ladder was also secured in the same manner. The rope which was attached to his waist would prove to be a very important factor later on.

The wolves were gathered in the huge lair, feasting on carcasses they had dragged in from the outside. They had practically eliminated the entire deer population; and they were finishing the last of the remains. And there was other prey inside the lair which they had killed, and were eating. Fortunately for the National Guard, today was a day that the wolves were occupied with eating. Tomorrow, over two thousand predators would be ready to hunt again.

Sally was walking through the dark, damp tunnel. She could see a faint light in the distance. She started to move faster, but slipped and fell. She got up slowly, and carefully moved towards the wall of the tunnel. She felt along the sides. She dug out a little sand from the rock wall, and let it slip through her fingers.

Alex continued his descent, and checked his GPS indicator. It registered two hundred and ninety-eight feet down. Then two hundred ninety-nine. Then three hundred. He was approaching the target level.

"Sally! Sally! Please!"

Missie started to cry again. She felt despair, grief, and fear all at the same time.

"I can't take this anymore! She's gone! She's gone!" Her voice tapered off. "She's gaw-hawn."

Tripp tried to console her.

"We're not giving up, Honey. We'll find her," he said.

Tom said, "We'll keep looking until we find her."

Missie stood up, wiped the tears off of her face, and began to move forward.

Alex aimed his headgear flashlight by turning his head left-to-right, and scanned the area. There was a rock wall just thirty feet away. He used the GPS indicator to mark the target spot. Then he took out the harpoon "hook" gun, and fired the lateral rope at the target area. The impact was powerful enough to penetrate the rock wall several inches. The claws of the hook instantly dug into the wall by expanding so that it could not be pulled out by the weight of a human being on this lateral rope. Alex then secured the lateral rope to the vertical rope-ladder, being careful to safely secure the hook gun, which remained attached to the lateral rope. He then attached the rope-chair to the lateral rope, attaching the mechanized pulley system to it. He then carefully positioned himself into the rope-chair, and buckled himself in. He committed himself to the security of this chair, knowing that he was also attached to a second rope: the one secured to his waist. He pressed some buttons on a small keyboard, inputting the password that activated the mechanized pulley system; and he began to move forward in the rope-chair, towards the target point.

Sally saw the light get brighter as she moved forward. She came out into a huge area. There were walkways on tops of ledges in front of her; and she could see that she had to walk carefully now. She instinctively sensed the danger she was in.

Alex set the CZ-14 securely to the wall, and set the detonator for 4:00PM. Then he put the rope-chair engine into REVERSE, and returned to the rope-ladder. He carefully moved from the rope-chair back to the rope-ladder. Then he detached the rope-chair from the lateral rope, and put it back in his backpack. Then he carefully detached the lateral rope, with the harpoon hook gun, from the rope-ladder. He released the catch-safety of the hook gun by entering a five-digit password, and pushed the REVERSE button. The gun sent an electronic signal to the claws of the "hook"; and they retracted. The hook apparatus pulled out of the rock wall; and the rope rewound into the gun's rather bulky interior. He then reattached the gun back to a side-strap. The GPS locator then gave him directions to the next target detonation point. He resumed his descent. As he descended, he noticed a beam of light in the distance, to his left.

Two hundred yards away, to Alex's left, was Jose. Jose was in a lighted area to the left of a huge rock ledge overlay, which looked like it was not too stable. He had set a couple of charges on the bottom of this overlay. He thought to himself, "I wouldn't want to be here when the charges go off."

To the right of the overlay were some ledges that looked like they had been pushed out of the side of the mountain and suspended in mid-air. It looked dark and foreboding over there.

One hundred feet below Jose, behind the dark ledges, and two hundred feet inside the rock wall, little four-year-old Sally was walking towards the lighted area. There was another corner to turn; and then she came to a straight rock ledge path with a steep drop to the left. She was afraid to go forward. She opened her mouth to scream.

Alex had just finished placing his second charge of CZ-14. He was getting ready for his third, just twenty feet down and fifty feet to his left, when he heard a faint scream. "Help me! Help!" The noise, although faint, reverberated throughout the expanse of the chasm. Alex couldn't tell where it was coming from. Jose heard the scream, and knew it was coming from his right, from the dark ledge area.

Art Hutchinson was also nearby. He stopped what he was doing, and radioed Jose.

"This is Art Hutchinson. Sector 25. Do you copy?"

"I copy. This is Jose Hernandez. Sector 24."

"Did you hear the scream?"

"Yes. Do you know where?"

"I've got a pretty good idea."

"It sounded like it came from the ledges to the north."

"That was my guess."

"Let's work together."

"Roger that."

Alex figured if he called Jose in Sector 24, he might get an answer.

"Alex Warfield calling. Sector 23. Calling Sector 24. Do you copy?"

"I copy, Alex. This is Jose."

"I heard a scream. Did you?"

"Yes. Inside our sector borders."

"The suspended ledges?"

"Yes."

"I can't see any openings on this side."

"I see an opening over here."

"Do you need help?"

"Please stand by."

"Copy that."

Jose was an accomplished mountain climber. But he was sure that this rescue attempt was not going to be easy. He turned towards the suspended ledge entrance and fired the "hook" apparatus into the wall near the opening. There was an outside ledge; but it was a narrow one.

Jose moved to the entrance, and entered the gigantic hollow suspended ledge. At first, there was a wide floor on which he could walk; but as he continued further into the interior of the suspended ledge, he noticed that there was a small crack or crevice in the rock floor. As the crevice widened, the width of the rock floor became narrower. He hoped that he would be able to find the person who was trapped inside. He felt a sense of urgency, because it was quiet in here, and he wondered why.

Tripp and Missie and Tom heard the noise of a helicopter approaching.

"Now we're in for it," Tripp said.

"Uh-oh," said Tom.

"What?" Missie asked.

"They're going to tell us to—"

"THIS IS A RESTRICTED AREA! YOU MUST LEAVE IMMEDIATELY!"

"What are we going to do?" Tom asked.

"LEAVE THE AREA IMMEDIATELY!"

Missie waved frantically at the chopper.

"Please!" she yelled. "My daughter! Please!"

They couldn't hear her pleas. And they were not disposed to stay there. They issued the order once more, and then left.

"We're not giving up," Tripp said.

"That's right," agreed Tom. "We're not leaving without our Sally."

Little Sally was so tired that she had fallen asleep. She had screamed for help several times, and then had given up to exhaustion. She slept, and dreamed that an angel came to her and told her that everything would be alright. In her dream, two men rescued her; but when she turned to thank them, only one man was still there.

CHAPTER FORTY-FOUR

Art Hutchinson moved towards the suspended ledges by hanging from his rope and moving along the rock wall. It took him about ten minutes to reach the entrance. He entered the tunnel and radioed Jose.

"This is Art. Do you copy?"

"Roger. This is Jose."

"I'm at the entrance. Do you need help?"

"I believe so. I haven't found anyone yet."

Jose waited for Art to catch up. They were both still attached to their waist ropes.

"We're going to have to detach," Jose said. "We won't be safe anymore."

"I understand," Art said. "There are too many turns in here, it looks like."

"Any more turns, and the ropes would not allow us to move freely," Jose said.

"True," said Art.

"We can attach both of our ropes to the rock wall with one of our hook guns."

"Then we save one hook gun in case we need it."

"Yes," said Jose.

They released their waist ropes, and attached them to the rock wall. Then they used their mountain-climbing gear to continue forward. Jose and Art were both experienced mountain climbers.

Sally suddenly awoke. She could hear voices about a hundred feet away. Someone was just around the corner!

"Help me!" she yelled. "Help me! Please!"

Jose rounded the corner, aimed his headgear flashlight, and saw a little girl about thirty yards away. He started moving towards her, and spoke to her in a soft and gentle voice.

"Hello, my name is Jose; and this is my friend Art. We're here to help you."

Sally remembered her dream.

"I knew you were coming," she said.

"Jose said, "What's your name?"

"Sally Crandall."

"Hi, Sally. How did you get here?"

"I crawled through a hole in the mountain."

"She's precocious," thought Jose.

"How long ago?" he asked.

"I don't know. Early this morning."

"Wow! You've been here for a long time. Maybe eight or nine hours!" Jose said.

"It's 14:07 hours now," said Art. "We'll have to call our superiors and let them know what's going on."

"Roger that. Go ahead and call; and I'll tend to Sally."

Art radioed Lieutenant Bob Richter, while Jose resumed talking to Sally.

"Everything is going to be okay. We've come to get you out of here," Jose said in a soft, friendly tone of voice.

"I want Mommy and Daddy!" She paused. "And Uncle Tom."

"We'll get you back to them," Jose promised.

"Okay," she replied.

Art was explaining their situation to the Lieutenant; and told him he had set all four of his assigned CZ-14 charges.

"Sally, are you hurt?" asked Jose.

"My head is sore; and I cut my arm."

The light here was dim; but he quickly examined her. Nothing too serious. He figured it would be better to get her to a safer spot, and then apply First Aid.

Art finished his conversation with the Lieutenant, who said he would relay the message to the other leaders.

"Time to leave this party," Jose said. He put Sally on his shoulders. "Hold on, Honey. Can you do that?"

"Yes."

"Whatever you do, don't let go. And don't look down."

"Okay."

"Don't be afraid," Art said. "We're here to rescue you."

"I know." Then she said, "I'm not afraid."

Jose started moving. Art was about four feet behind him. They moved halfway across the narrow ledge, each of them using a pick to stabilize their balance as they faced the rock wall and moved sideways on the ledge. Jose's feet were three sizes smaller than Art's, which gave him better leverage than Art had, while navigating on the treacherous ledge. There was a weak spot in the ledge about mid-point across; and it was virtually undetectable. Providentially, Jose didn't step on it. Art was not so fortunate.

The ledge gave way instantly, without warning. Art fell before Jose could even react. He fell four hundred feet with his pick still in his hand in a striking mid-motion position. Jose could hear his scream for several seconds. A lump formed in his throat; and he wanted to cry; but he kept his composure for Sally's sake. He could feel that Sally was shaking badly. He spoke to her.

"We're almost there, Honey. We're almost there."

He made sure that he tested his weight on every step before removing his pick from the wall. They were in a precarious place; and he didn't want to lose Sally.

Missie, Tripp, and Tom Crandall were still combing the mountain, and had not encountered any soldiers or the police. Fortunately, there were no wolves nearby, on the outside of the mountains. The Crandalls were getting tired, but pressed on. They were hungry, but were not interested in food right now. All they wanted was to find Sally.

Jose turned the corner, and safely set his feet on solid ground. He let out a huge sigh of relief. He was even more relieved once he had reattached himself to his safety-rope. Then he radioed Alex. Alex answered the call eagerly.

"This is Alex Warfield."

"This is Jose. Can you assist me?"

"Roger that. I'm on my way."

Jose treated Sally's injuries. By the time he was done, Alex was there.

"We lost Art. I couldn't save him."

Alex could see that Jose was broken up emotionally. He knew that his friend had just gone through a really traumatic experience. He spoke in a kind, reassuring tone of voice.

"I am so sorry, Jose. I'll pray for you."

"Thanks."

"And for Art's family."

"Thank you. You're a true friend."

Alex looked at the girl.

"Who's this?"

"This is Sally," Jose said.

"What's your name?" Sally asked.

"I'm Alex. Alex Warfield."

"I have a cousin named Alex," Sally remarked.

"She's precocious. That's for sure," said Alex.

"Very," said Jose.

"Well…. Let's get out of here," Alex said.

"I have a request."

"What's that, Jose?"

"Can you take her? I have to set one more charge; and I don't have much time."

"I want to stay with Jose!" Sally said.

"I know, Honey; but I have to do something dangerous. And besides, Alex is my brother. You can trust him."

Of course, Jose meant that Alex was his "Christian brother"; but Sally probably wouldn't understand that. But it gave her enough confidence to say:

"Okay. He can carry me."

So Alex put Sally on his shoulders, told her to hold on tight and not look down, and backtracked the way he came, secured by his rope. But he had to be careful, even though he was secured; because if he lost his footing on the rock wall, he would end up swinging like a pendulum, and would most likely lose Sally.

The wolves were almost done with their feasting; and they would be ready for tomorrow's hunt. They would move out of the lair in large groups, and destroy every creature in their paths.

When Alex reached the top of the rope-ladder, the nine fellow-soldiers clapped and cheered. It was 2:53PM. They had heard over their radio communication system what was going on. WCAX TV even had a reporter there who asked Alex some questions. But the most important question was: "Where are her parents?" Alex said he didn't know.

Missie, Tripp, and Tom were still searching for Sally; and they were getting discouraged. The search seemed hopeless. The area was so big! They were over a mile away from their camper.

The five hundred members of the National Guard demolition crew were airlifted back to the forty-mile perimeter. The moment of reckoning was fast approaching. The perimeter was presently three miles away from the target area; and just before the Air Force sortie, the Guard would move a mile further back away from the area. At 3:30, the line of soldiers began to back away; and they would watch the devastation from four miles away.

The Air Force base at Plattsburg was on full alert. The pilots had gone over all the checklists for their planes; and all twenty of them were ready for takeoff.

The F-18's were fast, well-armed, and had great maneuverability. They could fly at Mach Two, over fourteen hundred miles an hour. Each plane had two pylons—one on the right, and one on the left. Each pylon held four advanced Sidewinder missiles. These missiles could penetrate through over one hundred feet of solid rock. It was calculated that one hundred and sixty missiles detonating along with two hundred and fifteen CZ-14 explosions would collapse the entire cavernous area. The wolves would die in their lair.

At 3:55, all the fighter planes would be in the air. They would reach the target area in less than two minutes. They would circle around the area, line up with their respective target areas, and then attack all at the same time. Twenty jets, each with eight missiles, would attack from all four directions. Sixty-four Sidewinders would slam into the north; thirty-two into the east; thirty-two into the west; and thirty-two into the south. One hundred and sixty missiles would detonate at exactly 4:00PM, Eastern Standard Time.

The helicopter co-pilot, Lieutenant Bob Girard, spoke to the pilot:

"Sir, let's do one more scan of the area."

"Roger that," Pilot Barney Oulette replied. Then he added, "You don't think those people left either, do you?"

"No way."

"Let's see if we can spot them."

The chopper turned toward the northern part of the target area and descended to a level just over the trees. They spotted the three adults in less than two minutes.

"Go ahead and speak to them, Bob," the pilot said.

Bob Girard turned on the loudspeaker once again to warn them.

"THIS IS A RESTRICTED AREA! WE WILL AIRLIFT YOU TO SAFETY!"

Missie began to run away.

"This is not good," Pilot Oulette thought. "It's 3:54. Only six minutes to rescue three people; and one of them is running away!"

"THIS AREA IS GOING TO BE DESTROYED BY EXPLOSION!"

Missie stopped. Tripp went to get her. Tom signaled to the chopper to let down the rescue rope-chair.

"I wish we could land here; but the terrain is too rough," Pilot Oulette said.

"I know," Bob said. "The rescue would be a lot easier. And much quicker, too."

Suddenly, Missie said, "I can't leave her! My little Sally! I can't!"

Tripp wanted to save his wife. "Come on, Honey."

"No!"

Tripp lifted her up and began carrying her towards the chopper.

"I said No!"

"Please. We have to go."

Missie struggled and broke free, and ran eastward along the rough terrain.

"This is not going well," Bob said.

"I know," Barney replied. "It's 3:55. Five minutes to doomsday. That gives us just two minutes ; and we leave."

Tripp ran after his wife, afraid that he would lose her. It was bad enough losing his daughter; but to lose both his wife and daughter would be unbearable. He caught up to her.

"I don't want to lose you, too," he said, feeling desperate.

Tom helped Tripp get her to the chopper. As they approached the chopper, Missie was kicking, screaming, scratching, and biting.

"Ouch!" Tripp said.

"Go ahead, Bob, and climb down the ladder. Let's get her secured; and we're out of here!"

"I'm going down now!"

"We've got four minutes, Bob! We need to leave in sixty seconds!"

Bob went down the ladder, and secured Missie into the rope-chair in record-time. She looked like she was in shock. There was no time left; not even enough time to pull in the rope-chair. Bob and Missie would be literally suspended in mid-air.

"We have to go! Hang on, Bob!" the pilot yelled into the loudspeaker.

Bob signaled to Tripp and Tom, and yelled, "RUN! That way! NOW!"

As the chopper took off, Bob added, "You've got THREE MINUTES!"

Suddenly, they saw the twenty F-18s flying overhead. They would soon be circling around, and would break up into four groups to attack from all four directions.

"Let's go!" said Tom. Tripp hesitated.

"Sally's going to die," Tripp said, feeling helpless.

"I'm so sorry, Tripp. Sally's gone. But Missie needs you. Please. We've got to go."

"Okay," Tripp said through his tears.

Tripp suddenly felt a rush of adrenaline. He knew that time was running out.

They ran—two brothers in the race of their lives.

"My daughter's in there!" Missie screamed.

"She's been found!" Bob answered, as he held tightly to the rope-ladder.

"What?"

"She's been found! And rescued!"

"Where is she?"

"Safe with the authorities!"

"When can I see her?"

"As soon as we can get you there!"

She sighed a big sigh of relief, and relaxed. She felt much better now. And she felt safe and secure in the rope-chair. She imagined that it was like an amusement park ride. Then she looked back, and saw two tiny figures running. She tensed up again.

"Can they make it?" she asked.

"I don't know," Bob replied.

"What's going on?"

"We're blowing up the mountain area."

"Why?"

"We're eliminating the wolf population."

"There?"

"Yes."
"Where?"
"Inside the mountains."

Tripp and Tom ran furiously, over rocks and tree trunks, and down the mountainside. They ran with reckless abandon. The clock was ticking.

The wolves felt the vibration, and heard the noise, of the war planes flying overhead. Some of them ran towards one of the entrances of the lair.

The two brothers reached the base of the mountain. They were both breathing heavily now; but they were spurred on by fear. The CZ-14 timers were all registered at ninety seconds and counting. Tripp and Tom hit the ground running, and saw that they were in a huge meadow. They both ignored the pain of exhaustion, and ran as if there was no tomorrow. They could see the planes coming towards them: the messengers of death and destruction, devastating instruments of war. They ran until they couldn't run any more. They felt they could die from exhaustion. They feared they would die from the ordnance on the pylons of the F-18s. And when they looked back and saw a pack of wolves coming towards them, Tripp turned to Tom and said, "We are SO dead!"

Helpless, exhausted, they looked up and saw the Sidewinder missiles flying overhead.

"Plug your ears!" Tom yelled.

All the pilots reported successful delivery:

"Fox One, eight away!"

"Fox Two, eight away!"

"Fox Three, eight away!"

The reports continued:

"Fox Nineteen, eight away!"

"Fox Twenty, eight away!"

All over the world, people were watching the action live on TV, and on the Internet. Over a billion spectators worldwide held their breath as they watched the attack and listened to the newscasters.

President Allen Westcott, New York State Governor Paul Atkins, New York Senate Majority Leader Mark Weinberg, and New York Speaker of the House Greg Nemire were among the viewers glued to their seats. So were Jonathan Wilkes, Susan Morehouse, Marie Trombley, Jim Ellenberger, and Jack Leland.

The wolf pack slowed down and watched the instruments of death racing for their targets. Two hundred fifteen CZ-14 detonations went off simultaneously as one hundred and sixty Sidewinders slammed into the mountains.

The noise of the explosions was deafening, like a hundred claps of thunder at once. The foundations of the cavernous mountains were ripped apart; and the tops of the mountains caved in. Millions of tons of rocks and dirt and trees shook as if in an earthquake, and began to fall as the mountains imploded.

The ground shook underneath Tripp and Tom; and they fell to the ground like dead men. They could see the smoke and debris rising from the mountains as they collapsed northward, towards them. It looked like a huge avalanche was heading their way. The ground behind them ripped apart, and swallowed up the wolf pack that had been pursuing them.

"Hang on!" Tom yelled.

The ground kept cracking; and the fissure raced across the meadow towards them. Tom rolled out of the way. Tripp's eyes widened as the ground cracked underneath him. He let out a scream as he fell into the earth. Fortunately, he landed only a few feet down.

"Grab my hand!" Tom yelled.

His heart pounded as he saw the avalanche getting closer. They had only seconds left before they would be buried under tons of rock and dirt.

Tripp reached out, grabbed Tom's hand, and climbed out of the fissure. As he cleared the ground, more of it collapsed. He fell, kicked wildly, and found solid ground. He quickly climbed out again and ran, with Tom leading the way.

The wolves inside the lair were all deaf from the noise of the explosives. They could not hear the millions of tons of rock and dirt falling and crashing down towards them. They felt their lair shake like a leaf in the wind; and saw small dust and debris falling first. They whimpered and howled in those last seconds of life they had left; and the mountains collapsed on them. Death came quickly as they were instantly crushed. Over two thousand wolves were buried intact under the gigantic vertical avalanche.

TV reporters and viewers all over the world were jubilant as they watched the mission succeed. People were celebrating, calling and texting each other. The general atmosphere of the viewers was relief. The seven-day war was over!

This event would be played over and over again on the internet. In just a few short days, a record two-thirds of the world's population would have seen this spectacular event. It seemed like everyone was talking about the "Great Explosion".

"Please go back and look for my husband," Missie pleaded.

The pilot, Barney Oulette, steered the chopper around and headed back towards the target area. They could see the National Guard retreating. The battle was over!

Smoke and debris were rising from the mountains, spreading in the sky, and falling to the ground like volcanic ash. The chopper pilot spotted two men covered in dust walking away from the targeted mountains, just past a meadow that had been split in half and then partially buried under a huge mass of rocks and dirt. They landed and picked them up.

Alex Warfield, Max Williams, and Lieutenant Simon Martin were going home. They were exhausted, but pleased at what had been accomplished. Their mission had been a success; and they were all still alive. But their hearts were grieved for those who had given up their lives—military and civilian—because of human greed: the willingness of a multi-millionaire to put millions of people in harm's way in order to become a billionaire.

One thing really made them happy. A little girl's life had been saved.

"That little girl was something else!" Alex said. "I'll bet she grows up to be a leader in the Army Special Forces."

"Or maybe a Nuclear Physicist," said Simon.

"Yeah!" Max said.

"Well," Max added. "I've had enough excitement in the last seven days to last a lifetime. How about you guys?"

"You're absolutely right," Alex said. "I hope this never happens again."

"We lost a lot of good men," Simon said.

"I was stunned when Jose told me how Art died. That was awful," Alex said.

"We were all sorry to hear about Art," Simon said.

"We will never forget our fallen comrades: over two hundred dead," Max said.

"Let's pray," suggested Alex.

"Great idea," Simon agreed.

"Father, we are thankful that You protected us," Simon prayed. "We pray that You would comfort the families of those who died. And we pray for the speedy recovery of the wounded."

Simon continued in his prayer; and then Alex prayed. Then Max prayed, thanking God for his new-found salvation.

"Wow!" said Alex. "You didn't tell us you got saved. That's great!"

"I was saved two nights ago," Max said.

"I'm happy for you, brother," Simon said.

"Jose told me Bill accepted Christ, too," Alex said.

"Danger really does make people think more seriously about life after death," Simon mused.

"That's so true," Max agreed.

They continued to walk towards the nearest checkpoint, where they joined a convoy and climbed into the closest available military vehicle.

"Well, this is it," said Simon. "We'll keep in touch online. You're all on my Facebook page as friends; so I'll keep in contact with the ten of you: the whole First Squad. And the rest of my brave comrades-in-arms, also: all of Second Platoon."

"How are Al and Patrick?" Max asked.

"Doing better. Al can't walk without pain yet. And Patrick can't use his right arm yet.

But they're okay. Al texted me with his right hand; and Patrick with his left."

"Well, I'm just glad they're okay," said Alex.

"Me too," agreed Max.

The three continued talking as the convoy continued moving south through the Adirondack expanse. They could see some houses that were partly destroyed. And they wondered how many people had been killed in the last week by packs of wolves running wild and out of natural prey. They figured it could be in the hundreds. Or more.

Jonathan Wilkes, Susan, Marie, Jim, and Jack Leland were all at Jack's huge mansion, watching the news. They had watched the advanced F-18s fire off their missiles, and had felt the jubilation of victory as the plan worked and the mountains really did collapse. And they, along with millions of other viewers, had been really touched at the dramatic rescue of a little girl named Sally.

They watched as the National Guard receded and headed home. They had all accomplished a monumental task; and the awful nightmare was over!

The five of them listened as Jim Dwyer came on at 5:00 at the Fox News channel.

"This is Jim Dwyer at Fox News. We have exclusive photos of houses that have been invaded by marauding packs of wolves. It is believed that these predators have killed hundreds of people in the last week in the Adirondacks. It is also believed that they ran out of natural prey and therefore encroached into human territory, looking for food."

Millions of viewers saw pictures of houses with windows smashed. It was a scary thing to watch.

"If you have little children," Jim Dwyer continued, "you may want to remove them from the TV area, because the next few minutes of filming is very graphic."

Fox News next showed pictures of people lying dead in their houses: some partly eaten, some almost totally gone. It was gruesome to watch. There were pictures of the deceased being removed from their houses, and also from out of the woods. Jim Dwyer continued.

"All over the Adirondacks, as you can see, authorities are finding people dead in their homes and in the woods, eaten by hungry packs of vicious wolves. We will not know the extent of the body-count for several days. The Adirondack Park is about six million acres, or 9400 square miles. It is a vast area; and it is believed the death toll will be well over one thousand."

Jim Dwyer then mentioned former Governor Bruce Devane and the criminal charges that would be leveled at him.

"This is so awful!" Marie said. "So many dead."

"Probably fifteen hundred, plus the two hundred of the National Guard," said Jon.

"A lot of lawsuits will ensue," Jack remarked.

"Not just for the dead, but for loss of revenue, especially by small businesses," Jim said.

"There will be a suit involving the DIAC, because we were involved in the wolf reintroduction program," said Susan.

"That lawsuit should be against the Devane family," said Jim.

"Both the DIAC and Governor Devane will face charges on that count," Jack said.

"Well, I am thankful that it is over," said Susan. "Let's take time to pray and thank the Lord that He protected us and helped us to win this battle."

They all agreed.

May 31, 2026

The new Governor of New York State, former Lieutenant-Governor Paul Atkins, announced that people could move back into the Adirondacks right away. Most of the permanent residents returned within the next few days. Others trickled in later. A few hundred never returned, because the memories of lost loved ones were too painful for them.

In the first two weeks after the National Guard offensive, referred to as "Operation Wolfkill", ninety-nine percent of the Adirondack residents had returned. Local businesses were ordering more inventory; and residents were flocking to these outlets to buy much-needed goods. Schools reopened; and teachers and students crammed a month's schoolwork into a couple of weeks. Final exams would be at least a week late in the area. And students would have to try to pass their Regents exams with less preparation than other students outside the Adirondack Park.

The economy of the Park would boom this summer, because people from all over the United States and Canada would flock to the area to see what was now the most famous part of the country. Stores, restaurants, and other businesses would be literally packed with customers for the entire summer season. Some resorts, like the Sagamore Hotel, would be busy during the fall and winter, also.

Part of the National Guard stayed in the area for the cleanup. There were dead people, animal carcasses, and especially dead wolves, to remove from the area. The wolves were examined for drug enhancement, among other things, and then promptly incinerated. The vast majority of the wolves had the chemical "photonygenol-4" in their bloodstreams, a drug that remained in the bloodstream permanently through organic delivery and even duplication; and this drug radically altered the aggressive behavior of the host.

The human deceased were identified and given to their surviving relatives. There were over sixteen hundred funerals, many of which were done together: as many as ten funerals all in one. Finally, after three weeks, most of the public mourning was over; and people were moving on with their lives.

CHAPTER FORTY-FIVE

June 25, 2026

Jonathan Wilkes rose up later than his usual 8AM. He slept until 10:00. This whole wolf-population mess had taken a lot out of him, and he had dreamed about it and awakened several times during the night. He was still tired, but he decided he couldn't stay in bed any longer. He prayed for strength to get through this day, and opened up his Bible and read a couple of chapters in the book of Leviticus. He was amazed at how scientifically sound the laws were, preventing the Israelites from getting diseases through proper hygiene, which was not discovered to prevent diseases until thousands of years later, when germs were discovered. And their diet prevented them from getting Trichinosis, which leads to a painful death. Jonathan was struck by the fact that God knew all about germs and parasitic worms back then, because He knows everything! And that was precisely why God promised them that if they followed these hygienic and dietary guidelines, they would not get the diseases that plagued other nations around them, such as Egypt.

Jon then thanked the Lord for protecting his parents and bringing them back safely from their vacation in the Bahamas. They had arrived back home on June 15th. The house had not been bothered by looters, and was "no worse for wear". Everything in the house was in excellent condition, as if they had never evacuated. Bill and Marge had thoroughly enjoyed their vacation, and had only worried "a little bit" about someone looting the place. Jon had assured them that he was monitoring and protecting the house with his futuristic GPS security system; and that they should not worry about a thing.

When Jon was finished with his prayer and Bible reading, he had a quick breakfast, and then went downstairs to have coffee with his parents. Bill and Marge had some advice for him during their conversation. They told him that he should not let Susan slip away.

"You should propose to her right away," Marge advised. "She's a Christian; and you really need somebody for a companion. And from what you've told us, she seems to be the right one."

"As always, Mom, you're right. I will propose to her really soon. Just give me a couple of days."

"We're glad you forgave us for our failure as parents," Bill said. "And we have enjoyed your company. But we know that you have a life to live; and God has someone for you. Your mother and I think it's Susan. Please, Jonathan, don't let this opportunity pass you by."

"You're right, Dad. I DO need her. And I love her very much."

"We only want what's best for you, son."

"Thanks, Dad." Then he said something really profound. "And you were not failures as parents. You raised me well. You taught me dignity, honesty, and respect. And hard work. Your only failure was not understanding me. And I now see that it was hard to understand me, because I was so complex in my thinking."

"You were the genius of the family," Bill said.

"But I was not smart enough to understand how much the both of you always loved me."

"We loved you, even when we didn't understand you," Marge said.

"You have a way with words, Mom. Thank you. Thank you both. I love you so much."

Tears welled up in his eyes; and he hugged them both, and gave Marge a big kiss. They talked for a few more minutes; and everyone regained their composure. And then Jon left to go buy an engagement ring. He had been planning all along to propose to Susan, and had already decided on the time and place.

Susan was over at Marie's house on Cameron Road in Athol. They were talking about all that had happened in their lives during the past year.

"You know, this was the most exciting year I've ever had. It was the toughest year, but it was one I will never forget."

"Susan, you love him, don't you?"

"Yes. I really do," she said with emotion.

"Do you think he loves you?"

"I don't know…. Maybe."

"Do you think he'll pop the question?"

"I don't know. I hope so."

The man followed Jon from a distance. He didn't want him to notice that he was being followed. He was angry; and he had a gun with him. He had never killed anyone before; but he wanted to kill this meddler. He wanted revenge. He wanted Jon to pay the ultimate price. He wasn't sure how or when he would kill him. He would wait for the right time—for the opportunity to present itself.

Jon went into the Aviation Mall, went to one of the jewelry stores, and bought a beautiful diamond engagement ring for twenty-five hundred dollars. He then browsed around the mall, and bought some shoes and clothes. He also purchased some electronic equipment, with which he planned to program some more functions into his advanced GPS. Then he went to the dining center in the mall, bought some Chinese food, and sat down to enjoy his lunch.

The angry man was getting fidgety. He was trying to figure out a plan. He had been following Jon for a couple of days now. He wanted to catch him alone; so he would wait until the right time, catch him alone, and shoot him. He wanted to tell him why he was going to kill him; then he would do it. It was important to tell him WHY. He had to tell him WHY before he killed him; or else it would all be meaningless. He left the dining center, and headed out of the mall. He was long-haired, unshaven, and mentally unstable.

Jon left the mall, and went to visit some friends. He needed to make up for lost time, and see old friends he hadn't seen for twenty years. He had called 411 to get information, and had found a couple of his high-school buddies he could visit for the day. He dialed the first phone number: Bill and Emelia Harvey. One ring; two rings; three…

"Hello?"

"Hello, Bill?"

"Who's this?"

"Jon."

"Who?"

"Jonathan Wilkes, your old friend."

"Oh yeah! Hi, Jon! I didn't recognize your voice. It's been so long."

"I'd like to come over and visit."

"Sure! That would be great! You can meet my wife and kids."

"Great! I'll be over!"

"Wife and kids!" Jon thought to himself. "Maybe God IS trying to tell me something."

He drove to Exit 18, turned left, went down three lights, and turned left onto Southwestern Avenue. Then he kept going straight until he reached Cunningham Avenue, on the right. He turned onto Cunningham, drove past a couple of houses, and pulled into Bill Harvey's driveway. It was the third house on the left.

Jon got out of the Camaro, and looked at the house. It was a spacious new house surrounded by a beautiful combination of small trees, flowers, and bushes. There was a slate sidewalk leading to the back; and he could hear the sounds of people laughing and splashing around in water. A note on the front door read, "Jon, we're in the back, in the pool. Come join us."

Jon walked on the slate sidewalk, and followed it around to the back of the house. He was pleasantly surprised. The family was in the back, swimming in their in-ground pool. This pool was unusually beautiful; and all around it were hanging flowers and other vegetation, including some vines. There was a beautiful blue diving board; and to the right was a big slide into the ten-foot depth of water.

There were fountains spraying cool, clean water onto the shallow area; and it was a nice way to cool down and refresh oneself on a hot, sunny day.

Much of the pool was in the shade of a couple of large trees, and of the hanging vegetation. Jon had never seen a more beautiful in-ground pool-setting in his life. It was stunning. He wanted to jump in and join the family.

The kids looked like they were in their early teens. They were obviously enjoying themselves. "Bill has done all right for himself!" Jon thought.

Just then, the wife walked out from the back patio. She was about five-foot-four, slender, blonde, tanned, and very beautiful. But she did not appear to be enamored or obsessed with her beauty. She seemed down-to-earth, friendly, and easy-going. She had a big platter in her hand; and on the platter were ready-made burgers, already dressed in ketchup, relish, and hamburger buns. She smiled at Jon.

"Hello, Jon," she said. "Have one."

Jon had always been a big-eater; so he took one and said, "Thank you very much. They look delicious."

Bill spoke: "Hi, Jon. It's great to see you again." He smiled: "This is my wife, Emilia."

"Hi, Emelia."

"Hi, Jon."

"These are my twin sons, Adam and Jerry."

"Hi, guys."

"Hi, Jon," they said in unison.

The boys were both about five-foot-ten, tanned, slender, with blonde hair. They looked like they would make a great doubles team in tennis.

They're thirteen and two days," Bill said.

"Two young basketball forwards, I'll bet."

"Actually, Adam is a forward; and Jerry does better as a point-guard."

"Cool!"

The young girl with darker hair and brown eyes came over. She had a friendly, cheerful smile; and she put out her hand and said, "Hi, Jon!"

"This is my daughter Natalia."

"Hi, Natalia."

"Would you like to join us for both lunch and dessert?" Natalia asked.

She looked to be about fourteen: young, energetic, and cheerful. She was a slender five-foot-seven and unusually beautiful; but like her mother, was not narcissistic about her beauty. She appeared to be a very kind and caring person: one who wanted to help others live life to the fullest, as she appeared to be doing with her life.

"Natalia is our fifteen-year-old genius. She knows more about computers than any of us can even imagine."

"Interesting. The Pentagon could use someone like her," Jon said.

Jon's cell-phone rang.

"Pardon me for a second."

He pressed the "Talk" button.

"Oh, hi Dad….Oh, I remember. The party….Yes. Well, have a good time. Take care."

Bill and Marge were going to play "Bridge" with some friends of theirs, and wish the wife a "Happy Birthday". They had done this every year for over thirty years: a card-playing birthday party. It always lasted until about 9:30; and they would be back home around 10:00 that evening.

Jonathan did join Bill Harvey and his family in a short swim in the pool, because he happened to have just bought a swim-suit at the mall, among other articles of clothing. Then after swimming in the pool for a short time, he enjoyed Emilia's strawberry cheesecake, topped with a generous portion of whipped cream.

"Wow!" Jon thought. "I think I'll take up residence right here!"

Jonathan visited for a couple more hours, and found out that his old friend Bill was a trial lawyer, with a very successful practice. He had an office on Notre Dame Street in downtown Glens Falls.

Bill's wife, Emilia, was a secretary for the Warren County Chamber of Commerce. Something clicked in Jon's mind.

"Secretary for the Chamber of Commerce," he mused.

"What's your maiden name?" he asked.

"Brewer," Emilia replied.

"I'm about to propose to your younger sister's boss!"

"To Susan?"

"Yes. Susan Morehouse."

"What a small world!" Emilia said.

Jon talked with Bill and Emilia and the rest of the family until just after 3:00; and then Jon left. He had another old friend he really wanted to see. He stepped into the Camaro, and headed for South Street.

He went to the "Old Hotel" on South Street, a place for the homeless. He had found out that his old friend, Ed Hartley, was still living there. Ed had been a high-school buddy, who had played basketball with him, and had gone hunting and fishing with him, also. He had been a neighbor of his when they were growing up in Athol.

But tragedy had struck Ed. When he was seventeen, he was in a serious car accident. His mother and father were both killed; and he was their only child. Ed was in a coma for three weeks; and Jonathan had sat by his side every day. When Ed came out of the coma, the head trauma which he had suffered from the accident was found to be so great that his brain had been adversely affected. He now had the mental capacity of a ten-year-old. And the doctors said his condition would never improve.

Ed couldn't support himself; and Jon tried to help him. But even with disability checks from Social Security, Ed couldn't take care of the house his parents had left him. It was under a heavy mortgage; and the bank foreclosed on it; and Ed was homeless. He ended up living in the Old Hotel; and he had enough money to pay to live there and buy food; so he was okay.

But now in 2026, June 25th, Ed was thirty-eight years old, and not married. Jon had to visit his old friend and see what he could do to help him. He felt badly that he had not kept in touch with him over the last twenty years; but he had found out that Ed was still living there, in the same room at the Old Hotel: room 205.

A lump formed in his throat as he walked up the stairway to the second floor of the Old Hotel. He felt all the empathy flooding back into his heart and soul, after not seeing him for twenty years; and he missed his old friend Eddy. He hurt for him; and tears began to roll from his eyes onto his cheeks.

He regained his composure, walked to the door marked 205, and knocked. There was no response. He felt sorrow and panic at the same time. He knocked again, loudly.

"Eddy!" he called out. "Eddy! Are you there?"

He heard footsteps. Then the door handle turned.

"Hi. Who is it?" a soft male voice asked.

"It's me, Jon, your old friend!"

"Who?"

The door began to open.

"Jonathan Wilkes—your old basketball buddy. Johnny Rocket!"

"Oh!!! Johnny! Johnny Rawwwket!"

"Do you remember me, Eddy?"

"Johnny Rocket, my friend!"

The door opened wide.

Jonathan felt sadness at what he saw. Eddy was hunched over, with drool running down his unkempt black beard. His face was gaunt, and looked sad and tired. And by the looks of his old clothes, he looked like he hadn't been taking care of himself. The stench inside the room was almost too much for Jon to bear. Eddy looked like he had lost too much weight: perhaps from malnutrition.

"I've got to DO something!" Jon thought.

"Eddy, I'm sorry I left the state."

"That's okay, Johnny. I always knew you'd come back someday. Johnny, my best friend."

Jon couldn't help himself. He broke down and cried. Eddy tried to comfort him.

"That's okay, Johnny. Everything's all right. Jesus is right here with us."

"Yes," Jon said through his tears. "Yes, He is." He paused. "Eddy, can I pray with you?"

"Yes, Johnny."

Jon began, praying slowly.

"Dear Father, please forgive us for all of our sins that come between us and You. Help us, for we need Your help. Please, Heavenly Father, show us what You want in our lives—what You want us to do. We need You so much right now."

"And please help Johnny my best friend not to be sad."

"Thank You, dear God, for my best friend Eddy. He is such a good friend."

"Thank You, God, for my friend Johnny Rawwwket."

Suddenly, Jon's tears gave way to hysterical laughter. He wasn't laughing at Eddy. He was laughing nervously, because he didn't know what to say or how to feel. And so he burst into loud laughter. Then, Eddy said another prayer.

"Thank you, God, for answering my prayer."

Jon thought, "What is he talking about?"

Then Eddy said, "Thank You, God, that Johnny is not sad anymore."

Jon understood.

Then he prayed silently: "God, please help me!" He knew he needed God's help at this moment. "Please! Please!" he continued. "Show me what You want me to do!"

"Eddy, can I help you?"

"Help me?"

"I want to help you today."

"Do what, Johnny?"

"I'll show you, Eddy."

Jon spent the next two hours scrubbing and cleaning the place; and he took Eddy's clothes and bed-sheets down to the washers and dryers that were in the basement of the Old Hotel. Finally, at 5:30, he was finished. He felt exhausted, but happy to be helping Eddy.

He had talked Eddy into taking a long shower with lots of soap, and into shaving off his beard and mustache. And after he cleaned the room, he sprayed it with a lot of air freshener. He opened up the two windows to let in some fresh air. The place seemed transformed.

Jon had a plan for Eddy, but didn't tell him at that time.

He said, "Can I take you out to a restaurant to eat?"

"Steve's Place?"

"Sure, Eddy. That's a nice little place to eat."

"I like the food there, Johnny."

"Let's go then. I'm hungry."

"All right!" Eddy said, happy to be getting out of the Old Hotel for a while.

At Steve's Place, Jon studied Eddy for a while. He felt sad, because he knew what Eddy used to be like, and what he used to look like.

Eddy was the most cheerful, fun person whom Jon had ever known. At sixteen, Eddy was the "life of the party". And yet he was a devoted Christian. He was saved; and everybody knew it. But he could still have, and be, a lot of fun without all of the drugs and alcohol and other filth of the world. He didn't get any girls pregnant or use foul language. Some people made fun of him for that; but it didn't bother him.

For four years, all through high school, Eddy was an example to Jon; he never wavered, but demonstrated a genuine love for God and for the welfare of others. He was a person who "walked the walk", who lived the life. His exemplary life helped convinced Jon to come to Christ later on, in college. So, in a way, Eddy helped lead Jon to the Lord, by showing to Jon that being a true Christian was REAL, not phony. Even the so-called "atheists" had to admit that what Eddy had was "for real".

It was such a paradox. Jon was like a spiritual son to Eddy; but now Eddy was like a son to Jon, because of the accident. Jon felt responsible now for Eddy's welfare.

Jon remembered how Eddy used to be before the accident. He was tall at six-foot and six inches, super-fast, and a terrific shooter. He led the high school basketball team in scoring and in rebounds. He was the star player. He was of medium-build, yet fast, like a slender person. He could dribble the ball almost like a Harlem Globetrotter. And he was a terrific football and baseball player, also.

And, man, could he hunt! Jon used to be envious when Eddy got the bigger deer with the bigger rack. But Eddy was so generous that he gave Jon a twelve-point head, so that he could hang it up in his living room. That trophy was still there today; and he would always keep it there, above the mantle of the fireplace. Jon had felt guilty at first; but Eddy had insisted that he take it.

Eddy had also been a great weight-lifter. At six-foot-six and three hundred and twenty pounds, he could bench press just over five hundred pounds!

Eddy was a student who "had it all"! He was a super athlete with unusually great strength; and he also had very good grades. He graduated fifth in his class, with a 92.3 average. He was such a phenomenal talent!

And then the terrible thing happened. Two days after graduation, Eddy and his parents were driving to Cape Cod, Massachusetts for a vacation; and they were involved in a terrible crash. Their car rolled down over a cliff, and fell over a hundred feet. The parents were killed instantly. Eddy was in the back seat, and in a coma. The authorities thought he was dead, but then detected a slight pulse and breathing. He was airlifted to Albany Medical Center where he was comatose for three weeks.

But even in this bad situation, Eddy was phenomenal. First of all, most people would not have survived that crash; but he did. And secondly, he never appeared to feel sorry for himself, even after he learned that he had lost his mother and father, along with much of his mental and physical capabilities.

Right now, Jon was deep in his thoughts, and had stopped eating. He was feeling sorry for Eddy, because of so much that he had lost.

"Your food is getting cold."

Jon snapped back to attention.

"You're right, Eddy. I had better start eating again."

"You used to eat like a horse, Johnny."

"I used to eat more than you, I remember."

"Yeah," Eddy said, with his cheerful smile.

"Say, Eddy, maybe we could get out on the basketball court sometime."

"Okay, Johnny Rocket. We'll do it!"

They spent a little more time at Steve's Place; and then Jon drove Eddy back to the Old Hotel. They had a time of prayer and Bible study; and then Jon left, at about 7:15PM. He arrived home at about 7:45.

CHAPTER FORTY-SIX

The angry man had given up following Jon, and had driven up to Jon's parent's house. He had read the note on the outside of the door: "We'll be back at 10PM, son. We love you."

The vengeful man had moved his car to a secluded spot, and then had unlawfully entered the house. He had easily picked the lock and walked in, relocking the door. He had looked at his watch, which registered at 2:43. He had become hungry after waiting for a couple of hours, and raided the refrigerator. Then he had left his dirty dishes in the kitchen sink. With his stomach full, he had needed to use the bathroom. So he did; but had been ready for Jon's return. He kept alert in case anyone happened to come up to or into the house. By 4:00, he had again settled down to waiting for Jon. He even sat down in the most comfortable easy-chair, and picked out a book to read from the living room library. He was able to read and stay alert at the same time. At 7:45, he perked up. Somebody was here. He put the book away quickly, and hid behind the living room wall, and waited.

Jon parked the Camaro and stepped out. He walked to the breezeway door. It was partly open. "That's strange!" he thought.

But then, he figured that somebody had driven up to the house and then left, not knowing that he had to put pressure on the screen door to close it completely.

The intruder heard the screen door's creaking sounds as it opened and closed. Then he heard the main front door open. Somebody was walking in! The intruder expected that this "somebody" would walk towards him, but he didn't. He heard Jon's footsteps going towards the den. So he waited as patiently as he could, with the gun in his hand.

He could hear Jon turn on a computer. He thought about leaving the living room and heading for the den; but then he remembered that the floor squeaked in some places. So he continued to wait. After about fifteen agonizing minutes, he heard Jon get up and yawn and head towards the kitchen. He tensed up when he heard Jon coming.

Jon opened the refridgerator door and grabbed the milk container. He took a large glass and poured himself the two-percent milk. He grabbed a Granola bar, and unwrapped it. Then he walked over to the kitchen sink, and saw the dirty dishes. "That's strange," he thought, "They never leave dirty dishes in the sink." But his mind dismissed it. "First time for everything," he thought. He wolfed down the Granola bar, washed it down with the milk, and then washed the dishes. Then he walked towards the living room.

When he walked into the huge living room, a man with a gun suddenly rose up from a crouched position, next to the wall to his right.

"Freeze!" the man said. Jon practically jumped out of his skin.

"Okay, I'm freezing," Jon answered, instinctively. "What do you want?"

The man's eyes looked menacing. "Revenge," he said coldly.

"For what? I don't even know you!" Jon reasoned.

"It doesn't matter! You hurt me!"

"This guy is crazy!" Jon thought. He said, "How? What are you talking about?"

The man stared right through Jonathan with those angry eyes: eyes that looked like those of a killer.

"You hurt my father!"

"God help me!" Jon prayed silently.

"What? Who's your father?"

"I'm the Governor's oldest son, Jim. You took a fortune away from him!"

Jon spoke by instinct, already knowing the answer to his question: "How?"

Jim was livid. "Oh, you know how! You got the information somehow, and stopped my father from getting his gold!"

"HIS gold?"

"Yes, HIS gold!" Jim spat.

Jon could sense the conversation escalating, and decided not to argue about who owned the gold artifacts. This guy was riled up; and it looked like the slightest provocation might put him "over the edge". Jon decided on another avenue of thinking. He decided to test this guy's empathy.

"Your father hurt a lot of people. He—"

"It was my GRANDFATHER'S plan! Not my father's!"

"But he kept it going. He was compliant. He chose to follow and implement the plan."

"It doesn't matter. You hurt my father!" Not a very empathetic statement towards the victims of his father's crime.

He waved the gun and spoke again, in a low and menacing tone: "And now you're going to pay."

Susan Morehouse was at home; and Marie was visiting with her.

"Susan, please! Don't let Jon slip away from you."

"I don't know what to do. What do you think?"

"Give him a call. Tell him you love him."

"I told him already."

"Men are a little slow about love, sometimes. Tell him again."

"You think so?"

"Yes, Susan. Trust me. I know."

"Okay." She paused. "Maybe I should go over to his house and see him."

"Better to call. It's rather late."

"All right."

She dialed his cell phone number.

"Don't answer it!" Jim Devane snarled.

"Okay, I'm with you," Jon said, hoping that Jim would calm down.

Jon felt a surge of hope. He knew it was Susan who was calling. He immediately recognized the old sixties' song, "Little Darling". That was Susan's ring.

He also knew that if he didn't answer the call, she would try again a second time, then a third time. If he didn't answer after three times, she would assume that something was wrong. Sure enough, she called again.

"No answer," said Susan. "That's not like him. He always answers his cell phone."

"Is something wrong?"

"I don't know."

Jon knew he had to stall this guy.

"Can I do something to make amends?"

"Like what?"

"What do you want?"

"I want to KILL YOU!"

Jon's mind was racing frantically, trying to figure out how to placate this crazy man.

He said, "Well, you've got the gun. You certainly can. But what good would that do for you?"

"I'd feel better."

"It would make you a murderer."

"So what? I'd have my revenge."

"Would you? You'd just send me to Heaven."

Jon added, "And you would lose YOUR freedom, once you got caught. Your life would be over."

"I won't get caught."

"You'd be surprised."

Jim's eyes narrowed. "What? You have a camera here or something?"

"Could be. I might have audio, too."

He didn't have a camera; and he didn't have audio in the house. But he thought he might be able to spook this guy into not killing him. He felt like he could kick himself for letting his guard down.

He had had the house on surveillance from his GPS ever since he had been aware of "Roamer". But once the whole ordeal with Roamer was over, and once the danger of looters invading the house was over, he had turned off the surveillance function of his advanced GPS. He had never anticipated this unforeseen danger—a lone gunman whom he had never met, coming for revenge for a supposed "crime" against his father. If only he had kept the surveillance function on! He would have known this intruder was here, and would not be in this predicament. All he could do now was pretend he had surveillance on the house. He hoped that this man, Jim Devane, would not "call his bluff".

"Tell me where they are!" demanded Jim.

"Why?"

"Because if you don't, I'll shoot you right now!"

"You'll never find them."

Jon was telling the truth. Jim WOULD never find them, because they were not there.

Jon continued: "But if you leave, you won't be charged with murder." Then he added, "Why not leave peaceably?"

Jon's heart was pounding. Did God really want this to happen to him? Or would He deliver him again? He was not afraid to die; but he felt badly for his parents who would find him dead; and he felt badly for his "would-be" fiancé, Susan. How would these three cope with this? And what about Marie and Jim and Jack? And poor Eddy would be devastated!

"Dear God, please stop this man!" he pleaded in a silent prayer.

Immediately, the cell phone rang again. This was the third time. He didn't even try to answer it. He was sure God was stepping in.

"Who's that?" Jim asked.

He deftly answered: "A friend of mine who likes to call me a lot."

"Give me your phone."

"You can still walk away from this, and come out a winner."

"What are you talking about?"

"You don't have to lose your freedom. You don't have to go to prison. Just put your gun away; and let's have a civil conversation."

"Oh, no you don't! I'm not budging."
"Well, you have the gun."

"I'm really worried," Susan said. "I'm calling 911."
"Dial Mr. Daley," suggested Marie. "Remember. He's the Commissioner now."
"That's right. He is," Susan said.

Police Commissioner Charles Daley was at home playing video games with his two boys. His cell went off; and he fumbled for it.
"Commissioner Daley," he said gruffly. He didn't like to have quality time with his family interrupted.
"Mr. Daley, this is Susan Morehouse."
Suddenly, his voice became amicable. "Oh yes. Hi, Susan. What can I do for you?"
"Jonathan Wilkes is in trouble. I'm sure of it. He's not answering his cell-phone; and that's not like him. Can you help us?"
Commissioner Daley could think of a number of reasons why Jon didn't answer. He misplaced the phone. He turned it off. He was taking a shower. He left it in his car. But he didn't argue with Susan, because he could sense that Jon probably really WAS in trouble.
"Where do you think he is?"
"He's normally home."
"Are his parents home?"
"No. They're at a party. He told me yesterday. They will be gone until 10:00 tonight."
"That gives us time."

In just two minutes, five squad cars were racing down River Street towards Athol. Their ETA at the speed they were traveling was about five minutes. Larsen and Davey were on their way, too. They were being flown in by helicopter. They would be at the scene in fifteen minutes. They hoped Jon would still be alive by the time they got there. They would be there by 8:45.

"You'll never get away with this, Jim."

Jim was getting more agitated. And he had become more and more nervous.

"Just sit down, Jon."

"Okay, I'm cool with that."

Jon hoped that he could buy a little more time. He hoped that Jim would keep rambling on, and use up enough time for help to arrive. He was counting on Susan, sure that she had called 911 or Commissioner Daley. They would already be heading this way. Just a few more minutes.

"What's your ETA?" asked Commissioner Daley.

"Less than two minutes," Officer Riley said.

"Did you get the carfax?"

"Yes."

"Okay."

Mr. Daley called the other four squad cars; and all the officers affirmed that they could recognize Jon Wilkes, and would be sure to shoot "the other guy" if they had to discharge their weapons.

The squad cars parked out of sight of the house; and the officers continued on foot. Officers Riley, Craig, Weiss, Burke, and Hennessy, and their partners, converged on the house, surrounding it. Jerry Burke carefully used his one-sixteenth-inch periscopic magnifier camera to scan the inside of the house as much as possible from the outside windows. He saw an athletic, handsome man sitting in a chair, unarmed. About eight feet away, a short, stocky, mean-looking guy was seated and waving a gun.

"Don't shoot unless you have to," Commissioner Daley said quietly. "Snipers will be here in less than ten minutes."

The officers waited. Some of them knew how good Mr. Daley's snipers were.

Larsen radioed Commissioner Daley. He said, "Are there windows with curtains closed?"

"Yes. On the west side of the house."

"Is that the front or the back?"

"The back of the house. It's a big picture window."

"I'll take him from the west then."

"Okay with me." Then he asked, "What's your ETA?"
"The chopper's GPS says two minutes and thirty-five seconds."
"Good."

Jim was talking constantly to Jon. He would seem rational one second; and then suddenly, he would be in a rage. Jon tried to calm him down. And he tried to talk him into handing over his gun.

All of a sudden, Jon realized that Jim might be waiting for his parents to come home. He could use them as leverage. For what, Jon didn't know. But this guy was a sociopath. He might just kill all three of them, and then turn himself in. Jon couldn't let that happen. He needed to talk him out of this, just in case help wasn't coming. His final option would be to get the gun away from him forcibly, or die trying.

"I'm sorry I hurt you," Jon said. "I can assure you, it was not intentional. I was almost killed by wolves this past winter. I was only trying to make the area safe for everyone. The money was not the issue for me. I just wanted people to be safe."

"I don't care. My father is going to prison and maybe even get the death penalty because of you!"

"But—over a thousand people have died. Don't you even care?"
"No," he said, coldly.

Larsen and Davey jumped out of the chopper, and ran up the street to the driveway. They then went into the woods on the north side of the house and proceeded, undetected, to the west side.

Larsen was hidden from the view of anyone in the house by the edge of the tree line and by the thick brush. From his position, he could see the west side of the house. The curtains were pulled shut on the seven-foot living room picture window, but Larsen knew that the gunman and Jonathan Wilkes were beyond that curtain.

Larsen turned on the infrared switch to his goggles. He could see the two men's infrared heat signatures. He couldn't detect the gun; but he did know that the man on the left was the gunman, because of the movements of his arm and hand. Also, Commissioner

Daley had radioed that Officer Burke had confirmed the positions of the two men.

There was no time to lose. Larsen steadied his rifle against a tree branch, and clicked off the safety switch. He could see the gunman's head's infrared signature clearly through his scope. His index finger touched the trigger. He prepared to fire. And then the unexpected happened.

Jim Devane was unwrapping a Granola bar with his free hand, and dropped it. He quickly bent over to his left and downward to pick it up. He moved so quickly, that when Larsen fired, he only grazed the back of his head, and part of his right ear.

Jon heard the crash of the bullet through the glass and the ripping sound as it went through the curtain; and then the scream of pain from his enemy. And he saw the gun fall out of his hand.

Jon was still fast on his feet, like he had been when he was a high school basketball player. He wasn't going to miss this chance. He sprang out of his chair and pounced on Jim. They both ended up on the floor to the left of Jim's chair.

"What just happened?" Davey asked.

"I missed him! He moved just as I pulled the trigger."

"Those things happen sometimes."

"I think I grazed him."

"I hope so."

"I'm ready if I get a clear shot."

"Okay."

Davey knew Larsen could distinguish between the two heat signatures, and that he would only take a sure shot and, barring another sudden movement by the target, would certainly finish him off.

But then the order came from the Commissioner; "Hold your fire!"

Larsen backed off from taking a second shot. "Man, I HAD him!"

"Got to obey orders."

"I know. I know!" Larsen felt frustrated.

Davey tried to calm him down. "Daley's only trying to protect Jon."

"That's true," Larsen conceded. "I wish he'd given me one more second, though."

"Water under the bridge, my friend."

"Thanks, Davey."

The two nemeses were on their feet. Jonathan hit Jim with a hard right jab to the face. That put Jim into a crazed rage; and he clocked Jon with a right hook, then a left jab. Jon was backed up against a coffee table. He regained his footing, and kicked Jim in the groin as hard as he could. Then he crouched down and reached for the gun with his left hand. Jim was doubled over in pain; but he steeled himself and lunged for the gun. Jon pushed him away from it, and stood up. Jim then rolled towards the gun; but Jon kicked it out of the way, and belted Jim with a kidney punch.

Susan and Marie were running up the driveway, escorted by the police.

"Is Jon okay?" Susan asked in a pleading voice.

"He's fighting the guy right now. Our men are standing down."

Jim was still on the floor, and kicked Jon in the shin; and Jon went down on one knee. He knew he couldn't let Jim get the gun; so he ignored the pain and grabbed Jim's legs. He then stood up with Jim's legs still in his grip, and slammed them down onto the floor. He then stomped on Jim's knee; and Jim screamed. Then Jon pummeled him in the face until he was "out cold".

"There! Take that!" Jon said. He walked over to the gun, picked it up, and dialed the Commissioner.

"Mr. Daley?"

"We're coming in now."

"I thought you might be here. I'll let you in."

"Thank you."

Jon went to the side door, unlocked it, and opened it. Charles Daley stepped in, along with a number of his officers.

"Are you okay, Jon?" he asked.

"Yes."

"Where is he?"

"Over there. Lying on the living room floor."

"Who is he? Do you know?"

"Jim Devane, the Governor's oldest son."

Several officers went over to Jim Devane, cuffed him, read him his rights, and took him away. Jim had begun to wake up, but offered no resistance.

"Jon, do you know why he held you at gunpoint?"

"Yes."

"Go on."

"He was angry."

"Why?"

"He said I hurt his father."

"How so?"

"He said I took away his fortune, and put him in prison."

"I see."

"He refused to hold his Dad accountable for the loss of so many lives."

"That's typical of relatives of criminals. I've seen it hundreds of times. They'll blame the victims or the authorities or ANYONE ELSE but their criminal relative. It's amazing!"

"Human nature just won't admit sin."

"That's true."

Jon looked at the bullet-hole, after an investigating officer pulled back the curtain. He turned to the Commissioner.

"I'd like to thank your sniper. He saved my life."

"That was Officer Larsen."

"I remember him."

"He's a good man. He doesn't usually miss, but did this time."

"Jim dropped something and ducked down quickly and suddenly. But even with him doing that, your man Larsen still managed to graze him in the head. And that gave me a chance to get free."

"What exactly happened?"

"He was shot; and he dropped the gun. So I knew I had a chance; and I jumped him."

"And you won the fight."

"Thankfully."

The two talked for a few more minutes. Then Commissioner Daley radioed Larsen. And Jon thanked him profusely for saving his life. Larsen gave him a humble nod, and apologized for missing his target. Jon then said it was okay: that it still saved his life; and he was indebted to him. He said he would like to do him a favor someday; and Larsen told him to donate some money to his church or a charity. That would be enough compensation. Jon accepted that, respecting Larsen's wishes.

Finally, Susan and Marie were allowed to see Jon. They talked for a while, and comforted each other. Susan didn't talk about her romantic interest, because right then she was more interested in his physical wellbeing. They talked for about ten minutes, and then left. It was 9:45.

By 10:00, most of the officers had left. Commissioner Daley stayed at Jon's request, because Jon wanted him to be there to help explain to Bill and Marge what had just happened. Promptly at that time, Bill and Marge's 2024 Buick Regal came up the long, winding driveway. Bill and Marge saw Jonathan talking with Charles Daley just outside the breezeway door.

Jon introduced them, and then let the Commissioner do the talking. He was a very good PR man. He explained the situation completely and succinctly. He answered all of their questions, and assured them that this was just one man acting alone, and that they were not in any danger, because he had no accomplices. Bill and Marge accepted that. Then Jon said he would put his GPS surveillance back onto the house, just because it made good sense to do it.

Commissioner Daley left at about 11:00. Jon talked with his parents for a few more minutes, and then went upstairs to his computer system, and put the house back under maximum surveillance. Once that was done, he decided it was time to retire for the evening.

He took a shower, put antiseptic on his cuts, and cream on his bruises, and went to bed. His mind was thinking about tomorrow's agenda. What was most important to him now was his plan to "pop the question" to Susan. He believed tomorrow would be the day to propose. He fell asleep, in an attitude of prayer and thanksgiving to God for sparing his earthly life once again.

CHAPTER FORTY-SEVEN

Epilogue—June 26, 2026

Jon woke up early, and went onto the internet. He found a couple of window pane distributors who could install a window immediately. He was looking for a picture window; and he gave them the exact dimensions. The distributor that Jon chose promised to be there by noon. His conversation was through his Skype setup.

"How long will it take to install the picture window?"

"About an hour," the distributor said.

"Okay. I'll have a check ready for you when you get here."

"We'll be there at noon or a little earlier."

"Thank you. I'll see you then."

They arrived at just before noon, and wasted no time in getting to work. The whole project was done by 1:00.

Meanwhile, Bill and Marge decided to go to Walmart and buy a new curtain for the new picture window. By 2:30, they were back with the curtain, and a few other items they decided would be fun to purchase.

Jon called Susan at the Glens Falls DIAC office, and confirmed that she was available for a dinner date. He made a reservation for two at 6:00. He would pick her up at quarter to six; and they would be at the Gristmill restaurant ten minutes early. After dinner, but before dessert, he would propose to her.

At the Gristmill, they took their time eating. Then, at 7:30, as their dinner plates were being removed, he took a small box out of his inside suit-jacket pocket, opened it up, and showed her the sparkling engagement ring. He "popped the question".

"So, Susan Morehouse, will you marry me?"

She didn't hesitate. "Yes, Jonathan Wilkes. Yes! I will marry you!"

Jon breathed a sigh of relief. At the same time, the whole dining room erupted into applause. Some whistled and some cheered as Jon kneeled down and put the ring on Susan's shaking finger. They were both palpably nervous, but would get over that as their relationship grew. Time would make them more at-ease with each other. Jon and Susan both stood up and bowed to the crowd, and thanked them for their accolade. After numerous congratulations, the people quieted down; and Jon and Susan ordered dessert.

While they were waiting for dessert, they began to talk about their future as a married couple. During dessert, they talked about their views on having and raising children. Both believed in loving, and yet strict, discipline. And they both agreed that it was imperative for both of them to take the time to personally teach their children, to spend time with them, and to be good examples for them. They agreed on every issue down the line, showing that they were very compatible. They agreed on all they talked about, which covered a huge range of subjects. They talked until about 9:00, and had two desserts each. They set their wedding date for August 31, 2026.

Marie Trombley opened up an online business and found success, thanks to Jonathan Wilkes helping her to set up her website to reach millions of prospective buyers. He knew exactly how to reach the maximum number of online buyers for her business. She still retained her business of cleaning houses: at least, for a while. Once her internet business made a thousand dollars a week in profits, she scaled down her cleaning business to just a few preferred customers.

Jonathan, Susan, and Marie all became active members of a church in Warrensburg that faithfully preached the Gospel. That church grew to overflowing: filled to capacity, with hundreds of new members. One of those new members was Ed Hartley. Jon brought him up every Sunday, and twice during the week.

Jim Ellenberger celebrated his eightieth birthday at his new home on Bridge Street in Latham. Twenty family members were there; and so were four of his best friends: Jon, Susan, Marie, and Jack.

Jim decided to write about his life, in a book of memoirs. Maybe not many people would read it; but it would be a history of his life; and that mattered to him. He was active in a church in Latham where he had been a member for over thirty years. His wife had passed away from cancer about ten years ago; and he still visited her graveside every month. He would take his Bible with him and read a passage from it every time he went to visit her gravesite. Then he would replace the flowers and say a prayer for strength for himself and of thankfulness to God that he would one day see her again in Heaven. Then he would go home and relax.

Jim took the time to surround himself with good friends. He visited a lot of people and gave them encouragement, and good advice, when they needed it. He had a wealth of knowledge of how to live life and avoid serious mistakes and pitfalls; and if he saw someone headed for disaster, he would counsel them and keep them from getting into trouble. He lived a full life, and was a very happy man. He was never lonely, because God was always with him.

Jack Leland continued to practice law in Glens Falls. His office on Notre Dame Street did very well. He later on would run for the office of Mayor and win by over five hundred votes. His was a life of great worldly success; but he gave God the credit for it all. And he served in a good church in the area.

Governor Devane agreed to a plea-bargain; but then relatives of victims of wolf attacks filed multiple lawsuits. Consequently, he was given multiple life sentences, with no chance for parole. Two years later, he was murdered in prison by a crazed inmate.

His lawyer, Sam Lowell, was convicted of being an accessory to the conspiracy, and aiding and abetting the Governor's criminal actions; and he was sentenced to forty years to life in prison.

The Governor's campaign manager, Scott Franklin, was sentenced to two to four years in prison and five years' parole for his compliance with the actions of the Governor. His sentence was light, because he had cooperated with the authorities.

The Governor's son, Jim, received a ten-to-twenty-year sentence for attempted murder, criminal mischief, unlawful possession of a deadly weapon, criminal trespass, and a few other charges.

Lieutenant Simon Martin went on to become a Captain in the Army Special Forces and chose to have Alex, Max, Jose, Bill, and a few others with him as subordinate officers. Together, they oversaw and carried out missions all over the world, helping to save the lives of millions of American and foreign citizens as a result. They would all eventually retire; and several of them became active in Christian service.

Jonathan and Susan became Mr. and Mrs. Wilkes on August 31, 2026. They would have five children, and would live a very happy life together. They purchased a large, beautiful home on Library Avenue Extension in Warrensburg, and had visitors over constantly.

Marie Trombley didn't remarry until her ex-husband passed away. He died in a bar brawl as a drunken man in 2031. She went to his funeral, and then decided that it was time to "get on with her life". She married Adam Cleveland, a Certified Public Accountant who came to her church fellowship. They had two children; and she felt so happy to have them. The void of losing her Lizzy was never completely gone; but she found joy in having her two new sons, Jon and Jim, born twins in 2033.

The Adirondack Park returned to normal in 2026. It was a very safe place to live, now that the wolves were gone. Yes, there were still a few dozen wolves left. The DIAC decided to eliminate them and start over by introducing a dozen wolves that were free of chemical alteration. They would be tagged and studied over the next twenty years; and their population numbers would be kept at a "safe" minimum: under one hundred. With the DIAC importing deer, rabbits, and other ecological elements, these predators were not likely to encroach onto human territory. In 2028, Susan Morehouse Wilkes became the Head Supervisor of the DIAC in Glens Falls; and she vowed that "never again" would anything like Operation Wolf happen. In the Adirondacks there would never again be a "Year of the Wolf".